THE
MISTAKE
I MADE

BOOKS BY SAM HEPBURN

Gone Before

Her Perfect Life

A Good Mother

THE MISTAKE I MADE

SAM HEPBURN

bookouture

Published by Bookouture in 2023

An imprint of Storyfire Ltd.
Carmelite House
50 Victoria Embankment
London EC4Y 0DZ

www.bookouture.com

ISBN: 978-1-83790-405-1
eBook ISBN: 978-1-83790-404-4

For Debbie
With love

PROLOGUE

People are gathering: dog walkers, construction workers in hard hats, a group of mothers craning their necks and manoeuvring their buggies to get a better look, a teenager on a scooter and a genteel-looking old woman who elbows her way through the crowd, complaining loudly about the ambulance blocking her driveway. A second police car screeches to a stop, siren blaring. A tall, bald man in plain clothes gets out. Talking into his phone he scans the street before ducking beneath the police tape. He speaks briefly to one of the uniformed officers, who motions him towards a stocky man in an orange hi-vis jacket who's leaning against a cart full of cleaning equipment and pulling nervously on a roll-up. The boy on the scooter raises his phone as a ripple of silence spreads through the crowd.

All eyes lock on the gurney being wheeled out of the alleyway by two paramedics.

Vanessa edges forward, flinching as the wheels bump over the cobbled surface, as if the jerking and bouncing might harm the dead man strapped to the stretcher. She can't see his face, it's covered by a blanket, but for a moment she imagines his sightless eyes staring up at the canopy of scratchy grey wool, and feels a wave of sadness for all the bad decisions that lead to deaths as sad and lonely as this one.

She watches as the paramedics slide the gurney into the ambulance and slam the doors shut. The ambulance pulls away. No lights. No siren. There's no need for them now. It circles the central gardens and turns out of the square.

After it's gone she stays where she is, watching the police and the gawkers and the cars reversing and turning around, as if staring at the scene will answer the terrible questions shuddering through her head.

PART ONE

ONE

As a first-time hospice visitor, Vanessa had fretted about her ability to establish a rapport with the dying and there's no denying it, her early encounters with the patients at St Saviour's – who had all been male and elderly – had been excruciatingly stilted. So she's tense and fidgety as the head nurse, Deidre, a neat, birdlike woman with a bright smile and a strong Scottish accent, leads her down one of the long, light-filled corridors of the new wing to meet her first female patient.

'Don't take it personally if she doesn't want to engage,' Deidre says, quietly. 'She's been a bit withdrawn over the last few weeks, refusing to see family or friends – it happens sometimes, but I think it would do her the world of good to have a bit of company.'

Vanessa bites down on her lip. 'I'll do my best.'

Deidre knocks lightly on the door of room seventeen and, at the barely audible reply, she pushes it open.

Vanessa takes a sharp breath, smooths her hair and follows her inside.

The woman lying in the bed is as different from the other patients Vanessa has visited as it's possible to be. She can't be more than forty and she's startlingly attractive – fair, almost silver hair, green-grey eyes, full lips and high cheekbones. But illness has whittled away her flesh, carved out her cheeks and sharpened her features which, combined with her post-chemo crop and sun-starved complexion gives an ethereal, almost elfin quality to her beauty.

'Frances, this is Vanessa Dunn, one of our new volunteer visitors,' Deidre says, reaching up to adjust the drip. 'Vanessa, this is Frances Findlay.'

Frances Findlay. The name resonates through Vanessa's bones like a plucked guitar string, flinging up an image in her head – a snapshot of a flaxen-haired, green-eyed little girl in one of her mother's photo albums. 'Oh, my goodness,' she bursts out. 'You're not *Gordon* Findlay's daughter, are you?'

Frances eyes her coolly and her voice, although thin and breathy, is clipped. 'I am, actually. Why do you ask?'

'Well, it's either a huge coincidence or it explains why my mum had a leaflet about this place in her things.'

Frances's eyes narrow.

'I assumed she was thinking of volunteering here, but maybe she was actually planning on coming to see you.'

'I'm sorry?'

Vanessa knows she's gabbling but she can't stop now. 'She used to work for your father. As a housekeeper.'

Frances gazes at her, unblinking. 'What was her name?'

'Ellen Thomas.'

A shocked pause.

'You're *Ellen*'s daughter?'

'Yes. Do you remember her?'

Deidre stops fiddling with the drip and looks with concern at Frances, who's breathing fast and raising her hand to her mouth.

'I don't believe it,' Frances murmurs. 'How is she? Tell her I'd love to see her.'

'Sadly, that won't be possible,' Vanessa says, her voice steadying. 'She had a stroke a couple of years ago. Knowing how tough Mum is, I thought she'd make a full recovery, but the brain damage led to early onset dementia and now she's in a nursing home. She can't even speak.'

'I'm so sorry. She was a lovely woman.' Frances's face puckers. 'And so kind to me. Please send her my love.'

'I'm not sure if she even knows who I am any more, but I'll definitely tell her I've seen you.'

'Well, I'll leave you two to it,' Deidre says, with a little cluck of satisfaction. 'Buzz me if you need anything.'

'Thanks, Deidre.' Vanessa ignores the padded vinyl recliner by the window and pulls one of the hard plastic chairs over to the bedside. As she takes off her coat and sits down a little kink of tension untwists from her gut.

'I must have been ten when Ellen stopped working for us,' Frances says, sitting up a little. 'I was distraught when I came home after my first term at boarding school and Dad told me she'd left. She wrote to me at school for a couple of years after that – so sweet of her – but then, you know how it is... we lost touch.'

'Is your father still alive?' Vanessa asks.

Frances shakes her head, 'He died a couple of years ago, had a heart attack right in the middle of a board meeting. One minute he was hauling the director of R and D over the coals, the next he was gone.'

'That's awful.'

'Not really. I'd far rather go that way than this.' Frances flicks a dismissive hand down her emaciated body.

Vanessa flails for a response but before she can open her mouth Frances says, 'Tell me about you.'

'Oh, right. OK,' Vanessa says. 'Well, I'm thirty-three, I've been running my own interior design business since I left college and I've just opened an interiors shop in Notting Hill.'

She pauses and laughs. 'God, I sound like a contestant in a game show.'

'Are you married?'

'Divorced.'

'Your decision or his?'

A little taken aback, Vanessa looks down at her hands. 'All his. I thought we'd be together forever. But it wasn't to be. So I moped around for a while feeling totally sorry for myself and pining after everything I'd lost, then I did what the self-help books tell you to do when your world implodes.'

'Which is—?'

'Visualise "the 'you' you want to be, living the life you want to live".' Vanessa makes mocking air quotes with her fingers. '"Then direct everything you do towards becoming that person and achieving that life."'

Frances raises a pale eyebrow and says dryly, 'If only I'd known.'

Vanessa laughs. 'You're supposed to do it bit by bit by setting yourself smaller goals across all the key areas of your life – professional, social, emotional. As you achieve each of those you gradually build towards a final destination and a complete new you.' She grows serious. 'I know it sounds like a load of rubbish but it really helped me to reboot when it felt like everything had stalled.' She doesn't talk about the gaps and hollows she's still trying to fill, the lingering pain she's so desperate to ease.

'What were these smaller goals you set yourself?'

'To open my own interiors shop.'

'Hardly small, but it sounds like you've ticked that one off.'

'Put myself out there and do some volunteering.'

Frances nods. 'That one too.'

Vanessa grins, sheepishly. 'And find a new relationship that will give me everything I've always dreamed of.'

'How's that going?'

'Let's call it... a work in progress.'

Frances lets out a snort of laughter and, as the afternoon wears on, they bond over shared confessions about failed relationships and a mutual love of crime novels.

'Did your mother ever talk about my father?' Frances says, one afternoon a couple of weeks later as Vanessa gets up to examine the books lined up along the windowsill.

'Not really. She was incredibly discreet about her employers but she used to tell me about you.' She pulls out a battered Dick Francis novel and runs a finger over the silhouette of a horse rider outlined on the cover. 'Didn't your dad give you a pony one Christmas...? What was it called? Twizzle? Drizzle?'

'Sizzle.'

'That's it. God, I was envious.'

'Envious of me?' Frances shakes her head. 'I'd have given anything to have lived with Ellen. In fact, every time she put on her coat to leave I'd beg her to take me with her.'

She blinks unhappily, and in a very small, very hushed voice begins to talk about her past. Over the next couple of hours a shocking story of a privileged childhood fraught with separation, grief and unanswered questions comes out in wheezy dribs and drabs like dabs of paint on a grotesque canvas, starting with her mother's departure from the family home when Frances was eight, leaving her at the mercy of her overbearing, authoritarian father.

'Findlay's was just a small, single malt whisky distillery when he inherited the business from my grandfather,' she says. 'Only a man with a will of steel could have grown it into the vast luxury goods empire it is today, and my father used that same brutal determination to control me and my life.' Frances stops, brow furrowed as if suddenly realising what she's saying. 'I've never told anyone any of this before,' she says.

Painfully aware that she's being entrusted with the secrets

of a dying woman, Vanessa smiles gently. Frances doesn't return her smile. Instead, she heaves herself onto one elbow and fixes her eyes on Vanessa's. 'It must be because you're such a good listener.'

Vanessa blushes and experiences a genuine rush of pleasure. *This is why I'm doing this,* she thinks. *To give people like Frances the opportunity to unload their innermost thoughts and finally feel understood.*

Frances sags back into the pillows and stares up at the ceiling. 'It can't have been easy for Ellen working for a man like my father – I'm amazed she stood it for so long. I know my mother struggled in the marriage. She hid it well but even as a small child, on some deep subconscious level, I picked up on how unhappy she was. After she finally got up the courage to leave him he was so angry he stormed around the house destroying every photo we had of her. He'd have burned the ones I kept by my bed if I hadn't had the presence of mind to hide them.' She coughs into her hand before summoning the strength to go on. 'Every night I'd take out those pictures and tell myself that she'd come back for me but as the days went by I began to lose hope. Finally, I scraped up the courage to ask him where she'd gone and he just snapped at me and said: "There's no point hankering after that woman, Frances. If she'd ever really loved you you wouldn't have abandoned you. A clean break's much the best way." After that, whenever I cried or said I didn't want a clean break, he'd say, "It's for your own good, missy. More to the point, it's for the good of the family."' She closes her eyes and her jaw quivers. 'The *family*. Every heart-shattering decision he ever made about my life was for the good of the bloody family.' Her words are coming faster now, hissing and bubbling over the beep of the monitors. 'There was one afternoon, a few weeks before she left, when my mother took me to the park. She waved to me as I ran to the swings and then she sat down on a bench beside a young girl – she can't have been more than sixteen or seventeen – who was cradling a newborn, looking completely wiped out and utterly miserable. It was a beautiful autumn day, and as I swung backwards and forwards I leaned right back until I was almost horizontal and I could see leaves fluttering down like golden confetti against the shiny blue of the sky.' She yanks a breath from the air and lifts her hand as if reaching out to catch a swirling leaf. 'When I sat up again I saw my mother say something to the girl, and then she leant forward, put her hand on her arm and stroked the baby's head and the girl stopped looking miserable and started to smile. I think about that moment every day: all the gentle, caring loveliness that was lost to me when I lost her. It's made me realise something.' Her eyes open and fasten on Vanessa's. 'Something truly terrible must have happened to make her leave me without saying goodbye.'

'What sort of terrible?' Vanessa murmurs, embarrassed at how clumsy she sounds.

'I think she discovered something bad about my father.' Frances lowers her eyes. 'He was ruthless about most things, but especially when it came to making money. People who got in his way got hurt. Destroyed. Looking back on it now, I think she stumbled across something he'd done or someone he'd hurt and decided she couldn't go on living with a monster.' She blinks rapidly, her mouth quivering. 'After she left, our house was so full of his anger that over the next few weeks I began to absorb it – I suppose it was easier than allowing myself to feel the pain. A couple of months later, when he told me he'd had a call from the Portuguese police telling him that she'd been killed in a car crash in Lisbon, all I could feel was a terrible, all-consuming numbness.'

'Oh, Frances.'

Vanessa waits for her to pick up the thread again. When she doesn't they sit there, quietly listening to the thrum of the monitors and the tap of rain against the window. Slowly, Frances turns her head and fixes her eyes on Vanessa's as if trying to probe deep into her mind. When she finally speaks it's in a murmur so soft and rasping that Vanessa has to edge closer to hear her.

'Who knows that you come here?'

Surprised at the question, Vanessa shifts in her seat. 'Apart from Mum, I haven't told anyone at all.' She rubs the space below her knuckle where her wedding band used to be. 'I've not been seeing so much of my old friends since the divorce – you know what it's like when you're on your own and everyone else is coupled up.'

'Can you keep it that way?' Frances drags in a sip of air. 'I mean, not tell anyone that you visit me, or even that you volunteer at St Saviour's.'

Vanessa feels the tiniest shiver of apprehension. 'If that's what you want, but why?'

'I need you to do something for me' – Frances is wheezing hard but she keeps talking, forcing out words on shredded breaths – 'but it has to stay between us. No one must know that I've asked you.'

'You can trust me,' Vanessa says, softly. 'I promise.'

'Telling you... might put you... in a... difficult situation.'

'Consider me warned.'

Frances's body convulses – a shuddering heave that sets off the nerve-jangling shriek of an alarm. Vanessa jolts to her feet and cries out for help, her panicked voice slamming between the walls.

The door flies open. Deidre comes running in. Her eyes dart to the monitors. With swift, practised movements she jerks the oxygen mask over Frances's nose and mouth, shuts off the alarm and reaches for her wrist to take her pulse. 'You've exhausted yourself, hen,' she says, calmly. 'So whatever it is you two ladies were gossiping about, you'll have to pick it up next time.' She glances at Vanessa's frightened face and gives her a reassuring nod. 'She'll be fine, don't you worry. But you'd best be getting off now.'

Frances lifts her head from the pillow, straining the cords of her slender neck and stares at Vanessa over the dome of plastic, her chest juddering, her green eyes wide and pleading.

'Come on now, lie back,' Deidre says, firmly.

Vanessa reaches out and touches Frances's hand. 'I'll be back first thing tomorrow.'

Vanessa throws a glass of wine down her throat and steps beneath the shower, water gushing over her as the last few hours flood her brain: Frances's thin pale body trapped beneath the sheets; her burning need to spill out her pain, the horror of her childhood; her silent plea for Vanessa to come back; the task she wants her to do; the terrifying screech of the alarm.

She turns up the heat, presses her palms against the tiles and hangs her head beneath the scorching needles of water.

TWO

It's just after eight thirty the next morning when Vanessa pulls off her coat and drops into the chair beside Frances's bed. 'How are you?' she says.

Frances lifts a frail shoulder. 'Better. They've upped my meds. Shouldn't you be at your shop?'

'It's fine. My manager will open up and both assistants are in today. Anyway, I promised you I'd be back first thing so here I am, ready to hear whatever it is you need to tell me.'

Frances gazes at her, hollow-eyed, her lips moving as if words are backing up inside her, too painful to be spoken.

'You were telling me about your childhood,' Vanessa says, gently. 'Why don't you start where you left off.'

Frances nods gratefully and, with a sigh, she closes her eyes and drops back onto the pillow. 'After my mother died I became this hurt, angry, confused little kid who was desperate for affection. The only person who gave me any was your mother. In fact, for a long time Ellen was the only person who ever touched me. She'd plait my hair and put plasters on my knees when I scraped them. Sometimes she'd hug me for no reason at all.

Once, when I came top in an exam, she baked me a cake with a big gold star on top.'

Vanessa feels her eyes sting but looks down at her hands and says nothing.

'Then my father decided I needed proper discipline and he sent me to boarding school. It didn't work. By the time I was thirteen I was acting up so badly that he packed me off to spend the Easter holidays at a boot camp in the States. He said the kayaking, zip-wiring and fresh air would "sort me out".' Frances's eyes flutter open and she stares up at the neat white ceiling tiles. 'I hated all the outdoorsy stuff but I met a boy. He was sweet and shy and a bit of a loner like me. He told me he loved me. It made me feel wanted.' She pauses and lets her eyes slide back to Vanessa's face. 'So wanted that I came back pregnant.'

Vanessa reaches for Frances's soft, cold fingers. '*Pregnant?* At *thirteen?*' All at once she sees herself at that age – childish, gawky and totally clueless about boys. 'You weren't much more than a baby yourself.'

'Yes, and far too naïve to realise what was happening to me. I was so skinny that no one else realised it either. By the time I'd worked out why I was throwing up all the time and plucked up the courage to tell my father, it was too late to do anything about it.'

'What did he say?'

'That for the sake of the family no one must ever know. Findlay's is all about old-fashioned British values, you see, a brand that offers solid, straightforward certainty in an uncertain world.' She lets out a mocking laugh that sounds more like a sob. 'Once he'd sworn me to secrecy he did what he always did when he had a problem: he paid someone else to make it go away. In this case that meant hiring in a private midwife and arranging to have the baby adopted. I gave birth a week before Christmas in my bedroom at home, writhing in pain, surrounded by my books, fairy lights and Boyzone posters. The minute the baby was born the midwife whisked her away. She didn't even let me see her, let alone hold her.'

'You had a little girl,' Vanessa says softly, almost in tears.

Frances pushes herself up as an ember of old rage flares into life. 'That bitch refused to tell me the baby's sex. She said it would make the separation easier for me!' Exhausted, she falls back weakly and gasps for the breath to go on. 'But all through the pregnancy I thought of her as a girl. In my heart I call her Dora Mae. Dora after my mother, Mae after my grandmother. I imagine that she's grown up fair-haired like me, but with her father's beautiful dark eyes.' She puts her hand to her face as if overwhelmed by the image of the daughter she's never known. 'A week later, I was back at school surrounded by kids who'd spent their Christmas holidays skiing or cruising around the Bahamas. My father didn't tell my teachers or anyone else what had happened. In his eyes, the whole thing was over, never to be spoken of again.' She twists her bloodless lips. 'Another clean break, all bought and paid for with Findlay company cash.'

Vanessa gazes at Frances's emaciated face, the skin stretched over her protruding bones, the dips at her temples, then lets her eyes wander around the room. With its wipe-clean surfaces and pale blue walls, it's identical to every other room at St Saviour's: clean, neat, and functional, the only hints of Findlay money an exquisite emerald and diamond ring on Frances's finger and the tube of Elizabeth Arden moisturiser on the bedside table. In that moment she realises that for Frances, the simplicity of these surroundings, far from seeming austere, is probably a welcome escape from the world of wealth that had demanded so much sacrifice.

She shunts her chair closer to the bed and leans in as Frances rasps out more of her story.

'But I survived,' she says. 'I did well at school and university, joined Findlay's and discovered I was good at business. Very good. My career became all-consuming and for years I managed to convince myself that Dad had been right about the futility of hankering after a child I'd been too young to bring up, and a woman who hadn't loved me enough to stay. In fact, if you'd asked me how I felt about the loss of my mother and my baby I'd have told you it was all in the past and that I'd moved on, unscathed. The awful thing is, I'd have meant it too.' Her slender fingers pick at a loose thread in the bedcover. 'But there's nothing like looking death in the eye when you've just turned forty to rip the scab off an old wound.'

Vanessa tightens her grip on Frances's hand.

'It was as if the minute I accepted there was nothing more the doctors could do for me I freed up my brain to unlock all the memories I'd buried.' She gazes away to the wall. 'I started wondering how my life might have turned out if my mother had stayed. What if she'd persuaded my father to let me keep my baby? What if she'd brought Dora up for me? We could have grown up together, more like friends or sisters than mother and daughter. Perhaps then I wouldn't have been so frightened of having – and possibly losing – another child.

'By the time I realised that it was only fear of loss that was stopping me I was in my mid-thirties and getting pregnant wasn't as easy as it had been in my teens. I was on my third round of IVF when I got sick and it all had to stop. Then, once I came here and finally allowed myself to face the pain of giving up the only child I would ever have, I realised how badly I need to know what happened to her. It was all I could think about. So I started to search for her. I contacted adoption agencies, signed up to registers where birth parents and adopted children can leave messages for each other, and I hired a private investigator.'

Vanessa finds herself choking up, almost unable to speak. 'Did you find her?'

'So far we've come up with nothing, not even a birth certificate. I'm not surprised. My father probably got his fixer to arrange a hush-hush, no-questions-asked private adoption. Or maybe he gave her to someone who'd lost their baby and was willing to pretend she was their birth child. All that mattered to Dad was cutting the link between my child and the Findlay name and eradicating the shame. I bet the poor kid doesn't even know she's adopted.'

Her eyes, which have wandered away, dart back to Vanessa's face. 'You swear to me you won't say a word about any of this? Not to anyone.' There is an edge of panic in her voice.

'Of course I won't.' Vanessa's voice is soothing. 'But why the need for secrecy?'

'The family can't know I'm looking for her.'

'Do they even know she exists?'

'It was never, ever mentioned, not by any of them, and before I started to look for her it wasn't an issue. But I've been lying here thinking about it and I've realised that the one person my father might have confided in was his brother, Tom. He's been dead for years, and Dad was so ashamed about what had happened he probably didn't even tell him' – Frances regards her fiercely – 'but while there's a chance that my cousin Mark heard even the slightest whisper that I have a daughter, she won't be safe until she's been found and legally recognised as mine.'

'Why ever not?'

Frances glances at the door and whispers, 'I have to protect her.'

'From your family?' Vanessa asks, incredulous.

Frances's mouth sets in a tight line. 'If I die childless, ownership of the Findlay Corporation passes to Mark. If I find Dora, she'll be entitled to the lot. Even if she's found *after* Mark's inherited the company, it will automatically revert to her as the rightful successor.'

Vanessa drops her eyes. At the visitor induction training, she'd been advised to let conversations go wherever the patients wanted them to go, to listen to their anger, tears and fears and to respond with gentle questioning without trying to reason with them, so she takes a breath and says, 'Are you saying you think your cousin might go looking for your daughter and *hurt* her to keep hold of the company?'

'He's a greedy man who's wanted it all his life, with no expectation of it ever happening. So now that ownership is within his grasp, if he managed to find her before I did... well, who's going to lay it at his door if a young woman with no known connection to the Findlay family accidentally fell under a train or died in some other tragic accident?'

This seems so out of character for Frances that Vanessa can't stop herself from glancing at the catheter in the back of her hand, wondering if the pain medication pumping through her veins is affecting her brain.

'I'm not delusional, if that's what you're thinking,' Frances says, testily. 'You'd be surprised what even the most unassuming of people are prepared to do when there's a multi-million-pound company at stake.'

Vanessa blushes. 'Sorry. It's just that if you come from a family where the biggest inheritance squabble was over a set of teaspoons, it's a lot to get your head around. But if you're that worried about this cousin of yours, why don't you just cut him out of your will and leave the company in some kind of trust?'

'That's not how it works. My grandfather specified that the business would pass to his descendants in strict order of succession. Ironically, he did it to prevent strife within the family. So, since the day of my diagnosis, Mark has been sitting on the top floor of the Findlay Corp HQ counting the days until I die. Which is why I've banned the lot of them from coming to see me. Him, his wife, his grasping, hawk-faced mother and his spoilt, greedy kids.'

'I don't blame you,' Vanessa says, still trying to work out if Frances has suddenly lost her grip on reality. Maybe that's what happens when you're left alone for hours on end with nothing but pain and your own past for company.

'I'm not looking for Dora just because I want her to inherit what's rightly hers,' Frances says, her voice cutting through Vanessa's thoughts. 'To be honest, her life might be easier without it. I'm doing it because I want to hug her and tell her who she is and explain to her face to face that she was loved and wanted, that the night I got pregnant was one of the happiest of my life, and that I only gave her up because I was forced to. If I die before I get the chance to do any of those things I want her to know that I'm sorry from the bottom of my heart that I didn't start searching for her years ago.' She stares up into Vanessa's eyes. 'I've left money to pay the investigator to go on looking for her after I'm gone. But I haven't told him that she stands to inherit the company.' Her voice grows hesitant. 'So if – *when* – he finds her, she's going to need a friend who can break the truth to her gently, take her out to buy a fuck-you outfit to wear the first time she has to meet the family, and who'll stand by her when it all kicks off. Because, believe me, it will.' She draws in a laboured breath. 'I want that person to be you.'

'*Me?*' Vanessa says, starting to sweat.

'I've been thinking about it since the moment we met.'

'Frances, I'm truly touched but you must have loads of friends who'd be much better at doing all that than I am, and who know you far better than I do.'

Frances sighs. 'When you lose so much so young it makes you wary of getting close to people. It's as if there's a barrier stopping you from making yourself vulnerable. I think that's why my marriage failed. My ex, Daniel, is a decent man and we're still in touch but he wanted all of me in a way that I just wasn't capable of giving. I never even told him I'd had a child.' She grows quiet and her eyes droop downward. 'As for friends, I've got hundreds of them. Attractive, amusing, successful people who I used to see at dinners and parties and professional events, but there's no one I can trust the way I feel I can trust you.' Her voice grows so soft Vanessa can barely catch her words. 'I think it's because you're Ellen's daughter.'

Vanessa bites down on her cheek to stem the sudden wash of emotion. 'You said *used to see*. Don't these people visit you?'

'It would be too awkward. For me as well as them. They send me gifts, though. Extravagant bouquets flown in from God knows where, bottles of champagne I can't drink, and baskets of exotic fruit I can't eat.'

Vanessa gestures around the empty room and Frances laughs. 'I send the flowers to the lounge and divide up the fruit and booze among the staff. I don't even bother to read the cards anymore.' Her expression grows serious. 'That's why your visits have felt so special. They've given me a taste of what real friendship feels like. What I've been missing out on all these years.' She looks around her in a distracted sort of way. 'Anyway, it's safer if it's you.'

'*Safer?*'

'If Mark does find out about Dora, he might start keeping tabs on anyone he thinks might lead him to her, or even try to silence anyone who knows she exists. But the good thing is no one aside from Deidre has any idea that you and I even know each other, and she is the soul of discretion.'

Vanessa manages to make a small sound. She hadn't bargained on anything like this when she'd signed up to be a hospice visitor. It feels as if she's been driving along in one direction and her car has suddenly flipped over in a ditch and she's found herself hanging upside down, struggling to get her bearings.

A pause, then Frances's voice again. 'I know it sounds crazy but there's a lot at stake, Vanessa. Mark won't be happy about giving up the business, and I know he'll do whatever it takes to hang on to it.'

Whatever it takes. The words swell in the silence, filling every corner of the room.

She's serious, Vanessa thinks. She keeps her expression calm but her insides are squirming. 'Who else knows you had a baby?'

'The only people I've told are Roger Cheadle, my lawyer; Don Dexter, the investigator; and you. Three people who don't know each other and who, as far as Mark and the rest of the world are concerned, aren't linked in any way.'

'There's still time for you to be the one who's there for her,' Vanessa says, weakly. 'Dexter might have a breakthrough and find her in the next few weeks.'

Frances frowns: a hopeless, resigned expression on her wan features. 'We both know that's not going to happen. With so little to go on it could take months, years even. Time I don't have. I know it's a lot to ask but it would mean everything to me if I knew I'd be leaving her in your hands.'

Vanessa swallows a hard, rough swallow and wants so badly to tell Frances that she's picked the wrong person for the task. But, she reminds herself, she's now new Vanessa – bold, undaunted, post-divorce Vanessa who refuses to be fazed by unexpected challenges. 'I'd be honoured to do it,' she says.

'Thank you.' Frances's shoulders sag with relief. 'It goes without saying that if you have any expenses my lawyer will send you whatever you need. I'll text you his private number so you can message him, without having to go through his secretary and I'll write to him confirming our agreement and ask him to send you a copy of the letter.'

Vanessa looks down at her fingers laced in her lap. 'Have you got *any* leads to go on? What about the midwife?'

'I got hold of a list of all the private ones registered to practise in the UK in 1996, but without a surname it's impossible to know where to start.'

'If you send me the list I could make some calls. You never

know, I might get lucky. Can you remember her first name?'

'Moira? Maureen? Something like that, but she didn't arrive until I was well into labour and by then I was in so much pain it was all a blur. That's why Dexter thought it would be better for him to concentrate on finding the fixer my father used to arrange the adoption.'

Vanessa looks up. 'That sounds sensible. Was there someone he usually relied on to sort out his problems?'

'That's the thing. He kept all his employees in separate lanes, probably so he could limit the damage if any of them turned against him. For something as personal as this I think his instinct would have been to use someone outside the company.' Frances frowns. 'Then again, he'd have to have been sure they'd keep it secret.'

Vanessa looks away to the window. Through the polished glass she sees an elderly couple tottering across the hospice lawns, the man immaculately dressed in a tweed suit, the woman in a heavy brown overcoat thrown over a pink cotton nightie. 'Maybe he chose someone he had a hold over,' she suggests. 'You know – he'd keep their secret if they kept his.'

'Mutually assured destruction?'

Vanessa watches the elderly man grip the woman's arm and lower her onto a bench. 'Something like that.'

'It's definitely the kind of game he liked to play,' Frances says, thoughtfully. 'Anyway, I've given Dexter a list of everyone who was working at head office around the time I got pregnant. I told HR I needed it for a blog piece I'm writing about the history of the company. Like I said, I don't think my father would have involved a permanent employee in something as private as the disposal of his grandchild, but one of them might remember an outside contractor or a consultant he used for private jobs.'

'What happens if someone does come up with a name?'

'He'll contact that person and ask if any of the private work they did for Gordon Findlay involved a child. He won't mention me, of course, but if we throw enough money their way they might just open up. It's a long shot and there's a risk it might get back to Mark, but right now it's all we've got, so we just have to make sure that we stay one step ahead and get to her before he does.'

'How will I know if Dexter finds her?'

'I'll give him instructions to contact you. But just in case any of you are being followed, you have to promise me you won't try to meet either him or Cheadle in person, until Dora is actually found.'

'Right,' Vanessa says, uneasily. 'No contact with Dexter or Cheadle until she's been found.'

Vanessa rushes home after Frances's revelations and searches online for the side effects of morphine. Although the articles cite 'cognitive alterations' and, in a minority of cases, hallucinations and even paranoia, until today Frances has never given any hint of being anything other than rational. She switches her search to Mark Findlay: a pudgy-faced man in his late forties, who, from his photos, appears to have none of Frances's style or elegance. From what she can piece together he's spent his whole working life at the Findlay Corporation – but with no expectation of inheriting the company, and clearly no special treatment from his uncle, Gordon, he'd made a sluggish rise from an entry-level job in accounts through various middle-management roles to a junior directorship, before being suddenly catapulted to acting CEO when Frances received her diagnosis. Vanessa zooms in on his photo and stares into Findlay's small, expressionless eyes.

How *would* a man like that react when the prize that's been dangling just out of his reach all his life finally drops into his hands, only to be snatched from his grasp by a stranger?

THREE

TWO WEEKS LATER

'Hi, Mum. How are you feeling?' Vanessa puts her face close to Ellen's and thinks, as she always does when she arrives at The Laurels, that the saddest thing about her mother is her eyes: the dullness of them, the way they look past her or through her, or, on the rare occasions when Ellen's gaze grazes hers, the disappointment she feels when they drift away, and settle, unseeing, on the rug or the radiator.

But she refuses to give up and, every week, from the minute she walks into her mother's room, she pours out a stream of memories, thoughts, secrets and dilemmas, returning to the same well-trodden ground again and again. Sometimes she brings along little prompts and mementos to illustrate her stories because she has to believe that somewhere, trapped beneath those slack muscles and sagging lips, a spark of the woman that Ellen used to be lingers on, and if she only takes in a tenth of what Vanessa is saying, it will be worth it to keep that spark alive.

But she has to admit it: these chats are therapeutic for her too. It's not just that they give her a chance to say all the things she should have said before Ellen stopped being Ellen; it's that when she's with her she can leave bubbly, successful, outgoing Vanessa at the door and allow herself to be raw, honest – angry, even – in a way she just can't when she's with anyone else.

Sometimes she pretends that she and her mum are having a proper conversation – the way they used to before Ellen had her stroke – and she pauses and imagines her mother chipping in with one of her pithier comments or a piece of typically no-nonsense advice. Somehow it helps. In fact, without these one-way heart-to-hearts Vanessa's not sure how she'd have got through the last couple of years – the increasingly fraught discussions with Doug about starting a family, the shock when he'd asked her for a divorce and the discovery that her best friend Lisa had betrayed her.

She squeezes her temples and tries to breathe through the pain, counting the packs of pills on the bedside table the panes of glass in the window, the spokes of the wheels on Ellen's wheelchair. Of all the women her husband could have left her for, why did it have to be Lisa? Did he have any idea how that made her feel or the emptiness it left inside her when they both disappeared from her life?

'Everything alright, Mrs Dunn?'

She looks up, expecting to see Ellen's squat, sweet-natured carer, Phil, standing in the doorway, but through the blur of her tears she makes out tall, dark-haired Stefan from the nursing team. He's always faultlessly polite, and nice-looking in a remote, preppy sort of way, but there's something about the way he looks at her, his dark brown eyes enlarged by tortoiseshell glasses, that unsettles her.

She grabs a tissue from the box by the bed and presses it hard to her eyes, worried that he might have heard her spilling out her pain. 'Fine, thank you.'

'Really?' He steps towards her.

'I just keep thinking there must be something more I could

do for her.' A sob bubbles up. 'I feel so useless sitting here jabbering away to myself.'

'Don't put yourself down. You do an excellent job, coming to see her week in, week out.' He aims a thermometer gun at Ellen's ear and nods at the reading. 'Good – she was a bit feverish in the night but her temperature's right back to normal.' He reaches for Ellen's wrist and turns to look at Vanessa as he takes her pulse. 'It's a shame your sister can't take a bit more of the strain.'

Vanessa shifts uncomfortably, unsure how to respond to the criticism in his voice. 'I wouldn't want her turning down gigs, not at this stage in her career.'

'Is she a musician?'

'A singer-songwriter.'

'Any good?'

'She's definitely starting to build a following. That's why these tours she does are so important: even for the warm-up acts it's a chance to get noticed.'

'She's Izzy, right?'

Vanessa nods and blows her nose.

'I thought so. Next time you speak to her, tell her that Ellen has been saying her name. Quite a few times, actually.' He lays Ellen's hand back in her lap and regards Vanessa with his pene-trating gaze. 'Of course, it could just be a verbal tic, but I think your mother really misses her.'

Vanessa looks at Ellen and swallows to ease the sudden lump clogging her throat, unsure whether to smile or cry. Izzy always had been her mum's favourite, the late miracle baby that had arrived after two miscarriages and a heart-wrenching stillbirth.

'Still,' Stefan is saying, 'thank goodness she's got you. We've got plenty of patients who don't see a visitor from one year's end to the next. How about I bring you a cup of tea?'

'That would be lovely. Thank you.'

'How do you take it?'

'Black, please, no sugar.'

'Coming up.'

The Laurels is good like that, the way it encourages its staff to support the families as well as the patients during visits. But Vanessa makes sure it's not all doom and gloom when she's here, and always goes out of her way to tell her mother about the positives in her life as well as the negatives.

She bites a tear in the cellophane wrapped around the bunch of lilies she bought on her way, rips it away and fixes on a smile. 'Last week's feature in the *Sunday Times* has really driven up our Instagram following,' she says. 'And the enquiries about the design service have almost doubled.'

Ellen's head stays drooped, twitching to a rhythm of its own as Vanessa trims the stems of the lilies. She tosses the severed ends into the bin and takes down her mother's favourite vase from the shelf above the sideboard. Admiring the play of sunlight on the blush-coloured glass she carries it over to the sink and lets out a horrified gasp as the rim chinks against the tap. 'Oh, sorry, Mum!' she gasps. 'It's heavier than I thought.' She runs her finger around the place where it touched, and calls over her shoulder, 'It's alright, no harm done.'

The vase is one of her mother's treasures. Even when she became too wobbly and forgetful to go on living alone and they'd had to move her to The Laurels, Ellen had somehow found the words to insist on bringing all her most prized possessions with her, raising a shaky finger to point out the things she wanted and watching, beady-eyed, as Vanessa and Izzy swaddled them in bubble wrap. Vanessa, who definitely hadn't inherited her design sense from her mother, had despaired over the ugly knick-knacks Ellen had amassed over the years, but in Ellen's eyes, the holiday souvenirs, cheap china figurines and amateurish watercolours were as precious as this exquisite art deco vase. Of course, she'd refused to be parted from her photo albums, and Vanessa had even gathered up all the old snapshots she'd found shoved in the back of a drawer and stuck them in a new album for her, to make sure they didn't get lost.

Ellen had got a bit upset when she'd had to tell her that there wouldn't be any space at the nursing home for the boxes of paperwork they'd found squirrelled away in her attic. Izzy had headed off to Croatia that summer so it had been down to Vanessa to wade through it all, and she'd discovered it wasn't just personal mementos that Ellen had hung on to. There was a mountain of bits and pieces from her work: payslips, letters, menus, thank-you cards, even a child's painting of her wearing one of the smart black dresses she'd adopted as a sort of uniform.

Ellen had taken infinite pride in running the homes and lives of people who were too rich and too lazy to do it themselves. She'd been good at it too – every gourmet chef she hired in, 800-thread bedsheet she ordered, domestic crisis she averted, party she arranged, and drunken guest she helped into a cab – she'd done it with her trademark calm and good humour. There'd been nights when she'd bring back plates of canapés, and cast-off clothes that her bosses' offspring refused to wear, and Vanessa would wrap herself in the too-big designer dresses, serve the canapés to her guinea pig and pretend that she was rich enough to pay her mother to stay at home every day, so that Ellen would be the one who was there when she got back from school, cooked her tea and put her to bed instead of that old witch Mrs Richards from next door.

Along with the bumf about St Saviour's, Vanessa had come across some painfully private letters in Ellen's boxes, and bundles of leaflets about causes her mother had clearly been interested in since she'd been widowed, but had never spoken about: justice projects, addiction programmes and prisoner rehabilitation initiatives. It was reading through them that had prompted Vanessa to think about volunteering as a way to fill the empty spaces in her own life. In the long, lonely evenings after her split with Doug these thoughts of 'getting involved' had given her something to cling to.

She carries the vase back to the sideboard, drops the lilies into it one by one and stands back to admire her handiwork. 'Mmm, smell that gorgeous scent.' She turns to look at Ellen.

She's staring at the box of tissues on the bedside table.

'Shall I put on some music?' Vanessa reaches for the iPad she bought her mother when she first moved in and scrolls through the playlist she spent hours putting together; every piece chosen to evoke a meaningful time, place or person in Ellen's life. She'd read somewhere that with dementia patients, smells and music could trigger even stronger emotions than words, pictures or touch.

She finds the track she's looking for and smiles as the room fills with the deep-throated strains of Johnny Cash singing 'You are my Sunshine', then she takes the photo album she made from the bookshelf, pulls up a chair and reaches for Ellen's hand. Waving it to the beat of the music she gives it a little squeeze. With the other hand she flips open the cover of the album.

'Look, Mum, that's you.' She presses a finger to the plastic-covered page and points to a polaroid of a young woman in a short white wedding dress. The photo is faded and cracked across the middle but you can still see how beautiful her mother was as a young woman – auburn curls, perfect skin and willowy limbs.

Vanessa glances over at the sideboard where Izzy's sun-kissed face peeks out from beneath a wheat-coloured fringe. Her blonde, honey-skinned sister and her brunette, porcelain-complexioned mother. Both stunning in their own way. Vanessa smiles. She'd accepted long ago that with her mousey hair, hamster cheeks and what her grandmother used to call 'the Willis chin', the stunning gene had somehow passed her by.

Still, with the help of a clever hairdresser, an excellent eye for an outfit and a sadistic personal trainer, she does her best. She turns the page. 'And there's Dad at his passing out parade.'

There he stands, Charlie Thomas, lanky and painfully young in a box-fresh police uniform, eyes front, chest out, chin up, white-gloved fists pressed hard against his thighs.

'Look how handsome he is, Mum.' She sighs. 'I've been thinking about him a lot recently, imagining ways to put things right between us.' She flips to the next page. 'And that's you, me and him on holiday.'

It's a snap taken a few years later of the three of them on a beach, her father looking tanned and assured in tight black swimming trunks, her mum beside him in a striped bikini, balancing two-year-old Vanessa on her hip. 'That was taken before Izzy was born.' She stares down at her father's face and adds silently, *Before Dad started drinking. Before things fell apart.* She blinks hard, blindsided by a queasy swell of emotion, and quickly turns the page.

'There's Frances on Sizzle!' she says, brightly. 'She must have been about nine when this was taken.' She shakes her head. 'There's still no news on her search for Dora, but I have a gut feeling there's going to be a breakthrough in the next few months. It will be so sad if it comes too late for Frances.' She sighs. 'And such a shame that you can't go to the hospice to see her. After all, it's all down to her fondness for you that she asked me to befriend the poor kid. Let's just hope that when the time comes I manage to do you both proud.'

She's about to turn the page when her attention snags on the people gathered at the edge of the paddock watching Frances put her pony through its paces. Vanessa leans in, trying to make out their faces. Her eyes lock on a stocky, dark-haired boy of about eighteen or nineteen in jeans and a flannel shirt who's slouching against the gate, glowering at the scene through half-closed eyes. She stops cold. 'Mum, is that Mark Findlay?'

She lifts the album closer to her mother's face. 'Frances's cousin? Do you remember him?' She glances at Ellen to see if her questions are stirring any kind of response. 'What was he like?'

For one, heart-stopping moment she thinks Ellen might respond, but her mother's eyelids simply droop further and a trickle of saliva dribbles down her chin. Vanessa pulls a tissue from the box and dabs it away.

'I don't know why I've been letting what Frances said about him get to me. If Don Dexter, who finds people for a living and knows everything Frances knows about what happened isn't making any headway, what hope has an outsider got? As to thinking Mark Findlay's a threat to me, Dexter or her lawyer' – her eyes dart back to the photo in front of her – 'I'm sure that really is down to the medication. The man's an accountant, for God's sake! Still,' she says, with an attempt at a smile, 'I'm definitely not going to be telling anyone I'm in the know about the baby, and I'm pretty sure my secret's safe with you.'

Ellen turns her head a little and stares past her at the blue candlewick dressing gown hanging on the back of the door.

'Ooh, I forgot to tell you they've offered me a trial shift at Cranmore House. That hostel for the homeless I told you about —? The one looking for volunteers? A lot of the men there are ex-offenders so I'm a bit nervous about it, but I'm going to imagine that you're right there by my side, doing it with me.' Vanessa tosses the tissue in the bin and tries to recount some of the inmates' stories she's read on the Cranmore House website, but it's only a few minutes before she's distracted again, her eyes pulling back to the face of Mark Findlay as a teenager.

'One black tea.'

Vanessa startles as Stefan comes in with a mug. He sets it down on the table beside her. 'I wanted to say all credit to you that you manage to come here so often *and* keep up the stints at

St Saviour's. It's one thing looking after your own mother, quite another giving up your time to visit dying strangers.'

Vanessa snaps the photo album shut and curls her fingers protectively around the cover. 'How do you know I visit St Saviour's?'

'I saw you coming in the other day, then I noticed your name on the rota. I'm agency, you see – here most of the time, but I fill in over there when they need me.'

She feels a rush of blood to her cheeks. 'I... I don't really tell people I'm a hospice visitor,' she says, carefully.

'Sorry,' he says, smoothly, 'I didn't mean to—'

'Would you mind keeping it to yourself?' She hears the crack in her voice, and takes a little breath. 'I don't want anyone thinking I'm some kind of misery junkie.'

He considers her for a moment. 'Of course, but just so you know, I think it's... impressive. Hospice visiting isn't for everyone.'

Why doesn't it sound like a compliment?

She looks up and manages to find an embarrassed smile. 'It was something Mum was thinking about doing before she got ill, so I thought it would be good to, you know, pick up where she had to leave off.' *Slow down. Stop babbling.* She takes a breath and looks over at Ellen slumped in her wheelchair. 'I like to think she knows I'm doing it because of her. Anyway, it's only a few hours a week and it gives us' – the corner of her lip pulls and quivers – '*me* something to talk about that I know will interest her. Honestly, when I'm sitting with the patients over there, listening *to* them rather than talking *at* them, knowing I'm making a difference to their day, it kind of recharges me for when I come here.'

It's warm in Ellen's room, too warm, and the sweet scent of the lilies grows heavy.

'I know it might not feel like it,' Stefan says, 'but I'm sure Ellen knows you're here.'

Vanessa looks down at her mum's fingers lying limply in hers and cups them with her other hand. Almost too choked up to speak, she whispers, 'I just have to hope you're right.'

Later, as Vanessa walks through the well-kept gardens to her car, she's still jittery at the thought of Stefan seeing her at the hospice. Her excuse about not wanting to be seen as a misery junky was weak, but in the surprise of the moment it was all she'd been able to come up with. Will it be enough to keep him quiet? How would he even know that it's Frances she spends most of her time with when she's there?

FOUR

Vanessa parks in the yard behind her shop, her heart still beating hard. *Stefan's a nurse,* she tells herself. *He's trained to respect confidences.* She throws off her jacket, runs up the back stairs and pushes open the door to the showroom. 'Sorry it took me so long to get back. The traffic was awful.'

Stepping into Vanessa Dunn Designs and seeing her hall-mark mix of quirky vintage and carefully chosen designer pieces always calms Vanessa's nerves: glinting glassware, silk-shaded lamps, brightly glazed ceramics, lengths of velvet cascading from the old wooden stepladders she uses to display fabrics. Meghan, who is unpacking a box of light fittings, looks up. She's wearing a black jumpsuit that hugs her slim figure, and her smooth, dark gold hair looks good against the zesty blues and greens reflected in the huge age-spotted mirror behind her. 'Honestly, you shouldn't have bothered coming back at all. How was your mum?'

'Oh, you know.'

Meghan nods sympathetically.

'Has it been busy?'

'Not bad. Lots of interest in the new cushions, a couple of

people wanting leaflets about the decorating service and that woman who's been umming and aahing about the walnut dining chairs came back and I managed to get her to order six.'

'That's brilliant,' Vanessa says, and she means it. Meghan is proving to be a very persuasive saleswoman.

'Jody worked through her lunch break so I said she could go home early – I hope that's alright.'

'Of course.'

'You look drained. Do you fancy going for a drink after we close up?'

'That's sweet of you, but I should probably get home.'

'Oh, come on. It will do you good to relax.'

Is her tension that obvious? Perhaps going for a drink will stop her worrying about Stefan's sighting of her at St Saviour's getting back to Mark Findlay. At least for a little while. 'Alright, why not? Just a quick one, though.'

The door opens and a young couple bursts in, arms entwined. A huge square-cut diamond glitters on the woman's left hand as she gestures excitedly at the collection of antique mirrors arranged on the wall. These people are exactly the kind of customers the shop needs – stylish, affluent and about to set up home, but right now Vanessa's not sure she can cope with dewy-eyed exuberance. She glances quickly at Meghan. 'Is it alright if I catch up on some admin?'

'Sure.' Meghan hurries over to the couple, a beaming smile at the ready, leaving Vanessa to duck away between the shelves of glassware and slip downstairs to her office.

The desk she left strewn with fabric swatches, magazines and order books is unnaturally tidy, the wilting tulips have been replaced by a single stem of white orchids, and the dirty mugs have been washed and put away. The tidiness should please her, yet it jars. This sunny little office is where she does her thinking and planning and now everything is out of place – only very slightly, but enough to make her feel even more off-kilter than she does already. *Meghan was just trying to be helpful*, she tells herself, and it only takes her a few minutes to shift things around until the room feels like hers again. Then she makes herself a coffee, drops into the swivel chair and clicks on the computer. She's a little taken aback to find that the invoicing she was about to deal with is all up to date and the latest Twitter queries have been answered. Somehow Meghan has even found time to post shots of the gorgeous new rattan furniture range on the Vanessa Dunn Instagram account.

She takes a long sip of her coffee. Steadied by the hit of caffeine, she finds herself using these unexpectedly free moments to scroll on through Instagram, studying carefully curated glimpses of the lives, relationships, homes and obsessions of friends, family, acquaintances, competitors and strangers. Hovering here, zooming in there, she loses herself in a thumb-stopping barrage of faces, places and things.

After a while she tears herself away and clicks open the file of articles she's been saving in preparation for her meeting with Larry Cox, the director of Cranmore House: first-hand accounts of life on the streets, essays by experts on the reasons why people fall through the cracks and a blog written by a volunteer who delivers soup and sandwiches to rough sleepers from his van. *What if Larry decides I'm not good enough and I fail at this, like I failed at my marriage?* She can't let herself think like that. This is about new Vanessa, filling the gaps and hollows, making herself whole again.

Later, as they sit in a wine bar, Meghan takes a sip from her glass, taps her phone and turns the screen to Vanessa.

'What is it?'

'A new dating site.'

Vanessa groans and bats the phone away.

'It's not like the others, I promise – it's for professionals only. You can meet other singles one-on-one if you want to, but if you sign up for the app's group events they send you the profiles of everyone who's going to be there. That way you can meet people you like the look of without the pressure of going on an actual date.' Meghan swipes through a series of images. 'We could do it together. It's not just bars, they do cinema and theatre trips too and look' – she taps the screen – 'there's a day at the races coming up. That would be a laugh.'

'I haven't got time to go on outings.' The words come out a little more sharply than Vanessa had intended.

Meghan puts down her phone. 'That's the whole point. You've got so much going on at the moment. What with your mum and the business and the divorce, you don't have a minute to think about yourself. You can't go on like this, Nessa.'

She flinches. *Nessa.* The only person who ever called her that was her father and hearing it on Meghan's lips feels odd... intrusive. She looks up into her new manager's subtly made-up eyes. Meghan smiles back warmly and Vanessa feels annoyed at herself for overreacting. Meghan's just trying to be nice and right now she could do with some nice in her life. She runs a finger down the stem of her wine glass. 'It's not that I wouldn't love to meet someone new, but after what happened with Doug I'm scared to start trusting people again.'

'That bad, huh?' Meghan tips her head to one side. 'You never actually told me what happened.'

Vanessa sighs. 'I met him in my first term at university. We were together for nearly eight years, married for four. I thought I knew him inside out, and then he left me for...' She hesitates. '... someone I knew. They'd probably been seeing each other for months but I never suspected a thing. I still can't believe I could have been so blind and so stupid. To be honest, it's made me doubt my judgement about everyone and everything.'

Meghan nods, sympathetically. 'You don't have to tell me about the risk of letting new people into your life. But if you're

ever going to move on, it's one you've got to take. So what if you
have to kiss a few frogs along the way?'

Vanessa manages a half-smile. 'Moving on doesn't have to
be about finding a new relationship.'

'Oh, God, you're not thinking of selling up?'

'No, nothing like that. But after Doug left me I took a long
hard look at what I had left and I—'

'—saw you had a fantastic business, a stunning home, good
friends...'

'Yes, and I'm grateful for all of those things, but none of
them are very... meaningful.'

Meghan's eyes stay fixed on Vanessa's, clearly wary of
where she might be going with this.

'I'm nearly thirty-four.'

'Not exactly ancient.'

'No, but most of the couples Doug and I hung out with are
having kids, or at least thinking about it and—' She looks down
at her glass. 'When I realised that was no longer on my horizon
it left me feeling a bit, I don't know... lost? Directionless?
Empty?' She knocks back the last of her wine and places the
glass firmly on the table. 'So I'm looking to get involved with a
couple of charities.'

Meghan groans. '*Please* don't tell me you're going to turn
into one of those marathon bores who bangs about mileage,
carbs and hitting your fundraising targets.'

'God, no. I hate running. I want to do something hands-on
that' – she pulls an embarrassed smile – 'might help to change
someone's life.'

Meghan eyes her suspiciously. 'Like what?'

'Volunteering at a homeless shelter.'

'*You?*' Meghan doesn't even pretend to hide her astonishment.

'Why not?'

'You can't just blunder into a place like that. You need

training and experience.'

'Not if you're just volunteering. I've found this place called Cranmore House and their website says they've got all sorts of people helping out – taxi drivers, students, retired teachers, bankers.'

Meghan takes a glug of wine and swills it around her mouth as if to rinse away a sour taste. 'Why *homeless* people?'

Vanessa looks down at the table and wonders what it would be like to spill out the truth and explain the feelings of loss and regret that she's trying to erase, the wounds she's trying to heal. Instead, she says only, 'My whole life revolves around homes. I make my living helping the well-off to make theirs more beautiful, so I thought the best way to give back would be by helping people who don't have one. You could come too if you want.'

Meghan pulls a horrified face. 'No, thanks. But keep me posted about those big-hearted bankers. If any of them turn out to be single I might just change my mind.'

Vanessa gives her a playful slap on the arm. 'That's not what this is about.'

They break into giggles. 'Here's me baring my soul and I hardly know anything about you,' Vanessa says, taking another sip of wine.

Meghan shrugs. 'There's not much to tell. I'm single, my mum and dad still treat me as if I'm sixteen and incapable of looking after myself; yes, I wouldn't mind finding a rich, good-looking man to have fun with, but right now I'm not interested in anything serious as I'm totally focused on building my career. In fact, I've signed up for an evening course in interior professional practice – I did a bit of planning and detailing when I was at college, and I was wondering if I could get a bit more involved in the design side of the business.'

'Oh,' Vanessa says, mildly surprised. 'I thought you studied marketing.'

'I did, but interiors was one of my final year electives, and

since I've been working for you I've got more and more interested in it.'

Vanessa traces her thumb along the padded arm of her
chair, pushing her nail into the seam. 'The thing is, at the
moment I'm focused on promoting the specific Vanessa Dunn
look, so I'm a bit wary of involving other designers until my own
offer is a bit more established.'

'Oh, sure, I totally get that but maybe I could tag along to
some of your client meetings and get a feel for the process—?'
Meghan pushes back her chair and stands up. 'Let's have
another drink.'

Vanessa lifts her hand. 'Not for me—'

'Come on, we both need to unwind.' Without waiting for an
answer Meghan heads to the bar.

Vanessa lets her gaze drift around the room. It catches on a
man at a table by the door. He's on his own – dark hair, checked
shirt, brown jacket, a half-drunk pint in one hand and a folded
newspaper in the other. Only he's not looking at the paper. He's
looking over the top of it. At her. He drops his gaze. So does she.
Annoyance sluices through her. How can she unwind when she
can't even catch the eye of some harmless guy having a quiet
beer after work without fanning the fear that Mark Findlay is
having her followed?

Minutes later, Meghan's back with an open bottle of Merlot
and, despite Vanessa's insistence that she shouldn't drink any
more on an empty stomach, she fills her glass. 'Don't worry
about your stomach, I've ordered us a couple of burgers. The
food here is amazing, and their chips are to die for.'

Vanessa, who's had little or no appetite since Doug left,
suddenly realises how hungry she is and as soon as their food
arrives she digs in. Meghan was right: the crunch of the fat,
hand-cut chips is perfect with the juicy burgers, melting blue
cheese and salty strips of pancetta. Between bites she swigs her
wine and laughs as Meghan writes her a mock dating profile.

'Bacon enthusiast, interested in wild sex and saving the world, own teeth...'

Before she realises it, she has cleaned her plate and Meghan is pouring the last dregs of a second bottle of wine into her glass.

'I'm going to feel like hell in the morning,' she says, as she lifts it to her lips.

'Then don't come in. Jody, Sarah and I can cope. Have a lie-in, go to the gym. Take a few hours to de-stress.'

'But you'll be wrecked too.' Vanessa's tongue is dragging a little, slowing her words.

'I'll be fine. Constitution of a horse. Anyway, I'm not dealing with a sick mum and a shitty ex. I can't imagine how you cope.'

Vanessa feels a sudden pang of envy for Meghan's easy, uncluttered existence – her supportive parents and carefree optimism, but as she stretches her eyebrows to lift her drooping eyelids her thoughts snag on something she'd said earlier. 'It sounded like you've had your own problems with letting the wrong people into your life. What happened?'

There's a sticky little silence then Meghan laughs and leans back in her chair. 'How long have you got?'

Vanessa laughs too and glances blearily at her watch, yearning for the moment when she can kick off her shoes and collapse into bed. 'OK, we'll save the big confession for another night.' She wags a wavery finger. 'That doesn't mean I'm letting you off the hook – I want to hear all about it.'

She stands up, tipsier than she's been for a very long time. Swaying slightly, she heads towards the door. Her hip knocks against the table where the man in the brown jacket had been sitting, sending his abandoned newspaper scudding to the floor. Embarrassed, she bends to pick it up.

A sobering prickle of unease shoots down her spine. The paper is four days old.

FIVE

Cranmore House, once an elegant Victorian mansion, is now sad and dilapidated, its former red brick and sandstone symmetry destroyed by a jerry-built extension and a rusty fire escape that zigzags up the side of the building. Separated from the main road by nothing more than a narrow strip of car park, the noise and fumes from the traffic are overwhelming. *OK, Mum, wish me luck.* Vanessa gets out of her car, automatically glancing up and down the street as she locks the door. All she sees are fast-moving cars, a motorbike courier hitching up his backpack as he stops by the kerb to check his phone, and a couple of pedestrians looking the other way. Nothing to explain the feeling of being watched that chills her skin.

She hurries to the entrance and presses the bell. The door clicks open and she steps inside, hit instantly by the smell of stale sweat, cheap disinfectant and blocked drains. She fights the temptation to turn and run.

'Hey, you must be Vanessa.' A man strides towards her, his beefy hand outstretched. He's big, shaven-headed and wears a red sweatshirt with a Cranmore House logo printed across it in white.

'You must be Larry.'

'Yep. I thought you were going to be a no-show.'

'Sorry,' she says, 'am I late?'

'No, you're right on time.' He looks her up and down. 'But you'd be amazed how many bushy-tailed do-gooders get to the car park, take one look at the place and decide they can't hack it.'

His words sting, hitting deep into her insecurities. 'Oh,' she says, flustered. 'I wouldn't call myself a do-gooder. I just want to... help out.'

'Night, Larry!' A tall man in a well-cut suit comes past, swinging a battered briefcase.

'Night, David, see you next month,' Larry calls after him. 'David's one of our longest-serving volunteers,' Larry says, setting off down the hallway. 'CEO of a big accountancy firm in the City, but he's been coming in to do our books since the day we opened.'

A howl echoes off the peeling paintwork and a man stumbles down a set of stairs and lurches towards them. His eyes are wild and a scar runs livid through his stubble. Trembling and clearly upset, he thrusts an angry finger at Larry. 'You've got no right going in my room, no right taking my stuff.'

Larry stands his ground though the man is broad-set and at least a head taller. 'You know the rules, Matt.' His voice is firm and icy calm. 'No drugs. No alcohol. This is your second strike. One more and you're out.'

The man glares at him, then at Vanessa, a purple vein throbbing at his temple.

'Up to you,' Larry says.

The man's eyes shift, his shoulders slump and he turns and stumbles away.

'This way,' Larry says, without missing a beat.

Vanessa follows him into his office. It's a grim, airless space, carved out of a much larger room by flimsy partitions that cut through the dusty sash window and ornate plaster cornicing. A torn plastic lampshade dangles from an off-centre ceiling rose, giving the whole place a skewed, lopsided feel. An iron medical screen stands in one corner; beside it hangs a message board, shaggy with printouts and flyers. Larry points her to a grey bucket seat and lowers himself into the vinyl swivel chair behind the desk. There's a banner taped above the scarred whiteboard behind his head – *There's no such thing as bad people, just bad decisions.* Wondering if that's what this is going to turn out to be, she sits down.

Larry picks up a biro and clicks it with his thumb. 'Your email said you're offering to help with CVs and job applications.'

'That's right.'

'Well, the good news is you've passed the DBS check – looks like you're a model citizen. Not even a speeding ticket.'

There's a quick knock at the door and a woman pokes her head inside. 'Ginny's just called. She won't be in. Her kid's hurt his leg at football and she's got to take him to A and E.'

Larry's expression turns pleading. 'Could you—?'

The woman shakes her head. 'Sorry, not tonight.'

'Alright, Anna. Thanks for letting me know.' He lets out a sigh and turns wearily back to Vanessa. 'The bad news is we need an extra pair of hands to serve dinner. Would you mind? I know it's not what you signed up for.'

'That's fine,' she says. 'In fact, it might be a good way to get to know everyone.'

'That's the spirit. So, a quick rundown of what we're about. Forget the guff on the website about offering a home to the homeless. We're donor-funded so we're permanently broke, which means we can barely give a handful of rough sleepers bed and board for six months. That said, in the time they're here, we do our damnedest to help them find a job and a perma-nent place to live. We spend ninety per cent of our time fighting losing battles with social services and housing departments. We can't afford the staff we need, the place is falling apart and they're threatening us with more cuts, so we're pretty dependent on volunteers coming in when they can. But even sitting down for ten minutes with a new arrival and listening to his problems can make all the difference. Though it's not about telling them what's good for them – they've had a bellyful of that. It's about helping them to make good choices. Oh, and there's two basic rules. One – you never ask a guest how he ended up on the street.' *Guest*, Vanessa thinks, making a mental note. 'If they want to tell you their life story they'll do it in their own time. Two, if you're dealing with an ex-offender you never, *ever* ask him what he was in for. Understood?'

'Yes,' she says.

'Working here can be very rewarding, but it can also be challenging. Some of these men have never had a chance at life, others have been let down time and time again. That can make them difficult, angry, untrusting, and there are plenty who'll go out of their way to wind you up. If you can't deal with that then this isn't the place for you.' His gaze is frank and businesslike, yet non-judgemental. 'If I think it's not working out, I'll tell you straight. I'd rather be short-staffed than have the wrong people working here.' Vanessa swallows and nods. 'Most of the guests have lost contact with their families. Without family support they're far more likely to drift back into their old ways – drugs, alcohol, crime – so we try, as best we can, to fill that gap. But for every vulnerable rough sleeper we take in, there's at least fifty more we have to turn away.'

'More like a hundred and fifty.' A man comes in clasping a bunch of keys. He's in his twenties, lean – a little too lean – his black skinny jeans are ripped at the knee and his thick dark hair is tied back with a leather thong. 'And the ones we do take in need a hell of a lot more than six months to turn their lives around.'

'Don't put her off,' Larry says, cheerfully. 'She's offering to help out with job applications.'

The man, who is taking a pen from a tin on the desk, glances up at her through dark, heavy-lidded eyes and grunts, 'Good luck with that,' before opening one of the battered filing cabinets that block the fireplace and dropping the keys into the top drawer. His accent is difficult to pin down – rough edged, but as if it's by choice. As he signs his name on the chart hanging above the cabinet she glimpses a mesh of scars running down the inside of his arm.

'Is he a volunteer?' she asks, when he's gone.

Larry shakes his head. 'Jay? No, he's staff. Lives in.'

'What does he do?'

'Whatever needs doing,' Larry says, briskly. He opens a cupboard, pulls out a nylon overall, a blue tabard and a white cotton cap, snaps a pair of black latex gloves from a box on the shelf behind him and drops it all in a pile on the desk. 'Here you go. You can change behind there.' He jerks a thumb at the screen.

'Oh,' she says, frowning at the torn green curtaining.

'Don't worry, I'll lock your bag away then I'll leave you to it.'

He bends down to open a drawer at the bottom of the filing cabinet and as she leans across the desk to hand him her bag, her elbow sends a stack of files skittering to the floor. 'Oh, sorry.' She's bobbing down to pick them up when a crash of splintering glass sends them both swinging round in alarm. A panicked shout rings down the corridor.

Larry holds up a warning hand. 'Stay here.' He rushes out. Feet pound the stairs and the whole building shakes with angry shouts. She peers through the glass panel in the door. The corridor is empty. She turns back into the room and drops to her knees to retrieve the files from the floor. They're dossiers – one on every inmate; lives, careers, hopes and dreams reduced to a handful of scribbled notes and a mugshot clipped to a manilla folder. Gradually, as she gathers them up, the noise from upstairs subsides, replaced by a tense silence in which all she can hear is the ticking of the clock on the wall. She piles the files neatly on the table and wanders over to look at the big whiteboard, its stained surface covered with upcoming meetings, events and scribbled notes, before slipping behind the screen to change.

'What happened?' she asks, when Larry finally reappears.

'Matt wasn't too happy about having his stash confiscated. Took it out on his window.'

'Oh.' She adjusts the Velcro tabs at the sides of the tabard. 'Is he alright?'

'A few cuts. Jay managed to restrain him before he did himself any real damage, and Anna's bandaging him up. Don't forget the cap.'

She twists up her hair and perches the cap on her head.

Larry locks the door behind her. 'This way.'

The soles of her trainers cling to the sticky grey floor tiles as she follows him down a badly lit passageway painted a muddy shade of green and into a cavernous dining room that smells of cheap fat and over-boiled cabbage. The wall at one end has been knocked through into a smaller room that's been converted into a kitchen, separated from the eating area by a servery counter. Behind it, a boy who looks about nineteen, with pale, pockmarked cheeks and faded tattoos up his neck, is heaving steel trays into place, overseen by an elderly red-faced woman.

'Donnie, Beattie, meet Vanessa,' Larry says. 'She's going to help serve up this evening.' He turns to Vanessa. 'Beattie's been running our kitchen for the last ten years and Donnie's getting a bit of catering experience to put on his CV.'

'Hi, Donnie.' The boy nods at her shyly. Vanessa studies his face and tries to commit his name to memory as she snaps on the gloves. 'Hi, Beattie. What do you need me to do?'

'You can plate up the roly-poly.' Beattie dumps a pan on the counter. It holds two long grey logs of suet sponge. 'Bowls on the side.'

'How big do you want the pieces?'

The woman holds up her thumb and forefinger a couple of inches apart and turns back to the stove.

'Right.' Vanessa picks up a heavy knife from the counter and begins to slice into the sponge while Donnie stands at her elbow watching her.

'How long have you been at Cranmore House?' she says, keen to break the slightly unnerving silence.

'Two months.'

'Do you like it?' A thin smear of jam sticks to the knife as she lays it down on the counter and reaches over for the stack of bowls.

'S'alright.'

'How many guests are there here?'

He considers this and shrugs. 'Twenty? Thirty?'

'Larry says you're looking for a job in catering—?'

He nods again.

'Well, I'm here to help with applications so we can work on that together. Have you got a CV?'

He shakes his head, looking slightly panicked.

'Don't worry,' she says, quickly. 'I can help you with that too.' She plops the last slice of roly-poly into a bowl.

'Veggie option.' Beattie slams down a tray of baked potatoes topped with watery baked beans and a smattering of grated cheese. 'Don't stand there gassing. It's six o'clock.'

She thrusts a metal scoop into Vanessa's hand. 'Three of mash, two of peas. Donnie'll do the sausages. They help themselves to gravy, afters and custard.'

Vanessa's nerves pulse as she takes up her position behind the servery.

Donnie lifts the lids off the metal trays. The mash is grey and sloppy, the sausages shrivelled and the peas so overcooked they've turned almost khaki. The door bangs open, the residents file in, a rattling and scraping as they grab their trays.

Vanessa's hands grow clammy beneath the latex gloves. She plunges her scoop into the mash. The first diner shuffles along the counter and holds out his plate. She looks up at him and smiles. He's in his forties, stocky with a barrel chest and thick, pudgy fingers. He ignores her, keeping his eyes on the movements of the scoop, as if she might try to cheat him out of his allotted dollops of mash. The next man is younger – he could be anything between twenty and thirty, yet he walks with the lurching gait of an old man. This time she tries a quick, 'Hi, I'm Vanessa,' but he's already moving on, reaching for the jug of gravy. She looks down the line of men; a few wear overalls, others are in jeans or track pants and there's one in a baggy, brown suit. The queue speeds up. There's no time for niceties. These diners are hungry. Intent on their food, they swing their laden trays away from the counter and make for one of the two long plastic trestle tables set up in the middle of the room. The air fills with the clink of cutlery and the murmur of voices.

She gets into a rhythm and after a while she hears herself call over her shoulder for more peas. Gradually, the queue thins down to a few stragglers and she gets a chance to catch her breath.

'How's it going?' Larry stands before her, tray in hand.

'Alright – I think.'

She fills his plate. He shakes out a glob of floury gravy from the jug and pivots around to face the tables.

'Listen up, everyone – this is Vanessa.' His voice silences the chatter. Every eye turns towards her. She feels a flush creep up her throat. 'She'll be coming in once a week to run a job application and CV clinic.'

She looks nervously across the sea of stares. So many faces – fat, thin, dark, pale, bored, hostile, curious, appraising – yet they all have the same pasty gauntness about them.

'Hello.' To her annoyance, her voice comes out shrill and wavery.

The clatter and hum start up again. Larry moves away and calls over his shoulder, 'Get yourself something to eat, then join me over there.' He points to an empty space at one of the tables.

She's about to refuse the food when she catches the look in Beattie's eye. Stomach heaving, she drops a baked potato onto a plate, grabs a knife and fork and carries it over to the seat beside Larry. She sits in a tremble, looking down at the cigarette burns dotted along the edge of the table.

'You can use the staff meeting room for your clinics.'

'Great,' she says, excited and at the same time terrified. 'I thought I could do a mixture of general group chats about how to sell yourself, and then one-on-ones to help with specific applications. What do you think?'

'Sounds good.'

'Do you have any computers?'

'Two laptops, but you have to sign them out.'

'I can only really come in at weekends.'

'Sundays could work.'

'That's fine.'

'Won't your boyfriend mind?'

She looks away, taking in the faded strips of flower-sprigged wallpaper curling off the walls, the tobacco-stained paintwork, the plasterwork falling away like broken meringue and the general patina of gloom. For a moment she imagines it as the grand salon it was built to be, filled with glittering chandeliers, silken drapes and swathes of flowers. 'I don't have a boyfriend.'

'Husband, then.'

'Don't have one of those, either.' She prods the food on her plate and thinks of that last night with Doug; the final, heart-wrenching admission of infidelity that had ended her marriage. 'I've just got divorced.'

'Ah, so that's it.' He laughs, but not unkindly. 'You wouldn't be the first volunteer to turn up here trying to mend a broken heart.'

'Why d'you pick a dump like Cranmore House?' The man with the ponytail she'd seen in Larry's office drops into the seat opposite her. He's chewing on a toothpick, working it around his mouth, and there's a cockiness about him that irritates her.

'Why did *you*?' she says.

He laughs, as if genuinely amused.

'Why's that funny?'

He slides the toothpick to the other side of his mouth. 'Let's say it was picked for me.'

Larry grins. 'Vanessa, this is Jay. Any problems, he's your man.'

She nods at Jay and turns quickly back to Larry. 'If I could round up a few of the guests to help me, we could paint this room.'

The idea seems to startle him and he looks around, as if seeing its grimness for the first time. 'If we had money lying around for decorating, I'd get the rotting window frames in the rec room replaced.'

'There's been a lot of research into the effects of décor on mental health and self-esteem.' She winces, worried that her nerves are making her come across as snotty and superior, but she ploughs on. 'A clean bright colour in here would really cheer people up.'

'Yeah, well, like I said, there's no budget for it.'

Jay tips back in his chair, watching her with a sort of jaded amusement. She ignores him and focuses her attention on Larry. 'It needn't cost you anything. I've got plenty of paint left over from a client who changed his mind about colours at the last minute. If we made an early start I'm sure we could get it done in a day.'

Larry shrugs, as if he can't be bothered to object.

'Is that what you do then? Decorating?' Jay says, rolling the toothpick back the other way.

'Sort of,' she says, refusing to rise to the sneer in his tone... 'I'm an interior designer but pretty good with a paintbrush when I need to be.'

She turns away and crushes her eyes shut. *I won't let this guy get to me. Come on. Up.* Heart pounding, she hauls herself to her feet and moves along the table. *I can do this. I can, I can, I can.* Her legs feel wobbly but she keeps going, gripping the backs of chairs, grey plastic warm and tacky beneath her fingers. *One – two – three.* 'Is anyone up for helping me paint this room this weekend?'

A few heads shake. She falters forward, approaches a group at the end of the table. They're joshing each other, loud and lairy. Though still in their twenties, they have the same scooped-out pallor as the older men.

'Nice tabard.' The voice is mocking and the Scottish accent strong. Its owner is a scrawny, twitchy-looking guy with a gold ring in one ear and a DIY tattoo of a grinning skull on his left bicep.

'Thanks,' she says. 'Are you offering to help?'

He folds his arms and shakes his head. 'Nah.'

She glances at his companions. 'Any of you? You don't have to decide right now. You can just turn up on Saturday morning.'

One of them rolls his eyes; another pushes his plate away and stands up. 'You coming, Stu?'

The Scot gets up and leaves. Aware of Larry and Jay watching her, Vanessa scans the rest of the guests. For a moment she loses her nerve, and then she approaches a man who's bending so low over his plate all she can see is a shock of matted grey hair. 'Do you fancy helping me?' she says, a little desperately.

The head tips back. The man is haggard, his skin an unhealthy grey but the eyes that stare up at her are a fierce blue.

'*Please?*'

His voice is scratchy as though he hasn't used it for a while. 'What with?'

'Painting this room.'

His eyes dart away to the walls. He shrugs as if humouring her. 'Alright.'

'Great,' she says. 'Sorry – I don't know your name.'

'Mick.'

'Thanks, Mick. Are you around on Saturday?'

'Got nowhere else to be.' He goes back to sawing his sausages.

She makes her way along the rest of the table gathering a handful of half-hearted yesses, a couple of 'Dunno, maybes' and a lot of surly refusals.

Jesus, she thinks. *This isn't going to be easy.*

Yet an hour later, when she stumbles out to her car and catches sight of her flushed, sweaty face, smudged cheeks and messy halo of frizz in the mirror, instead of reaching into her bag for her hairbrush and a tissue to repair the damage, she sits in the driver's seat staring at her reflection. So what if she looks like a wreck and Larry and the rest of them think she's a daffy do-gooder who doesn't have a clue? She hasn't felt this elated in years, and she can't wait to share her excitement with her mother.

She pulls out of the car park, turns onto the main road and approaches the traffic lights, switching on the radio as the traffic slows to halt. She smiles a little as 'Dancing in the Street' – one of her father's favourites – blasts from the speakers. All at once she's back in the kitchen of her childhood home and her father's pulling her up, twirling her around, tossing her scarily high and catching her as she falls.

Lost in the memory she's rocking her shoulders and singing along with Martha Reeves when a biker pulls up beside her. He turns his head to look at her. She glances up at him, catches her bobbing reflection in the tinted curve of his visor and smiles, embarrassed, expecting a nod or a cheery thumbs-up in return. He makes no move. She can't see his face but she can feel him studying her even as she looks away. The lights change, he opens the throttle and screeches ahead.

SIX

'It's the sheer bloody arrogance of it, Vinnie – whizzing up behind you, crashing into kids and old people, acting like they own the pavements, and what do the police do about it? Nothing.'

Dave from Enfield is always angry, and tonight his fury has been whipped into incandescence by the riders of electric scooters.

It was her sister, Izzy, who introduced Vanessa to 'Late-Night with Vinnie Dalgliesh'. Between long-winded musings about life, and rambling chats with insomniacs, long-distance lorry drivers and harassed parents, he plays an eclectic selection of music by new artists and once, about two years, ago he'd played a tape Izzy had sent him of one of her songs. He'd liked it enough to repeat it a couple of times a night for a week and since Izzy had been staying at Vanessa's at the time, Vanessa had been forced to listen along. A week later, Izzy had flounced off to Greece with a busker she'd picked up on the Tube. As Vanessa lay awake in her empty house, raking over the smoking rubble of her marriage, she'd found herself tuning in to Vinnie's particular brand of aural cocoa to get her through the night.

Since Frances's revelation, however, it's not heartache that's been keeping her awake; it's a gnawing concern for the future of Frances's child, and the fear of what Mark Findlay might do to keep hold of a business empire that isn't rightly his.

She glances at her phone – 3.30 a.m. She slips out of bed and goes downstairs to make herself a steadying cup of herbal tea. Vinnie is on form tonight, wondering, arguing, banging on between tracks from a gravel-voiced blues singer and a grumpy grunge artist playing choppy guitar.

She takes her mug over to her kitchen table and clicks open Mark Findlay's LinkedIn page. She's visited it before – more times than she cares to admit – but she can't resist the urge to look at it again. She catches sight of his photo. That bland, unreadable face. Instinctively, she gets up to check that she's bolted the back door and set the burglar alarm, something she only ever used to do when she left the house. She drops onto the bottom stair and cradles her head in her hands.

This is ridiculous. Instead of letting her imagination run riot, she needs to take control of this situation and get the inside track on Findlay. It's the only way she'll be able to decide how much of a threat he might really pose to Frances's kid. How much of a threat he might pose to her.

Suddenly energised, she's back in the kitchen skimming through links, studying his interests, looking for a way into his life. He's a keen golfer, squash player and yachtsman, which is no help to her at all, and although he's a member of a number of private clubs they all have lengthy waiting lists. Oddly, though, there don't seem to be any properties registered in his name.

She goes back through his personal data and stops on the details of his current spouse. She's wife number three, her name is Amanda Mason-Findlay and she owns a gallery in Soho. According to the gallery's website it's currently exhibiting new works by Mexican artist, Miguel Sanchez, who 'explores the tensions between shape and space, utilising vivid colours and bold brushstrokes to represent reality in fresh and exhilarating ways'. *Who writes this twaddle?* She notes down the address and delves a little deeper into Amanda. It doesn't take her long to discover that the couple's London home – a townhouse in Chelsea – is registered to a company of which Amanda is the director and sole shareholder, and that the same company has recently purchased the house next door. A quick delve into the Kensington and Chelsea planning portal reveals an application to knock the two properties into one and dig out another layer of basement beneath both houses. Interestingly, after diving deeper, she comes up with another recent purchase made by the company – a derelict manor house in Norfolk set in eighteen acres of protected woodland.

Amanda Mason-Findlay has to be Vanessa's way into Mark Findlay's life. She gets up, opens the fridge, closes it again and shuffles into the sitting room, picking things up and putting them down again as she works out how best to approach Amanda.

It's nearly 5.30 by the time she's satisfied with her strategy. Too late to go back to bed, too early to get ready for work. Determined not to lose sight of her goals for 'new Vanessa', she opens the link to the dating site Meghan sent her. Bemused by the garish graphics and game-like design of the app she signs up, just for a month, and sits at her kitchen table, head cranked downwards, swiping through the faces of strangers. *Has the selection of prospective mates always been this brutal?* she wonders. *Snap judgements based on chins, eyes, lip shapes and hairlines?* She studies a few profiles: singletons trying too hard to impress; widowers with hearts still raw; wounded divorcés pretending that they are fine, fine, fine.

She drops her phone and leans back, rubbing her aching neck. How can she tell if a man even has the potential to be the special someone she needs right now, unless she meets him face to face and looks him in the eye? Even then, how can she ever be sure he's someone she can trust?

SEVEN

Vanessa tugs the wagon across the cracked concrete of the Cranmore House car park. It's a smart black canvas box on wheels, the kind her personal trainer uses to drag kettlebells and yoga mats around the park. It had seemed like a good idea when she'd ordered it, but when she looks up and sees Stu watching her, she feels like a total idiot. He's leaning against the wall rolling a cigarette. 'Hi,' she says.

His eyes slide down her body, and she's glad she's wearing her baggiest, most paint-spattered overalls.

'Have you changed your mind about helping me spruce up the dining room?'

He lets out a bark of laughter and pushes himself off the wall.

She hurries on inside and walks into the dining room to find Mick up a ladder scraping off wallpaper. He glances down and pushes a straggle of hair off his face. 'I... thought I'd make a start,' he says, his voice halting and low. 'This is the only wall that needs stripping completely. We can just patch the others up.'

'Why do I get the feeling you've done this before?'

He opens his mouth, closes it, then shakes his head as if to knock something free. 'Got any lining paper?'

'There's a couple of rolls in the wagon, and paste and a brush.' Kicking herself for mentioning Mick's past she hands buckets, scrapers and sponges to the trickle of men who wander in. By ten thirty, there are still only five of them: Mick; Donnie; Gibbo, a rangy Yorkshireman missing most of his front teeth; Gaz, a kid with liquid brown eyes who seems slightly bewildered by the whole enterprise; and Blakey, whose main contribution is to lug in an old ghetto blaster, crank it up to full volume and fill the room with ear-splitting heavy metal. But by lunchtime the walls are patched and scrubbed clean, the first layer of gloom seems to have lifted, she's managed to persuade Blakey to lower the volume and she's levering the lids off the tubs of emulsion.

'I don't like yellow,' Gibbo says, peering over her shoulder.

'Why not?'

'Turns my stomach.'

'Oh, come on, anything's got to be better than this dingy brown wallpaper.'

'I like brown,' he says huffily, and stomps away.

'Don't mind him, he's a miserable old so and so,' Mick says, coming over to inspect the colour.

Vanessa gives him a grateful smile. 'Here, have a roller and tray.'

He backs off, holding up his hand. 'If it's alright with you I'll make a start on the woodwork.' The practised ease with which he picks up a screwdriver and twists off the lid of the undercoat makes her want to burst out with all kinds of questions, though she knows she mustn't.

'What's going on?' It's Beattie, standing in her coat with her hands on her hips, surveying the room.

'We're going to freshen this place up,' Vanessa says.

'Where are they all going to eat, and how am I supposed to cook with all this mess cluttering the place up?'

'Larry's put the tables in the rec room just for today. And we're not going to touch the kitchen. Just the dining area, so we won't be in your way.'

'I should have been warned,' Beattie grumbles. 'I can't abide the smell of paint.'

Vanessa gazes around her, unable to suppress a smile. The fresh yellow walls make the room look twice the size. Even Larry seems impressed.

'Not bad,' he says.

'You wait till it's had a second coat,' Mick says, from the top of the ladder.

'Yellow's supposed to be calming,' Vanessa says in an excited rush. 'I was thinking we could hang some artwork along that far wall – maybe pictures done by the guests. I know a couple of artists who might be willing to come in and do some creative workshops.'

Jay slouches in the doorway, saying nothing, his hands thrust deep into the pockets of his jeans.

'Don't you approve?' she says.

'I don't see the point.'

'The point is to cheer people up and make them feel motivated.'

'Oh, right, so a lick of paint's going to stop this lot ending up back inside or sleeping rough the minute they get chucked out of here.'

Vanessa glances at the other men in the room, worried at the effect his words might be having, but no one seems to be bothered. 'Of course not but—'

Jay twists away and lets the door swing shut behind him.

She wants to run after him and ask him what his problem is.

Instead, she picks up her paint-soaked roller and slaps it hard
against the wall.

Vanessa leaves Cranmore House at 2 p.m. and rushes home to
shower and change. By 4 p.m. she's in Soho. Feeling uneasy and
conspicuous, she weaves between the cars and cuts across
Golden Square, crosses into Beak Street and sees the gallery on
the corner – a chic, understated shopfront with 'Mason Fine
Art' etched in small black letters at the bottom of the plate-glass
window.

Vanessa thrusts her hand into her pocket, squeezes her
phone so hard she fears it might crack and counts the lines
between the paving stones, the arrowheads on the railings, the
bollards on the corner. Breathing hard, she approaches the door.
A bell dings as she pushes it open and steps inside.

Three people are gathered in front of one the splodgy
explosions of colour lining the walls – two men in suits and a
woman who Vanessa recognises as Amanda Mason-Findlay.
Slightly older than she looks in her website photo, she's still at
least ten years younger than her husband – tall and slender,
with long legs and a narrow waist. Her red hair is cut short, with
soft wisps framing her heart-shaped face. She wears sharply
tailored black trousers and a cream silk shirt, gold studs in her
ears and a narrow gold chain around her neck.

'Hello,' she says, pinning Vanessa with a smile. Her voice is
low and husky. Vanessa smiles back. 'There are more paintings
through there and catalogues on the table. Do shout if I can help
you with anything.'

'Thank you.' Vanessa turns to inspect the nearest painting.
It's a mess of blues and purples. Like the rest of the pieces she
finds it clumsy and underwhelming, but she's not here for the
art. She moves slowly from canvas to canvas waiting for the men

to leave. It feels like an eternity before they finally kiss Amanda on the cheek and wander out into the street.

'These are very powerful,' she says, as Amanda returns to the glass desk in the corner.

'I love Miguel's work. This is the third time he's exhibited with us. He's becoming very collectible.'

Vanessa turns back to look at a particularly uninspiring mishmash of green and yellow blotches. 'Actually, I'm looking for a couple of pieces for a client.'

Amanda lifts her head and looks at her with a flicker of interest.

'I design interiors.'

'Oh.'

'Vanessa Dunn.' She walks across the stripped floorboards and lays her business card on Amanda's desk, her calm, controlled voice belied by the tremor in her hand.

Amanda picks up the card in her manicured fingers. Her nails are painted the palest pink. She slips a pair of black-framed glasses onto the tip of her nose and reads the name. A fine line creases her brow. 'Wasn't there a feature about you in one of the Sundays?'

'I've just opened a shop in Notting Hill. The paper used the launch to showcase some of my design work.'

'I remember now. Your interiors are stunning.'

'Thank you.' Vanessa hesitates. 'I've just commissioned a very talented young director to make some short videos for my website. He's going to film the creation of a Vanessa Dunn interior from concept to completion, alongside interviews with the makers and suppliers I use for each project.' It's a lie, of course, but actually not a bad idea. 'If my client decides on a Sanchez or two, might you be willing to be interviewed?'

'Of course.' Amanda beams. 'I'm sure Miguel would too.'

'Great! I'm hoping the client will sign off on the artwork in the next couple of weeks but he's proving a bit difficult to pin down.'

'If daytimes are a problem, I'd be happy to stay open after hours.'

'That's very kind.'

Amanda's smile is warm. 'Can I add you to our mailing list? I'd love to invite you to our next opening.'

'Can you put my manager on it too? Meghan Grey. Meghan with an H, Grey with an E. Next time you're out west you should drop in and take a look at the shop. If you let me know when you're coming in, I'll make sure that one of us is there to show you around.' Vanessa hitches the strap of her bag further up her shoulder. 'And if you're ever in the market for an interior designer, don't hesitate to give me a call.'

Amanda pulls off her glasses and lays them on the desk before meeting Vanessa's gaze. 'I might just do that.'

The door opens, and a couple with matching purple hair and nose piercings comes in. Vanessa moves away, returning to the mess of green and yellow as if she's taken a particular fancy to it.

She slips out into the street while Amanda is busy chatting to the couple. She's cast her bait. All she can do now is wait it out in the hope that Amanda Mason-Findlay will bite.

EIGHT

For the last few months Vanessa has dreaded Sundays. Waking up alone, dragging herself out to the gym, spending an hour being barked at and bullied by her trainer, then picking up breakfast from some overpriced deli on the way back and spending the rest of the day catching up on work emails and flicking through TV channels. Now and then she still gets invitations to join old friends for pub lunches and walks by the river, but they're mostly friends of Doug and Lisa's too, and she knows they'd much rather spend time with the fun new couple than the wounded ex-wife, so she stays away.

Today, however, she wakes up full of hope and possibility, eager to jump into the shower, down a coffee, and get back to Cranmore House. She's done her research on tips for writing CVs, and after running her own business for five years she's seen enough job applications to know what's likely to catch an employer's eye. With these men, however, she's pretty sure the first hurdle will be giving them the confidence to apply.

On her way to the staff meeting room she can't resist slipping into the dining room to see how the new décor looks. The room falls silent as she walks in. Her stomach twists when she sees why.

Across the upper part of the far wall someone has painted a giant pair of hands bursting through the pristine surface of the emulsion. The left hand has a handcuff dangling from its wrist, the right holds out a cup with a couple of coins in the bottom of it. The execution is crude but expressive, and there's no mistaking the message. She feels the heat of thirty pairs of eyes waiting to see her reaction.

'Who did this?' she says.

'I did.' There's a mixture of pride and challenge in the voice. She doesn't need to turn around to know it's Jay's. 'You said you wanted to see some art on that wall. I thought I'd oblige.'

Mick gets up from the table with his empty tray. 'Don't worry about it,' he grunts as he passes her. 'I'll sort it. It'll take a few coats, mind.'

She looks at Jay and struggles to control her voice. 'It must have taken you half the night. That's a lot of work for something that's going to be gone within hours.'

'No worries,' he says. 'I've got what I wanted.'

'Which is what? To wind me up?'

He eyes her scornfully and holds out his phone. She looks down at the screen. It's his Instagram page. On it there's a photo of the Cranmore House residents sitting at the tables eating breakfast with the mural of the handcuffs and begging bowl hanging over them like a threat. Somehow, he's managed to catch the light from the window and frame the shot to look like da Vinci's *Last Supper*, except in his version the diners are dressed in hoodies and the chalices have been replaced by chipped china mugs and bottles of ketchup.

It's a striking image, but before Vanessa can think what to say he's tucked the phone back into his pocket and sauntered away.

She walks over to Larry who's at the servery, helping

himself to tea from the urn. 'Are all your staff as negative about this place as Jay?'

He shrugs. 'Yeah, well, sorry about your paint job but Jay just sees things as they are. And he's a good worker – does everything I ask him to and a lot more besides. We're going to miss him.'

'Is he leaving?'

'Yep.'

'When?'

'Couple of weeks.'

She takes another look at the mural scarring the freshly painted walls that she and Mick had worked so hard to perfect. Telling herself to stay calm she pushes open the door and walks out to her car. The wagon full of painting equipment is still in the boot and she heaves it out and drags it back to the dining room.

Mick comes over to help her unload it. 'Don't upset yourself,' he says. 'I told you, I'll sort it.'

'If it was just about the art I'd leave it up there, but the whole point of painting the room was to make people feel better about themselves, not worse.'

Her phone buzzes. It's a text. The caller ID says 'John Mathis'. The name is vaguely familiar but it takes her a moment to place it. She's annoyed when she does – he's the old man who lives in the house opposite hers. A busybody with pet peeves about dog mess and bins left out overnight. She stuffs the phone back into her pocket.

She leaves Mick to strip the wall and spends the next hour with Donnie, helping him to fill out applications for minimum-wage kitchen porter jobs. Years spent bouncing between foster homes and institutions have left him desperate for anyone to show any kind of interest in his life and opinions, and as she struggles to shape ten different schools, a complete lack of quali-fications, a stint in juvenile detention and eighteen months living rough, into an appealing CV, he opens up to her about his dreams of becoming a chef and having a family of his own.

'You know what?' she says, reading through the pitiful list of positives she's managed to pull together. 'I might take this home and do a bit more work on it tonight. I'll have a look at day-release catering courses too.'

'Thanks,' he says. A broad grin spreads across his face – then falters, when he sees Stu's crony, Creeper, staring at them through the glass panel in the door.

'Do Stu and his mates push you around?' she asks, quietly.

'I keep out of their way,' Donnie says, a flash of fear in his eyes.

She follows him out into the corridor. Creeper has gone and there's no one else waiting to see her. She wanders back into the meeting room, sits at the table for a couple of minutes staring out at the street and listening to the shudder of traffic and the whine of sirens. Slowly, she picks up her phone and logs on to Jay's Instagram account. There are hundreds of images on his feed. Half a dozen are shots of his street art, done in the same stark style as the hands in the dining room, each image designed to comment on the world around it. He's painted the frightened faces of a mother and child – clearly refugees – peeking out of a slit in the side of a removal van parked in front of a white-columned mansion. Above their heads the company strapline reads, 'Your relocation means the world to us.' Another shows a shot of a homeless man asleep on a pavement with a chalk line drawn around his outstretched body, as if he's already dead. She studies the image then swipes on to a collection of nightscapes, each photograph framed around a single source of light – a neon sign, a street lamp, a bonfire in an alleyway, the flame from a cigarette lighter, an uncurtained window. There's another series, this time of shadowy silhouettes: men, women, foxes, vermin.

She returns the laptop to Larry's office and goes in search of

Jay. Unsure if the upper floors are out of bounds to visitors she climbs a steep, badly lit staircase. It seems to go on forever, performing awkward turns where the original building meets the extension, sprouting stray landings, odd dead ends and a warren of boxy little rooms along the way.

Eventually, she finds him swabbing out one of the shower rooms with a mop. She stands in the doorway. 'Why work at Cranmore House if you think everyone here's going to end up back on the streets?'

Jay stops mopping and looks up at her. 'That's not what I think. A few of them might make it. If they're lucky. Anyway, like I told you, I didn't choose to work here. As soon as I've done my time I'm out of here.'

'What do you mean, done your time?'

He jabs the mop into the bucket and gives it a sharp twist. 'I'm here on a community service order.'

'Oh,' she says, into the overly long silence.

'Since you're dying to ask, I had a drug problem. I started dealing to support my habit and I got done for possession with intent to supply.'

She still doesn't know what to say so she keeps quiet.

'That's my excuse for being here. What's yours?' That cocky look is back. 'A love of humanity? Some kind of religious thing? A Good Samaritan complex?'

Tired of his taunting she looks down at the grey water swilling at her feet and decides to offer him a taste of the truth. 'I was close to someone when I was a kid. Someone... in my family. He made a mistake, a big one, and he went to prison.' Above the shouts and murmurs from the floor below blood throbs in her ears. 'When he came out everyone he knew, including me, turned their back on him. He ended up homeless, drinking himself into a stupor, then he disappeared. It's haunted me all my life.'

'Who was he?' Jay says, after a blink of surprise.

She looks away, her eyes burning. 'Isn't there a rule here about not asking people about their pasts?'

'Only if they're guests.'

She flinches beneath his gaze. 'You know what? Mick put his heart and soul into making the dining room look good. The least you could do is help him to repaint it.'

She leaves him standing there and goes downstairs to find Mick. He's dragging a ladder towards the second pair of hands on the mural. 'I've asked Jay to come down and help you.'

'I'd rather work on my own.'

The door swings open and Stu sidles in. He grins at Vanessa, showing a mouthful of small, blackened teeth. 'I want to apply for college.' He comes closer.

She can see that his pupils have shrunk to pinpricks and there's a look of menace in them that unnerves her. She takes a step back. 'What sort of courses are you interested in?'

'Business,' he says, with a smirk. 'I've got what you might call a natural aptitude for it.' He gestures towards the door with his thumb. 'I'll have my session in private, same as Donnie.'

He keeps grinning at her but she refuses to meet his gaze. There's no way she's going to spend even a second on her own with this creep, especially not when he's high. 'Wait here while I fetch a laptop.' She reaches down to pick up her bag. 'We can work on your application in here.'

She straightens up to see Mick twisting Stu's hand hard up his back. 'Don't even think about it,' he says, in a voice that rumbles with threat, then he pushes Stu back towards the door.

Stu stumbles forward, giggling stupidly.

'Go on, get out of here, and don't show your face until the dope's worn off.' Mick turns back to Vanessa. 'I should have this finished in a couple of hours.'

Vanessa, who has no idea what just happened, hears herself say, 'OK. And thanks for whatever it was you just did.'

Mick shakes his head. 'That lad's a mess. If Larry catches

him using again he'll be out on his ear. If he catches him dealing he'll have him arrested and I tell you, for all his swagger he won't cope with another stretch inside.'

'Did you know him—' She hesitates. 'Before you came here?'

'Came across him a couple of times. Tried to help him once but he wasn't having it. Can you pass me that scraper?'

'I know I'm not supposed to ask—' Vanessa says, picking up the scraper.

Mick holds out his hand. 'You want to know how I ended up living on the street.' It's a statement not a question.

'I'm sorry.' Vanessa blushes and hurriedly hands him the scraper. 'It's none of my business.'

He shrugs. 'It's a fair question.'

He climbs back up the ladder and jabs the scraper into the mural, saying nothing more. Embarrassed, Vanessa turns away and busies herself checking through her phone messages.

Bracing herself for a harangue about lax recycling or parking violations, she opens the text from John Mathis.

Just recorded these on my door cam

She clicks 'Play' on the first of two video links he's sent her. A fish-eye shot of the exterior of her house appears. A biker in worn black leathers pulls up, dismounts and approaches her front door holding a parcel in his hand, which is odd for two reasons. Firstly, she's sure she hasn't ordered anything; secondly, if she has and she's forgotten about it, she always has her parcels delivered to a collection point.

The man presses the doorbell, waits a couple of minutes then drops the parcel onto her doorstep. Instead of leaving, he throws a furtive glance at the street, turns back to the house, lifts the visor of his helmet and peers through her front window. Then he drops the visor again and with his face concealed from view, he slips around to her side gate. To her horror, with another quick glance over his shoulder he lets himself into her back garden.

She plays the second video, recorded fifteen minutes later. The biker emerges through the gate, zipping a phone into his jacket. He retrieves the parcel from her step, saunters off down the front path and disappears out of sight.

Trying for calm, she holds the phone up to Mick. 'Mick, can you have a look at this?'

'What it is it?'

'My neighbour's just caught a bike courier sneaking into my back garden. I think he was checking to see how easy it would be to break into my house.'

Mick reaches down from the ladder, takes the phone from her and frowns at the footage. 'He's scoping out your house alright, but that bloke's no bike courier.'

'How can you tell?'

'Aside from taking back the parcel he brought with him, look at his hands.' He gives her back the phone.

She rewinds the footage, freezes a frame and zooms in on the man's hands. Mick's right. The black gloves he's wearing aren't thick leather. They're finger-hugging black latex.

'My house is really secure,' she says, more to reassure herself than him. 'I've got locks on every door and window, and a burglar alarm.'

'You still need to get a proper lock on that side gate.' He flicks her a cautious glance. 'Tell you what, if you pick one up this afternoon I'll fit it for you.'

She hesitates, just for a beat, but he sees it and she blushes crimson to the roots of her hair.

'No problem,' he says, and turns away to go back up the ladder.

She grabs his arm. 'You've got it all wrong. I only hesitated because I didn't know if it was allowed. But, yes. If you would, I'd be so grateful.'

On the way to Vanessa's house they drop in at a DIY superstore to buy a mortice lock and a security light. Mick hums as he scours the aisles for what he needs and he's still humming as he rifles through her toolbox for the right sized bit for her drill.

'I had a wife,' he says, as she places a mug of tea on the pathway by his foot. 'We were married for ten years.' Vanessa freezes, not daring to speak. 'Two kids, a nice house, and my own building business, employing three hardworking lads. All dependent on me to bring in the work.' He inserts the bit into the drill head. 'Then the jobs started drying up and the debts mounted. I felt powerless. Got depressed, started drinking and took my worries out on my wife. In the end she kicked me out – I don't blame her. Once I was on my own the drinking got so bad I was blacking out. Next thing I know, I'm homeless.' He grows still and stares down at the drill in his hands. 'It doesn't take much. That's the scary thing. One minute you're jogging along thinking everything's going to work out fine; the next, you're nothing and nobody.'

Later that evening, after she's raided her fridge and cooked them mushroom omelettes with sautéed potatoes – which Mick says is the best meal he's had in years – Vanessa calls an Uber to take him back to Cranmore House.

When he's gone, she throws the bolt on the front door and sags back against the wall, feeling the fear that's been pulsing inside her gain depth and texture. Why had the thief targeted her house? It's one of the smallest in the street and although it's full of vintage finds, they're not exactly priceless antiques. Panic rises in her throat. She runs from window to window checking the locks and tugging down the blinds and then she grabs a canvas bag and begins to stuff it with everything she'd hate to lose. Tomorrow she'll find somewhere safe to store it. She gathers up the jewellery she inherited from her grandmother but rarely wears, and all the personal documents she keeps in her desk, adding a clear plastic envelope full of papers she rescued from her mother's attic. She's about to zip the bag shut when she stops, retrieves the envelope, pops open the flap and pulls out a bundle of yellowing press cuttings.

She slumps onto the sofa and flicks through them, stopping to reread an article whose contents she almost knows by heart.

A former Metropolitan Police officer who abused his position to help an organised criminal gang seize money from other criminals has been jailed for eight years. Charles Andrew Thomas, 36, of Pinner, Middlesex wore his uniform and used marked police cars to travel to locations where he had been informed that "significant quantities of cash" would be exchanged. With the help of armed gang members masquerading as a police SWAT team, he seized the money while pretending to be undertaking his police duties. Judge Julia Harris said Thomas "abused his position of power, trust and responsibility" and his actions were an "exploitation" of his policing colleagues. Thomas, who wore a white shirt and black suit, did not react as the judge delivered his sentence, reduced from twelve years to eight due to an early guilty plea.

She can barely bring herself to look at the mugshot of her father printed at the bottom of the article. Taken just after his arrest, he stares into the camera with a look of shock and bewilderment. Like Mick said, one minute you're jogging along, thinking everything's going to work out fine; the next, you're nothing and nobody and the rest of the world is moving on without you.

She pulls out a second cutting.

Ex-wife of corrupt cop Charles Thomas weds top
detective who investigated husband's case.

*Mother of one, Ellen Thomas, tied the knot with DI Richard
"Rocky" O'Brien at a quiet ceremony at Southwark Register
Office yesterday morning. The pair said "I do" while her
former husband, Charles Thomas, begins the second year of his
eight-year sentence for conspiring with a criminal gang to
fraudulently seize significant sums of criminal cash. The
newlyweds, who are expecting a child later this year, were
unavailable for comment when approached.*

Vanessa gazes at the words, assailed by memories of the
misery that had descended on her forty-three-year-old mother
when that child had been stillborn; and Ellen's explosion of joy
when, by some miracle, Izzy had arrived the following year.

Only as she pours herself a large glass of wine does she
allow herself to face the ever-hovering spectre of Mark Findlay.
Could it have been him who sent the biker? Was he looking for
information about Frances's baby? She darts her eyes to the
window, opens her laptop and clears her web history, erasing
every trace of her recent activity.

NINE

Vanessa starts her day with a trip to a self-storage facility in Shepherd's Bush. There's a company in Barnes she uses to store the contents of houses she's gutting, but today she's keen to hire a smaller unit in a facility where nobody knows her name or her face. She's already paid online and, armed with her pre-set passcode, she manages to enter the building and lock away the bag of valuables without having to see or speak to any of the staff.

Shooting a wary look up and down the car park, she jumps back into her car and drives to Pimlico, where she's due to recce a penthouse. It's at the top of a small 1950s block recently renovated by Mathieson's, a firm of developers who specialise in creating luxury short-term rental apartments for the super-rich. Her brief is to give this overpriced two bed some warmth, character and quirkiness. If Mathieson's likes what she does with it there's a chance she'll get the contract to decorate the other eight flats in the block, using furnishings from Vanessa Dunn Designs. A contract which would give her fledgling business the certainty it needs.

She sits with her back to the wall and her notebook propped

on her knees looking from the terrace that overlooks the river to the wide expanse of white wall on the opposite side of the reception area. It needs bold colour she decides, lots of it, and something dramatic to draw the eye. She's trailing her fingers across the pristine white wall, re-imagining the space, when her phone buzzes a text alert.

She pulls it from her pocket and stares at the screen until the sender's name blurs and distorts: Amanda Mason-Findlay. She clicks open the message.

> So lovely to meet you the other day. We're planning a major redesign of our London house and I wonder if you might be interested in meeting up to discuss the project.

In a different mood Vanessa might have whooped out loud at the success of her ploy. Right now she's too scared for self-congratulation. She taps out a reply saying she'd love to talk more and suggests that they meet at the property to discuss what the job would entail. With a shiver of trepidation she presses 'Send' then she slides open the glass doors to the terrace, leans her elbows on top of the parapet and gazes out across the choppy waters of the Thames to the rooftops on the opposite bank; thousands of flats, houses and workplaces stretching for miles. Beyond them, a patchwork of villages, towns and cities seething with people.

After all this time and with no name, sex or even date of birth to go on, surely the chances of Mark Findlay finding Frances's kid out there must be practically zero. But all the time, like a dripping tap, the thought repeats in her head. *There is a chance. There is a chance. There is a chance.*

The route back to her shop takes her past D&D – Doug's architectural practice. It's housed in an old bakery that his father, Norman, had bought for nothing in the eighties and converted into an edgy, upmarket workspace. Originally Dunn and Co, it had become Dunn and Dunn when Doug's father had made him a partner. The old man had always joked about saving on rebranding costs when she and Doug eventually took over the practice.

She slows at the traffic lights and can't stop herself from turning her head to look it at. She remembers her excitement, after the wedding, when Norman Dunn had encouraged her to set up Vanessa Dunn Designs in one corner of the big open-plan office on the ground floor, and their heady plans for the company to offer a complete architectural and interiors service. Norman had died suddenly and unexpectedly a few months after her decree absolute came through, and the practice was all Doug's now. She scans the glinting windows. *Is he in there now*, she wonders, *helping himself to a coffee from the espresso machine that she'd installed, taking it back to the antique part-ners desk that she'd picked up at auction and sipping it while he fires off a smoochy text to bloody Lisa?* For a moment she feels bleak and defeated. The lights change, she rams her car into gear and roars away.

'How did it go?' Meghan asks.

'The rooms are smaller than I expected, but there's plenty of light and the terrace is amazing.'

'Not the recce, the homeless shelter. Weren't you there this weekend? Any cute bankers going spare?'

'There's a crusty accountant who comes in to do the books and a bad-tempered old bag who cooks vile food and shouts at everyone.'

Meghan laughs.

'I got some of the inmates together and we used the paint left over from that Muswell Hill job to paint the dining room.

There was this one guy, Mick, who did most of it. He's really good.' She lowers her eyes. 'I thought I might offer him some work.'

'You're kidding.'

'Just a one-off to begin with. If it goes well, maybe I could give him a regular contract.'

'What if he messes up?'

'Then I'll be down a couple of days' wages. So what? Anyway, he won't mess up.'

'If he's that good how come he's jobless and living in a shelter?'

'He lost his business, started drinking, then his wife threw him out and his life fell apart. You should see him, Meghan – he's a really lovely guy and it's like life just punched him in the gut and went on kicking him and kicking him once he was down.'

'He might have all sorts of... *issues*.'

'We've all got issues.'

'You're doing your bit by helping out at the shelter. Isn't that enough?'

'What I do there hardly touches the sides and after six months they all get chucked out. God knows what happens to them then.'

'That's not your responsibility.'

'I know. But if the business expands the way I'm hoping it will, employing more people from Cranmore could work for them *and* for us.'

Meghan opens her mouth, seems to think better of what she'd been about to say and closes it again. 'While we're discussing staffing – do you remember we talked about me getting more involved in the design side of the business?'

That's not quite how Vanessa remembers their conversation; in fact, she clearly recalls putting a dampener on the idea as soon as it came up, which is what she tries firmly but gently to do now. 'Right now I really need you to concentrate on establishing the retail arm and developing our online sales,' she says. 'You're so brilliant at it.'

Vanessa can feel Meghan's frustration and senses that this conversation is far from over, but she's got too much on her mind to worry about it now.

She looks past Meghan to the street outside. 'Before I forget, can you get in some estimates for installing CCTV in the shop? I've been meaning to sort it out for weeks.'

'So you can keep an eye on your sketchy new workforce?' Meghan's tone is teasing but there's nothing jokey about her expression.

'Of course not,' Vanessa snaps, unable to hide her irritation.

She spends the next couple of hours unpacking a set of bronze figures by Emma Dutton, a new artist she's working with – elegant fluid shapes with almost featureless faces – experimenting with ways to display them and debating whether a couple of the larger pieces might work in the Pimlico flat.

'Vanessa!' Meghan calls as she crosses the shop floor with a man in tow. 'Would you mind helping this gentleman? He's looking for a wedding gift for his niece.'

'Of course.' Vanessa smiles up into the craggy, well-used features of a man in his forties. 'Did the couple make any kind of list?'

'That's the problem. They're telling everyone they want gifts that "come from the heart", whatever that means.' He pulls a despairing face.

'Don't worry, I'm sure we can find them something they'll love. Can you tell me a bit more about them?'

'Oh... right. Well, he's in IT and she's a primary school teacher.'

'Interests?' Vanessa glances over at Meghan, who is grinning maniacally at her from behind a display of china. She glares back at her, morphing her expression back into a smile as she returns her attention to the customer.

'Erm, they do a lot of travelling, enjoy going to pubs and festivals, and they've just bought their first flat. But they've been living together for a while, so they've already got all the basics.'

Vanessa's gaze skips around the displays of merchandise and settles on a cluster of steel planters that have just come in. 'Do they have a garden?'

'A balcony, but it's really small. Barely room for a couple of chairs.'

Her gaze wanders on. 'We've got some beautiful silk cushions. Really great citrusy colours.' She leads him over to the pile of orange, lime and yellow cushions spilling out of an antique trunk.

He runs a hand over the delicate fabric and shakes his head. 'They've got a huge red setter who's allowed on the sofas. These would get destroyed in no time.'

'Do they like entertaining?'

'I think so – nothing formal, though.'

Vanessa spins around and walks towards the glassware. 'How about a dozen of these—?' She takes a blue-rimmed goblet from the shelf. 'They're made by a wonderful artist in Morocco, who only uses recycled glass. And they're a really good size.' She holds the goblet up to the light to show him the dimples and bubbles in the glass, and catches Meghan gawking at her over the shoulder of the woman she's serving. She turns her back to block her out. 'They're hand-blown so each one is slightly different. That's the joy of them.'

He smiles at her. 'Perfect.'

'Shall we gift-wrap them and send them directly to the couple, or would you like to take them with you?'

He hesitates. 'How about you gift-wrap them and send them to me.'

'Of course.' She leads him over to the till and reaches for the order book. 'What's the name?'

'Ralph Gilmore.'

'Address?' She jots it down and looks up at him, trying to square his wrinkled, slightly ill-fitting suit and loosened tie with the upmarket Kensington address he's just given her.

As she puts the purchase through the till he picks up one of the leaflets about the Vanessa Dunn interior design service.

'Are you thinking of redecorating?' she asks.

'Yep.' He folds the leaflet and stuffs it into his pocket. 'Although I'm about as clueless with décor as I am with wedding presents.'

'Sometimes it helps if you make a list of all the pieces of furniture or paintings that you're particularly attached to, and then think about how you can build your new scheme around them.'

'I don't have any furniture. Or paintings.'

'Oh.'

'I let my wife... ex-wife, keep the lot.'

'Well,' she says, dropping the pen back in the jar, 'that certainly makes things simpler.'

'Simpler choosing furnishings or simpler dealing with life in general?'

She blinks at him. 'I couldn't possibly say.'

'Why not?'

She laughs. 'When it comes to interiors my choices are always spot on. With life in general – not so much.' Instinctively she squeezes her ring finger, touching the bare flesh where her wedding band used to sit.

As soon as he's gone Meghan comes shooting over. 'Well?'

'Well, what?'

'Your cuddly new customer.'

'He was *not* cuddly.'

'There's definitely something a bit sad and squishy about him. I think he's lonely and looking for love.'

'Oh, stop it! He's ancient and totally not my type.'

'What did I tell you about taking risks, Nessa?'

'I'm not interested, alright? And I very much doubt that he was interested in me.'

TEN

'Hey, Frances.'

Frances looks up, pulling out her earbuds as Vanessa enters the room. 'Hey.'

Vanessa walks over to the bed, taking out her make-up bag. 'Which first? Nails or eyebrows?'

'Eyebrows, please. They told me my hair might grow back weirdly after chemo, but no one warned me my eyebrows would go wild.' She settles back against the pillow and closes her eyes.

'Hardly wild.' Vanessa takes a little brush from her bag, runs it through the pale down of Frances's brows and sets to with the tweezers. 'Any news from your investigator?'

'He's been working through that list of former Findlay employees I got from HR, but tracking them down after all this time is slow going and none of the ones he has managed to contact have been able to help.' She opens her eyes and regards Vanessa bleakly, her nose pinking up, her eyes reddening.

'He could have a breakthrough any day,' Vanessa says.

'I know.' Then, after a few poignant beats she forces a smile and says: 'How's that sister of yours?'

'Izzy? Oh, still on tour, still flitting from man to man, still refusing to take life seriously.'

'She's young, let her enjoy it while she can. And she's really talented. I loved that new song of hers.'

'Did you listen to it?'

'Of course. I used to sing a bit myself when I was younger.'

'Really?'

'I never wrote anything but some boys in the year above me at my boarding school got a band together. I was lead vocal, would you believe. Then they left and my singing career fizzled out.'

'You should have gone solo.'

Frances laughs. 'I can just see my father letting that happen.'

'There,' Vanessa says, passing Frances a little hand mirror.

'Thanks.' Frances inspects her brows then tips the mirror to the light, juts out her chin and runs her finger along her jaw. 'There's a crazy hair just here that's been driving me potty. Can you get rid of it? I don't want to die with a full beard.'

'Don't worry. If you do, I'll personally come over and plait it for you, like that Drogo guy in *Game of Thrones*.'

Frances bursts into giggles. Laughing too, Vanessa leans in and plucks out a tiny golden hair by the root. She zips the tweezers back into their little plastic case and as she reaches for the nail clippers, her eye catches the title of a book on the bedside table. She eases it from the pile. '*A Survivor's Guide to Toxic Parents.*' She lifts an eyebrow. 'I'm guessing this isn't a newly discovered Agatha Christie.'

'It's about men like my father,' Frances says. 'Powerful, charismatic and determined to win, whatever the cost to the people who love them.'

'My mother used to say that all successful businessmen have a psychopathic gene.'

Frances smiles, grimly. 'Then let's hope that the Findlay psycho gene died out with my dad.'

Vanessa thinks about Mark Findlay's dead, expressionless eyes and a coldness pools at the base of her spine. She turns the book over and scans the blurb on the back. 'I thought you thought self-help manuals were tosh.'

'I do usually, but this one's different. When I read it, it was like I'd been living in the shadows and someone had suddenly switched on a light.' There's a born-again brightness in Frances's eyes, a fervent certainty beneath the breathy quiver of her voice. 'Instead of searching for my own child, I devoted my whole life to trying to get a man who was incapable of love to love me, buying into his bullshit about clean breaks long after I should have realised how destructive his warped mindset really was. Now it's too late.' Her voice breaks but she holds up her hand to ward off words of comfort. 'Do you think for one minute he'd have come out with all that garbage about giving up my baby for the good of the family if I'd been knocked up by some preppy WASP whose father wore the right suits and knew the right people? Of course not. He'd have hired in an army of nannies to bring it up and bored the world rigid, boasting about his wonderful, chip-off-the-old-block grandchild. My mistake was telling him the truth about the baby's father.'

'Which was?' Vanessa lays a tissue on the bed, takes Frances's left hand in hers and with firm little snips of the clippers begins to trim her slightly ragged thumbnail.

'He was from Haiti.'

There's a long silence, which Frances breaks with a stifled sob. 'I hate admitting this, even to myself, but Gordon Blane Findlay wasn't just a tyrant. He was a bigot, a snob and a racist. He hid it brilliantly, of course – supporting international charities, funding community projects, donating to politicians whose views he despised but, deep down, he couldn't bear the thought of his precious company ending up in the hands of a kid whose grandmother was a refugee who worked in the kitchens of some backwoods boot camp. Because of that, he was willing to let me and my baby suffer a lifetime of pain. But I'm not going to let him win. Not this time.'

Vanessa moves on to Frances's other fingers. 'He's dead, Frances,' she says, softly. 'You can't beat him now.' Feeling a rush of determination she stops snipping and says, 'But I swear to you I'm going to do everything I can to ensure that Dora gets what's rightfully hers and that she knows exactly why you were forced to give her up.'

Frances pushes herself up on one elbow, her lips tensing with pain. 'The most important thing is that you tell her she was loved and wanted, and that I was wrong to leave it until I was nearly dead before I tried to find her.' A trolley trundles down the corridor outside, its small hard wheels creating a low rumble, quite different to the pneumatic tyres of a wheelchair. Vanessa realises how accustomed she's become to the sound-scapes of the hospice, how much a part of her life these visits to Frances have become, and it hits home that it won't be long now before they come to an end.

'Will you promise me something else?' Frances says.

'Of course.'

'If there's something in your life you need to do, do it now. By tomorrow it may be too late.'

Clippers in hand, Vanessa sits in the abrupt stillness that has fallen, staring at the mountains and valleys of the monitor. 'I'm trying,' she says, quietly.

Frances turns her head to look at her.

'I lost touch with my father when I was a kid. It's a long story but a couple of days ago, I finally managed to get hold of an address for him.'

'Where is he?'

'Spain. I've booked a flight for next week. Just a twenty-four-hour round trip but after twenty years, I couldn't just ring him up out of the blue. I need to see him face to face.'

Frances curls her outstretched fingers around Vanessa's, as if glad for once to be the one giving comfort. 'I'm so glad you tracked him down before it was too late. Whatever happens, you'll always know you did your best.'

'We're going to find Dora too,' Vanessa says. 'She's out there somewhere, and the lead we need could just be a phone call away.'

Frances squeezes the bridge of her nose. 'I can't stop worrying about you. Are you being careful?'

Vanessa bundles the nail clippings into the square of tissue and moves around the bed to work on Frances's right hand. 'Don't you worry about me. I guarantee that when the time comes I'll be here, all in one piece, to fight Dora's corner.'

Frances doesn't seem convinced. 'You haven't noticed anyone following you or acting suspiciously around you?'

'No,' Vanessa says quickly, feeling the lie stick in the back of her throat.

'No attempts to steal your laptop or your phone – old acquaintances who've suddenly got back in touch or new ones trying to worm their way into your life? People in need of money who Mark might be paying to keep tabs on you and report back to him?'

Vanessa gives her a reassuring smile and turns away. 'God, no. Nothing like that.'

ELEVEN

Vanessa declines Meghan's invitation to return to the wine bar after work and drives back to Cranmore House.

'I wasn't expecting to see you till next weekend,' Larry says, when she taps on his half-open door.

'I've been doing some work on Donnie's CV and I wanted to show him how much better it's looking.'

'He's probably in his room.'

'Thanks.' She shifts uncomfortably. 'While I'm here... could I have a word?'

'If you're quick. We've got our staff catch-up in ten minutes.' His phone rings. He raises a finger at her and she sits down as he takes the call. She's gazing around the cluttered office when her eyes catch on a box of black latex gloves sitting on top of one of the filing cabinets. An image flashes across her mind: the fake courier's latex-gloved hands. The words on the packaging swim and distort. *Safe... effective... textured fingers... extra grip.*

'So, what can I do for you?' Larry's voice jars her thoughts and she drags her eyes from the box to his face.

'Oh... I... I've been thinking... If they've got the right experience, I might be able to offer some of the guys here some decorating work. Maybe starting with Mick. He really knows what he's doing. Would that be alright? I'd give him a proper contract and pay him the going rate.'

There's a silence that lasts four or five seconds before Larry speaks. 'I know your heart's in the right place, Vanessa, but you're like all the other volunteers who come in here thinking they can offer these men a quick fix and sort their lives out overnight. That's not how it works.' He pauses. 'Not for them or for you.' Vanessa frowns and looks down at her hands. 'Sorry if that sounds harsh,' he says, more gently. 'But this isn't about making you feel good, or getting brownie points for your business. It's about doing what's best for these men. Mick's only been here a couple of weeks and when you've not worked for a while it can be tough readjusting to it physically, let alone mentally.'

'I understand what you're saying, but surely it would make him feel valued if I offered him a small project?'

Larry massages the back of his neck. 'Alright – well, you can talk to him and see what he says. But you mustn't pressure him. A day here and there would be more than enough to start with. And you'd have to let him work at his own pace.'

'Of course. But if there are any other guests with building and decorating skills—'

'Let's not get carried away. We do have relationships with a number of socially minded businesses, but any employer who's serious about employing ex-offenders or the long-term homeless needs to take things slowly – give them time and accept that there might be all sorts of blips and bumps along the way. There's no point trying to force people with troubled pasts to make the right choices. If it's going to work, they have to be ready to make those choices for themselves.'

'So, what are you saying?'

'Let me discuss it with my team. If we come up with anyone else with suitable experience you and I can have another chat.'

She leaves his office and goes in search of Donnie, her thoughts still revving and stalling on the box of black gloves. *For heaven's sake*, she tells herself, *every commercial kitchen in the country uses gloves like that.* She'd worn a pair herself to serve up Beattie's soggy mash and overcooked peas.

She sticks her head around the door of the recreation room. Blakey and Creeper circle a pool table, pool cues outstretched, while Stu and four other men sprawl on the shabby, mismatched armchairs, watching football on a wall-mounted TV. Two of the faces she recognises, two she doesn't, but from the nudging and sneering they all seem to know exactly who she is. 'Anyone here seen Donnie?' she asks.

Stu raises a middle finger and points it at the upper floors, a gesture greeted by a dutiful snicker of laughter from his mates. She backs away and hurries upstairs, checking the name on each door as she searches for Donnie's room. She finds it on the second floor, only two doors down from Stu's, which can't be much fun for a nervous kid like Donnie.

She sits with him for nearly half an hour, showing him the work she's done on his CV. He's so thrilled that she's gone to so much trouble just for him that he doesn't notice how distracted she is.

On her way out, she passes Larry's empty office. Her eyes shoot to the box of gloves sitting on the filing cabinet and then up to her name on the whiteboard – *Vanessa Dunn CV clinic 10–12 Meeting room.* Had the biker picked last Sunday morning to recce her home because he'd known she'd be here at Cranmore House? Fear grips her gut, rushes up through her heart and claws at her throat, sending her scuttling down the hallway to the staff room. As she gets to the door she sees Jay in there, perched on the edge of the table scrolling through his phone. She rushes past him to the sink, fills a glass from the tap and drains it. 'Sorry.' She coughs and puts her hand to her throat. 'I think I swallowed some dust.' She coughs again.

'Want a coffee?'

'If you're making one.' She glances away, unsure if he's making fun of her. But he leaps up, flicks on the kettle and turns around, leaning back against the chipped countertop.

Unsure how to play this, she opts for a weak smile. 'How was your staff meeting?'

He shrugs. 'Same old. Look, I'm glad I've seen you.'

'Really?' she says, warily. 'Why's that?' She rinses out the glass and stands it upside-down on the drainer.

'We kind of got off on the wrong foot and I'm sorry about that. Can we... start again?'

'Sure,' she says. 'Actually, I wanted to apologise to you. That mural you did was really good and I'm sorry if I came across as a snotty cow, but you can see why I thought it might be bad for morale.'

'Yeah, well, I have been known to get a bit carried away.' He grins. 'I had a look at your website. I didn't realise you've got a shop as well as a design business. How long have you had it?'

'I leased the premises about six months ago and we've been open for nearly four. It's been hard work but I'm getting there.' She winces. Couldn't she have come up with something less... trite? Her voice falters. 'Larry says you're leaving soon.'

'Yep.'

'What's the plan? Are you going to stay with family?'

'Family?' He laughs, short and sharp.

'Don't you have any?'

He levers open a battered tin of instant coffee, spoons some granules into a mug and pours on boiling water. 'Used to.'

'What happened?'

'I walked out and they didn't exactly bust a gut trying to find me.'

'How old were you?'

'Seventeen.'

'That's terrible,' she says, and feels a sudden burning desire to hear more of his story. 'So, what are you going to do?'

'Stay clean and find a job. Milk?' He waggles the carton.

'Yes, please. Where will you live?'

He lifts a shoulder. 'There's a couple of sofas I can crash on.'

'But—'

He raises a hand, cutting her off. 'Don't tell me. You've had the Larry lecture about ex-junkies without families being the ones most at risk at falling off the wagon. It's probably true for some of them. Not for me.' His expression hardens. 'I'll keep going to the meetings and I'll be fine.'

'Meetings?'

'Narcotics Anonymous.'

'Won't it be tough doing it on your own?'

'Look, I had an expensive habit. In the end, the only way I could support it was by running errands for my dealer. I got caught in the crossfire between him and a rival, things turned nasty and I ended up getting sent down. My lawyer appealed and after a couple of months I got lucky. They reduced my sentence to rehab and community service. It was part of a trial they were running. Next time, there'll be none of that and I tell you now, I'd rather top myself than do another five minutes in prison.' The vehemence in his voice startles her, as does the sudden glitter of anger in his eyes. 'You've seen the ex-cons in here.' He thrusts a mug at her. 'They might be human when they go down but by the time the system spits them out, they're the walking dead.'

She nods quietly, thinking of her father, and looks down at the grey liquid in her mug. A door bangs downstairs. Canned applause drifts up from the TV in the rec room.

'You should do something with your photography when you leave here.'

His dark eyes watch her closely. 'You've been looking at my Instagram.'

She smiles. 'Why shouldn't I? You checked out my website.'

'True.'

'I'm serious about the photography.' She takes a sip of coffee. It tastes like mud. 'Images like your nightscapes are very saleable.'

'Not when they're shot on a crappy old phone.' He runs a grubby cloth across the countertop. 'Thanks for the enthusiasm, but I won't get very far without a decent camera.'

Another burst of canned applause. A deep rasping voice shouts an obscenity that echoes down the hall. She puts down her mug. 'Thanks for the coffee. I need to catch Mick before I go. Do you know where he is?'

Jay gives her a sideways look. 'Last time I saw him he was out the back, having a fag.'

'Thanks.' She feels his gaze on her back as she walks away. At the door she stops and looks round. 'Does anyone here have a motorbike?'

Silence. His eyes on hers. 'Why do you want to know?'

Vanessa scrambles for a lie. 'I found a pair of leather gauntlets in the car park.'

'Oh, right. I think Dave, that City bloke who comes in to do the books, rides one sometimes. Apparently oldies and bikes are a thing these days.'

'Not... Stu or any of the other guests?'

He laughs. 'Not as far as I know. But given half a chance there's plenty round here who'd be happy to nick one and take it for a joy ride.'

TWELVE

When Vanessa offers Mick a couple of days' work sprucing up her office and explains it will probably mean bumping into customers, he agrees readily enough that a decent haircut will make it easier for him to fit in. But as they cut through the back-streets of Mayfair and approach the salon she's been going to for years, the sight of her hairdresser, Simon – black silk shirt, onyx earring, neatly trimmed goatee – sitting in the golden glow of the window seems to throw him into such a panic she worries he might run off into the night.

'It's OK,' she says, gently. 'There'll be no one else there – he's a friend, and he's stayed open late just for us.'

'Hey,' Simon says, looking up as they come in.

'Simon, this is Mick,' Vanessa says. 'Mick, Simon.'

'OK, Mick.' Simon leads Mick to a chair at one of the basins. 'Over here.'

Mick shuffles to the chair, avoiding his reflection as he passes the mirrors.

It shocks Vanessa that a man who, in his old life, must have had a thousand haircuts, should now feel so cowed by a salon. She drops onto one of the velvet sofas in the waiting area and watches as Simon whips out a gown and tucks it around Mick's hunched body. For once, her hairdresser's usual outpouring of snarky comments and outrageous celebrity gossip is silent and he frowns down at the frazzled mop before him with an expression, not of disgust, but of excitement. She knows that feeling well – the anticipation of transformation and the heady rush of satisfaction that the finished result will bring.

'I'm sorry,' Mick murmurs, blushing.

'What about?'

'My hair. I—'

'Hey, no worries. Head back.'

Mick complies and stares up, unblinking, at the spot-lit ceiling, silent save for a grunted 'Yes' when Simon asks him if the water temperature is alright. Vanessa reaches for a glossy magazine but forgets to open it; instead, her eyes drift across the brightly lit interior of the salon to the half-lit shapes moving murkily through the blackness of the street outside. Already anxious, she's been on increased alert since she saw the footage of the biker scoping out her house, and it occurs to her that anybody could be out there now, looking into the salon from the shadow of a doorway, a passing car or the saddle of motorbike, knowing that to the people on the inside, they would be invisible.

Simon is wrapping Mick's head in a towel and leading him back to his cutting station, where he picks up his scissors and begins to saw through the matted hunks of frizz. Vanessa watches them drop to the floor. Mick flinches at each snip and stares down at his gown-covered knees. But as the weight of his hair slowly lightens, his head seems to lift of its own accord, and slowly he's staring straight into the mirror, a look of bemusement on his weathered features as his ears and eyes appear.

Her eyes flick back to Simon who's trimming and cropping, combing and snipping with all the skill and concentration of a sculptor freeing a human face from a lump of stone, carving out the curve of Mick's lips from beneath his overhanging moustache and darting in with the tips of his scissors around his nostrils. Then he froths up a pot of shaving cream, slathers it around Mick's throat and cheeks and shaves the skin smooth, patting it off with a towel.

With a great sigh he pulls Mick's head upright again and the three of them gaze at the man in the mirror; a stranger with cheekbones, a jaw line, a strongly domed skull, a neat narrow beard and a crisp, slightly elongated crew cut, unrecognisable from the weary husk of a human being who had shuffled into the salon less than an hour before.

Doubt dampens Vanessa's smile. Mick's makeover is nothing compared to the transformation in store for Frances's child. How will they cope when they're ripped out of the life they know and catapulted into an alien world of unimaginable wealth and power? Will she really be able to rise to the challenge of helping them to adjust? She'll need to win their trust, and be kind but firm, supportive yet not indulgent. But in the end will ownership of the Findlay Corporation prove too much for someone not brought up to it?

But these are problems for the future. She lifts her eyes to the darkness outside. Right now, she has to focus on getting the inside track on Mark Findlay and working out how much he does or doesn't know, and whether he really is having her watched.

THIRTEEN

Vanessa scrolls through the work calendar on her phone, double checking that she's rescheduled every appointment she'd had for next Friday. She's marked it as holiday but the trip to see her father in Spain will, she knows, be anything but restful.

'Hi.'

She looks up. For a split second she fails to recognise the slim, dark-haired man looking at her across the counter. 'Jay,' she says, blushing. 'What are you doing here?'

'Having a look at your shop.'

'Do you approve?'

He pushes his hand through his hair – no ponytail today – and lets his eyes sweep the room. 'I thought it would be cutesy. It's not.'

'Thanks. I think.'

'Where do you find this stuff?'

'Auctions, house sales. Commissions from craftspeople. But I can't believe you came all this way just to check out my stock.'

He picks up one of the design service leaflets and flicks it open. 'It says on your website you're looking for a delivery driver.'

Vanessa's eyes follow an elderly couple who are ambling towards the fabrics, and braces for what she senses is coming.

'I came in to let you know I'd applied.'

She scoops up a couple of marker pens and drops them into the drawer beneath the counter. 'There's a lot more to the job than deliveries. It's putting stock together for mail order, overseeing the warehouse, looking after security. Maybe serving in the shop once in a while.'

He shrugs. 'I know. I read the spec.'

'Do you have any retail experience?'

'Plenty.' He shoots her a teasing look. 'Of sorts.'

She glances again at the elderly couple who are now browsing nearby and hisses, 'Jay, for heaven's sake. It's hardly the same thing.'

'I'm serious,' he hisses back. 'I can do all the things you need.' He gives her a slow smile. 'I can also be extremely persuasive when I want to be.'

'I've had a lot of applications from people with great references and years of warehouse experience.'

'I'm an artist. I'd have a feel for the merchandise.'

'I need someone reliable. The business is too small to employ anyone who needs constant supervision.'

'You're saying I'm not reliable because of my past?' His sharply raised voice causes Meghan to glance over from the other side of the shop.

'I didn't mean it like that,' Vanessa says, flustered.

His eyes narrow. 'You weren't worried about giving Mick a job.'

She tries to meet his gaze and not seem embarrassed. 'That's different. He's a highly experienced builder and decorator.'

'Well, he's certainly a changed man since you tucked him under your wing. New haircut, a spring in his step.'

'I'm glad. He deserves a break.'

'So this inclusive staffing policy you've been bending

Larry's ear about is fine when it comes to manual workers, but you can't have misfits rubbing shoulders with your precious customers.'

'Jay, that's not fair.' From the corner of her eye Vanessa sees Meghan moving towards them, straining to hear what's going on.

'Then give me a trial. If it's references you want I'm sure Larry will give me a decent one. You've seen for yourself how good I am at dealing with challenging situations.'

'What did you do before you—?' She stops and swallows.

'Before I got sent down for dealing?' He shrugs. 'Driving, bar work, a couple of stints as a barista. I got by.'

'I'll have to think about it.'

'I need this, Vanessa. It's not easy finding work when you've got a record.' His jaw tightens. 'It's not just about the money, either. If I'm going to stay clean I need structure. Deadlines, a sense of purpose.'

He really wants this, she thinks. And it would be so easy for her to just say yes, but like Larry says, this isn't about quick fixes and she mustn't be hasty. 'I promise I'll take a look at your application. Meanwhile, you should work on your photography.'

'Oh, for God's sake. I've already told you I can't get anything like a decent shot with the crappy camera on my phone.'

'Not so loud,' Vanessa murmurs. Meghan is hovering now, her face signalling concern and curiosity, like an actress in a silent movie.

'I'm sorry,' he says, though he doesn't look it.

Vanessa takes a deep breath. 'Actually...' she says.

'What?'

'Wait here.' She hurries away to her office. When she comes back Jay is leaning back against the counter, his arms folded tightly across his chest. She hands him a small canvas case. 'Here. You can use this.'

He snaps open the lid and eases out a digital camera. His expressions darkens. 'Whose is it?'

'Mine. Though I hardly use it.'

'Don't you get it? I don't want your charity! I want a job.'

'This isn't charity. It's a commercial proposition. I'm after a night shot of the Thames – maybe neon signs reflected on the water.'

'What for?'

'There's a penthouse in Pimlico I'm decorating for a client. It overlooks the river and I need a big, eye-catching image for one of the walls.'

'How much?'

'I don't want to buy it. I want to sell it.'

'What?'

'If you get me the kind of image I'm after, I'll get a limited edition professionally printed and hang one in the flat, charge the client five hundred pounds for it and take a twenty per cent commission.'

'Five hundred quid?' He fixes her with a cool beam of interest.

'Yes.'

'How about a thousand?'

'No,' she says, firmly. 'You'd need to build a name for yourself before you could start charging that sort of money.'

'And you'd take twenty per cent?'

'That's the deal I have with all the creatives I work with. Like I said, this is a commercial proposition. Purely professional. If the client likes what I do with the penthouse and I get the contract for all nine flats in the block, I'll commission you to create eight more river-themed images. I'll also showcase copies of the prints in here' – she gestures around her – 'and if they sell, we can talk about you doing another series on a different theme.'

'What if they don't sell?'

'I'll write off the loss.'

He studies her as if he's weighing this up but she's not fooled. They both know he's going to jump at the offer.

'Alright,' he says, not dropping his gaze. 'On two conditions.'

She laughs. '*You*'re giving *me* conditions?'

He tosses the leaflet back onto the pile. 'You give my application for the delivery job proper consideration.'

'What's the other one?' She waits uncertainly, her eyes on a jug of white daisies on the counter.

'You come with me while I try out this camera. That way you can show me exactly the kind of shots you're looking for.' The challenge is back in his voice, as if he's daring her to step out of her comfort zone.

There's a long, tense silence.

'Alright,' she hears herself say. 'When?'

He flashes her a surprised smile. 'Any night you want.'

She smiles right back. 'Fine. Let's do next Thursday.'

'You're on.'

Meghan watches him leave and comes over to the till. 'Who was that?'

'His name's Jay. He's a really good photographer and he does a bit of street art on the side.'

'It looked like you knew him.'

'I do, a bit. He works at Cranmore House. His contract there's about to end.'

'Good-looking, talented *and* a social conscience? Sounds too good to be true. Which probably means it is. What was he getting so pushy about?'

'He wants the delivery job.'

Meghan's expression darkens. 'So... what are you thinking?'

'I'm not sure.' Vanessa frowns, thoughtfully. 'He says he's done driving work in the past and that he has some retail experience.'

'If it was up to me, I'd say no.'

'Why?'

Meghan's gaze slides away to watch Jay saunter past the window, long and loose-limbed. He sees her looking at him and raises a hand in mock salute. She looks sharply away. 'Call it a gut feeling.'

FOURTEEN

The home that Amanda Mason-Findlay shares with her husband Mark is a four-storey townhouse in a leafy square off the King's Road in Chelsea, worth, Vanessa guesses, at least three million. A sweep of white steps, a pair of neatly clipped bay trees in terracotta pots flanking a glossy, black-painted front door; winter window boxes spilling over with eucalyptus, white cyclamen and ivy; and a glimpse through the first-floor window of a white marble mantelpiece, the painting above it – a single slash of bright red – the only visible colour in the room. 'Know your enemy,' Vanessa murmurs under her breath, then she raises her hand and presses the gleaming brass bell.

Amanda throws open the door. 'Vanessa!' she says, as if they're old friends.

'A coffee before we start? Or a glass of wine?'

'Coffee would be great. Thank you.'

'Let's go straight down to the kitchen then.'

Vanessa follows her down a hallway tiled in black and white, its walls lined with a series of framed abstract paintings, and down a set of wooden stairs into a gleaming, minimalist kitchen that takes up what looks like almost the whole of the basement. Her eyes sweep the room. No snapshots on the fridge, no child's paintings, no mess. Then she remembers: Amanda is the child-free third wife.

'Your home is lovely,' she says.

'Thank you.'

'How long have you lived here?' Vanessa asks, assuming they must have bought it after Mark had finally squirmed his way out of middle management less than two years before.

'Ooh, nearly eight years now,' Amanda says, fiddling with an industrial-sized coffee machine.

Amanda must have money of her own, Vanessa thinks.

'So, there are two jobs I want to talk to you about. Number one, we've just bought the house next door and the plan is to knock the two buildings into one, dig out another level of basement across the two buildings and put in a gym, spa room and cinema. Of course it's all subject to planning permission but there's plenty of precedent in the area so we're hoping to get all the permits through by the summer. I can send you the architect's drawings as soon as they arrive. As far as the décor is concerned, it will be a question of revitalising the whole thing so it feels like the new layout was meant to be. All quite straightforward. But the exciting project is the property we've just completed on in Norfolk – Garston Grange.' She raises her voice over the gurgle of the machine. 'It's a wonderful old manor house with barns and stables. At the moment it's a total wreck but the plan is to do something really exciting with the main building and convert the stable block into a satellite gallery, where I can exhibit sculptures and installations that are too big for the Soho site.'

Vanessa pulls out a steel bar stool and sits down at the kitchen island. 'That sounds like a major undertaking.'

'Exciting, though, especially if we get the right interior designer on board.' Amanda hands her an espresso in a tiny white cup and smiles, one corner of her carefully contoured lips tipping upward, as if tugged by an invisible string. 'My husband and I have been looking at photos of your work and we really think you could be that person. Sugar?'

'No, thank you.' Vanessa takes a scalding sip and snatches at the opportunity to press her a little more about Mark. 'Have you and... sorry, I don't know your husband's name—?'

'Mark.'

'Have you and he done a major renovation project before?'

'It's something I've always wanted to do and he's happy to go along with it. I think it's partly to keep me sweet. He's going to be travelling a lot more from next year.'

'Is that for his work?' She feels like a bad actor, saying lines.

'Yes. It's going to be crazy. He's taking over the family business.' Amanda purses her lips as if holding back a rush of excitement. 'The Findlay Corporation.' Her eyes hold Vanessa's.

'Gosh, he will be busy.' Vanessa looks away and glances up at the street outside. A sleek black car draws into a space across the road. The driver gets out and opens the back door to a passenger whose face she can't see. The two men talk for a moment, the exchange appearing to grow heated before the passenger walks away and the driver slams the door and gets back into the car.

'Will Mark want to be involved in the interior design?'

'Oh, don't worry about that. He's interested in the big picture but he'll leave the interiors to me.' Amanda takes an iPad from her bag. 'Let me show you some photos.' She strokes the screen, bringing up shots of the exterior of an imposing red-brick mansion, then flicking on to a wood-panelled hall with an enormous fireplace at one end, a stone-flagged scullery, a carved staircase, beamed bedrooms, attics swathed in cobwebs and finally an aerial shot of the whole house surrounded by acres of dense woodland.

Vanessa points to a cluster of rooftops hidden among the trees at the edge of the photo. 'Are these buildings yours too?'

'Yes. The larger one is an old mill and the smaller ones are grain stores and barns. My husband wants to convert them into offices and use them for confidential meetings. You know how difficult it is these days to get away from prying eyes.'

'It's certainly off the beaten track,' Vanessa says.

The door opens. Vanessa looks up. The room wobbles around her, a dizzying whirl; but after a moment it steadies and she locks eyes with Mark Findlay. *Does he know who I am? My link to Frances?* It's impossible to tell. His gaze flicks away to Amanda and he walks in, pushing his mobile into the pocket of his expensively cut beige jacket. He's shorter than his wife and he rocks forward on his toes a little as he kisses her cheek.

'I thought you had a client dinner tonight,' she says.

'I needed to pick up some papers, and I thought it would give me a chance to meet Vanessa.' Findlay's gaze swivels back in her direction.

Vanessa's heart thuds. Without taking his eyes off hers he offers her a small pink hand, which she shakes with what she hopes is a professional smile.

'Mark Findlay,' he says.

'Lovely to meet you, Mark.'

He leans in closer, invading her space. He smells of after-shave and alcohol.

'I've been doing my homework on you.' Perhaps he sees the alarm in her eyes. 'Don't worry, the feedback was *very* complimentary.'

'Can I ask who you spoke to?'

'A couple of clients who contracted you through D&D Architects. The Wallaces and a chap called...' He frowns, and looks over at his wife as if in need of a prompt.

'Bassett,' she says.

'That's the one. You did an excellent job on the interiors of his house in Provence, and I have to say I was bowled over by the work D&D did on the building itself. It's not easy extending a house that old without destroying its character.'

Vanessa gasps inwardly, dreading what he's going to say next.

'So impressed, that I got their director in for a chat about our Norfolk place. He's produced some extremely interesting preliminary sketches.'

Vanessa stares at him, aghast.

'Would it be a problem for you if we got them on board?'

'Um... no, not at all,' she lies. 'My ex-husband and I have an excellent working relationship.'

'That's good to hear.' He turns back to Amanda. 'I shouldn't be back too late but don't wait up.'

He walks out, letting the door swing shut behind him.

'Sorry about that,' Amanda says, clearly disconcerted. 'I thought we'd have the house to ourselves.'

Vanessa gazes at her dumbly, her heart stuttering. It's not just coming face to face with Mark Findlay that's disturbed her, or even discovering that he's been digging around in her life and questioning Doug – of all people – about her. It's the timing of it. If Doug has already produced preliminary drawings for Garston Grange does it mean that Findlay had been asking D&D about her *before* she'd approached Amanda?

She glances down at the aerial shot on the iPad in front of her as if the answer might be hidden among the impenetrable swathes of trees, and then up at the street as the sleek black car pulls out from the kerb and glides away.

Somehow she manages to make coherent noises about retaining the integrity of historic buildings and using traditional materials to create modern spaces, and promises to pull together some thoughts about spa rooms and cinema seating layouts for the Findlays' London house.

'That would be fabulous,' Amanda says. 'Give me a call when you've got something to show me.'

'Will do,' Vanessa says. She glances at her phone. 'So sorry, but I've got to get back.'

The minute she's on the street she whips out her phone and texts Doug.

Need to discuss Garston Grange ASAP.

Ten minutes later, his name flashes up on her screen, flinging her heart against her ribs.

Tomorrow 10.30 at the practice?

Vanessa had hoped he'd suggest a neutral space – a quiet café or a walk in the park – but her need to know what the hell is going on with Findlay overrides her dread of walking back into the place where she and Doug had dreamed so many dreams and made so many plans.

FIFTEEN

She knew it would be difficult to walk through the doors of D&D but she hadn't reckoned on it hurting quite this much. She looks across the lobby to the people milling around the office space beyond, bewildered by how familiar and at the same time how alien it all feels. A woman she doesn't recognise looks up from the reception desk. Young, with wide red lips and very short bleached-blonde hair, she eyes Vanessa with interest when she gives her her name. *What did I expect? Doesn't every divorced man claim his ex-wife is crazy? Who knows what stories this girl has heard whispered about me in the staff kitchenette.*

'This way.' The receptionist leads her into the glass-walled meeting room, as if she is a stranger. 'Do take a seat.' She gestures to the long white wood table and chairs that Vanessa designed herself and had made by a Swedish furniture maker; the same table that she and Doug had made love on one drunken night to celebrate him winning his first big tender.

'Doug won't be long. He's on a call, and Lisa said she'd join you as soon as she can.'

'Lisa... Arnold?'

'Our project manager.'

Vanessa closes her eyes. She should have guessed that Lisa would find a way to commandeer the space she'd left in Doug's work life as seamlessly as she'd slipped into the one she'd left in his bed.

'Can I get you something to drink? Tea, coffee, water?'

'No, thanks.' She gazes up at the steel 'D&D' hammered into the stripped brick wall. Alerted to Doug's presence by the same magnetic pull he's always exerted over her, her eyes flick sideways as he crosses the office floor, seeing him long before he sees her.

'Ness,' he says, as he pushes open the door. It's six months since she's spoken to him, six months since he turned up at the house with a Zip van to take away the last of his things. He's clearly nervous and he doesn't look her in the eye.

'Doug.'

'How are you?'

'Fine.'

'So, yeah, this Findlay thing,' he says, sitting down as far away from her as the small space will allow and running the fingers of both hands through his thick, unruly hair. 'Have you seen the house?'

'Just photos,' she said, glad that their attempt at niceties is over.

'Right, well, he got me down there for a look around a couple of weeks ago. It's a total wreck and stuck in the middle of nowhere but with money seemingly no object, its potential is extraordinary and, I'll be honest, I'd kill for the chance to work on it.'

'When will you know if you've got the job?'

'He's talking to a couple of other practices and should get back to me by the end of the month.'

'Do you know why he approached you?' she says.

'I gather I have you to thank for that. He said his wife wants you to work on their London property, so he checked into your former clients, discovered that a couple of them had contracted you as part of a deal with D&D, and gave me a call.'

'What did you tell him?'

'That you have a unique eye. That you're meticulous about detail and that you know exactly what you're doing. Always.' He glances up at her, making eye contact for the first time.

'Would you mind telling me exactly when he first got in touch?'

'Why?'

'I'm... curious.'

'He emailed me.' He reaches for his phone and thumbs the screen. 'On the fourth, so exactly three weeks ago today.'

She runs the calculation in her head and frowns. 'You're absolutely sure about that?'

'Yes. Is there a problem?'

It's the day *after* she'd visited the gallery, which should quell her fears. Only it doesn't. If Findlay had moved that quickly after she'd approached Amanda, did it mean that he'd been having her watched and had merely pounced on the opportunity to find out more? Or was he just a control freak who always rushed to gather personal information on people he was thinking of employing?

'No problem. It's just that he seems a bit... controlling.'

Doug smiles that wry, easy smile of his. 'Aren't all multimillionaires a *bit controlling*?'

'He's not a multimillionaire.' The words shoot out sharp and unfiltered.

He looks at her curiously. 'He's about to inherit the whole Findlay empire. Didn't you know?'

'Right, yes. That's what I meant. That he hasn't inherited it *yet*.'

'If he offers you the contract for the interiors, are you saying you won't take it?'

'I'm not sure.'

'Think of the publicity a job like that would generate.'

'Like I said, I'm not sure.' She knows she's sounding rattled and she takes a minute to compose herself. 'Look, if he asks you anything else about me... anything personal, will you let me know immediately and tell him to speak to me directly?'

Bemused, Doug drops his elbows onto the table and says, half joking, 'What? Do you think he's *stalking* you?'

'Not stalking, exactly,' she says, looking away, 'but I want to make sure that any interest he has in me or my life stays strictly professional.'

'Vanessa.' Lisa's voice cuts her off. She looks up and sees her former best friend standing in the doorway. She's clutching a file, hugging it to her chest, as if to create a barrier between herself and Vanessa.

'L-Lisa,' Vanessa stutters, automatically adding, 'how are you?'

If Lisa gives a response it's drowned out by the roar of blood in Vanessa's ears; but there was no need to ask. Lisa is blooming: pink cheeked and curvy, her thick dark hair even glossier than usual.

'I've been giving a bit of thought to the Findlay project,' Lisa says, planting herself in a chair halfway between Vanessa and Doug. 'It's far too good an opportunity for both our businesses to allow our... history to get in the way. So if Findlay does decide to contract you and D&D, I propose that we hire in an intern for a few months to act as a coordinator between the interior and exterior visions. Great experience for them and a simple way to keep communication between us as smooth and professional as possible.'

Vanessa ignores her frozen smile and looks past her at Doug, remembering the joy of working on past projects together, poring over every brick and fabric swatch, striving for integrity between the interior and exterior design in a shared mission to create buildings that were as pleasing to look at as they were to inhabit.

'I'm sure Doug would have been perfectly capable of passing that on,' Vanessa says, bristling.

'I realise that,' Lisa says, more gently. 'But that's not the only reason I wanted to be here. We'd been hoping to set up a meeting with you anyway in the next couple of weeks.'

Vanessa who had flinched at the 'we', flinches again as Lisa glances at Doug.

'We've got something to tell you that we don't want you to hear from anyone else.'

Oh, God, don't be pregnant. Please, please, please don't be pregnant.

'We're getting married,' Doug says.

In that moment, Lisa unclasps her hands and puts down the folder, revealing a big fat diamond on her finger.

Vanessa lays her palms on the table, pushes back her chair and stands up. Her knees are buckling, even though they're not because she's still on her feet. Words drop from her mouth – appropriate, congratulatory words – and somehow she's putting one foot in front of the other and walking to the door.

Emotion spins her out into the lobby, and as she gets to the front entrance she begins to shake, sweat breaking out beneath her T-shirt. She barely makes it to the corner of the street before she has to drop onto a low wall, head between her knees, looking down at the gum-scabbed pavement to stop herself from throwing up.

A motorbike roars past, its screaming engine yanking her back from the edge. She throws back her head, squeezes her eyes shut and murmurs, 'Visualise the you you want to be and the life you want to live, the you you want to be and the life you want to live.' Saying it over and over again until she has the strength to stand up.

SIXTEEN

'Look, Mum, I've brought you some *turrón* from Spain.' Vanessa rearranges the photos and ornaments on her mother's sideboard and angles the box so that Ellen can see it from her wheelchair. 'It's a sort of speciality nougat full of nuts and honey, and it's delicious.'

She sits down and waves a hand across her mother's empty, unfocused eyes. Desperate to find out how much of the old Ellen might still be there, locked inside her stroke-ravaged body, she's just had a chat with Dr Shepherd, the medical director of The Laurels. His responses to her questions had, as usual, been vague and unhelpful but, undeterred, she pushes on with her monologue, because today there's something really important she needs to get off her chest.

'Mum? Can you hear me? I can't stay long so *please*, try to concentrate.' She swallows hard and lays her hands on Ellen's knees. 'Do you remember I told you I'd finally got hold of an address for Dad? I know – after all this time! So, yesterday, I took a day off work and I... I went to see him. A twenty-four hour round trip. He's in Spain now – you know how much he always liked the sun. He's living in a scabby little bungalow on a semi-abandoned estate outside Malaga and working in an expat bar on the quayside. Part barman, part cellarman, part bouncer. It's a life, I suppose, but not much of one.' She pauses and draws in a jagged breath. 'When he came to the door I hardly recognised him. He's really flabby now, with broken veins on his nose, a scar under his eye, something funny going on with his jaw, like it's been fractured or dislocated and never set properly. And he's still drinking. A lot. Smoking too. I really wanted him to hug me and say he was pleased to see me. He didn't, of course. He's still too bitter about what happened. Bitter about you marrying Rocky. Bitter about me.' It feels good to admit how much it hurts that her father had been so distant towards her, and though her eyes are stinging, now she's started to open up about it, it's hard to stop the words spilling out. So she lets them come.

Eventually, she pauses for breath and pours herself a glass of water from the carafe by the bed. 'The only time he got animated was when he talked about going to prison. He said he could have done a deal when he was arrested, named names and had a cushy life in witness protection, but he kept quiet and now he's eaten up with fury that when he'd done his time the crook he'd worked for just left him to rot – even though he could easily have given him money to get back on his feet, or even a job in one of his legitimate businesses. He says it's like this man destroyed his life twice over and now he's powerless to do anything about it. It was awful seeing how angry and broken he is, but I'm not going to give up on him, Mum. I told him I want him back in my life and that I'm going to do everything I can to make up for the past.

'I tried to take him out of himself by telling him what I was up to – how I was sure you'd been planning to visit Frances before you got ill and how I was visiting her now, and all about the people I'm trying to help at Cranmore House. I thought at least he'd be interested in that, but he wasn't. In fact, he didn't take me seriously at all when I explained about the new life I'm working towards. It was as if he thought I haven't got what it takes to make it happen. But he'll be proud of me when I prove him wrong. I know he will.'

She glances at her watch. 'Before I go I've got a little surprise for you.' Vanessa unzips her bag and brings out a sturdy wooden box, lifts the lid and shows her mother a bulky, tissue-wrapped object. 'Can you guess what it is?'

The parcel is heavy and she cradles it with both hands as she lifts it onto her lap. Slowly she pulls away the tissue paper to reveal an exquisite ormolu clock, with a gilded cherub perched on the top. The numbers on the face are wreathed in delicate pink flowers and each of the black enamel panels encasing the base are painted with a picture of a peasant girl tossing hay. 'I found it in those boxes in your attic. It seemed such a shame for something as beautiful as this to be packed away out of sight just because it had stopped working. So I took it to this amazing horologist in Shoreditch who's managed to mend it! He took ages showing me the right way to wind it, explaining that it's all about the gears. I'll show Phil how to do it next time I come so don't worry, it won't run down.' She takes a key from the tissue, slides it into the keyhole at the back, turns it gently then sets the clock down in pride of place on the sideboard. The tick fills the silence. It's a rich sound. Not loud but penetrating.

Smiling, Vanessa gazes at the face, watching the delicate black hands move towards the hour as she finishes telling her mother about her trip to see her father. 'There!' she says, clapping her hands together as the clock chimes ten. 'Isn't that lovely? Does it bring back memories, Mum? I hope so. It sounds the quarter and the half hours too, so you'll get a little blast from your past every fifteen minutes.'

SEVENTEEN

Vanessa steps out of the cab and hurries, head down, towards Westminster Bridge. A whoosh of sound. She swings round. A couple of boys on electric scooters zoom up behind her. She shouts, telling them to back off. They circle her then swing away, laughing, into the darkness. She leans back against the iron parapet, closing her eyes until her breath steadies, then hurries on down the stone steps to the Embankment.

It's a relief when she sees Jay waiting for her by one of the benches. She waves as she runs towards him. Instead of waving back he lifts the camera hanging on a strap around his neck and raises it to his eye. His fingers move fast, and suddenly he's snapping off rapid-fire shots one after the other until she holds her hand up, laughing. 'Stop it! That's not what we're here for.'

He grins, lets the camera drop and grabs her sleeve, pulling her along the walkway. The Thames flows blue-black beside them, the breeze crisping the surface into ripples that catch shimmers of moonlight. They walk on and he points the camera at streaks of pink, violet, green and blue dancing on the water, stopping to frame reflections of light-dotted buildings, boats and distant cranes, or to thumb back through the images and squint critically at a particular shot before turning round and thrusting the screen towards her to gauge her reaction.

'This is the kind of thing I'm looking for,' she says, pointing to a shot of light reflected from a rope of bulbs strung between two lampposts. 'Maybe with a bit more skyline in the background.'

She stands back and watches him work, a tall slight figure, bobbing and weaving in the darkness.

'Why are you so into night shots?' she says, as she falls into step beside him.

He shrugs. 'There's something... precarious about the city after dark. When you turn a corner you've got no idea who might be there or what they might be doing, and, believe me, I've seen it all. It's like as soon people step into the night they think they're invisible.'

'Aren't you ever afraid?'

'Sure.' He looks away but not before she's caught a flash of something she can't quite fathom. 'That's kind of the point.'

It's almost midnight when they stop at a coffee stall. They sit at the water's edge cradling paper cups of lukewarm coffee and stuffing greasy chunks of the stallholder's last pastry into their mouths.

'I've been thinking about what you told me about your parents. Was there ever a time when you were happy at home?' Vanessa asks.

He shrugs. 'It was fine when they could drag me to church every Sunday and dress me up in a little cap and blazer and pack me off to the poncey prep school my father went to.'

Prep school, she thinks. *That explains the glitches in his accent.*

'It was when I got older that they decided I was a "disappointment".'

'That's horrible.'

'They were old when I came along, much older than my mates' parents, and they had a very set view of the way they wanted their only child to turn out. They thought that with enough discipline – or "guidance" as they called it – they could mould me into being just like them.'

'And?'

'It didn't work. I wasn't like the other kids at my school. I was bright enough but I was all over the place with schoolwork and I had terrible trouble concentrating in class – classic ADHD I found out later. I was the weirdo who preferred hanging out in the art room to tearing around a sports pitch and I got bullied for it. So I started truanting, looking for a place where I could... fit in and be myself, I suppose.' He stares out across the water. 'I thought I'd found it with this bunch of older kids who did drugs, and for a while getting stoned seemed to make things feel better. I had no idea they were grooming me for a local dealer who was part of a county lines drugs network. By the time I realised what was going on I was hooked and I ended up working for this guy to feed my habit. After that, things just spiralled out of control and instead of trying to get me the support I needed pretty much everyone, including my parents, gave up on me.'

'Weren't you envious when you saw other kids with happy homes and supportive parents?'

'Not really. You just have to look around you to see that families aren't all they're cracked up to be.'

He turns to look at her, as if he's waiting for her to share a confidence about her own childhood, but she jumps up and walks over to drop her paper cup into a bin.

'Have you thought any more about the delivery job?' he says, when she comes back.

'I have actually.' She draws in a breath. 'I've decided to give you a trial. Three months. I have to warn you, though, my manager isn't too happy about it. She wants me to give the job to someone she knows who has a lot more warehouse experience than you, so you're going to have to work hard to win her over.'

Jay's tension falls away. 'Thank you.'

'But if there's ever the slightest hint that you're using again—'

'There won't be.' He places both hands on the top of her arms and looks her straight in the eye. 'I'm done with all that. I swear.'

Vanessa finds herself blushing and wonders cynically if he's stolen this move from a film. She extricates herself gently. 'What about accommodation? Have you found yourself somewhere to live?'

'Larry's fixing me up with a bedsit. It's a sublet, just for a few weeks until I can find somewhere permanent.'

'Great,' she says, with a warm smile. 'Looks like you're all set then.' She glances up at the clock on Big Ben. 'Come on, we need to get back. We've both got work in the morning.'

'I'm going to stay out for a bit,' Jay says. 'But I'll wait with you while you get a cab.'

They hurry up the steps to the bridge and as they duck through a rowdy crowd of drunks, she's grateful for the steadying touch of his hand in the small of her back.

Vanessa wakes up to rapid pings from her phone. She reaches out to grab it from her bedside table and finds forty images on her WhatsApp, the first ten of which are of her own face, blinking, windswept, caught off-guard but smiling in a way she hasn't seen herself smile for a long time. The next batch are images of the Thames. She sits up and scrolls through them, delighted when she finds a shot that will work perfectly in the Pimlico flat. She needs to get up but takes a moment to look back through the shots Jay took of her. She usually hates seeing herself in photos but these are great. She's flicking through them, wondering if she might actually bear to have one of them printed and framed as a gift for her mother, when her finger stops.

There's a lone figure on the bridge behind her. She zooms in. In the glow of the streetlamps lighting the bridge she makes out a man in a motorbike helmet. No visor, but the lower half of his face is obscured by a mask that leaves only his eyes visible. She scrolls on.

He's in every shot.

In the final two he has a long lens camera raised to his eye, the kind used by the paparazzi, and he's pointing it directly at her.

This isn't a figment of Frances's paranoia or of her own overwrought imagination. She really is being watched, and this is the proof that she's been both looking for and dreading.

Is this man the fake bike courier who scoped out her house? Is he working for Mark Findlay? Did he follow her from her home, or had Jay let on to someone at Cranmore where he was going and who he was meeting? Whichever it is, there's one thing she knows for sure. She has to keep this from Frances.

EIGHTEEN

Vanessa is in her office trying, with dwindling success, to concentrate on the final drawings for the Pimlico job when she gets a text from Frances. *I have news. Can you come?*

She stares at the screen. *News?* Her heart flutters and her vision blurs. *Has Frances's investigator made a breakthrough?* She grabs her coat and dashes out to her car.

Frances leans over and beckons with her hand as Vanessa steps into her room. 'Quick, come in and shut the door.'

'What's happened? Has Dexter found a lead?'

'If only. No, one of my old classmates just called me, a woman called Mona Harding. She said that someone called Sarah Sachs, who claims to be a journalist from the *Business Post*, has been contacting people from my year, telling them she's writing my obituary—'

'*What?*'

Frances flicks her hand. 'The actual word Mona used was "tribute" but that's not important. What *is* important is that Sachs was asking questions about my school days, specifically whether I'd ever taken time off for a protracted family trip, or due to long-term illness.'

Vanessa stares at her. 'Fishing for a time when you might have given birth.'

'Exactly. But that's not the worst of it. Mona thought it was a bit strange so she looked this woman up. She had no trouble finding her by-line, but when she finally dug up a photo of her it turns out that the real Sara Sachs is about ten years older than this woman, looks nothing like her and left the *Business Post* about six months ago.'

First the biker, now this. Vanessa scrabbles for an answer that will calm Frances's panic and her own. After a painful few moments all she can come up with is: 'Maybe she's working for Dexter.'

'No, I checked with him as soon as I finished speaking to Mona. Anyway, he knows exactly when Dora was born.'

Vanessa closes her eyes and swallows hard. 'Do you think your cousin sent her?'

'Can you think of any other explanation? It means he definitely knows about Dora and he's definitely trying to find her.'

Vanessa gets up. Her heart's racing and she's scared now, really scared. She goes over to the window, grips the sill to hide the shake in her hands and looks down at the sweep of lawn below, trying to order her thoughts.

She turns to look at Frances and says, with far more conviction than she feels, 'Let's not get ahead of ourselves. So, yes, it looks like Mark does suspect that you had a child, but if he had anything concrete to go on he wouldn't be scrabbling around trying to find out when you might have given birth.' Frances stares back at her, thinking this through. 'Like you said, your father may have let something slip to his brother years ago, maybe a cryptic comment when he was drunk, and Mark's just trying to make sure he's not going to get a nasty surprise. The first thing he'll have done is look for a birth certificate. That's good, because we know there isn't one, so now, with no facts to go on – not even the year you gave birth – he's just fumbling in the dark. But look at it this way: if Dexter, who knows everything that you know about Dora, hasn't had any luck finding her, Findlay's got no chance.' It's the mantra she's been repeating to herself whenever she starts to panic, as if repetition will make it true.

'But why is he suddenly looking for her now, after all this time?'

'It could just be because he thinks the company's almost within his grasp,' Vanessa says, feebly.

'No. He thought I was going to let my secret die with me but somehow he's found out that I'm not going to do that, and he knows he's in a race against time to get to her first.'

She's right, Vanessa thinks. *It's the only explanation there is.*

'I have a really bad feeling about this,' Frances says, 'and I'm beginning to think I should never have dragged you into it.'

Vanessa says nothing, but she has a really bad feeling about it too.

'Oh, God,' Frances drops her hand onto Vanessa's arm. 'I've been so wrapped up with my own problems I never asked how it went when you visited your father.'

Vanessa twists around, surprised and touched that Frances had even remembered. 'It's really sweet of you to ask.' She lets out a long breath. 'I had some stupid fantasy that we were going to fall into each other's arms and it was all going to be the way it was when I was little.'

'That's not what happened?'

Vanessa shakes her head. 'He's angry and bitter. I can't blame him for that, any more than I can blame my mother for cutting off contact with him after they divorced. He had his faults, plenty of them, but as kid I adored him and I was devastated when I lost him from my life.'

'Do you think your relationship can be rebuilt?' Frances asks.

'It's going to take a small miracle. But I'm keeping in touch, telling him about my plans and dreams and trying to show him I'm serious about making amends. Baby steps. Hopefully we'll get there in the end.'

Vanessa leaves the hospice an hour later with three words ringing in her ears: *Race against time.*

NINETEEN

Mick arrives at the shop promptly at 8 a.m., looking smart in his new overalls – and gazes around him like a traveller who's blundered into a strange land. Meghan, who has stomped around emptying out the office in readiness for its refurb loses some of her agitation when she sees how neat he looks, but she's clearly wary of him. 'The office is downstairs,' she says, when Vanessa brings him over to meet her. 'This way.' She turns and walks ahead of him, her high heels clacking disapproval on the painted wooden steps.

Vanessa stays back. It won't help if she tries to interfere, and anyway she has a couple of errands to run.

She's away for a couple of hours. When she gets back she deliberately avoids asking Meghan how Mick's getting on, instead hurrying downstairs to see for herself. She taps on the office door and cracks it open. The scuffed white walls are now a warm antique pink and she finds him up a ladder putting a second coat of the same colour on the ceiling. 'Wow, this looks wonderful. Any problems?'

'Not so far.'

'Can I get you a cup of tea or a coffee?'

'I'm fine. The other girl... Meghan, is it? She made me one earlier.'

'Oh. Right.' She breathes an inner sigh of relief. Meghan bringing Mick hot drinks has got to be a good sign. She reaches into her bag and pulls out a new phone, still in its box. 'This is for you.'

He looks down at it, bewildered.

'It's so I can contact you if you're out on a job, and you can get hold of me if you have any queries or problems. Is that... OK?'

'It's been a while since I've had a phone.'

'I got the store to set it up and put my number and the number of the shop in the contacts. You can use it for personal calls too. No worries if it gets lost. It's insured on the company policy.'

He reaches down to take the box, pulls off the lid and lifts out the slim black handset, turning it over in his big red fingers. 'I got robbed,' he says, quietly. 'First night after my wife kicked me out. A couple of kids. They nicked everything worth taking. Set fire to the rest of it, gave me a kicking and pissed on my head. I was too drunk to do anything but lie there and take it.'

In the silence she hears the ding of the shop bell and the hum of traffic in the street outside.

'You're sober now,' she says. 'You're working, you've got a roof over your head and you're taking your life back.' She watches him trying out the keys, suddenly aware that to him this is far more than a phone: it's a piece of the normality that had slipped from his grasp.

'Mick, there's something I need to ask you.'

'Yeah?' He tears his eyes from the phone.

'Have there been any new guests or volunteers at Cranmore since I arrived?'

'I don't think so.'

'Any visitors looking around, or prospective donors coming in to see Larry?'

He runs his hand over his newly clipped hair. 'Not that I know of. Why?'

She's wary about telling him about the biker on the bridge, but she needs to know if there's a mole at Cranmore House passing information about her and her movements to someone on Findlay's payroll.

'I've been thinking about that fake courier who came to my house and wondering if he knew I'd be at Cranmore on Sunday mornings. I mean, my name and the time of my CV clinics are up there in big red letters on Larry's whiteboard for anyone walking past his office to see. So, whoever that guy was, he might have either seen it himself or been tipped off by someone who'd been at the hostel.'

'I s'pose,' Mick says, looking unconvinced. 'But why go to all that trouble just to rob your house? No offence, it's a nice place and everything, but it's not like you live in a mansion.'

Remembering Doug's first thought when she'd questioned him about Findlay, Vanessa looks down at her hands and says, 'I think I might be being stalked.'

'What? Have you been to the cops?'

'No.' She looks up at him quickly. 'At the moment it's just a hunch. I need more evidence before I tell anyone.'

'OK, well, I'll ask around for you and see if any strangers have been in lately.'

'Thanks, Mick, but promise me you won't mention my name. I... don't want anyone to know I suspect anything.'

Vanessa goes upstairs to find Meghan slitting open a packing case and pulling out a large mounted print. She studies it for a moment, then puts it down and takes out another.

'What do you think?' Vanessa says, going over to her.

'Are these the shots that bloke Jay took?'

Vanessa nods, enthusiastically. 'That one's going to look

perfect in the Pimlico penthouse.' She points to an explosion of pink and orange dancing on an expanse of dark, rippling river.

Meghan props the print against the side of the counter and takes out the others one by one. 'Hmm, not bad,' she says, deliberately noncommittal.

'Could you add them to the website and whip up a bit of buzz about them online?'

'I can try.' Meghan delves back into the box. 'Why have they sent all these duplicates?'

'I'm going to hang a set at Cranmore House – just for a few weeks. Now we've redecorated the dining room, I want to use the walls as a sort of exhibition space.'

'Are you joking?'

'Look, I know it sounds a bit yucky but I honestly think that art can make people feel better about themselves and, believe me, when it comes to improving self-esteem, the men at Cranmore need all the help they can get.'

Meghan gives her a long, quizzical look. 'You're really into that place, aren't you?'

Vanessa shrugs her shoulders and laughs. The sound is oddly happy. Then, like a chill gust of wind, the image of the biker blows into her brain and snuffs out her elation.

TWENTY

'Why didn't you tell me that Jay Brooker was a drug dealer?' Meghan hisses, ramming a new till roll into the card machine.

Vanessa stays silent, watching her snap the machine shut and jab the buttons.

'Well?' Meghan says, without looking up.

'It's not like that. He only sold drugs to support his habit.'

'Oh, so that makes it alright?' The machine spits out a blank receipt. Glowering, Meghan tears it off and scrunches it into a tight little ball.

'No, and he knows it, which is why he's desperate to sort his life out and stay clean. He can't do that unless somebody gives him a job.'

'That somebody doesn't have to be you.'

'You said that about Mick.'

'Mick's different. He's a nice guy who lost his business and had a breakdown. He's not a criminal.'

'Jay's served his sentence and now he's doing everything he can to make a fresh start. Anyway, how do you know about his past?'

'I read it online. Trials and sentences are on public record, *including* community service orders.'

'Why were you checking up on him?'

'I wasn't.' Meghan tosses the balled receipt into the bin. 'In case you haven't noticed, I've been adding a bit of biographical detail to all our maker profiles and I was trying to find some interesting hooks for his. Only I was hoping for something more along the lines of "street artist" and "care-worker", not "convicted drug dealer". *Please* don't tell me you're still considering him for the delivery job.'

'Without a job he'll never get back on his feet.'

'I thought you were going to interview those two women who want to do it as a job share.'

Vanessa frowns. 'Aren't they friends of yours?'

Meghan looks up with a vacant shrug. 'I knew one of them a bit in Southampton. She's super reliable and really nice.'

'Why do they want a job share?'

'They're trying to get their own upcycling business off the ground – she does joinery and her friend does this amazing reupholstery. You should take a look at their website. Some of their pieces might even work for the shop.'

'Sure, send me a link. But a job share wouldn't work for us, and Jay can commit full time.'

'But—'

'I think you should get to know him.'

'No, thanks.'

'I'm serious about this, Meghan.' An edge of annoyance creeps into Vanessa's voice. 'You need to put your prejudices about people like him aside.'

'So you *are* going to give him the job.'

'We had a long talk about it, he convinced me he's going to give it his best shot and I've agreed to give him a three-month trial. Starting next week.'

Meghan steps back and crosses her arms across her chest,

one hand tap-tapping against her elbow. 'Does he know about you and Doug?'

'What? No. Why would he?'

'Are you sure?'

Vanessa thinks back to that first night in the Cranmore House dining room – Jay sitting opposite her chewing a toothpick, Larry asking if her husband would mind her volunteering at weekends. 'He may have heard me mention I'm divorced.'

'You see!' Meghan throws up her hands. 'He knows you're lonely and vulnerable and he's homed in on you.'

'It's not like that.'

'I'm your friend, Nessa. Somebody has to make you see sense. Have you even thought about the risks involved in taking on someone like him?'

Vanessa has thought about them, a lot. In fact, she's thought about them pretty much non-stop since Jay told her he needed a job. 'Look, you and I are lucky. We've both been sheltered our whole lives but it doesn't take much to make a couple of bad decisions that send your life spiralling out of control. If either of us ever fell through the net like that, I'd hope there'd be someone out there who'd have the guts to take a chance on us. Anyway, you're the one who's always telling me that if I want to move on I need to start *taking* risks.'

Meghan is shaking her head, ready to argue, when the shop phone rings. She snatches it up. 'Vanessa Dunn Designs...' Impatience drains from her voice and she switches to professional charm. 'No, but she's right here. I'll hand you over.'

She holds the phone out to Vanessa. 'It's Ralph Gilmore.'

'Who?' Vanessa mouths.

'Mr Squishy,' Meghan mouths back.

Vanessa rolls her eyes and takes the phone. 'Vanessa Dunn. How may I help you?'

'Oh... hello.' The voice is gruff. 'Ralph Gilmore, here. I came in the other day looking for a wedding present.'

'Yes. I remember.'

Meghan raises an eyebrow. Vanessa scowls at her.

'My niece and her husband loved the wine glasses.'

'That's good to hear.'

'I've been reading up about your design service.' Tiny pause. 'I was wondering if you might have time to sort out my flat.'

Vanessa flips open her notebook and reaches for her pen. 'Of course. How many bedrooms does it have?'

'Two, and two bathrooms, a largeish reception room, a decent-sized kitchen and a dining room that I want to convert into a home office.'

'Are you thinking of signing up for our full service?'

'Does that mean you'd do everything?'

'If that's what you need. Some clients like to work with me closely on every decision; others prefer to leave it all to me.'

'You personally?'

'I do all the design work.'

'Well, ideally, I'd like to leave it to you. But with' – he pauses – 'plenty of personal updates along the way.'

Is he flirting with her? She's so out of practice she can't tell. 'Erm... why don't I check the diary and see when I could take a look at the property?'

'Great. So, how do we do this?'

'Once I've seen the space and we've discussed your needs in detail, I'll draw up some sketches and give you an estimate and an idea about timings.'

'Sounds good.'

She flicks through her diary. 'It will have to be next week, I'm afraid. How about Thursday afternoon, around two o'clock?'

'I'll look forward to it. It's Flat—'

'I have the address on file. I'll see you on Thursday.'

She cuts the call. Phone still in hand, she gazes out at the grey, rain-drenched streets, umbrellas bobbing, hunched figures jostling for space on the narrow pavement, awnings flapping in the wind.

'Excuse me. Can I pay for these?'

She blinks down at a set of turquoise bowls sitting on the bed of tissue paper in front of her. She drops the phone into its cradle and snaps on a distracted smile. 'Of course. Beautiful, aren't they? They're by a potter called Jenny St George. These striated glazes she uses are unique.'

Her eyes lift from the bowl to the face of the customer. Her body bucks, an involuntary jolt. It's Amanda Mason-Findlay. 'Amanda! You should have told me you were coming in.'

'I know, but I was at a meeting nearby and I thought I'd drop by and tell you that the architect's drawings for our Chelsea house have come back, and we've put in the planning application.'

'That's excellent news. Can you send me the drawings?'

'Of course. I also wanted to let you know that we've asked D&D to draw up plans for Garston Grange and that when the time comes, Mark and I would love you to work on that too. You already know I'm a fan but he's especially keen to get you signed up as soon as possible. We'd hate to lose out because we hadn't acted quickly enough.' Her eyes hold Vanessa's. 'Mark's meticulous like that. He wants to get everything in place before he goes from being the acting to the permanent CEO at Findlay's. For the sake of the business he's doing everything he can to make sure the transition is seamless. No loose ends to tie up. No annoying little snags to iron out.'

The Sellotape dispenser digs into Vanessa's hand as she grips it. *Is this some kind of warning?*

'Well, if it helps, please tell him I'll be very happy to work on the project.' The words come out in staccato little pops. The voice of a clockwork toy. Vanessa throws out a jerky hand. 'Can I show you around the shop?'

'Not today. I'm in a bit of a rush. I'll send you those plans as soon as I get back.'

'Great.' Vanessa's fingers flick up layers of tissue paper and tuck them between and around the bowls.

Amanda speaks again: 'Any word from your client who was thinking of buying a Sanchez?'

Vanessa snaps off a length of Sellotape. 'Oh... he had to go back to the States so the project's on hold until he gets back.' She fastens the package, lowers it into a Vanessa Dunn carrier bag and hands it to Amanda. 'Enjoy!'

Amanda gives her a tight little smile and disappears in a swirl of camel-coloured cashmere.

'We need to talk about Jay,' Vanessa says later that afternoon, when Meghan comes down to her office for their weekly meeting.

'What's there to talk about? I think he's trouble and you refuse to see there's a problem.'

'You've got this totally wrong, Meg.'

'Have you asked yourself why someone like him is so keen to get a delivery job? What better cover can you get than rocking up in a Vanessa Dunn van if you're delivering drugs to the doors of middle-class professionals?'

'You're being ridiculous. I'm not denying he's made mistakes in the past, big ones. But he's talented and all he needs is a bit of help. Something which isn't easy to come by when your family has turned their back on you.'

'He's a drug dealer.'

'*Was* a drug dealer,' Vanessa snaps. 'Look, if he messes up at any point over the next three months I'll sack him. If he proves he can do the job, I'll keep him on. Simple as that. Meanwhile, I want you to give him the benefit of the doubt and try to get to know him. In fact, I'm going to get you both over to my house for dinner.'

'No, thanks.'

'Please, Meg. I need you to make an effort with this.'

Meghan gives a weary shake of her head. 'Alright, I'll come. Just don't expect me to change my mind.'

'Are you busy tomorrow?'

'What's the rush?'

'I've got a lot on at the moment and I just can't deal with the stress when there are tensions at the shop.'

TWENTY-ONE

Blinking into the heat, Vanessa opens the oven door, takes out the casserole dish and lifts off the lid. Beer in hand, Jay comes over to inspect the dark, glossy beef bourguignon. 'Smells good.'

'I hope it tastes alright,' Vanessa says. 'I made it after I got home last night to give the flavours a bit of time to develop.'

'After three months of Beattie's offerings, let's hope I've got enough taste buds left to enjoy it.'

'The food at Cranmore is a bit grim.'

'Tell me about it. It's her kids I feel sorry for. Can you imagine being forced to eat that muck from birth?'

Vanessa giggles. 'It probably counts as child abuse. Can you grab some knives and forks from that drawer? And, Meg, could you get some plates down from the rack?'

Although her face is turned slightly to one side, Vanessa is aware of Meghan watching Jay with an expression that hovers between suspicion and open hostility, and she scrabbles for something to say to bring her into the conversation. 'Is your mum a good cook?' It's feeble, but it will have to do.

Meghan reaches down the plates. 'Pretty good. She did an

international cookery course when I was a kid. The trouble is she's been on a diet for years, so she'll whip up a wonderful curry or an amazing jambalaya then as soon as my dad and I sit down to eat it, she guilt-trips us by serving herself a stick of celery. Still, she's given me a taste for super spicy food. How about you, Jay?' Her tone is throwaway but her eyes, when she looks at him, are probing.

Jay shakes his head. 'Nothing spicy about the food in our house. My father's totally flavour-averse, and my mother thinks garlic's something you use to ward off vampires.'

'Vanessa said you don't see them.'

There's a charged silence. Vanessa catches her eye and gives a tiny shake of her head, annoyed at this betrayal of her confidence, but Meghan ploughs on. 'Do you ever think about seeking a reconciliation?'

'Not anymore,' Jay says.

'Why not?'

He adjusts a fork, squaring it up so it aligns exactly with the edge of the table. 'I wrote to them when I was in rehab. It was one of the tasks in this life-skills course they made us do – "Rebuilding Broken Relationships".'

'What did you say?'

'That I was sorry for what I'd put them through, that I was in rehab trying to turn my life around, and I asked them if they'd be up for coming to see me.'

'Were they?'

He laughs, though the sound is harsh. 'They never even wrote back.'

'Maybe they're sick,' Meghan fires back.

'Oh, don't you worry.' His voice is bitter. 'They might be getting on a bit but they're both in great shape. In fact, my father's just been elected chair of the parish council and my mother's running to be a school governor.'

Meghan sips from her wine glass and regards him with a

tight smile, as if she's caught him out in a lie. 'If you don't see them, how come you know so much about their lives?'

Jay looks straight back at her. 'If they'd ever bothered to get in touch I could have tightened up my mother's Facebook privacy settings – as it is, their saintly deeds are out there on the internet for the whole world to admire.'

Vanessa hurriedly turns on the mini speaker she keeps on the counter, flips opens her laptop and logs in. 'Why don't you take a look through my Spotify, Jay. Find us something relaxing to listen to.'

With a glare at Meghan, Jay moves over to the counter, the scorn on his face turning to a look of approval as he scrolls through Vanessa's playlist. Moments later, the room fills with John Coltrane's 'Blue Train'.

Meghan wrinkles her nose, as if she's caught a whiff of something rotten.

Jay looks up at Vanessa. 'Have you opened any dodgy links lately?'

'No, I'm really careful about things like that.'

'Not careful enough. There's a pop-up here saying some-one's trying to log into your laptop remotely.'

Vanessa peers over his shoulder as he nudges the little box with the cursor. She tries to breathe, only it feels as if there's a blade stabbing her lungs. This has to be Findlay, or someone working for him, trying to find out what she knows about Frances's child.

'That's so annoying,' she manages to say.

'Has anyone else been using your laptop? A friend? Your cleaner?'

'No. Anyway, no one knows my password.'

'Maybe you left it logged in somewhere.'

'No. If it's not here or in my office, it's with me in my bag.'

'Well, you'd better change the password.'

'I hate having to remember new ones.' She turns the laptop around and taps at the keys. 'There.'

She's churned up inside but she's invited these two here for a reason, and she can't let them see she's in a state. She lifts the casserole onto the table and goes back for the dishes of creamy mashed potato and buttered green beans – hot, steaming, comfort food that she hopes will thaw the thickening frost between them. 'Do you want to stick with beer, Jay, or move on to wine?'

'Wine's good.'

She fills all three glasses from the bottle on the table. 'Come and sit down. I hope you're both hungry. I've made loads.'

Her guests pull up chairs on opposite sides of her kitchen table and sit down awkwardly as she ladles beef bourguignon onto their plates.

'How long have you been working for Vanessa?' Jay asks, helping himself to mash.

Safe territory, Vanessa thinks, and throws him a relieved smile.

'A few months,' Meghan says.

'What were you doing before?'

'Visual merchandising.'

'Who for?'

'A department store.'

'Which one?'

'You wouldn't have heard of it. It's in Southampton.'

Jay reaches for the beans. 'Managing Vanessa Dunn Interiors is quite a step up for you, then.'

Their eyes meet. Meghan's narrow. 'What about you? I understand you used to be quite the entrepreneur.'

Whoa, Vanessa thinks. 'We've had a lot of interest in your nightscapes,' she says, hurriedly.

'No sales, though,' Meghan says.

'Not yet.'

The doorbell rings. Four sharp, impatient blasts. Vanessa half rises from the table, curious to see who it is yet loath to leave Meghan and Jay alone. 'Sorry, I won't be a minute.'

She dashes down the corridor and pulls open the door – astonished to see Izzy on the step, looking damp and dishevelled.

'You could look a bit more pleased to see me,' Izzy says, swaying slightly and slurring her words, a sharp blast of alcohol in her breath.

'I am... I just thought you were on tour.'

'The Stuttgart gig got postponed. Some stupid health and safety problem at the venue.'

Vanessa looks past her into the drizzly darkness. 'Are you with Gunther?'

'We broke up.'

'When?'

'About an hour ago. God.' Izzy bursts into tears.

'Izz, are you drunk?'

'Of course I'm not drunk. I'm upset.' She pushes past Vanessa and heads for the kitchen, dropping her tatty backpack on the way.

Vanessa hurries after her.

'Oh,' Izzy says, barely glancing at Meghan and Jay. 'You've got company.' She opens the cupboard above the sink, grabs a glass and fills it from the bottle on the table. She takes a deep slug, refills the glass and glugs it down with the bottle still in her hand.

'This is my sister, Izzy,' Vanessa says, apologetically. 'She's... a bit upset.'

She turns to Izzy. 'Don't you think you should eat something before you hit the wine?'

'What's wrong with you? My life's in ruins and all you can do is nag.'

'Let me get you some food.'

'I'm not hungry.'

'What's happened?' Meghan asks, shunting a little to one side and pulling back a chair so that Izzy can sit down next to her.

Izzy drops into the seat. 'It's my boyfriend, Gunther. My gig got postponed so I came back to London for a couple of days to surprise him. I thought he'd be pleased but when I walked into his flat – the flat we'd been living in together before I went on tour – he's there with this stupid slut who starts acting like *she's* his girlfriend and demanding to know who I am.' Tears run down her cheeks. She swipes at them with her knuckles. 'I asked him what the hell was going on and he got really nasty and said I didn't own him, and I should have warned him before barging in unannounced.'

'What a bastard,' Meghan says, sympathetically. 'But we've all been there. If you ask me, it sounds like you've dodged a bullet with the lovely Gunther.'

'I thought he was different,' Izzy sobs. 'I thought he was the one.'

Vanessa grabs a fork and a plate, heaps it with mashed potato, adds a mound of beef bourguignon and a spoonful of beans and pushes it in front of her sister.

Izzy swings back her pale gold hair, hunches over the plate and, mindless of the tears dripping into the gravy, begins to shovel the food into her mouth. Vanessa watches her and wonders how anyone who's clearly pissed, has red puffy eyes, smudged mascara and a mouth stuffed with mash can look so strikingly lovely.

She glances apologetically at Meghan and senses that she's thinking exactly the same thing.

'Why would he do that to me?' Izzy waves her fork at Jay, as if she suspects him of withholding information about Gunther's motivation.

Jay shrugs and raises his hands.

Izzy drops her fork with a clatter and bursts into loud, angry sobs.

'Come on, Izz,' Vanessa says. 'Why don't I take you upstairs and put you to bed? You'll feel so much better after you've had some sleep.'

'Of course I won't.' Izzy knocks back her wine and reaches for the almost empty bottle. 'What do you think I am? Five years old? You can't push me around like you pushed Mum into that horrible nursing home.'

'It's not horrible, Izz,' Vanessa says, calmly. 'It's one of the best in the country. You know that.'

'Yeah, yeah, until the visitors leave and then—' She scrunches up her eyes, pulls her mouth into a silent scream and claws at the air.

'Jay, more beef?' Vanessa says quickly, lifting the serving spoon.

'Sure.' He hands her his plate, clearly amused by the sibling drama being played out in front of him.

'It's not funny,' Izzy glowers at him, then slowly switches her foggy attention from him to Meghan. 'Are you two together?'

Jay smirks and Meghan nearly spits out her wine. 'God, no.'

'You should go for it. He's cute.' Izzy flops forward, her head dangling over her almost empty plate.

'Come on, you,' Vanessa says, gently. Taking her sister by the arm, she pulls her up and out of her seat and propels her firmly to the door.

Meghan picks up her handbag and looks meaningfully at Jay. 'We should leave them to it.'

'You don't have to go!' Vanessa calls from the hallway.

'It's fine. I'll see you tomorrow,' Meghan calls back. 'Don't rush in if you... have a tough night.'

Jay seems to hesitate, scowling slightly when Meghan grips his arm and ushers him out. 'Do you want a lift somewhere?' she says, as she kicks Vanessa's front door shut behind them.

'No thanks.' He shrugs off her hand. 'I'll walk.'

'You were mad to let Jay into your house,' Meghan says next morning, before Vanessa has even pulled off her coat. 'You could practically see the pound signs popping out of his eyes.'

'He was curious to see my home. That's not a crime.' Vanessa hurries away to open the door for a woman who's struggling to heave her buggy over the front step.

'Look,' she says, when she comes back. 'There's a motto they've got all over the walls at Cranmore House – "There's no such thing as bad people, just bad decisions." I didn't get it to begin with but the more I think about it, the more it makes sense. So, unless you find concrete evidence that Jay's making bad decisions again, I really don't want to hear it.'

'Well, don't say I didn't warn you,' Meghan murmurs, before beaming a smile at the woman with the buggy and ringing up the pair of cushions she's placed on the counter. 'Aren't these colours just gorgeous?'

'How was Izzy this morning?' she asks, as the woman leaves. Her voice is placatory and, at least for now, Vanessa decides to drop the argument.

'She's going to have the hangover from hell so I left her to sleep it off.'

'Poor kid. It can't have been much fun walking in on her boyfriend and finding him with someone else.'

'Izzy has the worst taste in men. She always picks total creeps, then she can't believe it when they cheat on her.'

'Unlike her big sister, whose taste in men is definitely improving.'

'What are you talking about?'

'Aren't you meeting Ralph Gilmore this afternoon?'

'How do you know that?'

'I was there when he called you, remember? And he's single and lonely and definitely not a creep.' Meghan waggles her eyebrows.

'Oh, stop it.' Vanessa bops her on the head with a roll of Sellotape.

Meghan laughs and ducks away. 'I forgot, this came for you.' She lifts a slim wooden box onto the counter.

Vanessa gazes at the words etched into the wood. *Findlay's, a triple distilled single malt scotch whisky with a light, distinctive nose.* She rips open the little card tied to the box.

Here's to a mutually beneficial collaboration. Mark Findlay.

Her hands grow clammy. Now he's failed to access her computer, is he testing the water? Trying see if she'll betray Frances's trust?

'Another admirer?' Meghan asks, tipping her head to one side.

Vanessa shoves the card into her jacket pocket and shakes her head. 'Just a client.' She picks up her bag.

'Where are you going now?'

'To the computer shop.'

'What for?'

Vanessa flushes. 'To get my laptop checked for spyware.'

TWENTY-TWO

Ralph Gilmore's flat is on the top floor of an imposing stucco-fronted building on the south side of Poultney Square. Vanessa presses the bell and waits.

He buzzes her in and meets her halfway down the stairs. Slightly out of breath, he holds out a bunch of keys. 'I'm sorry, Vanessa, I was really looking forward to this but I've been called back to the office to see a client and I'm going to have to leave you to it.'

'But we need to discuss the look you're after.'

'Can you come up with some ideas and give me a call?'

'Alright, but—'

'Sorry – it's a bit of an emergency.' He thrusts the keys into her hand. 'Leave them on the kitchen table when you go. I've got another set.' He hurries past her and she hears the front door slam.

Vanessa climbs the grand staircase with its slightly worn red carpet and lets herself into the top flat. Its proportions are beautiful and the basic fabric is sound, but the décor is tired and the furniture – what there is of it – is tacky. There's a bed, a chair, a wardrobe and chest of drawers in each of the bedrooms, all made of the cheap orange pine favoured by commercial land-lords, and a couple of sagged-out chintz-covered sofas in the reception room. The office is a bit more lived in – papers scattered across a large mahogany desk, a row of filing cabinets, a couple of leather club chairs. She sits at the desk for a moment taking in the feel of the place. Drawn by the pale sunlight slanting through the long sash windows, she crosses the room and looks down at the square. The view over the gardens is wonderful, though the exquisite symmetry of the pillared white houses is marred by a grid of scaffolding abandoned against the buildings on the eastern side, as if a developer had made a start on a major renovation then run out of money.

Turning away, she pulls out her laser measure and walks around the flat, sketching out a plan of each room on her tablet as she goes. When the floor plan is complete, she opens the French doors and steps out onto the narrow balcony. She takes out her phone with a fizz of dread: with everything that's going on in her life right now, it has come to feel like a bomb that might go off at any moment. There are a few pressing work emails but nothing from Frances.

Lifting her face to the thin autumn sunshine she calls Izzy. Her sister doesn't pick up. Worried, she calls again. Finally, on the fifth ring, she gets through. 'You OK, Izz? You were dead to the world when I left this morning.'

'Fine. Yeah.' She's breathless and a little giggly. 'Good, actually.'

'Did you eat something? There's plenty of bits and pieces to pick at in the fridge. I thought we could get a takeaway tonight and binge watch a box set.'

'Sorry. I'm... going to stay with a friend.' There's something suspiciously coy, almost defensive, about the way she says it, and what sounds like the click of a door being shut in the background.

'Is Gunther with you? You're not getting back with him, are you?'

'God, no. I'm never going speak to that creep again.'

'Good. Will I see you before you go back to Stuttgart?'

'Probs not. But thanks for last night. Got to go.'

'Izzy—'

'What?'

'Don't forget to put the alarm on when you leave.'

'Sure.' Izzy hangs up.

Amazed at the resilience of her sister's much-battered heart and overworked liver, Vanessa watches a truck manoeuvre in the square below, and then she goes back into the flat and does a second, more leisurely circuit of the rooms, this time taking photographs of everything she sees. She knows from experience that it's nearly always the little things that provide the greatest inspiration. The biggest problem by far is the bathroom. It's grim. The lighting is dull, the tiles vile, the fittings are in all the wrong places and it's an odd shape – one corner sliced off to accommodate a cumbersome built-in cupboard, which definitely has to go. She pulls open the door, curious to see how much pipework will need to be moved. Her view is blocked by a couple of large packing cases stacked one above of the other. The top one is full of bedding and pillows. She lifts it out and places it to one side. The one beneath it is heavier. She's pulling it out, dragging it by its half-sealed flaps, when a glimpse of navy and gold catches her eye. She pulls the flaps wider.

A Vanessa Dunn label stuck to a half-open package.

She eases out the package, dips her hand into the bed of tissue paper and brings out a hand-blown wine glass with a blue rim. She lifts away more tissue. Eleven more glasses – making up the complete set, still in their cardboard compartments.

Hadn't Ralph assured her that the happy couple had loved their carefully chosen wedding gift?

She quickly closes the flaps, replaces the packing cases and shuts the cupboard.

Perhaps his niece had hated them and he'd been too embarrassed to say.

TWENTY-THREE

Monday comes. Jay's first day. Vanessa wakes up gripped by nerves. She's got such hopes for her inclusive staffing plan. But what if giving Jay this job doesn't work out? After the strained atmosphere at dinner the other night, she's particularly worried about getting Meghan on side but given the way Mick managed to win her round, she just has to hope that, with time, Jay will be able to do the same.

That said, Mick is different: less angry, less defensive, less chippy.

She dresses carefully, selecting black trousers and a grey, fine wool jersey rather than one of her more cutting-edge outfits, aiming for professional yet approachable. She ties her hair into a messy bun and adds a favourite pair of antique coral earrings and a slick of coral lipstick.

She's arranged to meet Jay at the shop at eight, half an hour before the rest of the staff are due. When she pulls into the yard at ten to, he's already there, waiting by the back entrance, black hair damp and a little tousled, hands stuffed into his jacket pockets.

'Hey,' she says, getting out and pulling her bag from the boot.

He responds with a pinched smile and a single flip of his hand.

She strides towards him, clicking the key fob over her shoulder. 'Come on in.' She leads him into her office, scoops up a pile of files from the sofa and plonks them on the floor. 'Have a seat.' She turns away, flicks on the coffee maker and takes a phone from the drawer in her desk, identical to the one she bought for Mick. 'This is for you,' she says, holding it out to him.

'You're alright. I've got a phone,' he says.

She's been afraid of this – his knee-jerk resistance to anything he thinks smacks of charity.

'You said yours was old and crappy.'

'Yeah, but—'

'So you're going to need a company one. We have to be able to get hold of you at all times, and it's got the inventory software loaded onto it. You can use it for personal calls too.' She smiles. 'As long as you're not ringing Australia every night. If it's a problem lugging two handsets around I can get your old number transferred to this one.'

'Alright.' He takes the phone from her.

She holds his gaze. 'I really want you to make a success of this, Jay.'

'Me, too.'

'So, any questions or problems, don't hesitate to come straight to me.'

'OK.'

'I'll start by showing you around the stockroom. It's not enormous so it's important that everything is stored in the right place and the inventory is kept updated. We've got some more warehouse space for bigger items out in Brentford. I'll take you there tomorrow. Here, these should fit you.' She holds up a set of overalls.

He looks at them with disdain, then at her. 'Do I have to?'

'Not if you don't want to, but it can get pretty dusty in the stockroom.' She flashes him a smile. 'I wear them myself when I'm doing anything hands on.'

He puts down his mug, slings the overalls over his shoulder and follows her upstairs. She stops on the half-landing. 'Staff kitchen through this door.' She pulls it open. 'Feel free to make yourself a hot drink whenever you want.' She shuts it and pulls open a second door. 'Staff cloakroom. We'll be getting lockers, eventually; meanwhile, it's quite safe to leave your things in here.'

He shrugs off his jacket and hangs it on one of the hooks alongside the other coats.

The shop is busy, customers strolling around, Jody on the till, Sarah and Meghan greeting people and chatting.

'How much of your stock is vintage and how much new?' Jay asks.

'It varies. Right now, I'd say roughly forty per cent is vintage, sixty per cent new.'

'Where do you source the vintage stuff?'

'Auctions, mainly. Next time I go you should come with me. Nowadays you can bid online, but nothing beats the buzz of doing it in person.' Vanessa's phone vibrates in her pocket. She pulls it out and sees the number for St Saviour's flashing on the screen. She's hit by a wave of panic. 'Sorry, I need to take this.'

She ducks away from him, pressing 'Accept' as she hurries out of earshot.

'Mrs Dunn—'

'Has something happened to Frances?'

'She's asking to see you. We think now would be the right time to come.' The voice on the other end is steady and professional, but the urgency of her message – one this woman must have delivered a hundred times to the friends and families of the dying – plunges Vanessa into a sick, sweaty mess.

'Tell her I'm on my way.'

'Are you OK?' Jay asks, coming up behind her.

'Not really.' She spins around and beckons to Meghan, who sees her expression and comes quickly. 'Sorry, I've got to go,' Vanessa says. 'Can you take Jay down to the storeroom and get him started on the stock for tomorrow's deliveries?'

'Of course. Is it your mum?'

'A friend.' Vanessa blinks hard and swallows, already on her way to her office to fetch her coat and keys.

She feels bad abandoning Jay on his first morning but she has no choice. Five minutes later she's in her car swerving through traffic and speeding through amber lights.

TWENTY-FOUR

Vanessa has always known this day would come and she'd thought she'd prepared herself for it, but did it have to be so soon? Her hands shake on the wheel and her thoughts rev with the engine. She parks haphazardly across two spaces in the hospice car park and makes a dash for the reception, barely stopping to scribble her name in the visitors' book before pounding down the corridor and flinging open the door of room seventeen.

Frances is lying back against her pillows, her eyes closed, her hands clasped in her lap. Vanessa studies her from the doorway and thinks that if it weren't for the oxygen tube snaking from her nose, coiling around the bed and slinking into one of the many machines set up around the room she might be an effigy; a medieval martyr carved out of pale, blue-veined marble.

Frances turns her head very slightly. Vanessa rushes over and takes her hand. Her skin feels cool and waxy.

'I'm not doing goodbyes or if-onlys.' Frances's voice is frail and unsteady. 'My only regret is that I never had the chance to meet my girl. But we've both known for a while that I left it too late.'

'Oh, Frances.'

Frances holds her gaze. 'Seeing as we've got no idea what she's been through or what kind of life she's living, it's a real comfort to know that she'll have you to help her pick out that *fuck-you* outfit for her first meeting with the family, and ply her with wine and chocolate when she's feeling down.' While her tone is as playful as her failing lungs will allow, her eyes are deadly serious. 'If she's on her own and scared, you may need to do a lot more than that. I don't just mean protecting her from Mark's fury. Once the news comes out there'll be journalists and God knows how many lowlifes trying to take advantage of her.'

'I'll do whatever it takes. You know that.'

'Remember, if you need any help you mustn't hesitate to call my lawyer.'

'I will,' Vanessa says, struggling to collect her thoughts as she realises that this is the last conversation they will ever have. 'Look, I understand why you don't want to risk me and Don Dexter being seen together and I know that he has instructions to report back to your lawyer if he has a major breakthrough, but if he could start sending me updates, say once a week, to let me know how his search is going it would help me to stay in the loop and also keep him on his toes. Another set of eyes on the information might even see a connection that he's too close to it to notice.'

'That's a good idea,' Frances rasps. 'We can text him now, from my phone.'

Vanessa takes the phone from the bedside table and types as Frances dictates her instructions. She presses 'Send' and they sit in silence, unspoken thoughts swirling like smoke around the child Frances will never meet.

'When you find her, can you give her this?' Frances says at last.

Frances opens the fingers of one hand. A small red flash drive lies in her palm. Vanessa stares down at the little red rectangle, her mouth making silent shapes.

'It's a video message I made for her. I'd like you to sit with her while she watches it.'

Blinking back tears, Vanessa takes the drive and tucks it into her handbag,

'Perhaps you should take a look at it first so you don't get emotional,' Frances says, her thin voice matter of fact. Then she looks down at her hand and with great effort pulls at her emerald and diamond ring. It slides from her shrunken finger and she holds it out. 'For you. It was my twenty-first birthday present from my father.'

Vanessa pulls back.

'Don't worry, he had far better things to do than go shopping for a present for his only daughter's coming of age. He gave me his credit card instead, and told me to get myself something I liked. I bought the most expensive ring in the shop, thinking it would force him to take it back and pick out something for me himself. But he never queried the cost, or even asked me what I'd bought.'

'Even so, I can't possibly accept it.'

'Why not? Keep it, sell it, give it to someone you love.' Gathering her strength, Frances turns the ring this way and that so the stones catch the light and make it dance, before taking Vanessa's hand and slipping it onto her finger. 'It's yours now,' she says, looking away. 'Just don't get weepy about it.'

'Look, I know how much you loathe sentimentality, but I want to thank you for everything you've done for me.'

'Everything *I've* done for *you*?'

Vanessa nods. 'You have no idea of the state I was in when we first met, how deeply lost and alone I felt. But your friendship has meant more to me than you can ever know, and by entrusting me with Dora's future, you've given my life real meaning and purpose.'

Frances stares into space for a moment or two, then swallows and says: 'Will you read to me?'

'I'd like that.' Vanessa struggles to control her voice. 'What do you fancy? Christie, Allingham, or something a bit more recent?'

'Christie. The final chapter of *Death Comes as the End*.'

Despite herself, Vanessa can't stop a smile. 'Given the circumstances some people – not me, of course – might think that choice was a tiny bit near the knuckle.'

'It is – but not because of the title. What could be more suitable for the occasion than a mystery centred around a powerful, dysfunctional family in meltdown after a death?'

Vanessa gets up and bumps her finger along the books on the window ledge. She finds the well-thumbed paperback and takes it back to the bedside chair where she's sat so often. Pressing the heel of her hand to one eye, then the other, she opens the cover. Accompanied by the slow, steady bleep of the monitors she begins to read.

Frances's eyes close as she listens, her breathing soft and slow.

An hour later, Vanessa leaves St Saviour's, knowing that she will never see Frances again. At the exit from the car park she indicates right, ready to head back to the shop, hesitates then swings the steering wheel sharply to the left and turns the car towards home.

She kicks the front door shut behind her and says, 'OK,' out loud, to fill the silence. In the kitchen she makes a pot of coffee, sits down at the kitchen table and, with shaking fingers, slides

Frances's memory stick into her laptop. 'OK,' she says again, takes a deep breath and presses 'Play'.

An image of Frances fills the screen. She's sitting up in bed, cheekbones jutting through her smooth white skin as she stares into the lens of her phone. 'I'm so sorry I didn't start to look for you years ago,' she says, in a breathy whisper. 'If I hadn't spent my whole life in thrall to my father we might have got to know each other long ago, and developed a proper relationship. As it is, if you're watching this, then I'm already dead. My lawyer has the original recording, along with all my photographs and papers, but I've asked my dear friend Vanessa Dunn to give you this copy so that you can take as much time as you need to digest what I'm going to tell you, before you have to face the stress and formality of a lawyer's office.' Her eyelids tremble. 'I was thirteen years old when I had you. I met your father at a summer camp in the States. His name was Jean-Luc Baptiste. He was the only person I've ever loved who didn't abandon me.' She moistens her cracked lips with her tongue. 'He was fifteen and his mother, who was a refugee from Haiti, worked in the camp canteen. I have one photograph of him.' She holds up a tiny, bleached-out photograph taken in a booth. It's of a very young, very blonde Frances and a dark-haired, dark-eyed boy, the two of them squashed together and laughing.

As Vanessa leans in to look at his face the image freezes. She hits 'Play'. Nothing. She skips back a few seconds. The image unfreezes at the place she jumped to, plays briefly then refreezes when it gets to the photograph of Frances and Jean-Luc. 'Damn!' She scrolls to the beginning and tries again. Same problem.

Vanessa snatches up her phone, calls Frances's lawyer and leaves a message requesting a replacement copy of Frances's video.

For the next hour she sits, turning the ring on her finger and staring at the frozen faces of the two smiling teenagers, barely able to comprehend that Frances has gone.

Back in her office, Vanessa chases a couple of Nurofen with strong black coffee and presses a hand to her forehead, hoping to smooth away the dull throb in her skull. Thoughts of the last few weeks flood her brain: Frances on her deathbed, the note from Mark Findlay, the biker with his camera, the shabby gloom of Cranmore House, Jay's stark mural, her mother's empty stare, her father's indifference, Izzy's pert mouth hurling drunken insults at her across the kitchen table.

For one fearful moment she reverts to being lost, hurt, directionless Vanessa with a pain in her heart and no hope for the future.

Her phone rings. She hesitates for a moment and then picks up.

'Vanessa Dunn?' The voice is brisk and cheerful. 'Ralph Gilmore. Is this a good moment to talk?'

She pulls herself upright and reaches for her notebook. 'Yes, of course, Mr Gilmore.'

'Please, call me Ralph. Sorry I had to abandon you last week. What did you think of the flat?'

'It's beautiful and has a lot of potential. I've had a few ideas but before I go ahead with any drawings I'm going to need some kind of steer from you as to how far you want to go with the Vanessa Dunn look. Whether you're more interested in the classic simplicity end of things, or the full-on bohemian, and how much remodelling you want to do in the kitchen and bathrooms.'

'I think they both need a complete revamp, don't you? As to style, I suppose I'm quite traditional. I like a room that looks and feels comfortable, but with a few surprises thrown in.'

'Alright, well, I think it might help if I took you through some images.'

'I'm sure it would.' There's an odd little pause. He clears his throat. 'How about we do it over dinner?'

'Dinner?' She bites down on her lip, glad he can't see her. 'Erm... it would have to be somewhere informal. I need to be able to spread out my laptop and notebooks.'

'I know just the place. Are you... free tomorrow night?'

Vanessa tips her head back and stares at the bevelled moulding on her newly painted ceiling. 'Oh... yes, that should be fine.'

While the rest of her life strains at its stitched-with-secrets seams and she worries herself sick about Mark Findlay and doing right by Frances's child, dinner with an older, easy-going man like Ralph Gilmore might be just the diversion she needs.

TWENTY-FIVE

Vanessa flicks through the hangers in her wardrobe. Is she dressing for a date or a work meeting? She's pretty sure it's a date. Hair up or down? What if she's totally misread the signs? Trousers or a dress? What if he was lying about being divorced? Finally – it takes a pile of discarded outfits and a lot of twisting from side to side in front of the mirror looking at herself from all angles – she plumps for hair down, soft black pants, a black top, silver filigree earrings and a pair of red ballet pumps.

She sinks down onto the edge of the bed and checks her phone. Nothing from Don Dexter. She looks away to the mirror, then back at the phone and begins to type him a message.

> *Would appreciate an update on your search so far. As detailed as possible please. Thanks.*

The restaurant Ralph's picked is a friendly little bistro in Borough Market. He smiles, embarrassed, as he scours the menu and grills the waiter about gluten, lactose and a raft of other ingredients he claims he can't tolerate. Vanessa looks on in surprise. She hadn't had him down as the faddy type. Maybe, unlike most people she knows, his allergies are real. He doesn't seem to have a problem with wine though, and as she explains her initial design thoughts for his flat, they work their way through a bottle of red. He seems happy enough to go along with everything she suggests and she begins to worry that she's going to run out of things to say. She's just searching her phone for pictures of a bathroom she designed a couple of years ago when a text flashes up from Meghan.

How's it going with Mr Squishy? xx

She jabs the screen and quickly presses 'Delete'. It's great that Meghan is pushing her to start dating again but it's odd that she's so enthusiastic about Ralph. He's a nice enough guy, but hardly Meghan's idea of a catch. Not normally Vanessa's either, if she's honest.

She looks up. Ralph is filling her wine glass and she realises that silence has descended. She shifts awkwardly in her seat. Is this where they tell each other where they're from and what their favourite books, movies and TV shows are? She shudders inwardly.

'Can I ask you, something?' Ralph says.

'Of course.' She lays her phone face down on the table.

'Is there... anyone?'

She reddens and shakes her head. 'Not since my husband.' She feels sad as she says it, but it's a shadow of the bleakness that had engulfed her after Doug first left. 'The break-up hurt so much, for so long, but I've been making a huge effort to move on.'

'How?'

'Well, I've opened my shop and got involved with a charity. I'm finding ways to deal with my mum being in a nursing home and I've started to build bridges with my father, who I lost touch with when I was a kid. There's still a very long way to go but it feels as if my plans for a new and meaningful post-divorce life might finally be starting to come together.'

'That must be a good feeling,' Ralph says. Is that a hint of envy she sees in his eyes before he reaches for his glass. 'Any room in there for a new relationship?' He's trying to sound casual but there's an almost puppylike eagerness in his voice.

She hesitates. 'I'm not saying not ever, Ralph, but I don't want to rush into anything. Not yet.'

'So... if I hang in there, I might be in with a chance?'

She touches the back of his wrist with the tips of her fingers. 'Let's enjoy each other's company and see what happens.'

'Fair enough.' He sits back, resting one elbow on the back of his chair. 'So what are these charities you've got yourself involved with?'

'It's just one,' she says, quickly. 'A hostel for the homeless.'

'What made you pick that one?'

She shrugs. 'I was keen to step out of my comfort zone and I suppose I liked what I saw on their website.'

'Is it for men and women?'

'Just men.'

'What sort of age?'

'Anything from eighteen upwards.'

'Right. What's it called?'

'Cranmore House. Honestly, it's been really rewarding working there, and it's definitely helped me to put my own problems into perspective.' She looks up for a response.

He's staring at her, expressionless, and then his face crinkles into a smile. 'Maybe I should give it a try,' he says.

She smiles back. 'Maybe you should. They're always on the look-out for new volunteers.'

She opens her mouth, tempted to ask him about the wine glasses hidden in his bathroom cupboard. She closes it again. Why embarrass the poor man when he's making such an effort to be nice?

TWENTY-SIX

Not long after they got married, Vanessa and Doug had been invited to a glitzy fancy-dress ball by an old university friend of Doug's who, despite a prodigious weed habit and a chronic inability to turn up for exams, had gone on to start a hedge fund and make millions. While Doug had decided to go full mobster in a black shirt, white tie, wide-lapelled pin-striped suit and a fedora, Vanessa had channelled Louise Brooks, complete with a rope of pearls, a beaded sheath dress and a shingled black wig. It had been a terrible evening but she'd felt good in the wig – almost like a different person – so she'd kept it.

Now, she lifts it from its box and shakes it so the shiny black strands fall free. She eases it onto her crown, settles it over the elastic headband holding down her own hair and stares into the mirror as she pulls the back down into the nape of her neck. Tipping her head to one side she adds dark glasses, a neat felt hat with just enough brim to shade her eyes, and a slick of red lipstick. She looks unrecognisable. Which is exactly the result she'd been aiming for. How else can she attend Frances's funeral without being noticed by Mark or Amanda Findlay?

· · ·

Head down, Vanessa takes the order of service handed to her at the door of St Stephen's Church and slips into a pew at the back. Wired and twitchy, she glances around, glad that the church is packed. Glamorous mourners in figure-hugging black – probably the senders of the champagne and flowers that Frances had given away – glide down the aisle to take their places among the rows of bankers and businesspeople leaning over to greet acquaintances or whisper discreetly behind their own orders of service. On the other side of the aisle sit a sprinkling of what look like former employees and old retainers, all keeping a respectful distance from the family. Some of them sit quietly, while others dab away tears.

Is it possible that one of them really does know what happened to Frances's baby?

Her eyes travel across the ornate splendour of the candlesticks on the altar to the huge photograph of Frances displayed on an oversized easel set up beside the pulpit. The sleekly groomed woman with a wondrous head of thick blonde hair swept up into an immaculate chignon, who gazes out over the church, is barely recognisable as the frail elfin Frances she came to know.

Vanessa starts a little as a redhead a few pews down turns to whisper to her neighbour: it's Deidre, the head nurse at St Saviour's, and she's pretty sure the woman on her right is one of their receptionists. She drops her face into her order of service. A card slips from the pages. She picks it up and turns it over. It's a printed request asking all attendees to fill out their names and addresses so the family can know who was there. She taps the edge of the pasteboard and glances over at the rows of old retainers. If this is Mark's idea, it's a smart one. Worrying too. She crumples up the card, slips it into her pocket and makes a mental note to ask Frances's lawyer to see if he can get her a copy of the list. Surely if the request comes from Frances's estate, Findlay can't refuse.

She scans the congregation, wondering if Don Dexter might also have slipped in to see who's shown up.

The organ starts up and the elderly organist launches into the opening bars of 'Jesu, Joy of Man's Desiring'. The voices of the choir ring out and the bearers carry in the coffin. Dark mahogany with ornate brass handles, it's laden with an extravagant arrangement of waxy, hot-house flowers nestling in a bed of dark, glossy greenery. Not Frances's style at all. Behind it walk the chief mourners led by Mark Findlay, now proud owner and CEO of the Findlay Corporation. She stares at his back. Is she imagining a hint of triumph in the set of his cashmere-clad shoulders? He holds the arm of a very upright, white-haired woman – presumably his mother – while Amanda walks at his other side. She wears a tailored black frock with a matching pill box hat draped in netting and, to Vanessa's relief, keeps her eyes fixed straight ahead. Behind them come two men and a woman, who she assumes are Mark's adult children, not a tear or a hint of sadness for their dead aunt between them.

Briefly, Vanessa allows herself to imagine the moment they're confronted by Frances's child and forced to give up their newly acquired millions. *That will wipe the sheen off their smug little faces.*

The strains of the organ die away and after the priest's words of welcome Mark Findlay strides forward and takes his place at the lectern. Puffed up with self-importance, he announces that he has chosen to read from Ecclesiastes, chapter 3, verses 1 to 8.

Vanessa is surprised. She'd assumed that Frances would have chosen the readings. Perhaps when it came to it, she'd decided she didn't really care what was said over her earthly remains by the family she despised.

Mark, however, has a surprisingly strong speaking voice, and Vanessa gives herself up to the power and poetry of the words – '*A time to keep silence, and a time to speak, a time to love, and a time to hate—*'

Next up, there's a tribute from Mark's mother, who waxes lyrical in a warbly voice about *darling* Frances, her *dear* brother-in-law Gordon's only daughter, of whom he was so justly proud. It was Gordon, she says, who turned the whisky distillery he inherited from his father into a luxury goods brand, but it was Frances who cemented the company's reputation as a global leader. Not only did she inherit her father and grandfather's business acumen she says, she also inherited the legendary Findlay determination, which enabled her to endure the terrible burden of her illness. She dabs a dry eye with a neatly ironed handkerchief and steps down from the lectern. Although she looks perfectly capable of taking a solo hike up Ben Nevis, Mark – ever solicitous – rushes up to grip her by the arm and escort her back to her seat.

The organ wheezes back into action, another hymn, another prayer and then, as the mourners mumble the words of 'The Lord's My Shepherd', the coffin is borne back down the aisle, followed once more by the family.

Head low, Vanessa keeps to the back as the mourners make their way to the door. Out of the corner of her eye she watches Mark Findlay. He stops. He's turning around, exchanging greet-ings, accepting condolences. A man steps forward. It's Stefan, the preppy nurse from The Laurels who also works at St Saviour's. He's talking quietly to Mark, shaking his hand. Thoughts hiss in Vanessa's brain, murky and confused. Is Stefan here just to pay his respects like the other staff from the hospice, or do he and Mark know each other? Was Findlay paying him to report back on the people who came to see Frances? Did Stefan tell him that towards the end Vanessa was her only visitor? She studies the expression on Mark's face as he steps away from Stefan, watching him closely as he greets an elderly couple, only letting go of her breath as he walks out through the doors. Even then it's several seconds before she's able to move.

She steps behind a pillar, waits until all eyes are watching the coffin being loaded into the hearse, then she slips through the door, edges her way around the side of the church and hurries out through the back gate.

TWENTY-SEVEN

It's late when Vanessa gets back to the shop. She wanders down to the storeroom, where she finds Jay unbuttoning his overalls.

'You alright?' he asks.

She sighs. 'I've just been to a funeral.'

'Family?'

'A friend, not that much older than me. It was really sad.'

'I hate those things.'

'Me, too. I knew she was dying but the finality of seeing the coffin... it's really hit me.' Her face puckers and she turns away. 'Are you done for the day?'

'Yeah. Shall I lock up?'

'Don't worry. Now I'm here I might as well stay on and pick out a few pieces for the Pimlico job.'

'Are you sure you're up to it?'

'Not really, but I can't face going back to an empty house.' She lifts down a brass lamp base, cradles it on her hip and scans the shelves of cellophane-wrapped shades. 'I was rather hoping Meghan might be here to help me drown my sorrows. Have you seen her?'

'She's got her evening class tonight.'

'Damn. I completely forgot.'

He steps out of his overalls, hangs them on a hook on the wall and hovers by the door, long and wiry in his jeans and flannel shirt.

'I don't suppose you fancy grabbing a drink?' she says, tentatively. 'Or something to eat? My treat.'

There's a silence that lasts a few seconds but feels to her like much longer.

'Sure,' he says. 'Why not?'

They find a little Greek café by the canal. Tiny tables, bad art on the walls, fat white candles dribbling wax down the necks of empty ouzo bottles. They order kebabs and a plate of mezze to share. He's easy to be with, asking about her plans for the shop, the music she listens to, the best and the worst of the clients she's dealt with. When she asks about life in his new bedsit he responds with a stream of caustic anecdotes: damp on the ceiling, windows jammed shut, crazies down the corridor.

'Any luck with finding somewhere else?' she asks.

'Not yet. I need to save for a deposit. Then I have to be sure I can make the rent.'

'The money from your photos should help, and once your trial period is over, maybe we can talk about a raise.'

Jay skewers a cube of grilled lamb. 'Meghan won't be too happy about that. She's looking for an excuse to get me fired.'

'Whatever makes you think that?'

'I made a stupid mistake over some light fittings. I sorted it out as soon as I realised I'd delivered the wrong ones, but it's like she's never going to let it go.'

'It's her responsibility to keep an eye on new staff and to make sure that customers get the right goods on time.'

'I get that, but it's like she's willing me to mess up, watching me all the time as if I'm going to sneak off and get stoned. When

I suggested a couple of improvements we could make to the stock system, she dismissed them out of hand.'

'She's just a bit... wary.'

'Yeah, of people who can see right through her.'

She looks at him for several long beats. 'What do you mean?'

He tips back his head and drops a handful of shredded lettuce into his mouth. 'There's something off about her.'

'Jay, what is this? She's one hundred per cent trustworthy.'

'You think? How long have you known her?'

'I don't know – five, six months.'

'And now she's your best friend, hanging out around your house, running your shop, taking classes so she can muscle in on the design side of your business, poking her nose into everything you do.'

'That's not fair. It's her job to be across everything.'

'When you deal with the kind of people I've had to deal with, you learn to trust your gut. Mine's telling me that Meghan Grey is bad news.'

Vanessa rubs her eyes wearily. 'I know the two of you haven't hit it off but you've just got to convince her that any concerns she has about your past are misplaced.'

He scowls and sets his jaw. She reaches out and touches his arm. 'I might be your employer, Jay, but I'd like to think that you and I are friends and—'

His phone rings, making her jump. He whips it out, glances quickly at the screen and presses 'Reject'. There's a sudden tension in his face as he shoves it back into his pocket, a shifti-ness in the way he looks at her that could be guilt – or might equally be guile. Her heart sinks when she realises that she doesn't know him well enough to judge. 'Look, you're clearly more than up to the job and I know how determined you are to stay clean but... well, now and then we all make bad decisions. About work, relationships, money. So if you do make a mistake or something in your life gets... difficult, I want you to know that you don't have to deal with it on your own. There's nothing you can't tell me. I mean that, Jay – nothing. And if you need my help, you just have to ask for it.'

He looks at her. 'Why?'

Faintly she hears the clatter of plates from the kitchen. 'Because everyone needs someone who has their back. Now that my mother can't communicate anymore, I know how it feels not to have that.'

For a moment their faces are so close she can smell the wine on his breath and see tiny splinters of gold in the dark pupils of his eyes.

His phone rings again.

'Take it.' She pulls back and reaches for her glass. 'It's fine.'

He takes his phone, glances at the screen and presses 'Reject' again. 'It's OK. It's not important.' He slides the phone back into his jeans.

But he's edgy as she orders more wine and his eyes dither with impatience as she describes a new furniture line she's contemplating for the shop. With a murmured, 'Back in a minute,' he gets up when the waiter brings the wine and walks away, reaching for his phone before he's even halfway across the room.

While he's gone, Vanessa passes the time on her own phone, scrolling, checking, glancing through apps. There are no surprises. In fact, it's the dreary predictability of what she sees that leaves her feeling deflated and empty. She tosses the phone onto the table, takes a long swallow of wine and looks around for Jay. She sees him leaning against the wall of the narrow corridor leading to the cloakrooms, murmuring earnestly into his phone, making a call he was clearly desperate for her not to hear.

In her eagerness to fill the hollows in her own life, has she expected too much of him? Been too dismissive of the life he's lived and the damage it must inevitably have done to his judgement? Or is she right to have faith that he'll come through in the end? She rolls the stem of her wine glass in her fingers. And what is it with him and Meghan? On the face of it, he's a convicted drug dealer who's never held down a legit job for more than three months, while Meghan is hard-working, dedicated and brilliant at her job; so why had his insistence that there is something 'off' about her touched a nerve?

TWENTY-EIGHT

Vanessa wakes suddenly and sits up, straining her eyes as she looks at the time. It's 6 a.m. Something has roused her. A thought, a fear, a memory. It comes to her then: she'd been dreaming of Frances. Elegant, beautiful, damaged Frances spending years throwing herself into her career while all the people who might have helped her to find her child had slowly died, disappeared or slipped silently from her grasp. If Don Dexter had been at the funeral, is it possible that someone there had given him a helpful scrap of information – a tiny loose thread which, with a sharp enough tug, might enable him to unravel the truth? If so, how long might a determined, experienced investigator take to do the unravelling? Days? Weeks? Months? Years? She gazes at the clock, watching the numbers flip through the seconds and minutes. Dexter's response to her request for an update had been a one-line text telling her he's still following up on former employees of the Findlay Corporation. Can the man even be trusted? He could give this investigation his all or just as easily take Frances's retainer, claim ridiculous expenses and do nothing.

Maybe it's time for her to do a little investigating of her

own. It wouldn't hurt to at least find out what Dexter looks like. There has to be a way to do it without him seeing her.

She gets out of bed and presses her face to the window, picturing all the couples out there, entwined beneath the sheets, warm and safe. She thinks of Doug, hears his voice, sees his smile, feels his touch; and the contrast with the emptiness of the bedroom they'd once shared brings a sob to her throat. Knowing she'll never get back to sleep she pulls on her dressing gown, goes downstairs and switches on the light.

Blinking into the sudden glare, she flicks on the kettle, makes a large pot of tea and opens her laptop.

There's a military feel to the blocky monochrome text and sky-blue background of Don Dexter's website. No photographs, of course – just a list of the specialist services his company offers, including commercial and corporate investigations, infidelity issues, vehicle tracking, internet dating checks and missing persons.

It only takes her a couple of minutes to set up a fake email address, and not much longer than that to craft her message.

Dear Mr Dexter,

My husband is cheating on me and I want a divorce. Since he will do everything he can to stop me from getting a fair financial settlement, I need photographic proof of his infidelity that will stand up in court. Please let me know if you can help me and when we can meet.

Gina Cadogan

She rereads what she's written, presses 'Send' and goes upstairs to shower and dress.

When she comes down again at 7.30 a.m., Don Dexter – clearly an early riser – has sent a reply.

Dear Mrs Cadogan,

I am very sorry to hear about your problem. Unfortunately, I'm going to be tied up on other jobs for the next couple of weeks. However, if this matter is urgent my colleague is available to take your case. He's very experienced and specialises in infidelity issues. Shall I ask him to get in touch?

Don Dexter

Is one of the jobs he's so busy with looking for Frances's child? Vanessa wonders.

She taps out a response.

Dear Mr Dexter,

Although I would like this matter resolved quickly I would prefer to wait until you are available as you were personally recommended to me by someone I trust. Please get back to me when your current cases are resolved so that we can arrange a time to meet.

Gina

She squints at the screen, convinces herself that it doesn't look suspicious and presses 'Send'.

TWENTY-NINE

'It's going really well at Cranmore House,' Vanessa says, as she pulls a brush through her mother's hair. 'I was there yesterday and that boy Donnie wouldn't leave my side. He's a terrific kid but I think I'm the first person who has *ever* sat down and listened to him. How heartbreaking is that?' She glances at her mother's slumped reflection in the window and continues with her monologue. 'If you've been worrying about the tension between Meghan and Jay, there's no need. It's still a bit awkward and they're never going to be best friends, but he's really coming in to his own and she can't fault his work ethic.' She pulls Ellen's hair into a single rope, twists it up onto the top of her head and secures it with a tortoiseshell claw clip. 'I hope that's not too tight, Mum, only I don't want it coming down as soon as I leave.' She pauses, imagining a response. Her mother had always been so proud of her hair and even now it's still thick and wavy, with barely a thread of grey.

Her phone pings. She pulls it from her pocket. An email from the property developers who own the Pimlico penthouse she's working on. She holds her breath and clicks it open. Her gaze sinks to the message. Her body quivers. 'Great news,

Mum! Mathieson's are offering me the contract for all nine of the flats!' She allows a smile to lift the corners of her mouth. 'I think I'll carry the river theme through into each of them – Jay's photos, and lots of soft blues and aqua greens.'

She stuffs the phone back into her pocket. 'What were we talking about? Oh, that's right, how well Jay's doing. So, yes, right at the beginning he made a couple of wrong calls – and one extremely silly mistake.' She gazes off at the sad little water-colour behind her mother's head, with its chipped frame and faded mount. She'd never been able fathom why Ellen had refused to be parted from it. 'But it turns out he just needs the right handling. In fact, if our online sales go on expanding, I'll need to take on more staff and I really think he's capable of running a sizeable warehouse team and eventually taking charge of the whole stock management and delivery side of things.' She takes a packet of kirby grips from her bag. 'I wish you could have gone to Frances's funeral to say goodbye.' She lays her hand on Ellen's shoulder. 'Sorry, I know you wish it too. You'd have hated seeing those horrible, grasping Findlay cousins and that hawk-faced aunt acting like they cared, when all they wanted was her money.' She splits a kirby grip with her teeth and slides it up the side of Ellen's hair. Leaning round to check if she's caught all the stray tendrils, she does the same on the other side and gives the smoothed-out strands a pat. 'There you go, all neat and tidy.' She drops the brush into the top drawer of the sideboard. 'No news yet on the search.' She bumps the drawer shut with her hip, rattling the framed photographs lined along the top. 'Dexter says he's still concentrating on looking for the fixer who arranged it all. Frances was convinced it was someone her father had a hold over. "Mutually assured destruc-tion", she called it. Anyway, as soon as I find out anymore you'll be the first to know. It's like having our very own true crime podcast, isn't it? You used to love listening to those things. Waiting on tenterhooks for each new episode to come out.' She squeezes Ellen's hand. 'I still can't believe that Frances asked *me*, an almost stranger, to befriend her poor kid, and then, when she gave me this' – she rocks her fingers so the emerald ring catches the overhead light – 'I couldn't help thinking about that story you used to read to me when I was little. I can't remember what it was called, but basically a powerful king orders a young peasant girl to deliver a secret message for him and he gives her his ring so that if anyone challenges her along the way, she can prove that she really is acting on his behalf.'

She picks up her bag. 'Sorry, Mum, got to go.' She smiles, a little embarrassed. 'I'm having dinner with that guy, Ralph, I told you about. I know, I know, he's not my usual type, but, like I keep telling you, this is all about new Vanessa.'

THIRTY

Vanessa scans the text on her phone.

'Problem?' Meghan says, noticing her frown.

'It's my sister. I didn't even know she was back in the country. Typical Izzy. Totally ignores me for weeks on end and now she wants to come round for a "chat".'

'Does she say what about?'

'Knowing her she'll either want to move into my spare room with some deadbeat Gunther replacement or she's run out of money – again.'

'Do you give her money?'

Vanessa shrugs and pulls a face. 'She's promised to pay me back when she gets a record deal.'

Her finger hovers over her screen for a moment before she types back, *Sure. Home around 7 p.m. Will make supper. Do you need a bed?*

Izzy's reply pings back immediately. *Yes to food, no to bed.*

'I'm not doing much tonight if you need moral support,' Meghan says.

'That's sweet of you but I'll be fine.'

Vanessa always worries when Izzy turns up out of the blue

wanting to talk. For years her sister has lurched from crisis to crisis, all of her own making, and all involving unsuitable men, yet she can't help envying Izzy's ability to grab onto life and do exactly what she wants, without fear of the consequences.

She wanders up to the cloakroom and grimaces at her reflection. She's pale and drawn.

She's brushing a bit of colour into her cheeks when she catches a faint buzzing sound. She twists around. It's coming from Meghan's trench coat, hanging on the hook next to Jay's denim jacket. Her phone must be on silent. She goes to shout up the stairs to tell Meghan that she's got a call when she remembers something: Meghan had her iPhone with her just now, when they were talking about Izzy. The buzzing stops then starts up again.

Vanessa squeezes the pocket of the trench coat and feels a slim, hard rectangle vibrating through the folds of the fabric. Definitely a phone. She checks the coat again. Definitely Meghan's. She glances at the door and listens for footsteps. There's no one there. She slides her fingers into the pocket and draws out a small black handset. It looks cheap – the kind you can buy at a petrol station if you don't want anyone to trace your calls. But what would Meghan want with one of those? Who does she call with it? Who uses it to call her? Is she having an affair with a married man? Someone famous? Whoever it is, she clearly wants to keep it private.

It starts to buzz again and the word 'Unknown' flashes onto the screen. She slips the phone back into Meghan's pocket and hurries back down to her office.

On the way home she drops in at the deli on the corner and buys fresh pasta, homemade arrabiata sauce, a hunk of focaccia and a bottle of wine.

She's barely had time to unpack it all before the doorbell

rings. Wishing she had some idea of the mood her sister will be in, she puts on a neutral smile, walks down the hall and flings open the door.

'God, I'm dying for a pee.' Izzy, bright-eyed and pink-cheeked shoulders past her, a flash of black leather and purple velvet as she drops her bag and runs to the bathroom.

Back in the kitchen, Vanessa pours two glasses of red and readies herself for Izzy in whirlwind mode.

'Here' She holds out a glass as Izzy comes in.

'No, thanks.' Izzy pulls open the fridge and takes out a carton of orange juice.

'Don't tell me you've got a hangover. What on earth were you up to last night?'

Izzy kicks the fridge door shut and says, primly, 'Actually, I was in bed by ten.'

Not alone, I bet, Vanessa thinks. She pours boiling water onto the pasta and turns up the heat under the sauce. 'How long are you back for?'

'Just a couple of days.'

'Are you going to see Mum while you're here?'

Izzy digs an olive out of the focaccia with a purple-nailed finger and pops it into her mouth. 'I was there this morning.'

'Oh,' Vanessa says, unable to mask her surprise. 'That's good.'

'What's good about it?' Izzy tears off a piece of bread. 'I hate seeing her in that place.'

'It's got an excellent reputation.'

'I don't care. She shouldn't have to be in a home. Not at her age. Jesus, she's only a few years older than Madonna.'

Vanessa fetches down two large white bowls from the cupboard and says, gently, 'I know. What Alzheimer's does to people is horrible and unfair, but the staff at The Laurels are brilliant.'

'You can't know that. Of course they're going to act all kind and caring in front of visitors, but who knows what they get up to when they think no one's watching! Haven't you seen those documentaries about elder abuse?'

A gush of steam billows up into Vanessa's face as she tips the pasta into a sieve and breathes in its warm starchy smell. She shakes it back into the pan, pours in the sauce, stirs it around with a wooden spoon and takes a long glug of wine. 'Did Mum... say your name while you were there?'

Izzy tears off another piece of focaccia. 'Not this time. She was very tired. Some woman had been to visit her before I got there.'

Vanessa pivots round. 'What woman?'

Izzy shrugs. 'Dunno, but Mum got so agitated while she was there they'd given her something to calm her down. I mean, honestly, isn't she on enough drugs already?'

Vanessa's not even aware of the glass slipping from her hand until it explodes on the floor, spattering wine across the tiles.

Had this visitor been sent by Mark Findlay? Had she tried to grill her mother about Frances's childhood? Was she the same woman who'd been questioning Frances's former classmates about her school days?

Izzy looks from the shattered glass to Vanessa's bloodless face. 'What's the matter with you?'

'Nothing.' Vanessa reaches under the sink for the dustpan and brush. 'Do you know what this woman said to upset her?'

'No idea.'

Vanessa sweeps up the glass, fears and suspicions skittering through her head, sliding and colliding. She empties the dustpan and bends to mop up the wine. *Not now. I can't think about this now. Not while Izzy's here. I'll deal with it when she's gone.* She turns back to her sister. 'Can you pass me that blue dish?'

Izzy hands her a blue pottery serving dish, one of many that Vanessa and Doug had brought back from their honeymoon in

Sicily. She slides the pasta into the bowl, sprinkles on a couple handfuls of parmesan and places it on the table; quick mechanical movements to calm her shredded nerves.

They sit down facing each other across the scrubbed wood. 'Here.' Vanessa hands Izzy a serving spoon. 'Sorry it's not homemade.'

She watches Izzy heap her bowl high, her own appetite gone. 'So,' she says, pouring herself a fresh glass of wine, 'what did you want to chat about?'

Izzy shovels a forkful of pasta into her mouth and purses her sauce-smeared lips, looking very pleased with herself. 'You're going to be an aunty.'

Vanessa has readied herself to sound enthusiastic about the latest man in Izzy's life, but she isn't prepared for this. *A baby.* Her little sister is going to have a baby.

She closes her eyes then opens them, rocked by thoughts too raw to bear.

'Isn't it wonderful?' Izzy burbles, shovelling up another mound of pasta.

'Amazing.' Sitting there in her warm, pretty kitchen, with its handmade units and artisan tiles, Vanessa feels stunned and confused. 'How many weeks are you?'

'Nearly eight. I had a bit of spotting so they gave me an early scan this afternoon.' Izzy whips a flimsy printout from the pocket of her leather jacket. 'But they said everything's fine.'

Vanessa's fingers tremble as she reaches across the table to take it from her. 'Boy or girl?'

'It's too early to tell, but we've decided we don't want to know till it's born.'

We? 'The father went with you?'

'Don't look so surprised.'

'I'm not. I'm... pleased. Does that mean he's going to stand by you?'

'God!' Izzy drops her fork. 'This isn't nineteen fifty. But, *yes*, he is going to "stand by me". In fact, as soon as I get back from this tour we're going to get married.'

'Married!' Vanessa stares down at the photo. As she tries to make sense of the murky monochrome blur it crashes in on her, just how life-changing Izzy's news really is.

'You're not even three months gone. What if... if... the pregnancy doesn't... you know...' She trails off.

'It won't change anything. Don't you get it? It's not about the baby, it's about us. Him and me. Finding out I was pregnant just made us realise that we were meant to be together.'

'That's great, Izz.' Vanessa lays down the photo. 'Is he a musician too?'

'No.' Izzy picks nervously at the chipped purple polish on her thumbnail. 'He's working out what he wants to do with his life. But he's incredibly talented and he's got loads of ideas.'

Vanessa drops a portion of pasta into her bowl, a rush of questions tumbling from her mouth. 'So, come on, who is he? Where did you meet him?'

'Stop interrogating me.'

'Sorry, it's just that you can't have been with him very long. Last time you were here, you'd only just broken up with Gunther.'

'That doesn't matter,' Izzy snaps. 'What matters is the spark between us. We both felt it the moment we set eyes on each other.'

'Izz—' There's a question that Vanessa knows she must ask but she struggles to shape the words. 'What I meant was, are you one hundred per cent sure the baby isn't... Gunther's?'

Izzy rocks back in her chair. 'You are unbelievable!'

'I'm not making a judgement. I'm just trying to be practical.'

'If you want the gory details the dates don't work for it to be his. Thank God. The last time I slept with that piece of scum was the night before I went on tour. And before you ask, the baby's father is the only man I've been with since.'

'I can see how excited you are, but even if this new bloke *is* the right man for you, don't you think you should give yourselves a bit more time to get to know each other before you...?'

'Don't you dare!'

'What?'

'Suggest I get rid of it.'

'I wasn't suggesting anything! I just want you to take a moment to weigh up your options and think what rushing into a baby and marriage will mean for you, and him, and the rest of your lives.'

'I'm not stupid. I know exactly what it means. For once in your life can't you just be happy for me?'

'What about your career?'

'Getting married and becoming a mother won't stop me carrying on with my music.'

'It won't be easy going on tour with a baby.'

Izzy regards her fiercely with her wide brown eyes. 'Why are you always so negative about everything I do?'

'I'm not being negative. I'm all the family you've got and I'm just trying to look out for you.'

'Mum was happy for me when I told her.'

'Mum doesn't know what day of the week it is.'

'I could see it in her eyes.'

'She's not the one who'll have to pick up the pieces if it doesn't work out. Babies cost money, Izz. From the sounds of it, neither you nor this new man of yours has even got a proper job.'

'There are more important things in life than money.'

Vanessa takes a long breath and lets it out. 'Of course there are, and you know I'll do everything I can to support you and the baby, but what with helping with Mum's care home fees and getting the shop off the ground, I'm stretched pretty thinly at the moment.'

'Don't treat me like I'm a walking disaster.'

'I'm not, but I'm ten years older than you are and I've had a lot more experience of life.'

'Since when do a few wrinkles and a failed marriage give you the right to tell me what do?'

Her words hit like a slap. Vanessa looks away, tears burning in her eyes. 'I just want what's best for you.'

'No, you don't. You want to control me, like you want to control everything and everyone around you. Well, this is one decision that's out of your hands.'

'Izzy, that's not fair. Bringing a child into the world is a massive responsibility.'

Izzy snatches up the scan printout and waves it in Vanessa's face. 'This isn't about that, though, is it? This is about you being jealous because, for once in my life, I've got something that you don't.'

Vanessa hears herself gasp. After everything she's been through, how can Izzy be so cruel?

'Please.' She grips the edge of the table, counting the knots in the wood, the ridges in the grain. 'Let's not argue,' she says, weakly. 'It's your life, your body, your decision and whatever happens you know I'll do everything I can to support you.' She forces a smile. 'So do I get to meet this guy while you're in London?'

'He's not a "guy", he's my fiancé. And that's the thing. He wanted to come with me tonight so we could tell you together. But I knew what a bitch you'd be about it, so I told him I'd break it to you on my own.' Izzy pushes back her chair and stands up.

'Don't go. Not yet,' Vanessa implores her. 'It was a shock. I overreacted, I'm sorry. Let's talk it through calmly and make a plan.'

'I've already got a plan.' Izzy shrugs on her coat. 'And seeing as I knew you'd refuse to be happy for us, it doesn't involve you.' She turns and storms down the hall.

Vanessa braces for the slam of the front door but still

flinches when it comes. The words, 'I've got something that you don't' jangle in her ears as she tells herself that lashing out without a thought for the pain she's inflicting is just her sister's way. But this time it's different. It's not just about Izzy hurling herself into another doomed relationship – Vanessa had been ready to deal with that and she'd have done what she always did: waited it out and been there to offer sympathy. This time there's another life involved; a life that's going to get chewed up and spat out by her sister's careless belief that the whole bloody world revolves around her.

Vanessa grabs her coat and runs out into the rain. She looks up and down the street. There's no sign of Izzy. Her new 'fiancé' had probably been hovering outside, waiting to whisk her away the minute she stepped into the street. She shivers and closes her eyes, imagining him walking into her house arm in arm with Izzy, primed with stories of what a jealous, controlling bitch Vanessa is. At least she's been spared that horror.

Down the wet pavements she walks, her hands thrust into her pockets, her teeth chattering with cold, her thoughts ricocheting between possibilities: Izzy decides that she really has found her soulmate and lives happily ever after with him and their child. She gets married then decides nine months down the line that she doesn't want this man or his child and demands a divorce – on Izzy's past form, it's more than possible. Or this bloke dumps her and waltzes off with some other woman he's only known for five minutes.

Whatever happens, Vanessa will have to step in and care for the baby. The baby! She can almost see it in her mind's eye; a soft, helpless bundle. She steps off the kerb. Blurred car lights rise up out of the dark. A car blasts its horn. She stumbles back onto the pavement and bursts into tears.

THIRTY-ONE

Rain drums against the window, punctuating Vanessa's dream. She's running through the night, swerving down litter-strewn streets that refuse to take her where she desperately needs to be. Broken street lamps, illegible signs, cracked paving stones that trip her at every turn. A building looms through the shadows, blocking her path. She wheels round and sees figures in the windows: her sister with a swollen belly; Mark Findlay glaring down at her; a shadowy woman shaking her mother by her shoulders and screaming questions into her face; Frances beating her palms against the glass, howling in frustration; Jay muttering into his phone. She veers down an alleyway, sways, staggers blindly in the dark and slams into a locked door. Panic roars in. She rattles the handle and beats her fists on the wood. Sucking blood from her knuckles she turns, doubles back, stumbles into a pothole and falls hard on her knees. She raises her hands. Her fingers meet brick. Trapped, helpless, unable to see a way out, she hunches over, too stupefied with misery to move. There she stays, soaked through and numb, sinking into despair, darkness the last thing she knows. A gust of wind scuffs the edge of the silence, rattling cans, stirring up debris. A shiver runs through her. And then another. Her muscles unlock, she opens her eyes and raises her head. Above the black roofs of the buildings there's a ghostly sliver of dawn – as yet too pale and rain-smudged to see by, but bright enough to smear the surrounding blackness with just the barest tinge of blue. She gazes up from the muddy cold, a tiny glimmer of hope in her heart. Slowly, as the sliver grows more intense, streaks of pink begin to play against the sky and soon, in the pale early light, she makes out a narrow pathway between the overhanging buildings.

Vanessa wakes with a snap of her head as memories of the previous evening flood back. She reaches for her phone and texts Izzy. *Sorry, sorry, sorry. Would love to see you before you go back xxx* She slides out of bed, turns on the shower, steps into it while it's still cold and lets the water sting her skin. She brushes her teeth and downs an espresso from the machine in the kitchen. Cold water and black coffee aren't usually part of her early morning routine but after Izzy's news, their awful row and the terrible night's sleep she's had, she needs to clear her head. She contemplates the table still laid with the remains of last night's dinner and thinks ruefully what a fool she'd been to think that her new life might finally be coming together. Still, the situation could have been worse – Izzy could have sprung this ridiculous marriage on her without any warning at all. At least now she has until her sister's tour finishes to prepare herself. She knows there's not long to go – a few weeks at the most. She tries looking up the exact date online but she can't remember the name of the band Izzy is supporting and has no luck.

She decides to walk to work – it will give her time to untangle the thoughts still twisted up in her mind.

. . .

Vanessa arrives at the shop a little out of breath, but with a slightly clearer head, to find Jody on her own flicking a duster over the shelves.

'Where's Meghan?' she asks.

'Dentist. Emergency filling,' Jody says.

'Oh, right. I'll be in the office – shout if it gets busy.'

'I'm sure it'll be fine. Thursdays are usually quite quiet.'

Once downstairs Vanessa closes the door. Without even bothering to take off her jacket she calls The Laurels.

'Hello, this is Vanessa Dunn, Ellen O'Brien's daughter. My sister tells me that my mother had a visitor yesterday who upset her and left her very agitated. Could you check the visitors' book and let me have this woman's name?' She waits impatiently, tapping her foot against the leg of her desk.

'I'm so sorry, Mrs Dunn,' the receptionist says at last, 'the signature is illegible.'

Fear jabs the base of Vanessa's spine. 'Did she leave any contact details?'

'There's a number.'

The receptionist reads it out and Vanessa hurriedly jots it down.

'In future, can you make sure you get people's names and run them past me before you let anyone in to see her? I don't like the idea of strangers being allowed to walk into Mum's room unaccompanied and upsetting her.'

'I actually signed this particular visitor in myself,' the receptionist says, defensively. 'She said she used to work with Ellen years ago and she seemed very nice. I'm sure she meant no harm.'

'Then why did Mum get so upset?'

'It's the nature of her condition, Mrs Dunn. Ellen often gets agitated after a visit, even when the visitor is a close family member like yourself.'

'Well, I'd say it's better to be safe than sorry, wouldn't you?' Vanessa says, crisply.

She cuts the call and dials the number the receptionist gave her. A recorded message announces that the number isn't valid. In a panic she does the counting thing, her eyes flitting from the pencils in their holder to the cushions on the sofa and the files on the shelf. Once her breathing has settled she grabs a bottle of water from her fridge and gulps down nearly half of it, taking bitter comfort from imagining Mark Findlay's disappointment when this mystery visitor informed him that her mother was no longer capable of speech.

Calmer now, she opens her laptop and scrolls through her emails. She clicks open the one from Mathieson's. She tries to concentrate on the schedule they've sent her for the work on the rest of the Pimlico flats. She should be excited at the prospect but her head is too full of her other worries: Mark Findlay trying to probe into her life, access her computer, harass her mother and spy on her movements, Izzy's pregnancy and head-long rush into marriage. She jabs her keyboard and sends the schedule to the printer. While it hums and whirs, she closes her eyes and drops her head onto the desk, daunted by the size and complexity of the task ahead of her and the narrow window of time she has to complete it. *Calm down*, she tells herself. She can't mess this up. She already has the big idea, though that was the easy part – it always is. What she has to do now is plan, down to the finest detail, every single step she needs to take to turn her big idea into reality.

A couple of hours later she gets up from her desk, her head swimming from the intense burst of creative thinking. Fists in the pockets of her jacket, she's standing by the window staring fixedly at the yard – a brown paper bag scudding across the paving, a sad pigeon pecking at the dirt – when Meghan comes in bearing a large paper cup and a paper bag.

'One vanilla shot skinny latte. One cinnamon bun,' she says, holding them out in turn.

'Oh, my God.' Vanessa tears herself from her thoughts and walks over to take them from her. 'You're a mind reader.' She pulls off the lid, inhales the steam, takes a deep frothy sip and, with a satisfied sigh, sits down at her desk and gestures at her computer. 'Someone's just bought another of Jay's prints on the website. That's nearly two grand he's made.'

'Bully for Jay,' Meghan says, perching on the edge of the desk.

'It's great, isn't it?' Vanessa says, refusing to acknowledge the bite in Meghan's voice. 'If he's lucky that should be enough to put a deposit on a one-bed flat *and* pay a chunk of his first month's rent.'

'Let's hope he doesn't fall back on his old tricks to make up the rest of it.'

'No chance of that. How was the dentist?'

Meghan seems momentarily confused, then shrugs. 'Oh, you know – just a check-up. Have you heard anything back from Mathieson's?'

Vanessa draws in a breath. 'I got the contract.'

'Hey, that's amazing!'

'Scary, though. Especially when I've got so much else on.' Sipping her coffee, Vanessa walks around to the other side of the desk and taps her keyboard. 'These are the final drawings for Ralph Gilmore. What do you think? I've made this whole kitchen section quite industrial, then softened the look for the dining area.'

Meghan leans in to get a proper look. 'Gorgeous. Isn't he coming in later?'

'Yes, so I need to get these finished and the whole presentation printed, mounted onto boards and back here by the end of the day'.

'That's OK. Sarah's in soon. We'll manage fine in the shop.'

Vanessa scrolls on, checking through the drawings. 'You can sit in if you like.'

'On the presentation?' Meghan says, surprised.

'You've been saying you want to get a feel for the design side of the business.'

'I got the impression you weren't keen.'

'I wasn't, to be honest. But I've been thinking too small for too long. When surprises happen and circumstances change, you have to adapt your plans.'

'Surprises like getting the Pimlico contract?'

'Exactly. It's made me realise I should have been thinking on a grander scale all along.' Vanessa sinks her teeth into the bun, relishing its sticky warmth. 'If you shadow me on Ralph's job, we could think about you expanding your role and taking on a couple of small projects of your own.'

'Seriously?'

'Under my supervision; but if I'm going to need a second designer I'd far rather train up someone I know and trust than bring in an unknown.'

'I... don't know what to say.' Meghan's brow furrows and she looks over Vanessa's head at the yard outside.

Vanessa follows her gaze to where Jay is getting out of the van, his phone pressed to his ear. 'So you'll come to the meeting with Ralph Gilmore?'

'Of course.' Meghan's eyes swivel back to Vanessa. 'Though I wouldn't want to cramp your style.'

Vanessa blushes a little. 'Don't be ridiculous. There's nothing to cramp. Ralph and I have had a couple of working suppers, and a few chats over drinks to discuss budgets.'

Meghan grins. 'If you say so.'

Vanessa takes another sip of her latte. 'He'll be here around six this evening. You can join us once you've closed up. Just to observe, though.'

'Of course. He won't even know I'm there.' Beaming, Meghan swings her long legs off the desk and makes for the door.

'Meg, before you go—'

Meghan stops and turns around.

'I want to expand Mick and Jay's roles too.' Meghan's smile wavers. 'I think they've both got a future with the company. To make that work I'm going to need your backing.'

'For what exactly?'

'I'm going to offer Mick a full-time decorating contract. It will give him the security he needs. And I've told Jay that I'm planning to take on a couple more people from Cranmore House to work on our delivery and warehousing. When I do, I want to put him in charge of the whole distribution team. He's the perfect choice. He's had some great ideas about refining the stock system *and* he knows exactly how to get the best out of people with troubled pasts.'

'But—'

Vanessa looks up at Meghan and holds her gaze. 'I hope that's not going to be a problem.'

Meghan's thrown by this but tries hard not to show it. 'Of course not,' she says. 'Maybe I can get one of the papers interested in doing a piece on our socially-minded staffing.'

'I'm not sure about that,' Vanessa says, doubtfully, but she's already picking up her phone to text Izzy.

Please don't blank me, Izz. I can't bear the thought of not being part of your wedding. Let me know when and where it's going to be. I'd like to take everyone for lunch somewhere lovely after the ceremony and time is running out to book anywhere decent. I know someone who takes great photos too! xxx

THIRTY-TWO

Meghan walks into the office at five past six holding a bottle of wine, and sticks out her hand. 'Hello, Mr Gilmore, I'm Meghan Grey, Vanessa's store manager. I hope you don't mind if I sit in.'

'Not at all,' Ralph says. His smile is casual and relaxed.

'Great.' Meghan opens the bottle and takes down three glasses from the shelf behind the desk. She's pouring the wine when the delivery van swings into the yard outside. The loud slam of the door causes Ralph to glance up. He reaches for his wine glass without taking his eyes off the activity outside – Jay opening the doors to the storeroom, Mick getting out of the passenger seat, lifting a wooden crate from the back of the van and passing it to him.

Vanessa follows Ralph's gaze, smiling when she sees the easy way Jay and Mick fall into a rhythm as they unload. 'Alright, let's start with the living area.' She takes a large sip of her wine, picks up one of the presentation boards and turns it around.

As she talks him through the rich, dark colours she feels his eyes on her face. There's something intense in them, a warmth, and a touch of amusement. Perhaps giving Ralph Gilmore 'a chance', as he'd put it, wouldn't be so difficult after all. She looks away and forces herself to concentrate.

'I love it,' Ralph says, as she lays down the final board. 'Where do I sign?'

Vanessa purses her lips. 'Ralph, before I draw up the contract there's something I need to get out of the way.'

'Fine.' He leans back in his chair and crosses his legs.

'When I take on a new a job I always do a bit of due diligence on the property – it's something my ex-father-in-law drummed into me. I usually start by checking the land registry to see who holds the deeds. Just to make sure it's not a scam to make off with the furnishings.'

Ralph, who has his glass to his lips, slowly sets it down on the desk. 'It's fine. I can explain.'

Vanessa ploughs on. 'Your flat is registered to someone called Arlo Van Proht. I looked him up. He's a Dutch banker currently living in Paris.'

Vanessa sees Meghan dart Ralph a look. He's wearing an embarrassed 'you got me' smile on his face, like a little boy whose adoring aunt has just caught him with his hand in the cookie jar.

'Look, Arlo's an old mate,' he says. 'We were at school together. He found out I was living in a hotel after my divorce and offered to let me stay in his place in London if I got it refurbished for him while I was there.'

'Alright.' Vanessa doesn't return his smile. 'But why lie about owning it?'

He groans and runs his hand through his hair. 'I wanted to impress you.'

'What?'

'I was looking online for an interior decorator. I found your website, saw your photo and decided I'd really like to get to know you. So I came into the shop, hoping to see you in real life. As soon as I did, I knew I didn't stand a chance. But I couldn't stop thinking about you and I convinced myself that I might be able to persuade you to come out for dinner with me if you thought I owned a million-pound pad in Poultney Square.'

'Oh, God!' Meghan bursts out. 'That's so sweet.'

Vanessa opens her mouth, then closes it again. 'Ralph, that's totally ridiculous and actually slightly creepy.'

'Oh, come on, Nessa,' Meghan says, laughing openly now. 'I think it's one of the most romantic things I've ever heard.'

Vanessa looks from one to the other, not quite sure what to think.

'Look, I'm sorry,' Ralph insists, with a pleading smile. 'It was a dumb thing to do but it doesn't change anything. I still want to spend time with you, and I still want you to work your magic on Arlo's flat.'

Vanessa shakes her head at him.

'If you're worried about payment, don't be. Arlo's authorised me to settle the full invoice up front.'

'What about the wine glasses?'

A muscle tightens in his jaw.

'The ones you said your niece and her husband loved. I saw them. Shoved away in the cupboard in one of your bathrooms.'

'OK, I admit it.' He holds up his hands in a gesture of surrender. 'I used the wedding present thing as an excuse to have a proper conversation with you.'

'Do you even have a niece?'

'Yes.' He grins sheepishly. 'She's three.'

Meghan giggles. Vanessa glares at Ralph and shakes her head. 'What's wrong with you?'

Ralph rakes his hand through his hair. 'Look, can I take you for dinner after we've finished here?'

'I'm... not sure.'

'Please. I'd like to explain properly.' He glances at Meghan and then back at Vanessa, his expression growing serious. 'In private. If you'll let me.'

. . .

Ralph takes his time scanning through the menu and checking for allergens with the waiter. Vanessa watches him across the table wondering, a little uncharitably, if he's stringing this out just to put off the moment when he'll have to explain himself.

'Well?' she says, irritably, when the waiter has gone.

'What can I say? I'm sorry. It was a stupid thing to do but I... I haven't had a relationship since I broke up with my wife.'

'That's no excuse for lying.'

'I know, but I thought that my wife and I would be together forever. When she told me she'd fallen in love with someone else, it completely knocked the wind out of me. Her new bloke is someone I've known for a long time and, to be honest, if I were her, I'd happily have left me for him. He's charming, caring, rolling in money, funny, good-looking. So when she dumped me I didn't just lose a wife, I lost most of my confidence too.'

Ralph's hand seeks hers across the table. She moves it away. 'When were you going to tell me the truth?'

He shrugs. 'I don't know. Maybe when you'd fallen so head-over-heels in love with me you didn't care what I did or didn't own.'

'I'm sorry, Ralph. I was beginning to think that you and I might have a chance at something special that would help us both to heal. But I don't like lies and I don't like liars. I had enough deceit from my ex to last me a lifetime.'

'I *was* going to tell you, I promise.'

'When?'

'Soon. Look, I couldn't have kept it a secret much longer, anyway. The minute my divorce settlement is finalised I'll be buying a place of my own – not quite up to Arlo's standards, but something decent, and I was rather hoping you'd help me look.'

'Don't try to wheedle your way out of this. You thought I'd

be more interested in someone who has a lot of money than someone who doesn't. I don't like it that you see me that way.'

'I know. I messed up. But I'm not a liar, Vanessa.'

'But you did lie to me. It's hardly a basis for building trust.'

'Can we start again?'

'I don't know.'

Ralph leans in closer, desperation burning in his eyes. 'Look, I like you. A lot. I want to spend time with you. I want to get to know you properly and I want us both to find some happiness. Is that so wrong?'

Vanessa gives him a long searching look. 'No more lies?'

'I promise you. No more lies.' He lifts his glass. 'Here's to honesty.'

Vanessa lifts her glass and smiles. 'To honesty.'

He grins, relieved, and takes a large gulp of wine. 'Tell me more about this homeless shelter you volunteer at.'

She pauses before bringing her own glass to her lips. 'Actually, if we're going for full disclosure, there's something I'd like to come clean about.'

Ralph raises an eyebrow.

'If Arlo goes ahead with the contract, on his flat—'

'—which he definitely will—'

'—I'd like to use a couple of men I've met through Cranmore House to do the work. People who need a second chance. I'd vouch for them, of course, and make sure they were properly vetted. That guy you saw unloading the van this evening, the one with the crew cut, would be one of them. He's a brilliant decorator and a really nice man, but he ended up on the street after his divorce.'

They sit back to let the waiter serve their food: a medium rare, sauceless steak for him, seared sea bass with lemon and white beans for her.

'What about the other one?' Ralph says. 'The guy with the ponytail? Are you giving him a second chance too?'

She nods. 'He's on a three-month trial at the moment but he's doing really well and hopefully he's going to take over running my warehouse.'

'What was his problem?'

'Drugs.'

'Taking or supplying?'

'Both. He went to prison – but he's done his time,' she adds, quickly. 'And now he's one hundred per cent focused on staying clean, which is why he's determined to make a go of the job. He's also a talented photographer. You probably saw some of his nightscapes in the shop.'

'What about the woman who sat in on our meeting?'

'Meghan?' Vanessa laughs. 'As far as I know, her past is squeaky clean.' As they pick up their knives and forks, she grows serious. 'Is my inclusive staffing policy going to be a problem for you?'

'Absolutely not. I think it's impressive. The world could do with a few more employers like you.' He looks at her over his wine glass, the flicker of the candle reflected in his grey eyes.

She reddens and looks down at her plate.

'Maybe I could come with you next time you go.'

'Seriously?'

'Why not?'

'OK,' she says. 'You're on.'

Later, as he sips a coffee and waits for the bill she hurries to the loo, retouches her lipstick and checks her phone. Nothing from Izzy. Nothing from Don Dexter.

When she gets back to the table Ralph's paying the waiter, peeling off notes from a wad of cash.

She laughs. 'That's a bit old-school, isn't it?'

'I had my wallet stolen and the bank's taking forever to issue my new cards.' He grins. 'Anyway, what's wrong with old-school? As the queen of vintage I'd have thought you'd approve.'

After dinner he walks her home. The night is cold and damp, street lights catch the puddles, making them glitter in the gloom. A sickle moon rides high above the clouds. When Ralph slips a cautious arm across her shoulders she glances up at him, feeling as nervous as a teenager on a first date.

'Do you want to come in for a nightcap?' she asks, her mouth dry, her fingers clumsy as she fumbles for her key.

'I'd like that very much,' he says.

They stand in her hallway only inches apart. He slides a hand behind her head and pulls her close. Instead of melting into the moment she tenses up. It's been a long time since she's been touched like this, and her body feels awkward and unused. She stares past him and catches their entwined image reflected in the pitted glass of the hallway mirror. What is she doing? She hardly knows this man and he's here, in her home, about to kiss her. Can she trust him? Is he really what she needs in her life right now? He tilts his head lower. Her tension turns to panic. *I can't do this. I can't, I can't, I can't.* She thinks about the gaps and hollows she's so desperate to fill, Meghan's warning about never moving on if she doesn't start taking risks, Izzy's hurtful jibe that she has something that Vanessa doesn't – and her doubts begin to dissolve. *You can, you can, you can*, she tells herself and, as his lips brush hers, she gives in to the warmth of his kiss and the knowledge that letting Ralph into her world is another small step towards the change she's working so tire-lessly to achieve.

THIRTY-THREE

Meghan bursts into Vanessa's office waving a bunch of fat white peonies tastefully wrapped in tissue paper. She plonks them on the desk and stands back, rocking on her heels as Vanessa opens the little card and glances at the message.

'I take it they're from Ralph.'

'Yep.'

'So last night went... well?' There's an eager upswing in Meghan's voice.

Vanessa stuffs the little card back in the envelope and wonders if her cheeks are going red. 'Fine.'

'Just fine?'

'It was good, actually. Really nice.'

'Details, please. I want to know everything.'

'Well, we had dinner at a little French place he knows not far from my house. I had the—'

'I don't care what you ate.' Meghan reaches for the cafetiere and pours a cup of coffee for Vanessa and one for herself.

'Well, as you probably realised I was pretty pissed off with him for lying to me about owning the flat in Poultney Square – I mean, honestly! But he was so embarrassed and so apologetic about it and when he explained that his wife had gone off with this rich, amazing, good-looking, funny bloke who he'd known for years and it had shattered his confidence I knew exactly where he was coming from. So I decided to give him another chance. On condition that from now on we go for complete honesty. No more lies.'

'Did you... go on anywhere after dinner?'

'He came back to my house for a drink and he' – a smile breaks across Vanessa's face – 'stayed over.'

'Yes!' Meghan gives a little fist pump. 'When are you seeing him again?'

'Soon.'

'You see?' Meghan says, with all the pride of a coach whose rigorous training regime has finally paid off. 'I told you that you had to start taking risks on new people.'

Vanessa laughs. 'Can you ask Jay to pop down? I think I just saw him go upstairs.'

As Meghan leaves Vanessa glances at her phone. There's an alert from the email account she set up for Gina Cadogan. Her heart speeds up.

The only person who has that address is Don Dexter. She clicks open the message. He apologises for the delay in getting back to her, says he'll be free to meet for a preliminary chat next week and gives her the address of a café in south London.

She feels a stab of impatience. The sooner she gets a handle on this man the better, but she'll just have to wait. Her attention drifts away to Frances, to the child she lost and the promises she made to her, the sense of time ticking by.

If Mark Findlay goes on hitting a brick wall in his search, what then? Might he really get desperate enough to eliminate the people who know that Frances had a baby?

Suddenly she hears Jay's voice, raised as if he's trying to rouse her from sleep. 'You wanted to see me?'

'Sorry, I was miles away. Come and sit down. Can I get you a coffee?'

He shakes his head and drops into the seat opposite her. 'Meghan's been bitching about me, hasn't she?'

'Of course not. She thinks you're doing brilliantly both with the job *and* with staying clean. As do I.'

'I hear a "but" coming.'

'I'm going to be honest with you – and I'm saying this as a friend, not an employer – I think it would really help to keep her on side if you increased the number of NA meetings you go to.'

'What the hell has me going to NA meetings got to do with her?'

Vanessa keeps her voice low and measured. 'She knows that you're looking to make money so you can rent a flat and she's worried that when you're delivering Vanessa Dunn merchandise to wealthy customers there could be a temptation to deliver... other merchandise as well.'

He jerks back his chair and jumps up, tossing the hair out of his eyes. 'What the—?'

'Sit down and calm down, Jay. She has a point. It would be the perfect cover.'

He makes a derisive noise but drops back into the chair. 'Sure it would, and she'd know all about that.'

'What are you talking about?'

'Jesus, Vanessa. It's not me you want to worry about – it's stuck-up, two-faced cows like her! A few lines in the pub with a glass of wine on a Saturday night, a few more at a house party, a bit of, "Oooh, I can't relax when I get home until I've had a few more." They don't even think it's a problem because they're snorting, not injecting. And when it arrives on their doorstep, hidden in an overpriced bunch of flowers or a gourmet pizza box, they don't have to think about the gangs who are bringing it into the country, or the kids wielding knives to see off the competition, or the damage wreaked by the drug cartels in some far-flung place they prefer not to think about. But, yeah, point the finger at people like me. Jesus, you know how much I've got to lose if I screw up! I'm not going to risk going back inside for the sake of a quick high or a few measly quid, so you can tell Meghan to back off.'

Vanessa sees the fury in his face and there's nothing she can do but hold her ground. 'I get it, Jay. I'm not doubting you and I'm not having a go at you. But you and I both want to make this inclusive staffing thing work, so it makes sense to set the bar high when it comes to the company's drug policy. Overkill, if you like. I've been reading up about supporting former addicts so if you want time off in the day to go to a meeting that's fine with me. If you want me to go with you that's fine too, and if you need someone to talk to my door is always open.' Her throat feels so tight she can hardly speak. 'And before you go storming off to confront Meghan, two NA meetings a week was my idea, not hers. She wasn't accusing you of anything either – just flagging up a possible temptation.'

Temptation. The word sits in the silence, sour and resonant, sparking a memory of Jay's phone ringing that night in the Greek restaurant, the call he hadn't wanted to take in front of her. The shifty way he'd sloped off to ring the caller back.

'If you and I don't respect each other enough to get potential problems out into the open and discuss them before they get out of hand, without you flying off the handle, we might as well give up now.'

He's breathing fast, still angry, but at least he's listening to her.

'Come on, Jay, do this for me. I've also found some meditation sessions for recovering addicts. It's a small group that meets online. I'll send you the link. We'll put the bill on the company tab.'

'Whatever you say.' He gets up, his jaw set hard. 'Two meetings a week and online meditation.'

She opens a drawer, takes out a glossy catalogue and slides it across the desk. 'I'd also like you to come with me to this auction.'

His eyes drop to the catalogue then rise to meet hers. 'Is this supposed to be some kind of peace offering?' There's a snarl in his voice that Vanessa has never heard before.

She pulls back. 'I'd like you to come because you've got a good eye and I'd appreciate your input but also because, well... I think that you and I make a good team.'

She turns away and taps at her keyboard. He hesitates, then picks up the catalogue and stomps out of her office.

THIRTY-FOUR

On Saturday morning, Vanessa leaves the house early and drives to Kensal Green Cemetery. Grasping a simple posy of lily of the valley, she stands at the entrance and glances around. Save for a groundsman sweeping the path there's no one else in sight. Hitching her rucksack a little higher on her shoulder, she makes her way down the winding paths, past stones half-buried by foliage, broken columns corded with ivy, and winged angels pitted with lichen, until she sees the mound of brown earth that marks Frances's grave rising like a scar from the surrounding green.

The funeral flowers are long gone, replaced by a single dark-leaved wreath interwoven with crimson roses whose petals shiver in the breeze – the kind of expensive, impersonal tribute more suited to a municipal cenotaph than the grave of a loved one.

Beside the mound stand two imposing gravestones of brilliantly polished granite, one inscribed simply *Gordon Blane Findlay*; the other, *Dora Elizabeth Findlay – Beloved wife and mother – Taken too soon* above their respective dates of birth and death.

Judging by the burnished perfection of the stones and the perfectly manicured planting on each grave, the Findlay family plot is maintained by a contractor. *Of course it is*, Vanessa thinks. Gordon Findlay, for whom appearances were everything, probably stipulated it in his will, and she's sure that Mark is only too happy to keep up the veneer of monied respectability.

Vanessa turns back to Frances's grave, squats down and takes a white cube-shaped stone vase from her rucksack. She presses the base into the damp soil and carefully arranges her posy of lily of the valley and baby's breath in the brass reservoir. When she's finished, she runs a finger across the engraving on the front of the vase and rereads the lines she'd thought so long and hard about; words she'd chosen with care to mark the loss of what might have been.

> *Footsteps echo down paths we did not take*
> *Towards doors we'll never open*

Given the fast turnaround offered by the online supplier, she'd been worried the finished lettering would be shoddily carved or badly spaced. To her relief it's neatly done and the whole effect, like Frances herself, is elegant and understated.

Using one of the metal watering cans provided by the cemetery, Vanessa fetches water from the central tap and fills the vase. As she inhales the sweet scent of the lily of the valley, she thinks about the thrillers that she and Frances had read together, the talks they'd enjoyed, the secrets they'd shared, the friendship they'd kindled. She stands up, dusts herself down and gathers up her things.

There's every chance the contractors will report the appearance of the vase to Mark Findlay and he'll instruct them to remove it. It doesn't matter. She's done what she came to do.

THIRTY-FIVE

'Do you like it, Mum? I found it in one of those specialist "mother of the bride" websites. The minute I saw it I thought, *That would be perfect.*' With one hand Vanessa thrusts out an emerald-green dress with a cream trim, dangling it from its hanger; with the other she holds up a matching jacket. 'The fabric's a special mixed fibre that doesn't crease. Ideal for wheelchair users. Next time I come, I'll bring you the shoes I've ordered.'

She waits for a moment, imagining her mother reacting to her new outfit, asking about the shoes and demanding to see the hat she's chosen. Smiling as if in response, Vanessa opens the wardrobe, hangs the dress and jacket on the door, and then pulls a straw cloche with a matching emerald-green band around it from a carrier bag. 'I thought a smallish one would work best.' She sets it on Ellen's head and adjusts it a little so it sits jauntily to one side. 'We don't want it tipping into your eyes.' She takes out a hand mirror and holds it in front of Ellen's face in the hope that some relic of her mother's life-long pride in her appearance might trigger a Pavlovian response to her reflection.

Vanessa sighs as Ellen's eyes stay fixed on the tartan rug on her knees. She puts down the mirror and drops onto the edge of the bed. 'Sorry I was in such a state last time I came. But, honestly, Mum, you must have been as shocked by Izzy's news as I was. When she said she wanted to come over for a chat it was the last thing on earth I expected her to tell me, and it completely threw me. She's never cared about the effect of her craziness on me or my life, or ever bothered to thank me when I've had to step in when it all goes wrong, so I suppose there's no reason why she should start now. But getting pregnant and marrying the father within weeks of meeting him—? It isn't like when she crashed my car, or lost her passport in Bali, or got arrested at that demo. I can't just throw money at the situation and sort it out. This is life-changing. Of course, my instant reaction was to panic about the baby – but then I realised that no, that poor little mite isn't a problem. It's a blessing.' She reaches out and squeezes Ellen's arm. 'If it comes to it – and I really hope it doesn't – I'll remortgage the house and convert the attic. There's enough space up there for two decent-sized rooms and a bathroom, so whatever happens I can be there to keep an eye on him... or her. Though I have a really strong feeling it's going to be a boy.'

She glances up as the delicate French clock clicks, whirrs and chimes the quarter hour. 'No. The problem is this ridiculous rush into marriage. I just don't understand why she can't wait. Single women have babies all the time and no one gives a damn about it. I mean, going on her past form, this relationship won't last more than a few months, but, take it from me, you can't just snap your fingers and get a divorce. These things take time and money, especially if there's a child involved, and spouses are entitled to walk away with fifty per cent of everything their other half owns, including' – she squirms a little and lowers her eyes – 'everything they inherit from their parents. But it's alright. I've kind of got my head around it now – "readjusted to the new reality", as my old therapist used to say. You know me – hope for the best, but plan down to the smallest detail for the worst.'

She lifts the straw cloche from her mother's head and lays it on the bed. 'What with Izzy's news and the deadline on the big Pimlico job, on top of the shop and everything else that's going on, I was worried that all the work I'm doing to achieve my personal goals would get thrown off course. But I'm totally on it.' She ticks off the list on her fingers. 'I told Jay I had plans to expand his role, and he went straight round to tell Larry how much he's looking forward to taking on the new responsibility. I even convinced him to start going to two NA meetings a week, instead of one, and to do these meditation sessions for recovering addicts I found online. They're just small things but they'll help. I've got your wedding outfit sorted – big relief – and Ralph and I are now officially an item. He's even offered to come along to Cranmore House with me on Sunday *and*—'

'Is that your mother's dress for the wedding?'

Vanessa twists round. She freezes. It's Stefan with the medication trolley. She can't meet his eyes, sure he'll see her secrets written across her face. 'Green is Mum's favourite colour.'

She wonders if he's going to mention Frances, unsure if it will be more worrying if he does or if he doesn't.

'Hello, Ellen, how are you doing this morning?' He takes Ellen's arm, gently rolls up her sleeve and swabs the inside of her elbow before turning back to Vanessa. 'It's great that your sister wants to have your mother with her on her big day.'

Vanessa wants to scream at him and demand to know there and then if he's working for Mark Findlay. She wants it so badly she can feel the words forming in her mouth. 'Every girl wants her mother at her wedding,' she says, her voice stiff and unnatural.

'You know she rang Matron from Stockholm to ask about hiring wheelchair transport and a carer for her?' He uncaps the

needle of a syringe and sticks it into a little ampule. 'I'd have
volunteered to do it myself but I'm away that weekend. A
family christening. Still, we're all looking forward to seeing the
photos.' He draws back the plunger and taps the syringe with
his nail. With a glance at the picture of Izzy on the sideboard he
pushes the needle into Ellen's arm. 'Your sister's going to make a
beautiful bride. You must be so pleased for her.'

'I'm trying to organise a nice lunch for everyone – somewhere a bit special, for after the ceremony,' Vanessa says,
flashing a smile. 'But it's not easy finding anywhere decent at
such short notice.'

'I'm sure you'll manage. You've still got two weeks.'

Two weeks. At least now she's got some idea of the actual
date.

She watches him leave and feels like crying as the tensions
of the last few weeks break over her. 'God, I shouldn't have to
pretend that I've been invited to my own sister's wedding! It's
more than embarrassing, Mum. It's humiliating and hurtful.
Really hurtful. I can't believe she's shutting me out like this. I
really thought she'd relent, maybe even ask me to be her maid of
honour. When I got married she was my bridesmaid, and when
you married Rocky I was yours. But she's so bloody stubborn
she won't even answer my texts.'

THIRTY-SIX

The weekend comes and there's still no response from Izzy, but Vanessa refuses to allow her row with her sister to overshadow her time with Ralph. On Saturday night they share a lactose-and gluten-free gourmet pizza – which, surprisingly, is pretty good – drink too much wine, and make love on the sofa, before staggering up to bed and making love again.

It's still dark when Vanessa wakes to find herself alone. She blinks into the gloom, wondering if she's imagined the presence of this new man in her life, her home, her bed, before realising she's naked and that the dim mounds on the floor are a trail of his dropped clothing. She rolls out of bed, pulls on a T-shirt and walks over to the door.

Ralph's not in the bathroom but there's a faint bluish light seeping up from downstairs. Blearily she pads down the stairs, the old boards creaking a little beneath her bare feet. She turns into the hallway. It's now in darkness, though the kitchen door is ajar. She pulls it wide and flicks on the light.

Ralph stands by the sink, a tumbler of water in his hand. 'Sorry, did I wake you?'

'It's OK. I'm pretty thirsty too. Too much red wine.'

He takes another glass from the draining board and turns on the tap. As he fills it, her eyes pull to her laptop. It's sitting on the table, lid closed. She's certain she left it open on the counter after she'd logged on to look at take-out options.

Ralph follows her gaze and says, quickly: 'I hope you don't mind. I had to check for an urgent email I'm expecting from the States, and my phone's dead.'

She takes the glass from his hand and looks up at him, her unease disappearing as he kisses her. 'It's fine. Did it come?'

'Sorry?'

'The email.'

'Not yet.' He slings an arm around her shoulders, switching off the light as he leads her out of the kitchen. 'Come on. We can't turn up at Cranmore House knackered as well as hungover.'

Later, as she lies curled against him, listening to the soft rasp of his breath, she stares into the dark and her thoughts pull back to Izzy and her baby. When the hurt bites too deeply she distracts herself by going over everything left on her mental checklist for next week. As she said to her mother, hope for the best, but plan down to the very last detail for the worst.

In the morning, Vanessa sets about making Ralph breakfast. Scrambled eggs with smoked salmon. It's what she used to make for Doug on Sunday mornings. She beats the eggs, assailed by memories of the life that has gone forever: lolling on the sofa, newspapers scattered across the floor, Doug barefoot in a T-shirt and track pants, sipping coffee.

'You look very fetching,' Ralph says, when he comes down.

She looks down at her faded jeans and baggy sweatshirt. 'Frankly it's a relief not to have to care how I look when I'm at Cranmore.'

'I like you with no make-up.' He bends to kiss her. 'It makes me feel as if I'm seeing the real you.'

She laughs and kisses him back. Hard and happy. 'What do you want to do for dinner tonight? Shall we try that new fish place around the corner?'

'I can't. I'm off to Manchester. That conference—?' He gives her an odd, slightly hurt look. 'I did tell you.'

Vanessa screws up her face. 'Oh, God. Of course you did. I even factored it into the work schedule and told Mick to do as much as he can on your flat while you're away. Sorry, I've had so much going on my head's a sieve.' She stands on tiptoe to plant a kiss on his cheek. 'Do you want me to drop you at the station this evening?'

He smiles, placated. 'Don't worry. I need to go home first to pick up my suitcase, so let's take both cars to Cranmore House.' He catches her gently by the chin. 'Can I see you when I get back on Thursday? After four days of unadulterated tedium I'm going to need something to cheer me up.'

She leans in and kisses him again. 'It's a date.'

THIRTY-SEVEN

On Monday morning Vanessa drives to the office with thoughts of Ralph in her head – the effort he'd made to get on with everyone at Cranmore House, the kindness he'd shown to Donnie, the smile he'd managed to squeeze out of Beattie. She turns into the yard and slams on the brakes when she sees Meghan running out of the back entrance, waving her arms. She lowers the window. 'What's wrong?'

'We've been burgled!' Meghan wails. 'Why didn't you answer your phone? I've been trying to call you.' She turns and dashes back inside.

Vanessa jumps out of the car and races after her. 'Have you called the police?'

'They're on their way.'

Vanessa looks down at the smashed lock on the back door and steps into her office. It's in total disarray: leather swivel chair slit across the seat and overturned; desk lamp smashed; filing cabinet on its side with all its drawers pulled out; assorted pens, pencils, pairs of scissors and files strewn across the floor; the computer monitor shattered; every sample vase, pot, dish and candlestick swept from the shelves and thrown onto the floor; a stack of mounted prints slashed with a knife. She rights the little padded armchair she's just had reupholstered and inserts her fingers into the hole where the seat has been sliced open and its stuffing ripped out. Horrified she runs upstairs to the shop. Tripping and lurching she crashes through the door, steps over the toppled stepladders lying in pools of fabric – and freezes where she stands. Her shop is still. Her world is still. Broken pottery, shattered glasses, drawers flung open, baskets upturned, cushions trampled. She feels angry, violated and afraid.

She stumbles forward, glass crunching beneath her feet, reaches the counter and watches Meghan key her passcode into the till. The drawer shoots open. The fifty-pound float they always leave overnight is untouched.

'This table's been cleared,' Mick says, righting one of the step ladders. 'Anyone remember what was on it?'

Vanessa swerves towards him. Mouth dry, she stretches out a shaky hand and runs it across the empty tabletop. 'The Emma Dutton bronzes. There were six of them.'

They glance around as a police car pulls up outside and two police officers jump out. One looks like a schoolboy – jug ears and bad skin; the other, a woman, is older, with over-plucked eyebrows and dyed red hair, cut short. She leads the way to the counter, looking around her with an expression that hovers between bafflement and disdain. Clearly not a fan of the Vanessa Dunn style, her eyes snap to the banknotes in the till. 'I'm DS Doulton, and this is PC Woolacott.'

Vanessa puts her hand against her chest and feels her heart beating heavily. 'I'm the owner, Vanessa Dunn.' She forces herself forward. 'This is my manager, Meghan Grey. She's the one who called you.'

The redhead turns and casts an eye across the front door and window. 'No sign of a break-in up here. Any idea how they gained entry?'

'Through the back door,' Meghan says. 'They smashed the lock.'

'You got CCTV?'

Meghan shakes her head. 'It's being installed in a couple of weeks.'

'Any witnesses?'

'I don't think so – the back yard's pretty secluded.'

'Alright, let's take a look.'

'Down here,' Vanessa says, leading the way.

The two officers pick their way through the mess on the office floor. 'Is there a safe in here?'

'We don't have one,' Vanessa says.

'That's the door they broke in through.' Meghan points down the narrow lobby. 'It looks like they took a hammer to the lock.'

The two officers wander over to the back door and take a cursory look at the splintered wood before stepping out into the yard and looking around at the open gate and the high brick walls enclosing the gravelled space. 'Easy enough to get a vehicle in and out of here without being seen. You should upgrade your security and get that CCTV installed pronto. What's in there?' She points to the door to the storeroom.

'Stock.'

'Can you open it for me?'

Meghan hurries inside for the fob and raises the roller door. The shelves look undisturbed.

'Check your inventory, anyway,' Doulton says. 'Did they take much from the shop, Ms Dunn?'

'I won't know for sure until we do a complete stock take, but all the bronzes have gone. Six figurines by a really important artist. They were worth a lot of money.'

Doulton nods and makes a note in her notebook, finally showing a flicker of sympathy. 'Scrap bronze fetches a fortune these days. Three or four grand a ton.'

'They were pieces of art, officer,' Vanessa snaps, following her back inside. 'Worth a lot more than the price of the metal.'

Doulton waves her pencil around the office. 'Anything missing from down here?'

Vanessa frowns. 'Not that I can see.'

'What about your hard drive?' The jug-eared PC is pointing at the cables dangling from the back of the computer. 'Anything of particular importance stored on those drives, Ms Dunn?'

Despite the rushing in her head, Vanessa manages to murmur, 'Stock inventories, accounts, customer contacts... nothing of value. At least, not to anyone other than me.'

Doulton is rapidly losing interest. 'If you discover any other missing items let us know. Meanwhile, I'll give you a crime number for your insurance.'

'Is that it?' Vanessa says, incredulous.

'With no CCTV and no witnesses, the chances of identifying the culprits are pretty much zero.' Doulton tucks her notebook into her breast pocket. 'If I were you, I'd get yourself some steel shutters. Front and back.'

When the police have gone Vanessa calls a locksmith, and while Meghan and Jody clear up the shop floor and make a list of all the damaged and missing stock, she and Mick go downstairs to tackle her office.

She leans against the doorjamb and stares wearily at the mess.

'Are you alright?' Mick asks.

What she wants to say is that she's tired and agitated and her heart is in overdrive, but his worn face shows such concern she says, 'I'm fine.'

Together they right the furniture, clear away the broken crockery and gather up the scattered contents of the drawers. There's something infinitely calming about carrying out a task like this with Mick; the quiet thoroughness with which he sweeps and tidies, the delicacy of the movements of his rough, calloused hands, his refusal to catastrophise. Vanessa drops to her knees and peers under the desk. 'Have you seen a bundle of memory sticks?' She holds her thumb and forefinger a couple of inches apart. 'There were three of them about this big, in the bottom drawer, tied around with an elastic band.'

Mick shakes his head. 'Sorry.'

She sits back on her haunches. 'They were definitely here yesterday.' Her gaze drifts to the gap beneath the desk where the hard drive had stood.

Vanessa pushes herself up from the floor and glances at the time. 'You'd better get off to Ralph's and start stripping the hall-way. I promised him we'd have the wallpaper up by the time he gets back from Manchester.'

Upstairs she finds Meghan in a state, flitting between displays, running her hand through her hair and snapping at Jody. She flaps a dismissive hand when Vanessa asks her if she's seen the memory sticks.

'That's the least of our problems. How are we going to tell Emma Dutton that six of her sculptures are going to be melted down for scrap? Do you want to do it, or shall I?'

'The thing is, one of those sticks has got all the hi-res versions of Jay's photos stored on it,' Vanessa says.

Meghan mutters something inaudible and turns away.

'What time is he due in?'

'Surprise, surprise, he's not in at all today.'

'What do you mean?'

'He's doing a pick-up from Brentford, delivering to Bath and Cheltenham, then going straight on to one of his NA meet-ings. It's in the diary.'

'I meant, what did you mean by, "Surprise, surprise"?'

'Oh, so you don't you think it's suspicious that this happened on a day when he doesn't have to show his face?' Meghan flings out her arm. 'Whoever did this knew there was no CCTV, knew they could get in through the back unseen and knew that the Dutton statues were the most valuable things we have.'

Vanessa backs up, raising her palms. 'That's ridiculous and you know it.'

'Is it?' Meghan regards her coldly. 'Anyway, what do you need him for?'

'There's some custom-made wallpaper arriving later that I need him to drop off at Ralph's. Mick's going to need it first thing tomorrow.'

'I'll send it by courier.'

'You know how delicate that stuff is *and* what it costs. It needs expert handling.'

'Then he'll have to do it after his NA meeting.' Meghan's tone is exasperated, as if Jay having commitments outside work hours is a personal affront.

'I'll be in my office,' Vanessa says and turns away.

Alone at her desk, she wrestles the tumult of thoughts surging through her head. The break-in wasn't Jay's doing, she's sure of that. It was Mark Findlay's. Just as she's sure that the Emma Dutton bronzes were snatched to make it look like a normal burglary, and stealing the hard drive was another of his fishing expeditions. It's the theft of the memory sticks that troubles her. *Has Mark found out about the deathbed video message Frances recorded for her child?*

Her thoughts flit to the little red flash drive – now locked away in her secret storage unit with all her other valuables.

Vanessa gets home early and sits on the edge of her bed, rain spitting against the window. What with the burglary on top of the stress of the last few weeks, she feels too frazzled to think straight and she knows from experience how counterproductive that can be. She needs to calm down.

She goes downstairs and cooks herself a proper supper – a pan-fried chicken breast with salad leaves, which she eats at the table with a glass of very cold white wine. Then she runs a bath, lights some candles, fetches herself a cup of herbal tea and a thriller she's been meaning to read for ages and slips into the warm, fragrant bubbles.

By the time she emerges from the bathroom, an hour later, the stream of troublesome thoughts has slowed to an almost manageable trickle and when Ralph calls she's able – almost – to laugh when she tells him about the break-in and DS Doulton's attitude to the missing sculptures.

'I take it you're insured.'

'Yes, we shouldn't lose out financially, but that doesn't stop me feeling violated or imagining the damage the intruders could have done to the stock if they'd really put their minds to it.'

Or the damage they could do to me if Findlay thinks he's losing the race to find the real heir to the Findlay Corporation.

THIRTY-EIGHT

'Vanessa Dunn Interiors, how may I help you?' Meghan's eyes dart around the shop, her brow puckering as she listens to the voice at the other end of the phone. 'I'm so sorry about that, Mrs Henson. Yes, yes, of course. I'll speak to our driver and call you straight back.'

Vanessa, who is manning the till, smiles at her customer, hands her a beautifully wrapped pair of candlesticks and her receipt and waits until the woman is out of earshot before calling out to Meghan. 'Something wrong?'

Meghan has dialled another number and she's standing with her phone pressed to her ear, her face taut with annoyance. 'Where are you? Call me as soon as you get this.' She cuts the call and comes over to the counter. 'Julie Henson's paint hasn't arrived. She's threatening to charge us for her decorator's time because he's sitting in her house with nothing to do. What the hell does Jay think he's up to? He promised he'd get it there by eight.'

Vanessa checks the time. It's nearly 9.30. She runs downstairs to her office and peers out into the yard. It's empty. She goes outside, presses the fob on her keyring and waits while the doors to the storeroom rattle open. The Hensons' order of speciality paint, all ten cans of it, is still where she left it last night, ready for Jay to collect first thing.

A faint flutter of adrenaline grips her as she walks back upstairs to the shop. 'The van's not here but the paint is,' she tells Meghan, who is standing by the door looking out into the street, her phone still clamped to her ear.

'Jay's not even picking up. What the hell, Ness?'

'Hang on.' Vanessa reaches for her bag and pulls out her own phone. There are three missed calls, all from Mick. Her tension kicks up a notch. She dials his number. 'Hey, Mick, it's me. Is there a problem with the wallpaper? Did Jay forget to drop it off?'

'The wallpaper's here, but he's left the van in the square, parked on a double yellow. It's already got a ticket and they'll probably be back any minute to tow it away.'

Vanessa groans. 'Any idea where he's gone?'

'None at all. What do you want me to do?'

She can hear the tremor of anxiety in his voice and says, soothingly, 'Don't worry about it. You get on with the wallpaper. I'll come over and move the van.'

She grabs her bag and calls to Meghan. 'Can you put the Hensons' paint in a cab?'

'I've just ordered one. Where are you going?'

'To get the van. Jay's left it parked in Poultney Square.'

'For heaven's sake.'

Vanessa scowls at her. 'He's been totally reliable up until now. I'm sure there's a perfectly good explanation. Have you seen the spare van keys anywhere?'

'On the hook in the office.'

My office, Vanessa thinks as she grabs the key, then chides herself for being so childish. She runs out into the street, darting in front of an oncoming Mercedes when she sees a cab.

The Mercedes driver slams on his brakes and blasts his horn at her.

'You're in a hurry,' the cabby says, as she drops onto the back seat. 'Where to?'

'Kensington,' she gasps. 'Poultney Square.'

'What's the big rush?'

'My van's about to get towed.'

'Oh, right.' The cabby spins the cab around and launches into a lengthy tirade about the evils of traffic wardens. His rant is petering off into a generalised moan about high-handed authority when he swings left into the square.

It's a one-way street and something is blocking the road ahead, causing the cars to back up. He slows down behind a shiny 4x4 and looks across the central garden to where a couple of policemen are taping off a section of road outside the scaffolded houses. Behind the cordon sits a police car and an ambulance, their blue lights flashing.

'Where's your van?' he asks, sticking his elbow out of the window and craning his neck to get a better look.

'Leave me here. I'll be fine.' Vanessa jumps out and thrusts a handful of notes into his hand. It's far more than the fare but she doesn't stop to get change.

She's walked half the length of the railings enclosing the garden when a second police car screeches past, travelling the wrong way, siren blaring. She watches it pull up. A man in plain clothes gets out, talking into his phone. He ducks beneath the tape and disappears down a narrow alleyway that leads behind the houses. Vanessa hurries over and calls out to one of the uniformed policemen: 'Excuse me, officer. I'm here to pick up my van.' She points to the navy-blue transit parked just inside the cordon. 'Is it alright if I take it?'

The policeman, who is young and skinny shakes his head. 'Sorry. You'll have to wait until we get the all clear.'

'All clear about what?'

'A body's been found in the alleyway. We've got to keep the whole area secured until they've confirmed the cause of death. Seeing as he's still got a needle hanging out of his arm it shouldn't take long.'

Vanessa grimaces, appalled by his indifference. All around her people are gathering, gawping, jostling for space on the pavement. A street cleaner in an orange hi-vis jacket slumps against his cart. Sirens whine, a second police car swings into the square. A man in plain clothes – tall and bald – gets out and strides around, taking charge, a phone clamped to his ear.

Silence grips the crowd. Two paramedics in lime green overalls appear in the alleyway wheeling a gurney, bumping it over the cobbles, the body between them faceless beneath a thin grey blanket.

'Alright, step back, please.' The skinny officer is bearing down on her, arms flailing, a flush of importance flaring red on his cheeks.

She feels tears brim in her eyes as the paramedics slide the gurney into the ambulance and slam the doors shut. The ambulance moves slowly away, strangely silent – no lights, no sirens. Vanessa stands immobile, watching it roll over the speed bumps carrying the nameless body away.

She walks back across the square and rings the bell of Ralph's flat. Mick buzzes her up.

'The police won't let me move the van,' she says, panting a little from the exertion of running up the stairs.

'Why ever not?'

'They've found some poor guy dead in the alleyway and they've got to secure the area until they're certain he died of an overdose.'

Mick goes over to the window and stares down. 'Do they know who it is?'

'I don't think so.'

He turns to look at her. 'I tried calling Jay again. He's still not picking up.'

Their eyes meet, a shared flicker of concern.

'Give me his address,' Mick says, gruffly. 'I'll nip over there now and see if he's alright.'

Vanessa looks up at him and says, very quietly: 'Why don't we go together?'

THIRTY-NINE

They don't have to wait long before the front door of Jay's building bangs open. Three men emerge, heads down, collars up, hands thrust into the pockets of their jackets. They barely glance up as Vanessa and Mick slip past them and hurry up the stairs.

The door to Jay's bedsit is slightly ajar. Vanessa knocks and calls his name. No response. She takes a breath, pushes it wide and steps inside.

There's no sign of Jay, and the room is a mess: clothes scattered across the floor, the bin jammed with takeaway boxes, the bed unmade. Mick throws her a look which she understands as plainly as if he'd spoken the words aloud.

She unlatches the rickety wardrobe and flicks through jeans, shirts and hoodies while Mick pulls open drawers, one by one, and runs his hands through the contents. Finding nothing in the wardrobe, Vanessa moves on to the kitchen area, rattling through a box of cutlery and peering into the fridge and oven.

Mick reaches the bottom drawer and removes a crumpled black sweater. Underneath it there's a canvas bag. He tugs back the zip and pulls opens a parcel wrapped loosely in newspaper. His shoulders stiffen. 'Vanessa. You need to see this.'

She puts down the coffee jar she was unscrewing and scurries over to him. Nestling in the newspaper there's a syringe, a pack of disposable needles, a lighter, a charred metal spoon, a leather strap and a little heap of stained cotton balls.

'No.' She twitches her head away as if she can't bear to look at them, and steps away from the drawer. 'He wouldn't. He swore to me he wouldn't.'

Mick drops a hand onto her shoulder. 'Let's go.'

Vanessa wriggles free and looks wildly around the room. 'I have to go to the police.'

'What for?'

'I need to know what's going on.'

Mick looks down at the drug paraphernalia and kicks the drawer shut with his boot. 'I think that's pretty obvious,' he says.

Vanessa blinks up at the fluorescent lights as they wait in line at Kensington police station. Mick stands a couple of feet behind her. After years of sleeping rough, being moved on and intimidated by the police, he's cowed and uneasy.

'I want to report a missing person,' she says, when a desk sergeant with a sagging jaw and tired eyes beckons them up to the desk.

'Age?'

'He's um... twenty-seven.'

'How long's he been missing?'

'Since last night.'

'Does he have any mental health problems? Disabilities, impairments?'

'Not that I know of.'

'How do you know he's not sleeping off a hangover on someone's couch?'

'He works for me. He left my company van in Poultney Square last night. That's not like him.' She draws in a gasp of air. 'It was parked right near to where they found a body this morning.'

There's a snap of interest in the sergeant's eyes. 'Poultney Square?'

'Yes.'

'Is this employee of yours a known drug-user?'

'No. Well... he used to have drug issues but he's clean now. He's been through rehab.'

'Can you give me his name?'

'It's Jay... Jay Brooker.'

'And your name is?'

'Vanessa Dunn.'

He flicks his gaze to Mick. 'Are you with this lady, sir?'

Mick nods and shuffles forward, eyes scraping the floor.

'This is Michael Morris,' Vanessa says.

'If you could take a seat over there, someone will be with you as soon as they're free.'

Ten minutes later, the plain clothes officer Vanessa had seen at the scene comes striding through the glass doors. He seems taller, and his bald head shines beneath the fluorescent lights. 'I'm DCI O'Halloran. Ms Dunn, Mr Morris, if you'd like to come this way.'

He takes them down a corridor into a small, scruffy meeting room that looks out onto the car park. The air is warm and stale and the only furniture is a brown, Formica-topped table and four plastic chairs. O'Halloran sits down on one side and gestures to them to take the chairs opposite. 'Ms Dunn, we've just received confirmation that the body discovered this morning in Poultney Square is that of your employee, Jacob Brooker.'

Adrenaline shoots through Vanessa's veins and her eyes fill with tears. This is real. It's not a dream or a nightmare. It's really happening. She rocks forward and grasps the edge of the table. Beside her Mick emits a low groan.

'Are you sure?' Vanessa asks, her voice cracking.

'I'm afraid so. Brooker had a criminal record which enabled us to identify his body from the fingerprints we have on file.'

'How did he—?'

'Preliminary tests on the substance in the syringe found in his arm indicate that he died of an overdose of heroin that had been cut with Rohypnol and a highly dangerous synthetic opioid. There's been a spike in these kinds of deaths over the last few months. Our concern is to find the supplier before anyone else dies.'

Vanessa reaches in her bag for a tissue and wipes her cheeks. 'I understand that, but Jay didn't inject himself. He wouldn't have.'

'Brooker was a registered addict, Ms Dunn.' O'Halloran's voice is kind but insistent, as if pushing her to accept the obvious.

'I've already told the desk sergeant, Jay was clean. He had been for months. There's no way he would have done this to himself. In fact, Tuesday is one of his NA nights. That's why he couldn't do the delivery earlier. Why would he bother going to a Narcotics Anonymous meeting if, two hours, later he was going to buy dodgy drugs and shoot up in an alleyway?'

'How long have you known Mr Brooker, Ms Dunn?'

'A few months.'

O'Halloran makes a note on his pad. 'Did you know him before he started working for you?'

'Yes. I volunteer at a shelter for the homeless. Cranmore House. I met him while he was working there.'

'When he was carrying out a community service order for possession of class A drugs with intent to sell.'

She raises her chin, defiantly. 'That's right. He went there after he completed a successful stint in rehab, and I employed him as part of an inclusive staffing initiative I'm piloting.'

'Can I confirm that it was your delivery van that was left in the square?'

'Yes.'

'Did he drive it on a regular basis?'

'Yes.'

'Did he keep it with him overnight?'

'Now and then, if he had an NA meeting to get to straight from work or a particularly early start time.'

'Is he the person who was driving it last night?'

She nods. 'He used it to drop off some wallpaper at a flat I'm decorating in Poultney Square. I tried to move it this morning but the police told me I couldn't.'

'Do you have keys for it with you?'

'Um... yes.' She fumbles in her bag and takes out the spare set.

He holds out his hand. 'We're going to need to take it to Forensics.'

'Whatever for?'

'To see if the vehicle was being used by Mr Brooker or his accomplices to transport and sell drugs.'

'It wasn't, I can tell you that now.'

'Who else from your company drives that vehicle?'

'Mick and I both use it now and then.'

'Would you be willing to give us your fingerprints? Purely for elimination.'

'Of course.' Vanessa struggles to keep control of her voice. 'But I'm telling you, Jay Brooker was not involved in taking or dealing drugs.'

'He died of an overdose, Ms Dunn.'

'One that *he* didn't administer. He'd been clean for months.'

'Because abstinence was a mandatory condition of his community service order.'

'Which he saw as a chance to turn his life around.' An edge of irritation creeps into her voice.

'There's always an increased risk of drug-related death soon after release.'

'Jay isn't a statistic,' Vanessa says, heatedly.

O'Halloran raises a placatory hand. 'I understand that, Ms Dunn. All I'm saying is that enforced drug reduction over a sustained period lowers tolerance.'

He turns his attention to Mick. 'How well did you know Mr Brooker, Mr Morris?'

'Well enough,' Mick says. 'I'm living at Cranmore House.'

Vanessa notes the reassessment in O'Halloran's gaze.

Mick shifts uncomfortably. 'I'm doing the decorating work at number forty-seven.'

O'Halloran examines him closely and frowns. 'Are you aware of any drug-related activity at the hostel? Any of the inmates dealing?'

Mick looks down at the floor. 'I wouldn't know what goes on. I keep myself to myself.'

'What about Mr Brooker? Did he appear to be involved in anything suspicious?'

Mick scrubs his hand over his face. 'Look, Jay was a good bloke but it's hard for these lads. It doesn't matter how long they've been clean or how determined they are to stay that way, the temptation is always there, hanging over them. Most of the time they give in to it.'

'No,' Vanessa says, on the verge of tears. 'Not Jay.'

'What about the syringe and strap we found in his bedsit, Vanessa?' Mick says.

O'Halloran looks up. 'He had a syringe in his room?'

Mick nods. 'We went over there this morning when he didn't bring the van back.'

'Can you give me the address?'

Mick gives it to him and Vanessa watches the detective write it down.

O'Halloran stands up. 'Thank you for coming in. I'll make sure that your van is returned to you as soon as practicable, Mrs Dunn. If you wait here, someone will come in to take your fingerprints.'

'You've got mine already,' Mick says, quietly.

Vanessa turns sharply to look at him.

'I got done a couple of years ago for being drunk and disorderly and smashing a shop window.'

O'Halloran merely nods and turns back to Vanessa. 'If we need to speak to either of you again, one of my colleagues will be in touch.'

'I'd better get back to Poultney Square,' Mick says, when they get outside. 'There's a lot to do.'

'I'll get you an Uber.'

Mick says nothing as they wait for the Uber to arrive. He thrusts his hands into his pockets and stares down at the pavement. Vanessa blinks into the wind, her throat hot and sore as if she's coming down with the flu.

FORTY

Vanessa bursts through the shop door. 'He's dead, Meghan.'

'Who is?'

'Jay. They found his body in an alleyway behind Poultney Square.'

Meghan's hands fly to her mouth. 'Oh, my God. What happened?'

'The police are saying he overdosed. But I don't believe it. Don't look at me like that. He was trying his hardest to stay clean.'

A young couple trying out the steel and walnut wood chairs turn to see what the commotion is about.

Meghan grips Vanessa's arm and motions to Jody to take over at the till. 'Stop shouting,' she hisses in Vanessa's ear. 'You're scaring the customers. Come on.' She steers her down the steps to the office. 'You're in shock. I'm going to make you a cup of tea and I want you stay down here and drink it. Promise me you won't go back upstairs until you've got yourself under control.'

'It's easy for you. You never liked him.'

'Nessa, come on. Whatever doubts I might have had about him I'm sorry he's dead. Of course I am.'

Vanessa fumbles for her phone. 'Larry will back me up.'

She stabs the keys with her finger and puts the call on speaker. 'Larry,' her voice is little more than a gasp. 'I've got some terrible news. Jay's been found dead. The police are saying it's an overdose.' She presses her knuckles to her mouth.

'I know what the police are saying,' Larry says, gruffly. 'They're here now, interviewing the guests.'

'Is it that tall, bald detective? O'Halloran?'

'Yes. The heroin in Jay's system was contaminated. They think he bought it from someone at the hostel.'

'Why would they think that?'

'They got an anonymous tip-off a few days ago that one of our guests is selling dirty drugs.'

Breath judders in her throat. 'Did they follow it up?'

'They searched the place and found nothing but as soon as the trustees heard about it they started kicking off about lax safety protocols, which is a headache I could do without. And now this.'

'What if it wasn't Jay who bought the heroin? What if some-body killed him and made it *look* as if it was an overdose?'

Kettle in hand, Meghan turns abruptly, her eyes wide.

'The cops say they found syringes and a strap in his bedsit,' Larry says.

'That doesn't prove anything. He could have had that stuff for years.'

'It was wrapped in a three-day-old newspaper.'

'Somebody could have planted it.' Vanessa hisses out the words through gritted teeth.

'Who'd go to the trouble of doing that?'

'I don't know. Someone he'd crossed in his old life, or owed money to. A dealer?'

Larry snorts, losing patience. 'If a street dealer wanted

someone dead, believe you me, they wouldn't bother making it look like an overdose.'

'But—'

'Come on,' he says, wearily. 'None of us want to believe that Jay was back on smack but there's no point denying the facts.'

Meghan places a mug of tea in front of Vanessa and stirs in three spoonfuls of sugar. 'Shout if you need anything,' she mouths and turns and hurries back upstairs.

'It takes a hell of a lot of willpower to come back from where he'd been,' Larry is saying, 'and falling off the wagon doesn't make him a bad person.' Someone in the background calls his name. 'I have to go.'

'Call me if you hear anything more,' Vanessa says, but the line is dead.

She stands up and circles the room, her heart hammering against her ribs. She's taking a swig of the tea Meghan made her, shuddering at the syrupy sweetness of it, when her phone rings. Ralph's name flashes on the screen. She hesitates for a moment, then picks up.

'Hey, it's me.' His voice is calm and reassuring. 'Meghan just called me. She told me what happened. Are you alright?'

'No.' The word comes out in a shapeless sob.

There's a silence before he says, 'Are you at the shop?'

'Yes.'

'Go home. You're in no fit state to work. Get Meghan to call you a cab. I'll jump on a train and come over as soon as I can.'

'There's no point in you walking out of your conference. There's nothing you can do.'

'I'll have to come back for the keynote speech tomorrow afternoon, but I really don't think you should be on your own right now. I'll bring food.'

He hangs up.

Is it really only three days since Ralph left? It almost

frightens her how much has happened in that time. How much has changed.

Ralph arrives at 6 p.m. with a bottle of good red and a carrier bag packed with delicious things he's picked up from his favourite restaurant. He hugs her hard then spreads out the paper cartons on her coffee table: stuffed tomatoes, roasted broccoli and chicken with mushrooms. The smell is wonderful. 'I'll grab some plates,' he says, heading for the kitchen.

On the way back to the sofa his phone beeps. He pulls it out and checks the message. 'It's Meghan. She wants to know how you are.'

'Tell her I'm fine and not to fuss.'

'But you're not fine, are you? When she called me she said you don't believe that Jay overdosed.'

'I don't.'

'Do you want to tell me why?'

'Oh, God.' She buries her face in her hands. 'There's a million reasons, but they're all muddled up in my head.'

He pushes the takeaway boxes aside and says gently, 'Can you fetch me your laptop.'

'What for?'

'We're going to take everything out of your head and put it down in black and white. All the reasons why you think he didn't do it and a list of all the facts surrounding his death. Things always look clearer when you write them down.'

'Does this mean you think I might be right?'

There's a long silence before he speaks. 'I think you need peace of mind,' he says at last.

Peace of mind, she thinks. It's a long time since she's had any of that. She stands up dazedly and goes out to the kitchen. In the silence the refrigerator hums. She looks down at the dirty coffee cup she dumped in the sink that morning before she left the house – sky-blue glaze with a smear of lipstick on the rim. Head throbbing, she picks up her laptop from the counter, takes it back into the sitting room and settles on the sofa beside him.

'You talk, I'll type,' Ralph says, gently taking the laptop from her. 'When you've given me everything you've got, I'll shape it into two lists of points.'

'I don't know where to start.'

'How about you tell me who Jay was? Everything you know about him: his past and his present, his hopes, dreams, strengths and weaknesses.'

She gazes at him. This new lover of hers with his soothing voice, reassuring smile and practical businessman's approach. She takes a gulp of air and lets the words spill out, describing the rigid upbringing that Jay had rebelled against, the gang who'd groomed him and his years as an addict, then his arrest, determination to reform his life, fear of getting sucked into using again and horror of going back to prison.

Ralph doesn't interrupt, try to challenge her or tell her what to think. He just listens and types. She weeps as she goes through the grim details O'Halloran had given her about the way Jay had died, the drug paraphernalia that she and Mick had found in his room and the tip-off about dirty drugs being sold from Cranmore House.

Ralph makes a final note and sits back. 'Why don't you have a bath while I knock this into shape. I'll run it for you.'

'You don't have to do that.'

'I want to. You look completely done in.' He runs a knuckle down her cheek.

'Thank you,' she says, gratefully. 'A bath would be good.'

She flops back against the cushions and closes her eyes. Moments later she hears his footsteps on the stairs and the sound of running water from the bathroom.

. . .

Vanessa feels a little calmer after her bath. She tightens the sash of her soft white dressing gown, pulls the towel from her hair and peers in the mirror. Wild, strained eyes stare back from a white set face. She goes downstairs to find that Ralph, who's leaning over her desk, has opened a bottle of wine, closed the curtains and lit the log burner, which throws comforting flickers of light across the richly coloured rugs and cushions.

'Ralph?'

He spins round, a sheaf of papers in his hand. 'Sorry, I was trying to get your printer to work and managed to knock these onto the floor.' He points to her laptop. 'Have a look at what I've written so far while I heat up the food.'

She pulls the laptop onto her knees and skims his notes. Somehow he's managed to condense her ramblings into concise points, and she has to admit that the evidence pointing to an overdose is overwhelming.

'It's pretty conclusive, isn't it?' she says, bleakly, when he comes back with the reheated food decanted into two bowls. 'You must think I was crazy to question it.'

Ralph looks at her, his expression grave and attentive. 'Don't they say that anger and denial are the first stages of grieving?' He hands her a bowl and a fork, sits down beside her and begins to eat, chewing hungrily. Vanessa prods her chicken, loses interest and casts her eyes across the glowing wood burner and the basket of logs.

Suddenly, she puts down her food, reaches for her laptop and opens Facebook.

Her profile picture is a photograph of herself and Izzy as children – a serious, heavy-browed nine-year-old and a golden-haired, golden-skinned toddler playing together on a beach. The image stays with her as she taps the keys.

'What are you doing?' Ralph says, putting down his empty bowl.

Vanessa looks up at him, her eyes brimming with tears. 'Setting up a campaign page for Jay. Accepting that he overdosed doesn't mean that I have to accept the circumstances that caused his addiction.'

Ralph opens his mouth, closes it again and puts a hand on Vanessa's arm. 'If that's what you need to do. Shout if you want anything. I'll be in the kitchen.'

'Hold the line, Vanessa.' The radio researcher's voice is clipped and slightly bored. 'Vinnie will be with you right after this track.'

With one ear, Vanessa listens to the music coming down the line; with the other she listens to the comforting clank and thud of Ralph moving around the kitchen, scraping leftovers into the bin, filling the dishwasher.

She blinks and does a little double take as she hears the familiar voice of Vinnie Dalgliesh saying her name.

'I've got Vanessa calling from west London. What's on your mind, Vanessa?'

She takes a deep breath. 'A friend of mine died last night. His name was Jay Brooker. He was twenty-seven years old and his body was found in an alleyway, pumped full of adulterated heroin.'

'I'm very sorry to hear that, Vanessa.'

'It should never have happened. Jay had been clean for months, he had a good job with excellent prospects, he was bright, personable and talented and should have had a great future. But he was targeted when he was a teenager by a gang he met in a park who groomed him aggressively over a period of months and forced him to become a mule in the county lines drugs trade. Once they'd got their hooks into him he never stood a chance, because no one – not his parents, his teachers or social services gave him the help he needed. Rather than seeing him as a clever kid with ADHD who was truanting because he was struggling to fit in at school, they dismissed him as a delinquent whose problems were all of his own making, telling him that everything would be fine if he just pulled himself together and learned a bit of discipline. Which is why I'm setting up a lobby group in Jay's name to campaign for coordinated support for vulnerable children and underage addicts to help them to break away from these groomers before they're sucked into a lifetime of addiction.'

'OK, let's hold it there, Vanessa. If people want to support this campaign, how can they get in touch with you?'

'So far there's just the Jay Brooker Memorial Facebook page, but if it's OK with you I'll phone in tomorrow to share full details of the other social media accounts I'll be setting up.'

'Fine by me. So can you give us some details about this coordinated help you're calling for?'

'I want mental health support to run in parallel with rehab. Currently, these kids have to come off the drugs before they can access mental health schemes, which is ridiculous when the two are so often intertwined. It's really common for kids with ADHD or other undiagnosed concerns to end up using drugs to self-medicate to deal with their fear of not fitting in.'

'I hear what you're saying, Vanessa, and I'd be happy to run a discussion about the issues you're raising. I'll try and get some experts on the line for later in the week.'

'Thank you, Vinnie. The more debate around this issue the better. As I said, until tomorrow, the best way to contact me is via the Jay Brooker Memorial Facebook page where you can also share your own thoughts and experiences, and find out how to get involved in our campaign.'

'Thank you, Vanessa. Anyone else out there tonight got a view on this? Darren from Stockport, what have you got to say to Vanessa?'

Darren's voice is loud, aggressive. 'Sorry, Vinnie, whatever happened to taking responsibility for your own actions and just saying no? Nowadays everyone's out to blame someone else for their own weaknesses. If these kids were in school instead of hanging around the streets they wouldn't be targeted.'

Vanessa digs her nails into her palm and cuts in. 'That's the whole point, Darren. We need to find out *why* these children aren't in school, and to develop ways to help them to fit in.'

'I've got Carol, calling from Bath,' Vinnie says. 'Carol, what's your take on this?'

'I'm with Vanessa. These county lines gangs need to be rooted out. You've got to remember that someone buying a bit of weed from their friendly neighbourhood dealer is only two links away from evil gangs who are exploiting vulnerable teens to make millions.'

'Thank you, Carol. We look forward to hearing from Vanessa again tomorrow night. Before we go to our next caller let's hear some music. This is a track from newly formed band, Random Hearts. It's called "Distraction"...'

Vanessa hears a creak behind her and whips round to see Ralph coming in holding a steaming mug.

'I made you some camomile tea,' he says. 'I thought it might help you to sleep.'

FORTY-ONE

Ralph leaves early the next morning to get back to Manchester and, at his and Meghan's insistence, Vanessa agrees to take a few days off work. But she has no intention of following their advice to take things easy. She'll go mad if she doesn't keep herself occupied and, anyway, she has an appointment in south London later that morning with Don Dexter. At least the fictitious Gina Cadogan does. An appointment that she is determined to keep. She might have promised Frances not to meet Dexter in the flesh until her child has been found and legally recognised, but there's nothing to stop her from watching him from afar.

She's booked her car in for a service, purely so she can swap her navy blue Micra with the Vanessa Dunn logo on the doors for the anonymity of a courtesy car. She arrives over an hour early and drives around the block until a suitable parking space comes free. She backs into the space, looks in the rear-view mirror and adjusts her trusty black wig. Even without the hat and dark glasses she wore to Frances's funeral she is unrecognisable.

She slips her phone into the handset holder on the windscreen and positions the adjustable arm to give the lens an unfettered view of everyone entering and leaving the Electric Café. On the face of it it's an odd choice of venue for a business meeting. For a man in Dexter's line of work, however, this old-fashioned greasy spoon, offering bubble and squeak, full English breakfasts, tea the colour of mahogany and no-nonsense coffees in thick china mugs, located in a suburban backwater of south London, makes perfect sense. A downmarket eatery frequented by a loyal band of locals that does little or no passing trade, in an area so out of the way she'd barely even heard of it until she'd driven over there to check it out after Don's email, reduces the chances of either him or his prospective client being spotted by anyone who knows them to almost zero.

Ignoring the barrage of *Call me!* and *Are you OK?* and *Do you need me to come over tonight?* texts from Meghan, she uses the time to make a hands-free call.

'Hi, Larry. I was just wondering if you know who's organising Jay's funeral.'

'His parents.'

'Have you spoken to them?'

'I went round to see them last night.'

'Were they upset?'

'Not so as you'd notice. Though his father seemed to be taking it a bit harder than his mother.'

'What was she like?'

'A real piece of work – cold, self-righteous, detached. It hadn't occurred to her that the way she and her husband treated him as a kid might have contributed to him growing up feeling lost and confused. She'd read some book about tough love and seems to think it meant breaking a child's will.'

'He told me they thought he was a disappointment.'

'Yeah.' He lets out a snort of derision. 'Faulty goods. Couldn't return him so they washed their hands of him.'

'When is it?'

'The funeral? Thursday week. The Brookers want to keep it low-key, but a lot of the lads want to go. Will you be coming?'

'I'd like to. Have the police made any headway with tracing the supplier?'

There's a pause. She hears him swallow. 'They've arrested Stu.'

She scrunches up her face. 'Oh, no.'

'He's admitted to dealing class A drugs but he swears blind he never sold any to Jay.'

She hears the distress in his voice and quickly changes tack. 'Did Jay's mother really describe him as faulty goods?'

'Not in those exact words, but it's what she meant. If you ask me, she and her husband didn't want a kid, they wanted a clone. I'll let you know as soon as I get a time and venue for the funeral.'

She hangs up and fires off a text to Meghan: *Thanks for the offer but I'm going to have a long bath, take a sleeping pill and have an early night* Vanessa switches her phone's camera to record and sits back to watch the passers-by. A few lone men wander past but it's mostly mums with buggies, elderly women dragging tartan shopping trolleys and groups of workmen. She turns her attention to the cars pulling into the nearby parking bays and she's got her eye on the driver of a black 4x4 when a motorbike draws up on the other side of the road.

A wave of nausea rolls through her.

The rider, who's wearing a black leather jacket and a visored helmet, leaves the bike idling while he looks around him, as if he might kick it into gear and roar away if he sees anything that makes him uneasy.

Vanessa drops lower in her seat as his head turns in her direction. Seemingly satisfied, he turns off the engine and sits with his back to her as he pulls off his helmet and runs his fingers through his hair. She cranes forward and wills him to turn around so she can see his face.

Swinging the helmet by its strap he walks towards the café. At the door he glances quickly over his shoulder before he steps inside. It's enough. She rewinds the video, freezes the frame, enlarges the shot and zeros in on the pale eyes of Don Dexter PI.

Through the plate-glass window she seems him order at the counter and take his mug over to a table by the wall. He sips his drink and, every couple of minutes, checks his phone. After exactly half an hour he gets up, puts on his helmet and walks out of the café. At the door he scans the street before walking over to his bike. She turns on the ignition.

When he pulls into the traffic she nudges her car behind a van a couple of spaces behind him and follows him back towards town. He loses her in Kennington, roaring away as the lights turn red.

On a whim she drives to the office address on his website. It's a walk-up above a seedy barber's shop in a litter-strewn street in Southwark. *Honestly, Frances, what on earth were you thinking entrusting the destiny of your child to a man like this?*

And why the hell has he been keeping watch on me?

FORTY-TWO

Vanessa parks outside her house and scans warily up and down the rain-swept street. Save for her elderly neighbour putting out his bins, there's no one in sight. Head down, she dashes inside, kicks off her shoes and heads into the kitchen. She hasn't eaten all day but she ignores her hunger. All she can think about is Don Dexter and the trust that Frances put in him. Why hadn't she asked Vanessa to find an investigator for her? Wind flinging rain against the windows, she pours wine into a glass and paces up and down, her fingers pushing through her hair. Shaken by fears for the present and the future she looks up and catches her reflection. She looks terrible – pale and overwrought. The shriek of the doorbell pierces her spiralling thoughts.

Oh, God, it'll be Meghan refusing to take no for answer. The bell rings again, shrill and insistent. Vanessa hurries down the hallway and yanks open the door, ready to tell Meghan to go away.

Izzy stumbles in out of the rain, her old brown coat sodden and her hair plastered to her head. Her eyes are red and her face is swollen.

'Izzy! Oh, my God.' Vanessa pulls her inside, glancing

quickly down the street, before she slams the door. 'What's happened, has somebody hurt you?'

'I can't believe it. I can't believe Jay's dead.' Izzy falls back against the wall and slides to the floor, her voice a wail.

Vanessa drops to her knees beside her and takes Izzy's face in her hands. 'It's terrible, but why are you so upset? You barely knew him.'

With trembling fingers Izzy unbuttons her coat and presses her hand to her belly. 'It's his,' she says.

'What?'

'My baby. It's Jay's.'

Vanessa gazes dumbly at the stretch and shrink of Izzy's lips. 'That night I broke up with Gunther and Jay was here having supper. He came back the next day to see if I was alright and... we slept together. We stayed in touch, texting and calling, and we realised we had something... special.'

Vanessa's head feels suddenly too heavy for her neck as it moves from side to side. 'Why didn't you tell me?'

'He... didn't think you'd approve.'

'Why ever not? He'd have been a vast improvement on the Gunthers of this world.'

'He'd got this idea into his head that you wanted him for yourself. He was scared you'd fire him if you found out about him and me.'

Vanessa shivers a little, feeling nauseous. 'That's ridiculous.'

'I know. You're, like, a million years older than he is. Then I found out I was pregnant and he was so happy. It was like it was the best thing that had ever happened to him. He said we were going to be together and we'd bring up the baby and he'd find a way to make money and look after us.' She bursts into tears again. 'Then I heard you on the Vinnie Dalgliesh show saying he was dead.'

'Oh, Izz.' Vanessa pulls her sister into her arms and rocks her back and forth, pierced by a sudden sadness for what might have been. She pulls gently away. 'Let's get you out of these wet things before you catch pneumonia.'

Izzy turns and presses her wet cheek to the wall. 'What am I going to do?'

After the strain of the last few days Vanessa is ready to break down in tears as well, but somehow she finds the strength to say firmly: 'It's going to be fine. I'm here and I'm going to help you.'

'I want Jay.'

'I know, sweetheart, I know.' Vanessa pulls off Izzy's coat, leaving it in a heap on the hall floor as she helps her sobbing sister up the stairs. She sits her on the edge of the bath, drops in the plug and turns on the big brass taps. Kneeling down, she unzips Izzy's muddy ankle boots and works them off her feet. 'Arms in the air like you just don't care.' It's what their mother used to say when she undressed them as children. Obediently, Izzy raises her arms and sits like a floppy doll while Vanessa tugs off her clothes. Still weeping softly, Izzy lifts a foot to step into the bath.

'Wait!' Vanessa holds her back, testing the water with her other hand. 'It's not good for the baby to have it too hot.' She shakes her fingers dry and grips Izzy's hand, steadying her as she lowers her into the water. With a pang she looks down at the pale curve of her sister's stomach.

Fresh tears spurt down Izzy's cheeks. 'I can't believe Jay will never see him.'

'Are you certain it's a boy?'

Izzy wipes the back of her hand across her nose. 'Pretty much. I did that test where you tie a ring to a string and hang it over your bump.'

'Right.'

'Jay wanted to call him Thaddeus. You know, after Thad Jones, the trumpeter.'

Vanessa doesn't know, but smiles sadly at the thought of Jay picking out a name for the son he'll never see. 'You lie there and relax. I'm going to heat you up some soup.'

Vanessa takes a clean towel from the cupboard, lays it on the chair beside the bath and hurries downstairs.

In the kitchen, she presses her burning forehead against the cool of the fridge door before she opens it, takes out a carton of soup and empties it into a pan. As it begins to bubble she lifts a spoonful to her mouth. She tastes nothing. With trembling fingers she pours herself a glass of the whisky Mark Findlay sent her, takes a sip and feels the burn slide down her throat.

Fifteen minutes later, Izzy comes into the kitchen wrapped in Vanessa's dressing gown. She sits down heavily at the table. 'You look awful.'

'I haven't been sleeping.'

'Because of what happened to Jay?'

Vanessa nods. Tears start in Izzy's eyes again and she holds up her left hand. On her ring finger she wears a chip of red stone set in a narrow band of gold. 'He bought me this with the money from the first photograph you sold for him. It's a ruby.'

'Your birthstone.' Vanessa takes her hand and straightens the ring as she looks at it. 'It's beautiful. Come on, eat your soup.'

Izzy dashes her hand to her eyes and picks up the spoon. 'I don't understand what happened. Jay was saving every penny he could lay his hands on for me and Thad. He'd never have wasted money on heroin or gone and shot up in a back alley.' She sniffs hard. 'I'll talk to the police. Once I tell them about the baby, they'll have to launch a proper investigation.'

Vanessa lifts her glass to her mouth and listens to the noises drifting in from outside. The slam of a car door, the passing traffic, the distant rumble of a train. People coming and going, making plans, living their lives, unaware that all their precious hopes and certainties could be snuffed out in a heartbeat.

She has no idea how long she stands there, but at last she puts the glass down and speaks.

'Look, Izz, my reaction was the same. I was absolutely certain he didn't OD, but I talked to Larry – he's the director of Cranmore House – and the police about it, and the evidence is pretty conclusive. Even Mick, who knew him from the hostel—'

'I want to talk to them. All of them.'

'Of course – I'll take you to Cranmore tomorrow and we can drop in at the police station on the way back. But—'

Izzy looks up from her soup. 'But what?'

Vanessa's throat is so constricted she has to take another gulp of whisky before she can speak. 'Now that I know he was going to be a father maybe... maybe it makes sense that he was dealing again – just to get the deposit for a decent flat for the three of you and to buy things for the baby. Once he had the drugs in his possession perhaps he couldn't resist the temptation to—'

'No!' Izzy drops her hands onto the table and leans closer, a deep V cutting her pale, perfect brow. 'It was *because* of the baby that he swore he'd never go back to that life.'

'There was drug paraphernalia in his bedsit, Izz, wrapped in newspaper that was only three days old.'

'How do you know?'

'When he didn't turn up for work Mick and I went there looking for him.'

'I still don't believe it.' Sniffing hard, Izzy heaves herself up, goes over to the counter and tears off a piece of kitchen roll, pressing it to her swollen eyes. 'I keep thinking this is all a nightmare and that I'm going to wake up and Jay will be there – the Jay I loved, not this... this stranger.'

'Izz, listen to me. He may have made some bad decisions but that doesn't make him a bad person. That's what we have to hold on to and, when he grows up, that's what we're going to tell Thad.'

Izzy's lips tremble and she leans her hand against the door of the fridge as if she no longer has the strength to stand up.

'Come on, finish your soup. You need to eat for the baby's sake.'

Izzy pushes herself up upright, pressing her fists into the bow of her back. 'Who's that?'

'Who?'

'The old bloke in this photo.' Izzy pulls a snap of Ralph and Vanessa off the fridge door and peers at it.

'His name's Ralph,' Vanessa says. 'I'm... seeing him.'

'Is it serious?'

'I'm kind of hoping it is. He's not that old and he's really nice. You'll like him.'

Izzy turns around to look at her. 'So you really weren't interested in Jay?'

'God, Izz, what do you take me for?'

'Sorry. It's just that he was so sure about it and he was really worried you'd be upset when you found out about him and me.'

Vanessa sighs. 'If you have a childhood like his you probably grow up thinking that anyone who tries to help you must have an ulterior motive.'

'I suppose.' Izzy sticks the photo back onto the fridge.

'But your baby is going to grow up surrounded by love. From his mum and his aunty. You know you can stay here as long as you like, don't you? Permanently, if you want to.'

'It's OK. Ross Ritter, the lead singer in one of the bands I was supporting, is going to pay me to look after his house in Spitalfields for a few months while he's in Australia.' Her face crumples. 'I was planning on staying there with Jay while we looked for somewhere permanent.'

'If you're sure.'

'I have to get used to being on my own.'

'You'll never be on you own,' Vanessa says, gently. 'I'll always be here for you and Thad.'

'I wish Mum wasn't the way she is.'

'Me, too.'

Izzy looks away to the window, her fingers worrying at her ring. 'It's strange... it's like she sensed Jay was in danger.'

'Mum did? What do you mean?'

'I came back a couple of weeks ago to see Jay and I took him to The Laurels to meet her.'

'Mum met Jay?' The words clump together in her throat.

'I thought it would be nice for them to get to know each other before the wedding. But as soon as she saw him she got really agitated and she kept making this strange little noise, over and over again.'

'Was she asking him for something?'

Izzy shakes her head. 'That's what's so weird. It sounded as if she was telling him to run.'

PART TWO

FORTY-THREE

'It's exhausting being a killer. Honestly, Mum, you have no idea. So many lies to remember, so many baffled faces to pull. Especially when you can't write anything down in case some interfering busybody finds your notes, and your own mother is trying to warn your victim what you're planning.' I give her wheelchair a sharp little kick. 'But then I always knew that at least some of what I tell you seeps into that shrivelled excuse for a brain. How did it feel, Mum? Sitting in the same room as Jay Brooker, mouthing and grunting at him, unable to make him understand what was coming his way? But, come on, we both know he brought it on himself with all those terrible decisions he made.'

I turn away to the sideboard and help myself to a piece of the *turrón* I brought her back from Spain, biting through the wafer-thin covering of rice paper to the sticky, nutty nougat beneath. For a moment I close my eyes, enjoying the feel of the sweet chewiness wrapping itself around my gums. This stuff really is delicious. I start talking again, my mouth still half full.

'I'd been banking on the police being prejudiced against people with pasts like Jay's, but it's shocking how certain

everyone is that he fell off the wagon and overdosed by mistake.
I mean, yes, he used to have a drug problem but no one, not one
single person, gave him a moment's credit for all the hard work
he'd put in to getting himself clean. Talk about giving a dog a
bad name.' I suck a sliver of toasted almond from my teeth. 'It's
also been a bit disconcerting – more than a bit, actually – how
quick everyone was to decide that I'd lost the plot as soon as I
suggested that his death might have been a set-up to make it
look as if he'd OD'd. I had to put it out there though, to test their
reactions and make sure that, down the line, no one would stir
up trouble by pointing out some pernickety little flaw in my
otherwise perfect murder. Still, I did worry that with me being
such a sensible upstanding businesswoman, I might come over
as just a little too convincing and plant a seed of doubt. But I
could see it in their eyes, hear it in their voices – Mick, Meghan,
Larry, Ralph, the police – they all thought I'd gone completely
batty. On the other hand, even though I say it myself, my perfor-
mance so far really has been rather spectacular. Hardworking,
put-upon, gullible Vanessa; a woman in pain just trying to
believe the best about someone she'd tried to help.' I sigh,
happily.

'But you know what? Pulling off the perfect murder isn't so
different from creating the perfect interior. You have to let your
imagination run wild to spark the concept, but once you've got
the big idea you have to take control and plan everything down
to the finest detail. It's no good relying on fancy final touches –
it's the preparation that counts. And you definitely can't give in
to anything rushed, impulsive or unthought-through, nothing
last-minute or second-rate. Even so, I thought when it actually
came down to doing the deed, that it might prove too hard for
me and I might chicken out. But it wasn't and I didn't. In the
end, it was just the next task to tick off the list.' I take another
piece of *turrón* from the box, and inspect it closely as I drop into
the chair by the bed. 'Not that different from buying you an

outfit for a wedding that I knew was never going to happen, and telling everyone that I was planning to promote Jay to distribution manager. Then slipping his house keys out of the jacket he left in the cloakroom and getting them copied, and arranging for him to do a late-night wallpaper drop in Poultney Square so that Mick could make an early start the next morning.' I snap off a chunk of the *turrón* and pop it into my mouth. 'Good old Mick. I knew from the moment I read his file in Larry's office that getting him on board would be a good idea. Aside from encouraging Jay to apply for the warehouse job *and* making it look like employing the two of them was part of some "inclusive staffing plan", he's come in useful time and time again. What's that expression the Russians use for patsies?' I chew thoughtfully as I rack my brain. '"Useful idiots." That's the one. Sorry, there's me rabbiting on about Mick when I'm sure you're dying to know how I actually did the killing. Alright, since you insist...

'So, that night, to get myself in the "zone", I cooked myself a light but delicious supper and had a lovely soak in the bath – candles, bubbles, a good book. Around nine I pulled on a set of Vanessa Dunn overalls – a baggy old coat and a low-brimmed hat I bought a few weeks ago from Oxfam, and I put on that old pair of your glasses, the ones with the cracked lens, swapped my contract phone for the new burner I'd bought and walked to Kensington. Picture it, Mum – a dowdy, forgettable figure, hunched under an umbrella. The kind of woman that no one was going to look at twice. Once I got to the high street I hung around keeping one eye on the spy app I'd installed on the phone I'd given Jay. As soon as it told me he was pulling into Poultney Square I bought a couple of coffees, nipped into the loo in the coffee shop, shoved my coat, hat, glasses and umbrella into my bag, added a navy baseball cap, similar to the one he wears for work, and made my way to where he'd parked the van. I let myself into it with the extra set of keys I had cut last week, took off the cap and sat in the driver's seat, sipping my vanilla

shot latte and waiting for him to finish the delivery.' I settle back
and close my eyes. It makes it easier to picture the scene.

'He smiled when he opened the driver's door and saw me
sitting at the wheel. But there was something slightly pitying in
that smile – barely detectable, but just visible enough to stiffen
my resolve. *He'd got this idea into his head that you wanted him
for yourself.* Arrogant prick.' I snort, softly. 'As if I'd have given
someone like him a second glance if it hadn't been part of a
bigger plan!

'I told him I'd been passing by and thought I'd see if I could
catch him as I had some fantastic news to tell him and I wanted
to take him somewhere to celebrate. Eager to hear it, he walked
around to the other door and slipped into the passenger seat.'

Footsteps echo in the corridor. I open my eyes, lean forward
and tuck Mum's rug a little tighter around her knees. 'Just in
case anyone's watching,' I whisper, and sit there holding her
hand in mine until the footsteps fade and it's safe to go on. 'It
was cold that night and Jay seemed grateful when I handed him
the decaf Americano I'd laced with Rohypnol. He drank it
quickly. I turned up the heater and we sat in the darkness
watching raindrops slide down the windscreen while I told him
I'd just been to see Amanda Mason-Findlay, and that she
wanted to include some of his photographs in a major exhibition
she was putting on next spring.' I give Mum a conspiratorial
wink. 'I know, I thought slipping her name into it was a nice
touch, too. You should have seen him preening as I doled out
the flattery. *She's so excited about your work... if the exhibition
goes well she wants to represent you, with a view to giving you a
solo show next year.* I had to spin it out to give the Rohypnol
time to kick in, but he was more than happy to sit there lapping
up the praise. I watched his smile widen and his eyelids droop. I
snapped on a pair of latex gloves, eased the cup from his tilting
hand and waited for him to pass out completely. Then I rolled
up his sleeve, wrapped his belt around his arm and injected him

with a massive dose of the dodgy heroin I'd bought from creepy Stu at Cranmore House.' I pause, savouring this part of the story. 'Of course, Stu has no idea that I was the buyer. I just slipped an envelope under his door stuffed with a couple of hundred quid in cash and a note saying I'd do the same with another couple of hundred if he left me what I needed under a bin by the lock-ups down the road from the hostel. I'd read about a spate of deaths from a batch of heroin spiked with Rohypnol – you can't beat thorough research if you want to do something convincingly – so using a pinch of the pure stuff to knock Jay out before I injected him with adulterated heroin was a no-brainer. It worked in double quick time *and* it's keeping the cops busy looking for his supplier, when they should be trying to find his killer.' I smile to myself. 'Oh, in case you're wondering, it was Stu who got me the extra Rohypnol. He really is a nasty piece of work. If you ask me, I did the world a favour when I tipped off the police about him dealing drugs from Cranmore House.

'Anyway, once it was completely dark I drove the van into the alleyway behind the houses they're renovating, opened the passenger door and shoved Jay's body out onto the cobbles. He's only slim but you'd be surprised how difficult it is to manoeuvre a dead body. It took me at least a couple of minutes to arrange it the way I wanted it, and a couple more to reinsert the needle into his artery, but you know me, Mum – never skimp on detail. Once I'd re-parked the van in the square, I slipped the Oxfam coat and hat and your glasses back on over my overalls. If anybody noticed any of my comings and goings, they'd have seen a scruffy old woman and a delivery driver. No sign of anyone remotely resembling groomed, stylish Vanessa Dunn.'

I suck a smear of icing sugar from the tip of my finger. 'All in all, I'm pleased with the way it went. In fact, the whole thing couldn't have gone more smoothly. But, a week later, here I am, still trembling from the adrenaline rush. If I'm going to pull this off I need to get my head straight, and what better way to do that than by having one of my special little chats with you, Mum?'

I squat down in front of her bookcase and pick randomly from her photo albums. It doesn't matter which one I choose. All her pictures will lead one way or another to the reason I had to kill Jay. I drop into the visitor's chair and turn the page.

'Oh, look there's Doug dancing with you at our wedding – you always did have a soft spot for him – and there he is with me in Greece, all sunburned and laughing, holding my hand and leading me down a narrow cliff path to the sea.' Good looking, sweet-souled Douglas Dunn, with his winning smile, lofty ideals and wayward hair. It hurts just to look at his face because losing him ripped off the thin scab that had covered another, much older wound, that has never properly healed; the one inflicted by the loss of the only other man I've ever loved. My handsome, larger-than-life father, Charlie Thomas. 'And guess whose fault it was?' I edge a little closer to Mum and hiss in her ear. 'Yours. Both times.'

She doesn't flinch.

I take in a long, slow breath and reach for the accusation I often start these sessions with, in the hope that by the process of attrition it will eventually wear through to what passes for her conscience. Sometimes it takes me a minute or two to get started, but today I'm so worked up the words fly from my mouth, tumbling and bouncing. 'The minute you found out that Dad had got himself involved in organised crime you just couldn't wait to go sneaking off to betray him to that pinnacle of rectitude DI Richard "Rocky" O'Brien. You didn't even warn Dad you were going to do it. You just stood there when the police turned up and watched as they carted him away.' I reach for the coffee Stefan brought me earlier. It came with a couple of biscuits arranged on a flower-patterned saucer. I dip a Bourbon into the cup and bite off a soggy chunk. '*Betray*. It's a

good word, don't you think? I read it in a book not long after
Dad's arrest, and when I looked it up the dictionary said: *"To
expose one's country, a group, or a person to danger by treacher-
ously giving information to an enemy."* As far as I was
concerned, DI Rocky O'Brien was definitely Dad's enemy –
and therefore mine too. So when I got home – I bet you don't
even remember this – I asked you why you'd turned traitor and
told him about Dad.' I drop into the annoying singsong voice
people use to speak to the very old and the very young. 'Do you
know what you did?' I raise an eyebrow, high and inquiring, and
stare into her face. 'You lied to me, your own daughter, and
swore blind that it wasn't you who'd done it. I didn't believe you
then and I certainly don't believe you now. In fact, I was sure
you'd had your eye on "Rocky" for a while, and what better way
to wheedle yourself into his bed than by handing him Dad's
head on a plate? You didn't waste much time either, did you,
Mum? Dad had barely done eighteen months of his eight-year
stretch before you and Rocky were waltzing down the aisle with
a kid on the way. And once you got back from your honeymoon
– Mauritius, wasn't it? – all paid for by that big, fat bonus Rocky
got for combating police corruption and restoring public confidence, Charlie Thomas's name was taboo in our house. Forgotten. Erased. Expunged.

'*Expunge.*' I dunk the Bourbon again and take another bite.
'That's another word I found in the dictionary: *"To obliterate or
remove completely something unwanted or unpleasant."* For
nine-year-old me, there was a sudsy kind of soapiness to the
sound of it, the squelch of a frantically wielded sponge scrub-
bing out the unwanted unpleasantness that was my father. But
however hard you tried, you couldn't scrub *me* out, could you? I
was an ever-present reminder of the shameful past you were so
desperate to escape. A maggoty apple you feared hadn't fallen
quite far enough from the rot-ridden tree.' I swipe away tears of
fury.

'You never admitted to yourself, or anyone else, that it was all *your* fault that Dad got sucked into organised crime. Oh, yes, Mum, he told me all about it. The secret Mr Big he'd been working for when he seized all that criminal cash was your boss, Gordon Findlay. That upholder of "old-fashioned British values". Dad said he'd often wondered why the syndicate picked him when the crime unit was full of officers who'd have jumped at the chance of making the kind of money that was on offer. But when he got to jail and heard from another prisoner that Findlay was the man at the top, it all started to make sense. They'd picked him because of you! Miss Goody-Two-Shoes. You'd obviously told Findlay where Dad worked, maybe asked him for an advance on your wages, and let it slip that we had cash-flow problems because of Dad's gambling. You know what you were like back then – always moaning about money. Dad thinks Findlay must have used his chats with you to keep an eye on what he was up to. How that man must have loved having the inside track on one of his pet bent coppers.' I stop to take a breath and glare at Mum's smooth, expressionless face.

'Don't sit there playing the innocent! You might not have known at the start that Findlay was a crook, but I'm bloody certain that somewhere along the way you worked it out. I'm sure Rocky knew it too, even if he couldn't prove it. How upsetting for DI Rocky O'Brien. Not only had his lovely new wife been married to a criminal, she'd spent years running the household of a gangster. The strange thing is, Frances never quite worked out that her father had been leading a double life – at least, not on a conscious level, though it's pretty clear that he'd had her mother bumped off because she threatened to expose him. Perhaps there are some things that even the most disillusioned of daughters can't bring themselves to admit.'

I flash my sweetest, most martyred smile and lift my hand to wave as a face appears at the glass panel in the door. Thankfully, it's not Stefan but Mum's relentlessly cheery carer, Phil. Seconds later, he comes in with a pile of clean laundry.

'Back so soon?' he trills.

'A client cancelled on me so I thought I'd pop over and keep Mum company for a bit.'

He smiles approvingly. 'Ooh, more lilies,' he says, noticing the fresh stems I've just arranged in Mum's favourite flesh-pink vase. 'I always think of Ellen when I smell that smell.'

I slide a glance at Mum. She loathes lilies. She used to shiver whenever she saw them and say the smell reminded her of death.

Phil slides open the top drawer and arranges her clean nighties, blouses and socks in three neat piles. He closes it again and runs his fingers over the gilded head of the cherub on the top of Mum's clock. 'This is such a beautiful piece. Worth a bit too, I'd imagine.'

'I found it tucked away in her attic and had it mended because I knew what it would mean to her to have it here in full working order, bringing back memories with every tick and chime.' I give my mother's arm an affectionate pat and smile down at her.

'What a lovely thing to do. Is it a family heirloom?'

'No, a leaving present from someone she used to work for.'

'That's the sort of boss you want. I'll be lucky to get a box of Quality Street when I quit this place.'

'You're not leaving, are you?'

'Nah, not me. I'm a glutton for punishment.'

'That's a relief. I'd really miss you. I'm sure Mum would too.'

He grins appreciatively. 'Aww, thanks.'

I keep up the smile until Phil has hung a fresh towel on the heated rail beside the sink and bustled off to the next room. I get up, turn the clock over and slowly peel back the oval of green felt I keep glued over the base plate. Inch by inch, I reveal the inscription engraved in the brass. There it is, as sharp and shiny as ever. I turn around and read the inscription aloud. *'To Ellen, in appreciation of your years of loyal service. Gordon Findlay.'* Another of my little rituals just to keep her wandering memory on track. I take a tiny tube of glue from my bag, squeeze a couple of dabs onto the edge of the felt, press it down and put the clock back in its place of honour on the sideboard. As its brain-jarring chime sounds the half-hour I toss the album onto the bed and pop down to the canteen to get myself another cup of coffee. All this talking is making me thirsty as well as hungry.

FORTY-FOUR

'Where were we, Mum?' I kick the door shut, set down my cup and retrieve the photo album. 'Oh, yes, you and Rocky O'Brien. Well, to give him his due, once the two of you were married he did do his best to step up. Do you remember when he tried to get me to call him Daddy? That didn't last. Not when he hit a brick wall. I hated him when I was a kid, really hated him, but, looking back on it, I don't blame him for what he did to Dad. After all, he was just doing his job. It's you I'll never forgive.' I prod her arm and feel her bones beneath the rough synthetic fibre of her beige, chunky-knit cardigan. It's the kind of garment my stylish mother wouldn't have been seen dead in before her stroke, which is why, when she moved in here, I donated most of her clothes to charity and bought her three of these cardigans, just to be sure she'd always have one on, one waiting in her drawers and one in the wash. They go so well with the olive, old-lady slacks and dun-coloured roll neck jumpers I picked out specially for her.

She hates all shades of green, loathes beige and can't stand the feel of anything around her throat.

'There was one good thing about you marrying Rocky – or so I thought at the time. You gave up work. I'd spent years waiting for you to find time for me, to put your own daughter before the families you worked for, with their big houses, oh-so pressing needs and spoilt kids who had everything I didn't. But what happened the minute they were out of the picture? Izzy came along. Isadora Jane O'Brien. Chubby and glorious, monarch of all she surveyed, sucking up every second of your time and every ounce of your attention.' I squeeze out a slug of the hand cream I gave Mum last Christmas and work it absently over my knuckles. 'I grant you that bringing her into the world wasn't all plain sailing, what with the false starts and the miscarriage and you being the wrong side of forty, but I'll never forget the day I came home from school and went running into the living room to ask what you were making me for tea and there you were, still in your dressing gown, bed-head hair, baby propped up on your arm, goofy smile on your face, gushing misty-eyed into the phone. "I never knew that motherhood could feel like this," you said. "When this little one came along it was like falling in love for the very first time. She's the apple of my eye."'

I pause. 'Well, thanks a bunch, Mum. You hadn't noticed me come in and surprise, surprise, you didn't notice when I turned around and crept out again. You were so wrapped up in her every burp and dribble that for the next six months it was easy for me to completely ignore her. Of course, it got more difficult once she started crawling because she'd follow me around, but I'd just slam my bedroom door in her fat little face and refuse to open it, even when she tried to burble my name through her tears. It was when she started talking properly that the power balance shifted. It started off slowly enough, but it didn't take her long to realise that *her* daddy wasn't *my* daddy, that there was a gaping great hole where my daddy should have been, and that the more gleefully she pointed this out to me the more it hurt. You, of course, never said a word to shut her up. If I close my eyes I can still see her climbing onto Rocky's lap, fixing me with those big brown eyes and taunting me that she had her daddy and I didn't have mine.'

My mother stares half-lidded at the cuff of her cheap, nasty cardigan and I glance back at the photos of my ex-husband. Suddenly I feel drained. I cast a slow glance around her room, at the framed photographs crowding the sideboard, the medicines lined up on the shelf above the sink, the naff little paintings on the walls. I'm wondering if I might call it a day when, out of the corner of my eye I see her hand twitch, just a fraction. It gives me the strength to go on.

'As for the thing with Doug – well, you insisted it wasn't you who told him I'd had an abortion. But I've thought about it long and hard and who else could it have been? He'd been going on and on about us having kids, starting a family, becoming a father, blah, blah. He'd never have understood it if I'd told him that I didn't want to share him with a demanding little brat and that for once in my life I wanted to be the apple of someone's eye, not the maggoty windfall that nobody wanted. So it was just easier to pretend that we were having problems conceiving. Nobody, and I repeat nobody, could have been more conscientious about taking the pill than I was, even though it meant hiding the packs and swallowing them in secret; and nobody could have been more shocked or appalled than I was when I discovered I was pregnant. I have no idea how it happened. But, somehow, Mum, after thirty years of looking through me, past me or over me you took one look at my face and you guessed. God knows why you picked that particular moment to actually notice me. I swore you to secrecy and told you it wasn't going to happen, that the time wasn't right, that I wasn't ready, that it was my body, my choice, my life, and what Doug didn't know couldn't hurt him. If you remember you agreed to keep it quiet, to respect my decision. But keeping other people's secrets isn't your way, is it, Mum? You proved that pretty decisively when you betrayed Dad. In fact, you probably convinced yourself that telling Doug was "the right thing to do". Then, to cap it all, six months later I found out that the person he'd turned to for comfort was my best friend, Lisa. What. A. Bitch. Of course, when I confronted her about it she came up with some bullshit excuse about them both having felt uneasy about me for a while, that I wasn't the person I'd always pretended to be, that they'd both sensed a darkness in me that they found disturbing. What's that even supposed to mean? The room grows silent, the steady tick of the ormolu clock a steady pulse. I look up and see my face, my outward face, faint and hazy reflected in the darkened screen of Mum's television.

'Still, you know what they say about silver linings. It was only after Doug walked out – what with all the free evenings and weekends I suddenly had on my hands – that I started going through the boxes I'd taken from your attic. I'd been at it on and off for a couple of days when I found the flimsy sheet of paper that jolted me out of my stupor and set me off on a brand-new path to personal fulfilment.' I pause as I always do when I get to this point in the story, take the folded paper from the hidden pocket in the lining of my bag and thrust it under her nose. 'The letter that Gordon Findlay wrote to you, three years after you stopped working for him, telling you all about Frances's baby and begging you to help him to get rid of it.'

I stop to take a deep breath. This bit always shakes me up.

'I met Findlay once, do you remember? It was a night when you had to work late – yet again – and for once the old witch next door couldn't babysit. There I was, sitting in a corner of the kitchen of that bloody great pile he lived in, trying to make myself as small as possible because you'd warned me that staff weren't allowed to bring their kids to work, when he walked in – all compact and scary – as if a much larger man had been compressed into his boxy little frame, white shirt, black tie, green velvet dinner jacket, dark darting eyes that seemed to take in everything and give nothing away. When they landed on me he just stood there, staring. I was terrified, and I could see you getting hot and flustered.

'"This is Vanessa, Mr Findlay," you said. There was this odd, loaded silence. "My babysitter called in sick at the last minute and I couldn't find a replacement."

'He kept on skewering me with those eyes for another few seconds then, with a sour little smile, he turned to you and said – and I'll never get the words out of my head: "Well, she certainly missed out on your good looks."

'I wanted to tell him that *he* was ugly and mean and I opened my mouth to do it, but you threw me that look of yours, the one that said, *Keep quiet, you're not wanted*, and he just picked up a couple of bottles of wine from the table and walked out. I watched him swagger away down the hall and, just for a second, I felt a twinge of sympathy for his daughter. But it didn't last.' My fingers dig into the padded arm of my chair. 'I'd spent far too long listening to you going on about "poor motherless Frances" and how worried you were about her. Do you remember that time she caught chicken pox and you left me with the witch for a week so you could stay at her bedside? And you cried, yes, sobbed real tears, when her father packed her off to boarding school.'

I flip through the album, find the all-too familiar page and shove it in her face. 'You even stuck photos of her in your bloody albums! That spindly streak of nothing with her white-blonde hair and her big green eyes and her pony! A sodding *pony*, while I'd practically had to get down on my knees and beg for a ratty little guinea pig that was going cheap because it had a squinty eye.' My heart is hurting and my breath comes fast. To calm myself, I unfold Findlay's letter and rub my thumb back and forth across the felted crease. 'At first I couldn't work out why he'd taken the risk of putting his request down on paper. But I'm guessing that now you were married to Rocky you were refusing to take his calls and, given his obsession with secrecy about Frances's baby, I can't imagine him wanting to run the even bigger risk of coming to your house or involving a third party, which rather limited his methods of communicating with you.'

I look at the letter again, although I could recite the contents with my eyes closed. 'He thought he was smart though, typing it out and leaving it unsigned so it couldn't be traced to him. But you were so loyal – at least when it came to your employers – that in fifteen years you only worked for three families and, seeing as the Findlays were the only ones who'd had a daughter, it didn't take a genius to work out who'd written it.'

I look at her again. No matter how many times she and I have this conversation, I still love saying this next bit: 'I have to say, I was pretty shocked to find out that Frances had got herself knocked up at thirteen, the slutty little tramp.' I let out a snort of disgust. 'But I was truly gobsmacked to discover that three years after you stopped working for him, Gordon Findlay still expected you to jump to it and do his dirty work for him. I don't believe you did it for the nice little pension he set up for you, because you never touched a penny of that money, did you? I think he had something on you.' I hold up the letter and pretend to read a line that I know by heart. '"I know I can count on your discretion, Ellen, just as you have always counted on mine."' What *was* that about, Mum? Was Frances right about him giving the job to someone he had a hold over? Someone whose secrets he promised to keep as long as they kept his? *Mutually assured destruction?* Did whiter-than-white Mrs Ellen O'Brien, the woman who'd so self-righteously denounced her errant husband, have her own shameful secrets to hide?'

I take a long gulp of my rapidly cooling coffee, frustrated that my mother's secret is the one vital piece of this puzzle that she'll take to her grave. As I put down the cup, Findlay's letter slips to the floor. I snatch it up. 'Do you remember this bit he wrote about the baby's father? "All I've managed to find out is that he's a lad of 'Haitian' extraction."' I make air quotes with my fingers but she doesn't look up. 'Was that supposed to justify him dumping his own grandchild? Frances was right. Findlay was a racist, as well as a bully, and pompous with it. "For the good of my daughter and my family, I want you to find a priest,"' I read aloud, mimicking his grating arrogant growl. '"Tell him he can have a ten thousand pound donation to any cause he cares to name if he'll hand the child over to social services and claim it was abandoned on the steps of his church. That way we'll be sure the mother can never be traced, and only you and I need ever know the truth. However, from now on I want you to cut all contact with my daughter. I know you've been writing to her at school"' – I swallow hard – this bit always sticks in my throat – '"and sending her little gifts, but once you stop she'll get over it. A clean break will prevent you from getting sloppy and letting anything slip. You're the only person I can trust with this, Ellen."'

I look up at Mum. 'Oh, dear – poor Frances. Losing her mother, then getting pregnant, and now her trusty old house-keeper was ghosting her. But she didn't get over it, did she? At least, not at first. I read all those heart-rending notes she wrote you. *"Please write back to me, Ellen. Oh, Ellen, why haven't I heard from you?"* Though I'm not sure Findlay would have put quite so much trust in you if he'd known what an obsessive hoarder you were. It was bad enough keeping this letter, but plain crazy to hang on to those photos of Frances's baby – all dark-eyed and bud-lipped – and the notes from Father William Newman. That one thanking you for the generous donation you'd passed to the Good Hope Refugee Centre on behalf of an anonymous donor, not to mention the card he sent you a few months later letting you know the "wonderful news" that a couple from his parish had been successful in their application to adopt a baby that had been abandoned on the steps of his church. He even gave you their names. I mean, honestly, Mum? What were you thinking? Anybody could have nipped up to your attic and found that information. As it was, it was me.' I shake my head in mock disgust.

'Of course, as soon as I'd read your stash of secret letters I did searches on Newman and Findlay. Father Newman had been elderly even back then, and it didn't surprise me that he'd died a few years after he wrote to you. I felt oddly disappointed, however, to discover that Findlay had also died just after you had your first stroke, and I was more than a bit pissed off to read that it was Frances who'd inherited the family business. I mean, I'd barely forgiven her for the pony and there she was inheriting a multi-million-pound company. I remember standing in the kitchen in my grubby old track pants – I hadn't bothered much about getting dressed since Doug left – staring out at the traffic while I waited for the kettle to boil, when a thought crept in on me. With Findlay out of the picture and your brain too addled to remember your own name, let alone what you'd been up to more than twenty years ago, it looked to me like I was the only person in the world who knew what had happened to Frances's baby. Perhaps the only one – aside, of course from her – who knew she'd even *had* a baby. That's when, in an idle sort of way, I decided to get to know her.

'I'd always imagined the Findlays living a gilded life of elegant homes, luxury holiday and glitzy parties, and getting their health care from exclusive private clinics so I was surprised when I discovered you'd stored a leaflet about a char-ity-run hospice in the same box as Gordon Findlay's note. At first, I thought he must be one of their donors but when I made a couple of calls and discovered that Frances was a patient there, I realised exactly what you were doing with it. All these years you'd been keeping an eye on her from afar, waiting for her father to die so you could finally ease your guilt and tell her why you'd stopped writing to her and what you'd done with her baby, without fear of reprisal from him. But by the time he finally popped his clogs, you couldn't even get out of your chair. When I told you how desperate she was to find her kid before she died it must have been almost unbearable for you, sitting here, trapped inside that useless body of yours, unable to say a word, knowing how little time she had left.'

I pick up my coffee cups and the empty saucer and take them over to the sink, keeping up the stream of chatter as I rinse them out. I like to do these little things to ease the burden on the staff.

'Like I've always told you, the first time I went to visit her, I didn't have a plan. Not really. All I knew was that for once in my life I had something that Frances Findlay didn't, and the thought of it made me feel just a little bit excited. Of course, I knew that any child of hers would probably be up to inherit a few bob if the truth ever came out, but I hadn't realised they'd be the rightful heir to the whole Findlay Corporation.' I pause. This next bit is always hard. 'Neither had I stumbled across that last box of papers in your attic, the one you'd gone out of your way to hide. I cried after I ripped the packing tape off that box and found all those unopened letters to Dad written by nine-year-old me. It wasn't just that you'd lied to me about posting them, and then lied to me about Dad receiving them and deciding not to write back – it was that the fallout from your lies has made me feel worthless, unwanted and unlovable ever since.' I place the cups upside down on the edge of the sink to drain and balance the saucer against them. 'When I managed to stop crying, I decided to track Dad down and deliver those letters in person. And that, Mother dearest, is when everything changed.'

. . .

I give Mum's wheelchair another discreet little shove with my shoe. 'I'd hated you for such a long time. For never loving me, for betraying Dad, for marrying the man who sent him down and, worst of all, for treating Izzy like she was God's gift and leaving me out in the cold. I hated Frances too, for taking all your time and affection when I was growing up, and, after hearing Dad's side of things, I had good reason to hate her father for what he'd done to mine. And as I sat there in his scabby little Spanish villa I thought, "I don't care how rich and powerful the Findlays are, they don't get to do this to me." So I came up with a way to make them pay. A way that wouldn't just compensate me and Dad for what the Findlays and you and Rocky had taken from us, but would strike at the heart of everything Gordon Findlay held dear.' My eyes flick away to my reflection in the television screen then they swerve back to Mum. 'The first step was to find Frances's child and, thanks to you, I had all the information I needed to do it. A date of birth and the name of that couple in Father Newman's parish who'd adopted an abandoned baby later that year.'

I stifle a smile. 'I could hardly keep a straight face when Frances asked me to befriend her kid once it was found, and it made me laugh that her little fantasy about her baby being a girl was so wrong. So much for maternal instinct. I'd known from the letters from Findlay and Newman that her "Dora" was in fact a boy, and he hadn't inherited her flaxen hair and his Haitian dad's dark eyes. Quite the opposite. He was dark-haired and dark-eyed with very little – bar a delicately chiselled nose and mouth – of Frances in him at all. And the name his new parents had given him? Jacob Arthur Brooker. Though it didn't take me long to discover that as soon as he walked out of their mock-Tudor, double-fronted executive home he'd dropped the Jacob for the far cooler, far more street-smart, Jay.

. . .

'It was a shock to discover how Frances's son had turned out. You'd think with pushy, well-heeled pillars of the community like Clive and Rita Brooker for adoptive parents, he'd have grown up to be a banker, a lawyer or at the very least something in real estate or advertising. It must have broken your heart when he ended up in prison. You must have seen it coming, though, what with criminality – albeit on a slightly grander scale – running in the Findlay blood. But full marks to you for the close eye you'd kept on him when he was growing up. All those leaflets you kept about the institutions and programmes he'd been involved with after he went off the rails and started truanting from school. What did you do, Mum? Hang around his school gates, show up at his parents' church on a Sunday? Volunteer to serve tea at whichever rehab centre he happened to be in that week?

'Still, his community service order at Cranmore House made it far easier for me to get to know him than if he'd been living the life of a typical City boy. Though I nearly bottled it when I realised I'd have to volunteer at a hostel for the homeless. I pulled it off though – broken-hearted Vanessa eager to do her bit and inject some meaning into her sad, empty life. Places like that really ought to be a bit more careful about their selection processes. Just because someone doesn't have a criminal record, it doesn't mean their intentions are everything they seem.

'The plan was to marry him. Imagine that, Mum! Me married to your darling Frances's long-lost son. The boy you'd angsted over for nearly three decades. There was only a seven-year age gap between us – that's nothing these days. Look at Barbara Windsor and Joan Collins. Once we'd safely tied the knot, I was going to discover a sudden interest in helping him to look for his birth mother, then I'd feign shock and surprise when I discovered that this ex-con kid of a Haitian refugee was the long-lost heir to the Findlay fortune. We might even have made a go of it, Jay and I. If we had, then all well and good. He was easy enough on the eye, and I'd have enjoyed having a seat on the board – Vanessa Dunn, the power behind the Findlay throne. If we couldn't make it work I'd divorce him and demand a huge payoff and a big chunk of the company's yearly profits as part of the settlement.' I inhale, exhale, thinking of the paths I never got the chance to take, the doors that will stay forever closed.

'I decided that the best way to avoid raising suspicion about my real motives for volunteering at Cranmore was to cause a bit of friction between Jay and me at the outset, and I knew from the minute I saw his awful street art plastered all over his Instagram account that he wouldn't be able to resist the temptation to make his mark on a freshly painted wall. After that I was going to take it very slowly – a few months at least – and make it seem as if our relationship – like all the best interiors – had grown organically.

'The next step was to get him working at Vanessa Dunn Designs. Letting it be known that I'd taken poor old Mick on as a decorator, as part of my "inclusive staffing scheme", was the perfect way to draw Jay in and make it look as if asking me for a job was all his idea. To put him at his ease I also needed a casual love interest in my life – nothing too serious or demanding, nothing I couldn't ditch when the time was right. When Ralph came along – well, why not, I thought. He'll do just fine.

'I won't lie to you, Mum – I never do these days – after all that precision planning it pretty much floored me when Frances told me she'd hired an investigator to look for her kid. But I brazened it out – after all, I kept telling myself, you and Gordon Findlay had made such a good job of severing the ties between her and poor abandoned Jay, it would take a miracle for even the most gifted investigator to track him down. If by some outrageous stroke of luck Don Dexter's investigation did finally lead him in your direction I knew you wouldn't be spilling any beans any time soon – or, in fact, ever. It was when she told me that Mark Findlay might be looking for Jay too, that I got worried. I had no idea what rumours he might have picked up on the family grapevine, and I kept imagining him getting to Jay and wiping us both off the board before I got the chance to make my move. He knew I'd been visiting Frances – that was pretty clear from the get-go, and from what I could tell he was doing his damnedest to find out what I knew about her baby.

'My concern about Findlay got so bad it started to keep me awake at night, so I decided to turn on the charm and speed things up with Jay. It was going pretty well, too: jokes, chats, shared confessions about our shitty childhoods, late-night walks. We even talked about him being adopted.

'But then, guess what? Izzy poked her nose in and, once she started sniffing around, she just couldn't stop herself from taking what was mine.' I pick up the photo of her from Mum's sideboard and picture the little baggage batting her big brown eyes at Jay that night in my kitchen. A burst of fury rips through my veins. I hold my breath and do the counting thing. The panes of glass in the window, the pill packs on the nightstand, the spokes on Mum's wheelchair. Calm again, I put the photo back in its place and arrange it, just so.

'Do you know how I found out they were seeing each other? Through the spy app I'd put on the phone I'd given him. I'd installed it partly to keep an eye on where he went and who he contacted, but mainly so I could find out his likes and dislikes and pretend that we were soulmates. Jesus, his taste in music was dire. But that's how I saw the texts. Jay and Izzy. Izzy and Jay. Mindless, flirty exchanges that began the day after he came round to supper. I wasn't happy about it, not happy at all, but I knew her relationships never lasted more than a couple of months and if by any chance this one did start to drag on, I was pretty confident I'd find a way to split them up. Comforting Jay after the break-up might even have been a way to cement things between the two of us.

'It was Izzy who called him the night of Frances's funeral when he and I were at that Greek restaurant. I saw her number on the spy app when he slunk off to call her back. I knew something was up from the look on his face when he got back to the table. I tried to get him to admit that he was seeing her by assuring him that if he'd made a bad decision about something I'd do everything in my power to help him sort it out. But he clammed up and of course it never occurred to me that the careless little cow had gone and got herself pregnant.

'When she called me a few weeks later and said she wanted to come by for a chat I was expecting her to tell me all about her and Jay. Then she sprang it on me. Not only was she seeing him, she was having his bloody baby. *And* he was over the moon about it *and* they were getting married. Married!' I squeeze the word from my throat, tasting the sourness of it as it passes over my tongue. 'Apparently making your own family is a thing for adopted children, a way to heal the "primal wound" inflicted by being rejected by their mothers. But you and I both know you don't have to be put up for adoption to be rejected by your mother, and I'd say I'm living proof that maternal rejection can do the opposite of making you want kids of your own.

'So you see, it's your precious Izzy's fault that I had to junk my plans to marry Jay. Izzy's fault that I was forced to work out another way to get my hands on the Findlay fortune. Izzy's fault that Jay had to die.'

I hear the creak of a trolley coming down the corridor. I lean in closer and whisper in her ear: 'I'll let you know how plan B is going next time I come.'

I swing round as the door opens. It's Phil, back with Mum's supper. A brown slop main in a red plastic bowl, with a pink slop dessert in a blue one. A meal as soft and slippery as Mum's control over her faculties. He's all togged up in a rubber overall, ready for feeding time. Rather him than me. I don't know how these people do it.

I glance at my watch. 'Goodness, look at the time. Sorry, Mum. Got to go. Things to do.' I air kiss the top of her head and shoot out of the door.

FORTY-FIVE

It had been a bit of a worry that, after all my painstaking work, Izzy might rock the boat by demanding to give evidence at Jay's inquest – not that she'd stopped weeping and whining for long enough to ask if there was going be one. If she did turn up, who knew what doubts a beautiful, grief-stricken young woman, pregnant with the baby of the deceased, might sow in the mind of a receptive coroner? So it was a relief when Larry called me to say that seeing as the police had decided it was an open and shut case, Jay's parents had agreed to what they call a rule 23 inquest. That's where it's all done using paperwork apparently, with no witnesses called. Good old Clive and Rita. They'd never doubted for one minute that their embarrassing disappointment of an adopted son had OD'd, so as far they were concerned a no-fuss, fifteen-minute slot involving the coroner reading snippets of the medical and police reports into evidence and delivering a conclusion to an empty courtroom was just the ticket.

But Izzy always had been one for surprises and I wasn't going to take any chances, not when I'd come this far, so on the day of the hearing I took her shopping for baby things. Tedious, but it gave me a chance to give my "nice Vanessa" persona a little buff, while making sure that my unpredictable little sister was safely tucked away in the bowels of an out-of-town shopping mall, miles from the ears and eyes of the coroner.

Next morning, however, as I'm texting Ralph to arrange to see him on Thursday and flipping through Instagram, the Google alert I'd created for all things Jay Brooker flags up a report on the inquest on a local news website. I tense up and click it open.

A drug addict from west London who was found dead in an alleyway off Poultney Square in Kensington died from an overdose of heroin mixed with the synthetic opioid, fentanyl, and the date rape drug, Rohypnol.

A council worker found 27-year-old Jacob Brooker of Shadwell, slumped in Poultney Passage in the early hours of 4 November 2023, an inquest at Westminster Coroner's court heard today.

An ambulance crew called to the scene found the young man slumped on the ground with a needle lodged in his brachial artery – which they removed, with the permission of The Metropolitan Police.

Brooker, who had recently completed a community service order, was pronounced dead at the scene.

The court noted that to date, there have been at least 46 poisonings from similarly contaminated heroin, resulting in 16 deaths, but investigations are still ongoing into the source. The areas affected include south London, and the south east, south west and east of England.

Recording a verdict of death by misadventure, London coroner Peter Mitchum said it was unfortunate that such a young man died in this fashion.

He said: "It seems that his tolerance levels while on community service had dropped and that he took the same amount of drugs as before, which his body was unable to cope with."

It's perfect! Not just the 'death by misadventure', but the way the report ignores all the months of hard work Jay put into his recovery: it totally fails to mention that he was holding down a responsible job for a reputable company and connects his death to a wave of similar tragedies across the region. No one reading this could think for one second that his death had been due to anything but a self-inflicted overdose.

I drive over to Spitalfields to show the report to Izzy and offer her a sisterly shoulder to cry on once she's read it. It irks me every time I walk into the enormous Georgian pile she's looking after for that overhyped singer Ross Ritter that my spoiled little sis has lucked out yet again. The building itself is stunning and the décor far more tasteful than you'd expect from a flashy rock star – beautiful antique rugs, stripped floors, reclaimed bathroom fittings, wonderful French furniture and interesting explosions of colour in unexpected places. I'd die for the chance to decorate Ritter's next home, but this probably isn't the right moment to ask Izzy for an introduction.

'I'm so sorry,' I say, as I forward the link to her.

She slumps onto the faded velvet sofa, scans the report then flings her phone onto the cushions.

I stroke her hair. 'I'm sure it was a one-off lapse and that he meant all those promises he made to you about turning his life around.'

She shrugs, distant and preoccupied, barely listening to a word I'm saying.

'What's wrong?'

'Jay's birth mother doesn't even know he's dead.'

I slip my expression into neutral. 'I know, it's really sad.'

'When I told him I was pregnant it got him thinking about her. He said he'd talked to you about it and you'd offered to sign him up to a couple of those sites that use your DNA to link you up to relatives.'

For one heart-stopping moment I think she's found me out and she's testing my reaction. I mutter something unintelligible but quickly realise she's not even looking at me, and there's nothing challenging or combative about the way she's reaching beneath the cushions and bringing out a snaggle of white wool attached to a knitting needle.

It's a half-finished bootee, for God's sake.

She fumbles again and retrieves a second needle.

The tension in my chest eases and I hear myself saying, 'I thought it was worth a try. Did they ever send him any matches?'

She shakes her head.

Of course they didn't. Why would they, when the cheek swabs he'd given me to send off were locked away in my secret storage unit, along with all the other samples of his blood, hair and sweat I'd made it my business to collect.

'I'll chase the companies and make sure they received the samples. You know how rubbish the post can be.'

Izzy draws out a strand of wool. 'I can't stop thinking about his poor mother. She must have been desperate to dump her baby like that and run off. Not even a note to tell him she loved him.' She puts down her knitting and her hand finds her belly. 'To do that to your own child. I can't imagine the pain she must have been in.'

I can't meet her eyes. 'It's really sad. Did his adoptive parents know anything about her?'

She shakes her head again. 'He said they didn't have any interest in his birth family at all.'

'The more I hear about the Brookers, the more I dislike them.'

'He was obviously mixed heritage, with those gorgeous dark eyes and that beautiful black hair.' And then she says the words

I've been dreading: 'Even though Thad will never know his dad, it would be amazing if he could meet Jay's real family and get a sense of his roots. But Jay didn't even know his real birthday, let alone where his family were from, so if I'm going to have any chance of finding them I'm going to have to hire a professional researcher.'

My heart goes into overdrive. 'People who do that kind of thing charge a fortune.'

'I'm sure Ross will lend me the money.' With childlike concentration she winds the wool around one of the needles, pulls the stitch through with the other, slides it off and repeats the process. *Click.* Clack. *Click.* Annoying, but it gives me time to think.

In my mind I see Don Dexter stumbling blindly down a darkened tunnel and Izzy and some paid researcher groping their way towards him from the other direction. If by some hideous alignment of stars they were to meet in the middle, I'd have an awful lot of explaining to do, and the whole Findlay Corporation would go to her baby. Which is definitely *not* the plan B I've been taking such pains to concoct.

'What's wrong?' Izzy asks.

I look up, sharply. 'Nothing... I was just thinking about the expenses we're going to have once the baby comes. Before we splash out on a researcher, why don't I see what I can do to find Jay's mother?'

'You?' Izzy throws me a doubtful look.

'Actually, I've had a bit of experience searching for missing people.'

'Really?' She still looks sceptical. 'Who?'

'My dad. I started looking for him a few months ago. It took some doing, but I finally managed to track the old bastard down.'

She's curious now. 'Have you seen him?'

'Not yet,' I lie, 'but we're planning to meet up very soon. If you send me everything Jay told you about his birth family I'll follow up the leads and see what else I can find out.'

Her face lights up with gratitude. 'That would be amazing.'

She's never been the brightest button in the box, but I can't believe she's buying into this crap. It must be early onset baby brain.

Congratulating myself on my quick thinking over the researcher business, I step jauntily into the rain-slicked street, put up my umbrella and turn towards Spitalfields Market. There's a new vintage clothing outlet that's been getting rave reviews and I thought I might buy myself a little reward for all my hard work – a velvet jacket, a silk shirt, or maybe, if they've still got them in stock, the two-tone Chanel pumps I spotted on their website.

My umbrella jolts and dips. A woman in an ivory trench coat, clutching an enormous bouquet of flowers and a huge JoJo Maman Bébé carrier bag, has bumped into me, almost knocking me off balance

'I'm so sorry, I wasn't—' She stutters and stops. 'Vanessa!'

Blue eyes peer at me through strands of wet dark hair. A tip-tilt nose spattered with raindrops. Damp glowing cheeks.

Anger wells inside me.

It's Lisa.

'What are you doing here?'

She looks down at the wet pavement, shifty and ill-at-ease. 'I've... come to see Izzy.'

'How do you know where my sister's living?'

'She invited us to her wedding and the poor thing called me last night to explain why it's been cancelled. I can't imagine what she's going through.'

Us? 'Izzy invited *you* and *Doug* to her wedding?' The anger inside me swells and crests.

'Look,' Lisa says, switching from downcast and nervous to

wide-eyed and patronising, 'we know you're still hurting but we want you to know—'

'Stop it! Stop saying *we*! You *stole* my husband, and now you have the cheek to stand there rubbing it in my face.'

Something flickers in her eyes – a spark of anger – and her lips turn white, but her voice when she speaks is strangely measured, as if she's finally getting the chance to say something she's been rehearsing for a long time. 'I didn't steal your husband. You chewed him up and spat him out and I picked up the broken pieces. Do you have any idea how devastated he was when you had a termination without even telling him you were pregnant? If you'd been open with him he'd have respected your decision not to have children, maybe found a way to come to terms with it, but what he couldn't deal with was the years of lies and pretence, the tears every month when you got your period, the baby things you left hidden in obvious places as if you were hoping against hope it was going to happen.' Her eyes lock on mine, narrow with disdain. 'The moment when you screamed at him that the termination didn't matter because the baby might not even have been his was the moment when he finally saw you for what you really are' – she's on a roll now, picking up steam – 'a sociopathic liar who creates endless fake Vanessas to get you what you want: the doting wife who had affair after affair; the heartbroken would-be mother who craved a child but had a termination; the dutiful daughter-in-law who was counting the days till Norman Dunn died so she could get her hands on a slice of his company; the loyal friend who used me time and time again as a prop and a tool in her devious little schemes. Who are you today? Oh, don't tell me. The protective big sister who bullied and tortured Izzy all through her childhood.'

I lunge towards her, glaring into her face. 'It was you, wasn't it?'

Lisa jerks her head away, as if my nearness sickens her.

'I always thought it was my mother who told Doug about the termination! But it was *you*! Because you've always been jealous of me.'

'No.' She shakes her head. 'Doug found out for himself because you pretended to be sick that day and you turned off your phone. Being the kind, caring guy that he is he came home to see if you were alright and he saw you driving off so he followed you, thinking you were going to the doctor's. He saw you arrive at the clinic and go inside. He was devastated but it wasn't till later that night, when he confronted you and you admitted that he might not even have been the father, that he realised he couldn't take being with you anymore. I know you've cooked up one of your elaborate "poor me" fantasies about him and me having an affair when you were married, but it's just another of the psycho lies you love to tell. You know full well that it was months before he could even face seeing his friends, let alone bring himself to start another relationship.'

I flick a glance to the left. A taxi is coming down the street, headlights bright in the haze of rain. I push past her, fling out my arm and swipe her stupid flowers and baby gifts into the road, timing it perfectly so they hit the tarmac at the precise moment the taxi swerves past. I keep walking. When I look back I see her crouching over a mangled mess of petals, cellophane and squashed gift boxes, the hem of her designer trench coat trailing in the wet.

FORTY-SIX

'Looks like your week off did you good. You look great. Love the new haircut.' Meghan gives me a hug.

I shrug off my coat and look around the shop. *My* shop. Gilt, silk, wood, glass, bronze. Gorgeous textures, beautiful things. It won't be long until I'll be able to expand, maybe take the lease on the building next door or move the business somewhere larger altogether.

'I can't tell you how much better I'm feeling. You were right – I'd completely stressed myself out worrying about this place and dealing with Mum and taking on the volunteering, so all it took was Jay's death to tip me over the edge.' I push a wisp of newly highlighted, freshly blow-dried hair behind my ear. 'Cutting myself off from the world for a few days was exactly the rest-cure I needed.'

'So you didn't see much of Ralph?'

'I didn't see him at all, but we talked a lot on the phone and he's coming over on Thursday to make me dinner.'

She smiles. 'Great. He really seems like one of the good guys.'

'One of the best.' I let my gaze wander away in a dreamy,

aren't-I-lucky-to-have-him-in-my-life sort of way, then I snap out of it and clap my hands together. 'But right now it's all about getting the Pimlico job done. If it's OK with you, I'm going to hole up downstairs and work on the drawings now.'

I don't tell her that, far from taking my eye off the ball, I've been working on them all week.

Once in my office I bolt the door and take out the package I picked up from the post office on my way to work. I pull out a compliment slip from Frances's lawyer which I rip into tiny pieces, and a thumb drive which I slip into my laptop. It contains one file: a fresh copy of the video Frances made on her death bed. I scroll forwards to the point where the copy she'd given me had frozen: the photo booth snap of her at thirteen, embracing Jean-Luc Baptiste, the fifteen-year-old Haitian kid who had fathered Jay. He's handsome, just like his son. The same dark, heavy-lidded eyes, the same sculpted cheekbones. But, unlike Jay, Jean-Luc's expression is guileless and full of hope.

I stare at the faces of these two lost, lonely outsiders, barely more than children, who look so thrilled to have found each other. 'The night I got pregnant was one of the happiest of my life.'

Frances's words echo in my head, filling me with sudden doubt and regret. *Oh God, oh God, oh God. What have I done?* I wrap my arms around myself and rock forward, counting the pens in the jar, the books on the shelf, the beats of my heart.

Frances's voice murmurs on in that faint half-whisper of hers, talking about her childhood, her overbearing father and the loneliness she felt after she lost her mother, her words washing through me as she holds up more photographs. There's one of her mother, slim and lovely, standing in bright sunshine beside a red, open top car; and one of her with Frances aged about five – the two of them walking hand in hand on a vast sandy beach. She holds up another. My body stalls. I unclasp my arms and hit pause. It's a photo I've never seen before of Frances, aged about nine, with *my* mother. They're standing side by side, Mum's arm flung protectively around her as the two of them gaze dotingly into each other's eyes. 'This is Ellen, our housekeeper,' Frances rasps. 'After my mother died she was the only person who ever showed me how it felt to be truly loved.'

Fury squeezes my heart. I jab pause, slip on a pair of latex gloves, reach for a pen and paper and start to write a letter, using neat block capitals, quite unlike my usual, exquisitely formed italics.

It takes several drafts but finally I hit the sweet spot. The perfect point midway between threat and vulnerability:

> *As you may or may not be aware, your cousin Frances Findlay gave birth to a son when she was very young. When she was dying she asked me to help her to trace him. Since her death I have managed to find him and I have informed him that he is now the rightful heir to the Findlay Corporation. Before resorting to lawyers he has asked me to speak to you on his behalf to discuss a way forward that could be beneficial to both parties.*

I add a date, a time to meet, and the name of a restaurant, which I tell him I'll book in his name.

One by one I feed the discarded drafts into the shredder beneath my desk. Then I fold up the unsigned letter, slip it into a plain white envelope, address it to Mark Findlay at the Findlay HQ and mark it 'Private and Confidential. To be opened by addressee only'.

That's the great thing about a letter. It can't be hacked, and if the recipient decides to destroy it – which I'm sure Mark will – the contents can never be recovered.

FORTY-SEVEN

The restaurant I've picked is vegan with an edgy enough vibe –
I hope – to throw Mark Findlay off-balance. It's noisy, bright
and crowded. Despite my need for a clear head I'm sipping on a
large glass of white when I look up and see a hip young waiter –
dragon tattoo, heavy eyeliner – pointing Findlay to my table.
He's the only diner in a suit and he looks around in distaste
before focusing on my face. There's a pause. I can almost see
the cogs of his brain whirring beneath his broad, shiny brow.
'You!' he says. 'What the hell were you doing coming to my
home?'

'Frances told me all about you and I was curious to see for
myself what kind of man you were,' I say with a bland, nothing-
to-hide-here smile. 'Just as you made it your business to find out
everything you could about me.'

He doesn't respond, just sits down opposite me and orders a
mineral water from the hovering waiter. Slightly regretting the
effects of the white wine, I order one too.

'I don't take kindly to fraud or blackmail,' he says.

'I'm sorry?' I say, after a blink of surprise.

'You know exactly what I'm talking about.'

Fear quivers down my spine although I take care to keep my eyes on his. 'Mr Findlay, I don't stand to make any financial gain whatsoever from this negotiation.'

He lets out a sharp, incredulous laugh. I throw him a look of bewildered hurt – one I practised a few times in the bathroom mirror before leaving the house. 'I'm here because Frances asked me to befriend her child and, if necessary, to act as an intermediary between him and her family.'

'Why on earth should I believe that?'

'Because it's the truth, and because she left a letter with her lawyer to that effect. I've brought you a copy.' I take the letter from my handbag, unfold it and slide it across the table, tilting my hand very slightly so that the emerald in Frances's ring catches both the light and his attention.

'Beautiful, isn't it?' I say, with a fond glance at the ring. 'She gave it to me just before she died.'

He glowers at the ring and then, without a word, he shifts his focus to the letter and casts his eyes down the paper.

'Now that Frances's child has been found—' I continue.

'So you claim.'

'It's a fact, Mr Findlay. One that you are going to have to deal with.'

'I want proof.'

'Of course.' I take two small plastic tubes from my handbag and set them on the table in front of him. The first contains one of the cheek swabs Jay gave me to send off to an ancestry tracing site; the other holds three of his hairs, roots still attached, teased from the hairbrush I took from his room when I planted the drug paraphernalia in his drawer. 'I could give you that proof by taking these samples to Frances's lawyer and asking him to have them tested against the certified samples of her DNA which she left with him. Of course, once the maternal link was confirmed – which it most definitely would be – he'd be legally bound to carry out the terms of the Findlay family entail and arrange for the business to pass immediately to Frances's direct heir.'

'Yet you've come to me first,' he says, his icy calm belied by a muscle working overtime near the back of his jaw.

'Because her son hopes that we can resolve this... situation without involving lawyers or causing unnecessary disruption to the current ownership of the Findlay Corporation.'

A ripple of something between curiosity and suspicion passes across Findlay's face. It settles into a sardonic little smile. 'While neatly avoiding the need to verify that he really is Frances's son. Nice try, Ms Dunn, but I'm not an idiot.'

I roll the stem of my wine glass between my fingers. 'There's a way to prove his identity without troubling Frances's lawyer.'

He raises one eyebrow.

'As I'm sure you are aware uncles and nephews share twenty-five per cent of their DNA, so you could test a sample of his DNA against a sample of yours.'

His eyes switch right to left as he thinks this over.

'Just to be absolutely certain you could then cross-check those results against these samples Frances gave me of her DNA.' Like a conjuror pulling tricks from a bag I place a third plastic tube in front of him. It contains the hairs I plucked from her eyebrows and the clippings from her nails.

He stares down at the tube.

'Parents and children share fifty per cent of their DNA and first cousins twelve and a half,' I say. 'Since Frances had no other children and you have no other cousins on your father's side the combined test results will be definitive.'

His fingers hover over the tubes for a moment as if they might be primed and ready to explode, then he picks them up, slips them into the pocket of his immaculately cut suit and folds his hands on the table in front of him. We sit in silence while I think about the day I took those samples from Frances. I only did it so that I could prove to Jay that he was her son, before we hightailed it to the lawyers to lay official claim to the Findlay Corporation. The ultimate gift for my brand new, soon-to-be multi-millionaire husband from his astonished and ever-loving bride. My plan had been so simple, so perfect so... innocent.

Until he and Izzy went behind my back and spoiled everything.

'The flowers and the white vase left at her grave,' Findlay says, interrupting my thoughts. 'Were they put there by this son of Frances's?'

I almost want to smile. It's these tiny details, the exquisite little flourishes like the inscription I'd chosen for that vase, that give heft to the lie that Jay is still alive.

Footsteps echo down paths we did not take
Towards doors we'll never open

A perfect choice for a long-lost child whose mother had died before they could be reunited.

I shrug as if I have no idea what he's talking about. 'I'll ask him and get back to you.'

The waiter arrives with our water and whips out a pad. 'Are you ready to order?'

Findlay makes no move to touch the menus propped between the salt and pepper grinders.

'We'll both have the special,' I say, with a hurried glance at the chalkboard.

'Great choice,' the waiter says, and disappears through the packed tables.

'What's this man's name?'

I shake my head. 'That's information I'm not at liberty to share, Mr Findlay. Why don't you and I call him Dorian? A nod to Frances's late mother, Dora.'

His face darkens, a vein pulses at his temple. 'I want to meet him. Face to face. Just the two of us.'

I hold my nerve. 'That won't be possible.'

'Why not?'

'He doesn't want anything to do with you, your family or, if our little chat goes the way he hopes, your family business.'

Findlay blinks at this, clearly thrown. 'So what *does* he want?'

'An income. A payout, a dividend – call it what you will – paid annually into a discreet, numbered Swiss bank account, and a guarantee of life-long anonymity.'

'How much?'

'Considering that if he chose to, he could claim the whole company and kick you out as CEO, he's instructed me to ask for two million.'

I'd thought long and hard about the amount to ask for. It had to be life-changing for me and Dad, yet at the same time affordable enough to make paying me off a no brainer for Findlay.

'A year?' He's just going through the motions now, pretending he's not going to jump at the offer.

'We both know you can afford it.'

'Why the anonymity?'

I'm all teed up with an answer for this too. 'He's an artist and very happy with the life he has. Coming out as a Findlay would warp that life out of all recognition. Also' – I slow my words as I come to the kicker – 'he's actively involved in a number of social justice projects, something he wants to use the money to support, and he has concerns about being publicly associated with a man like his birth grandfather.'

'Meaning?' Mark Findlay's voice is oddly cold and flat and his eyes, behind his frameless glasses, shine hard and unblinking.

I unfold my napkin and spread it across my knees, as if I consider our negotiations done and I'm now focused on the important business of lunch. 'He has it on excellent authority that Gordon Blane Findlay wasn't quite the squeaky-clean pillar of British industry that the public imagined him to be... Don't worry,' I say, into the deadly silence that follows, 'he's got no plans to expose the truth. It's just that if it ever came out, he'd prefer not to be tarnished by the scandal.'

Mark Findlay's eyes drill deep into mine, showing no flicker of surprise or hint of disbelief. I think of his swanky townhouse in Chelsea and wonder if his lacklustre career at the Findlay Corporation might have been a front for a more lucrative role in his uncle's shadier business dealings. 'What authority?' he says.

'His mother's. Frances had been compiling a dossier on her father's criminal activities for years.'

Despite practising this lie a hundred times before I got here, as I say it, I'm as afraid as I've ever been about anything.

'Where is this "dossier"?'

'Don't worry, it's quite safe. Right now, Dorian has no more interest in it seeing the light of day than you do.' Like a dog signalling appeasement, I look away and lower my head, my heart jumping in my rib cage as I wait for him to speak.

'How do I know that *Dorian* won't keep sending you back for more?' he says, clearly as keen as I am to shunt the conversation into safer waters.

'If he'd wanted more, he could have asked for it upfront.'

He takes a slow sip of his mineral water. 'Why did Frances choose you to act as an intermediary?'

'My mother was Ellen Thomas.' I watch for recognition. His face gives nothing away. 'She was the Findlay's house-keeper when Frances was a kid. She looked after her after Dora Findlay had her' – I look away – 'tragic accident. They were very close, and for a while Frances and I were playmates.'

I allow myself another sip of wine. 'Who's to say that Frances and I didn't forge a childhood friendship that endured into adulthood? No one. Certainly not my silent, incapacitated, brain-addled mother.

'I should warn you, Mr Findlay, that if anything... *untoward* should happen to me, Dorian won't hesitate to come forward publicly to stake his claim. If anything should happen to him, the dossier Frances compiled on her father's criminal empire will be sent to every media outlet in the country. Why risk any of that when all you need to do is to stump up a paltry two million a year?'

I hand him a slip of paper with the details of the numbered Swiss bank account I've set up.

He glances at it, stuffs it into the pocket of his jacket and stands up.

'Aren't you going to wait for your beetroot falafel?' I say.

He doesn't bother to reply.

At ten o'clock the next morning I receive a text from an unknown number.

Four sweet words.

Terms agreed. Money transferred

I check the Swiss bank account. Two million in credit. Six beautiful little zeros.

I want to weep with relief. But there's just one more fissure I need to fill to make myself whole.

I've been taking Ralph for granted for too long, barely thinking about who he is and what he wants from our relationship, never repaying him for everything he did to look after me the night Jay died. It's time to change all that. Time to take the final step in the life-changing personal journey I've been on since the day Doug walked out.

.   .   .

On my way home from the shop I stop off at Waitrose to buy everything I need for a chicken biryani – Ralph's all-time favourite, so he tells me. Excited by my plan for the evening ahead I load chicken, yoghurt, cardamom, chillies and coriander into my trolley, and throw in a few Indian beers as well as a decent bottle of pinot noir. There's something infinitely pleasing about spreading out the ingredients on my kitchen table, turning up the music on the speakers and sipping a cold glass of wine as I chop, dice, shred and pound.

Leaving the chicken to marinade, I take a quick shower and slip into jeans and a loose jersey top. I don't bother with much make-up. Ralph likes the natural look and tonight... well, tonight is all about him.

The doorbell rings as I'm putting the finishing touches to the biryani. Gripped by nerves I let him in. He kisses me on the mouth and then stands back, holding me by the shoulders and making appreciative noises about the way I look and the appetising aromas permeating the house.

'Hungry?' I say.

'Famished.'

'Glad to hear it.' I take him by the hand and lead him into the kitchen. It's such a welcoming room with its clever mix of old and new, subtle colour palette and natural textures and I see him smile with contentment as he scrapes back a chair, shrugs off his jacket and loosens his tie. I scoop up the jacket. 'I'll hang this in the hall – we don't want it smelling of curry. Help yourself to a drink,' I call over my shoulder. 'There's beer in the fridge or wine on the counter.'

I hang up the jacket, rush upstairs, spritz a little perfume onto my neck and wrists and look at my reflection in the mirror. 'Ralph, there's something I want to say—' I push my hair behind my ears and tilt my head the other way. 'Ralph, I've been thinking...' I grip the edge of the sink and close my eyes. *This is such a huge step*, I tell myself, *but the time has come to take it.*

'How was your day?' I ask, as I hurry back into the kitchen.

Ralph's scrolling through his phone while he sips from a tall glass of beer. 'Not bad. I managed to follow up on a couple of promising contacts I made in Manchester. How about yours?'

I lift the pan of biryani onto the table. 'Mine was great. I had lunch yesterday with someone I've been hoping to do business with for a while and this morning he got back to me, agreed to all my terms and made the whole payment upfront.'

'Good for you.'

I pile his plate high with biryani. 'Help yourself to poppadoms and raita.'

He pulls the dish of raita towards him. 'Is the yoghurt in this lactose-free?'

'Of course.' I tut and shake my head, enjoying the teasing intimacy that comes from knowing – and accommodating – a lover's quirks and imperfections. 'So, now that I've got a bit more money behind me, I had a preliminary chat with the agent who's letting the building next door to the shop.'

'Are you thinking of expanding?'

'That's the dream. It used to be a noodle restaurant but it's been empty for nearly six months. Mainly because of the ridiculous rent the landlord's asking, but the agent says he's keen to find a new tenant and for the right person he might be willing to compromise.'

'If it's been empty that long he'll be haemorrhaging money on business rates.'

'Exactly.'

He forks a mound of chicken and rice into his mouth and briefly closes his eyes. 'This is so good.'

Relishing his enjoyment I watch him chew, swallow and scoop another forkful into his mouth. I take a bite myself. The meat is tender and the fiery spices leave a slight numbness on my tongue. 'Not too hot?'

'Never too hot for me.'

'Ralph.' I snap a poppadom in half.

'Hmm?'

'When we first met, I had no idea quite how... well matched we'd turn out to be.'

He grins. 'Me, neither.'

'But...' I pause and put down the poppadom. 'Oh, Lord, this isn't easy.'

He raises an eyebrow.

'I thought we'd agreed there'd be no more lies between us.'

'We did,' he says, after a waver of surprise.

'So why have you been pretending to be Ralph Gilmore, dull, reliable financial advisor, when in reality you're Don Dexter, motorbike-riding, sketchy-as-hell private investigator?'

He stops eating, his fork halfway to his mouth, and darts the tip of his tongue across his upper lip. 'How long have you known?'

'Long enough.'

'How did you find out?'

'Remember Gina Cadogan, the woman with the cheating husband who failed to turn up for your first meeting?'

He frowns. 'That was you.'

'Yep. I wanted to see what Don Dexter looked like in the flesh, so it was quite a surprise when you rocked up. Do you want to tell me what's going on?'

He spears a chunk of chicken and chews it slowly, a touch of smugness in the sharp grey eyes he's lifting to mine. 'Seeing as I'm not the only liar in this relationship, I could ask you the same thing.'

'True,' I say, affably. 'But fair's fair. I asked first.'

'Alright.' He takes a gulp of water. 'When Frances hired me, she offered me a large retainer, generous expenses and a hefty bonus, payable if and when I found her kid. But then I did some digging, found out about the family entail, and worked out that what she was offering me was nothing compared to what her cousin Mark would be willing to pay for information about the real heir to the Findlay Corporation.' A sheen of sweat breaks out on his forehead and he dabs at it with his napkin. 'So I went to see him. It turns out he'd suspected for a while that his cousin had given birth to a secret child at some point in her youth. He'd tried to find out more but had got nowhere, so he was happy to pay me a retainer with a promise of a whacking great payout if I found the kid and brought the information to him, rather than to Frances or her lawyer.'

'What was he planning to do with that information?' I study his face. Despite the familiar, crinkly smile there's a hardness in his eyes that I've never seen before.

'That was his business. Not mine.' He takes bite of poppadum and leans forward, coughing slightly as the crumbs scatter onto his plate. 'Though at the time, considering how little information there was to go on, I didn't rate my, or anyone else's chances, of tracing the kid. But then Frances called to tell me that one of the hospice visitors had turned out to be the daughter of her former housekeeper, and she'd asked her to befriend the kid once she... or he, was found. That niggled at me.' He refills his water glass from the carafe I'd put on the table. 'Something didn't sit right about someone with a connection to the family suddenly turning up out of the blue, so I decided to get to know you. I asked your advice about a wedding present, followed you around, hired you to do up Arlo's flat—'

'—scoped out my house, broke into my shop, stole the server from my computer, put remote viewing malware on my laptop and what? Paid, threatened, or cajoled my manager, Meghan, into fighting your corner?'

'Don't blame Meghan! She's got no idea I'm not poor love-struck Ralph, and you can't blame a girl for being ambitious. She wants in on your business.'

'What's that got to do with you?'

'I promised her that if you and I got together I'd do whatever I could to persuade you to make her a partner. I also gave her the money for that pricey interior design course she's doing. It's a complete rip-off but she seems to think it's worth it.' He's relaxing now, and so am I. 'But you were good – there was nothing to find. Or if there was you'd done a bloody good job of hiding it.' He takes a long drink of water and chuckles to himself.

'What's so funny?'

'If you must know, I wondered for a while if your sister Izzy might be Frances's daughter, hidden in plain sight by her doting former housekeeper.'

'*What?*'

'Right kind of age, right kind of colouring, Izzy short for Isa*dora*.' He laughs hoarsely at my astonishment, which I admit is perfectly genuine. Izzy Frances's kid? That really would have been something.

'I was so sure about it I ran some tests on a glass she left in a bar one night. But no. It turns out she really is your mother's daughter.'

'Good to know,' I say, entering into the jocular spirit of things.

'Then I discovered that you were volunteering at Cranmore House. I had my suspicions about Jay Brooker as soon as I saw the two of you together. Late-night walks along the Embankment, driving him to NA meetings, giving him a job. So, naturally enough, I did a bit of digging into his past too. And guess what?' He coughs sharply. 'Aside from being male, his backstory fitted exactly with everything Frances had told me about her baby – abandoned as a newborn, no way to link him to his birth parents, mixed race, mid-twenties.' He pours himself another glass of water and takes a long swig. 'So I told Meghan I thought Jay was a wrong 'un, got her to get me a pair of his dirty overalls, did a test and bingo! You'd clearly known who he was all along but at that stage I couldn't work out what you were waiting for. You certainly hadn't told Frances when she was alive and once she was dead you hadn't contacted her lawyer to certify Jay's claim to his inheritance. And although you'd hooked up with Mark Findlay's wife, you hadn't tried to sell Mark what you knew – I knew that, because he was still paying me a retainer. So what *were* you playing at?' He gazes at me, a hint of sly enjoyment in his smile. 'I thought about going to Mark myself, telling him about Jay and claiming my reward.'

'Why didn't you?'

'Because I'd fallen for you.'

'Oh, please—'

'I'm serious. You're not just smart and attractive; you're artful, ruthless and conniving.'

'Thanks a lot.'

'Which is why we'd make a great team. I was scraping up the courage to come clean and suggest that we join forces and split the money from selling Jay's identity to Findlay when' – he gives me a slow teasing smile – 'you killed Jay.'

His words sit in the silence.

'You don't know that.'

'Actually, I do.'

'You can't prove it.'

'I have footage. Shot on a long lens, I grant you, but your face is clear enough.'

I take a sip of wine and let it sit on my tongue before I swallow it down. 'Filmed in London when you claimed you were in Manchester.'

'Yep.'

'Show me.'

He takes his phone from his pocket, presses the keys and turns the screen towards me. Like a rerun of a half-forgotten nightmare I see the Vanessa Dunn delivery van draw up in Poultney Passage. The door opens, Jay's body tumbles onto the cobbles. The door pulls shut. Someone in overalls jumps out on the driver's side. Ralph presses 'Pause' as the figure bends over Jay's slumped body, their head turned slightly as if startled by a sound.

I stare into my own pale, exultant face.

My fingers twitch, barely able to resist the impulse to snatch the phone from his hand and dash it to pieces on the tiled floor. As if reading my thoughts he opens his palm and offers the phone up to me. 'Be my guest. There's a backup copy locked away in the safe in my office. Just so you know, if anything happens to me, a colleague of mine has instructions to open the safe and send the pictures to the police.' He throws me a boyish smile and presses on, enjoying his advantage. 'I was stunned by what I'd seen and more than a little intrigued to find out what you'd do next.

'But then, once you'd killed Jay, you *did* meet up with Mark. I admit it took me a while to work out what was going on but when Mark called me straight after your cosy little lunch and dispensed with my services, I began to piece things together. You'd been planning on getting your hands on the whole Findlay fortune by marrying Jay. But he'd got your sister up the duff and he was going to marry her instead. Oh, dear. That must have hurt.' His tone is taunting but I don't rise to it. 'So you killed him.' He grins. 'I suspect there was a touch of pique in there somewhere – hell hath no fury and all that. I mean, there's no getting away from it, Jay was a nice-looking lad and he and your Izzy made a lovely couple. But revenge wasn't enough of a motive. Not for a woman like you. No, you'd worked out another way to get your hands on Findlay's money.' He tips back in his chair a smug little half smile tugging at his glistening upper lip. 'I think you're blackmailing him. I mean, all you'd need is a sample of Jay's DNA to prove he's Frances's kid, and since Findlay has no way of knowing if he's alive or dead I imagine he's agreed to pay up.'

I say nothing and take a mouthful of biryani, impressed, despite myself, by his powers of deduction.

He's resumed eating too and I see a shred of fresh parsley caught between his teeth. He swallows and points at me with his fork. 'But seeing as you're not someone who *ever* does anything without a reason, it begged the question, why were you seeing me? And why, after weeks of arm's length coyness, did you suddenly decide to take our relationship to the next level and sleep with me?'

I keep my eyes on his, still saying nothing.

'I took a look through my notes and realised that it happened the day after Jay and your sister went for a scan at the hospital and she'd turned up on your doorstep, presumably to tell you she was pregnant. That's when the penny finally dropped. I was your decoy, wasn't I? I had been all along.' There's a looseness to his words, a wheeze in his breath. 'To begin with I was a casual dalliance to put Jay at his ease and scotch any suspicion that you were some desperate divorcée with your sights set on a younger man. Then, when he got your sister pregnant and you decided to kill him, I was promoted to being your publicly acknowledged lover, there to keep you out of the frame as a possible murder suspect motivated by jealousy. Oh, don't get me wrong. I don't object to being your sloppy seconds. In normal circumstances you'd be way out of my league. But these aren't normal circumstances, are they? So I have a proposition for you.' He starts to cough and runs the back of his hand across his lips. 'A variation on your original plan for Jay. You marry me, we split your payout from Mark, and combine our considerable talents to develop mutually beneficial future projects.'

'What if I decline this gallant proposal?'

He lifts one shoulder and takes another bite of spiced chicken. 'I send the film of you killing Jay to the police.' He coughs again. And then his face contorts, violently and painfully, and his body convulses in a desperate attempt to suck air into his lungs. He reaches wildly for his glass of water and sweeps it and his half-full plate of biryani to the floor. I get up from the table, step over the mess and take a Tupperware box from the freezer. 'I made blueberry ice cream for pudding. I thought it would be cooling after all the spice in the biryani.'

His hand flies to his throat, with the other he gropes for his jacket. 'My pen,' he wheezes. 'For God's sake. It's in my jacket.' His head is lolling, his face erupting in dark blotchy hives, and he's struggling to breathe.

'Of course. Hang on.' I walk down the hall, taking my time as I lift his jacket from the hook. His EpiPen is in his inside breast pocket where he always keeps it. His keys are there too. I take them and the pen back to the kitchen and dangle the bunch in front of him, holding it by the heavy brass key that I'm guessing is the one to his office safe. 'Oh, Don – it is alright to call you that, isn't it? – old-school tech leads to old-school mistakes. You really should have got yourself a digital safe.'

I see rage flash over him, confirming my guess. 'Fuck you,' he wheezes.

I tilt my head to one side. 'You really don't look well, Don.' He drags in a jerky breath and lunges for the pen, falling forwards off his chair as I jerk my hand out of his reach.

I look down at his crumpled body writhing on my beautiful Italian tiles in a mess of chicken and rice, and count slowly and loudly to twenty before kneeling down and pushing the pen into his hand. He struggles to pull off the cap, wheezing and bucking as his body contorts for one final time before he loses consciousness.

It's really extraordinary how much harm a drizzle of peanut oil can do to a grown man with allergies.

When he's almost stopped breathing I return the blueberry ice cream to the freezer – no point wasting it. Then I cup my hands around his, do another slow count to twenty and, when

I'm sure the effect will be too late, I plunge the pen through his trousers into the flesh of his thigh.

I stand up, practise a few hurried, panicky breaths and dial 999.

'Oh, my God!' I wail. 'My partner cooked supper, took a couple of bites and he's gone into anaphylactic shock. I don't understand what happened. We're always so careful—'

FORTY-EIGHT

There's a lightness in my step as I head down the corridor to Mum's room, a sense of elation that lends a brightness to the wallpaper with its two tones of scrubbable beige stripe, badly hung reproductions of the world's most overrated paintings, carriage-style wall sconces and subtle notes of talcum powder, stewed mince and piss.

'I've done it, Mum,' I say, before I've even shut the door behind me. 'Mark Findlay paid up. Oh, come on.' I bite through the wrapping of this week's lilies and tear back the cellophane as I cross the room. 'Aren't you going to congratulate me? All those months of hard work. All that plotting and planning, and the drastic rethink I had to do when your precious Izzy got herself knocked up with Jay's kid and threatened to marry him. Weren't you on tenterhooks, wondering if my new plan would work out? Waiting to see if all those carefully crafted threads would finally knit together into a seamless, organic whole or if I'd slip up somewhere and get caught. Well, now you can relax. Think how thrilled Dad's going to be when I tell him the news. "Hi, Dad, guess what? I've finally got you a million quid and the revenge you always dreamed of for everything Mum, Rocky and

Gordon Findlay did to you. All that father–daughter time they took from us when you went to prison."'

I throw last week's lilies into the bin and rinse out the precious pink vase. Precious because it was a gift from Frances. A present she picked out herself at some upmarket antiques fair she'd been dragged to as a kid by her businessman-of-the-year, two-faced, psycho, crime-boss father.

I approach Mum's chair. She sits there, head drooped, eyes unfocused, hands palm upwards in her lap, one on top of the other like she's begging in the street. 'I know you're in there, Mum.' I tap her temple lightly with the tip of my finger then, just in case anybody is walking past and glancing in, I lean closer and use the same finger to smooth back a strand of that still luxuriant hair. 'I know you can hear me. I know it because you speak when you're with Stefan. You say Izzy's name, you even tried to warn Jay to run when she brought him to see you.'

Anger stabs my gut. It starts with a flash and then it swells and rolls, gathering up a lifetime of being ignored, neglected and overlooked by this woman who'd rather play dead than acknowledge that I've finally won. It's a battle of wills. She knows I want a sign, a reaction, something, anything, to show that she knows me still and acknowledges my triumph.

'I tell you what,' I say. 'Why don't you hold your vase for me while I arrange these lilies?' I make as if to place it into her hands and then I let go. I want her to reach out, to grab it as it falls, but the vase slips through my splayed fingers and smashes to the floor, scattering shards of blush-coloured glass across the shiny brown vinyl like shrapnel from a grenade.

She does not move.

'Oh, you're good, Mum,' I say. 'I'll give you that, but you don't fool me.' I turn away to look for something else among her knick-knacks to put the lilies in. I'm reaching for the crystal decanter that used to sit on my grandmother's sideboard when I sense movement behind me.

I spin around. Mum has raised her head. She's looking at me, actually looking at me, straight in the eye. I gasp, certain she's finally going to speak. She doesn't. But it's enough.

She has finally conceded defeat.

I shut my eyes, rocked by a rolling wave of satisfaction. I'm smiling when I open them. The smile splutters into a gasp.

Like some washed out, geriatric zombie, she's slowly lifting her hand. I watch in wonder as she points a quivering finger at the framed watercolour hanging above her bed.

'What is it, Mum?'

Her hand trembles with the effort she's putting into raising it, then it drops back into her lap.

Unsure what she wants me to do, I take the painting from its hook. Her eyes bore down on it. I scan the picture, see nothing but crudely daubed roses in a wonky jug. I flip it over. The frame has a wooden backing held in place by four brass clips. I snap them open and lift away the backing.

There's a sheet of brittle, yellowing paper pressed against the underside of the painting. I recognise Mum's tight, sloping handwriting. It's a letter, addressed to *My daughter, Vanessa*.

I drop onto the edge of the bed and read it.

Every time I look at you, I see your father in your eyes, your nose, the line of your chin, and it shames me that I let Charlie Thomas believe that you were his. He was hurtful and careless, a gambler and a drunk, but he was my husband and it horrifies me that in a single, fleeting, moment of madness I took comfort from my misery in the arms of Gordon Findlay. It happened just after I started working for him and, like everyone else, I fell for his outward display of kindness and charm. It was only later that I discovered that beneath his charismatic mask lay a cruel, ruthless monster who took pleasure in inflicting mental and physical pain on the people around him, stringing out punishments so he could watch his victims squirm.

He agreed to keep your paternity secret, but he used it to force me to go on working for him long after you were born. The true extent of his cruelty became apparent after he married Dora. She was miserable and desperate to leave him but she knew he would never grant her custody of their daughter, Frances. When she threatened to expose what she knew about his criminal empire, he had her killed. When he discovered that my husband had been transferred to the organised crime squad it amused him to recruit him behind my back. I know you always thought it was me who shopped Charlie to the police. It wasn't. It was Findlay. He'd decided that Charlie was unreliable and "getting above himself" as he called it, and he wanted him out of the way. Rocky had been on to Findlay for a long time, but he could never find the evidence he needed to prove it or to break through the wall of corrupt senior officers who were on Findlay's payroll. Later, when Findlay discovered that I was seeing Rocky, it amused him to threaten to tell him that he was your father, knowing that I could never have born the shame.

They say psychopathy is genetic and I was sick with worry that you would turn out just like him. But I took heart from looking at Frances and seeing that there was nothing of her father's twisted nature in her. I told myself that if I shielded you from the truth and showered you with love there was no reason why anything of Gordon Findlay should blossom in you either. But it did. I saw that same manipulative cruelty in you from when you were tiny, coupled with that exact same ability to hide it, when it suited you, beneath a mask of smiles.

So this was the sordid little secret that Mum had been hiding all these years. I tear my eyes from the paper and stare into her blank, motionless face. She stares back, waiting for me to retreat, wounded, to contemplate the hollowness of my victory.

A snort of laughter erupts from my mouth. She thinks she's outplayed me. The laughter froths and bubbles into a guffaw. Sure, it's ironic that I risked so much and spent so long plotting, scheming, even killing to win back the love of a father who wasn't even mine, but can't she see? With this letter and my own DNA I can walk right in and take the whole Findlay Corporation from under Mark Findlay's nose.

Another rush of giggles, tingly as the bubbles in a celebratory glass of champagne, bursts through my nose.

'Bye, Mum, I'll see you next week.' I leave her to the stench of lilies and the sound of Johnny Cash belting out 'I Walk the Line' – another of Dad's all-time favourites – set to play on an ever-repeating loop until Phil arrives to put her to bed. Which should, by my calculations, be at least an hour from now.

I walk down the corridor almost delirious with excitement at the thought of what lies ahead. Should I take a solicitor with me when I spring the news of my paternity on Mark Findlay? Or should I take him out for another of our intimate little lunches? How about Ethiopian this time? One of those funky little back-street places with plastic tablecloths and no cutlery, where you get stuck in with your hand and lumps of sour, spongey bread. 'It came as just as much a shock to me as it has to you, Mark. I mean, who'd have thought that someone like my mother would have kept a secret like that for over thirty years?'

If he asks about 'Dorian', I'll tell him he's dead. I giggle aloud at the irony.

'Mrs Dunn.'

I look up to see the matron of The Laurels, Janice Adams, emerging from her office. She's a mousey little woman with a perma-smile and limp, nondescript hair. Her navy trouser suit is creased, polyester, and cheap, and the collar of her pale blue shirt pokes up against the folds of a second chin.

'Could I have word?' she says.

I glance at my watch. 'Actually, I need to make a call... but if it's urgent—'

'It is rather,' she says, and pivots back into her office on stumpy brown heels. Not a good look with black and blue but, let's face it, style isn't exactly Janice's thing.

I follow her inside and stop short, annoyed to see my sister sitting very upright in one of Janice's ugly, wing-backed armchairs, the budding swell of her belly straining against her skimpy brown sweatshirt. 'Izz, what are you doing here? Why didn't you tell me you were coming?'

Izzy doesn't reply. No surprises there. This pregnancy has turned her into even more of a moody cow than usual. Beside her – stiff, bespectacled and oddly nervous – stands Stefan, the two of them looking for all the world like a couple in a badly posed vintage photo.

Has she got her hooks into him now? I wouldn't put it past her. She's probably banking on a male nurse being willing to stay home looking after her screaming brat every night while she swans off to 'further her career' in some hokey music venue.

'Do take a seat, Mrs Dunn,' Janice says.

'Thank you.' I drop down into the second armchair. God, it's uncomfortable. Who on earth designs these things? I look from her, back to my sister and then at Stefan. The three of them are looking decidedly tense. If my sister and I have been summoned to hear news about a deterioration in Mum's health – well, frankly, Janice, I don't give a damn. Not anymore. Yes, as Mum's legally appointed guardian it was worth keeping her alive when I needed access to her savings – and I stand by my decision to sink the pension money she'd had from Gordon Findlay into setting up the shop. She'd been letting it pile up untouched for years and where else was I supposed to get that kind of investment from? But it's no problem if she snuffs it now. I adjust my expression to one of perfectly calibrated concern. 'So, what's this about?'

There's a short, oddly charged pause. I look questioningly at Izzy. She ignores me and glances up at Stefan. I get it now. Her obsession with elder abuse must have led her to make some wild accusation against one of Mum's carers and she's managed to inveigle Stefan into backing her up.

The phone rings on Janice's desk. She picks up, listens for a couple of seconds and says, 'Thank you, can you send them in?'

All eyes swivel to the door. I'm expecting Phil to walk in with a lawyer or a union rep to plead his case. Poor guy. This has to be a mistake. I can't imagine anyone less likely to hurt a frail old woman than dim, smiley Phil. Why the hell didn't Izzy talk to me first? I'm the one who's here week in week, week out – not her. The door swings open. *Whoa.* The accusations must be bad. It's not Phil standing there, it's Detective Inspector O'Halloran accompanied by a rangy female sidekick, who he introduces as PC Watts.

He tips his head in my direction, 'Ms Dunn.'

I respond with a curt, 'Inspector.'

Janice, who seems to have shaken off some of her mousiness and lost the perma-smile, offers them seats and they each perch a buttock on one of the metal chairs placed on either side of the door.

'Mrs Dunn,' Janice says, 'your sister has been worried about your mother for some time now. She thought she seemed to be getting increasingly anxious and upset and she was concerned that it might have something to do with the treatment she was receiving from her carers.'

I knew it! I glower at Izzy. Far from being contrite, the crazy cow's looking positively bullish.

'I have complete faith in my workforce,' Janice is saying, 'but I also take the concerns of families extremely seriously, so when she asked me if she could install a camera in your mother's room I agreed.'

My body stiffens. I sense the room shifting gears. I can practically hear it.

'She gave me the password so I could also access the footage and I made a point of scrolling through it on a regular basis. All I saw were people coming in and out, and either chatting to Ellen or attending appropriately, and with kindness, to her needs.'

My thoughts swing wildly between relief and fear like a compass needle torn between two poles.

'However, your sister found time to watch the footage in real time and she discovered some extremely troubling interactions. She showed them to Stefan who, it turns out, has had concerns of his own about your mother's well-being for some time. He kindly went back through weeks of footage and made a compilation of the more disturbing sections, which he sent to me a couple of hours ago. Having viewed it, I had no option but to call the police.' She comes around to the front of her desk, turns her computer screen to face into the room and clicks her keyboard. 'As you will see, it paints a picture of a campaign of sustained and pernicious abuse.' A silent, grainy image with a strip of time code along the bottom appears on the screen. It's Mum in her chair, staring into space, and there's me sitting beside her, my hand resting gently on her arm. It's a poignant little tableau, carefully staged so that anyone glancing through the glass door panel would see exactly what I wanted them to see – a loving daughter chatting intently to her invalid mother in a selfless bid to keep her failing brain alive. As I will the scene to change I glance at Janice and give her a small, self-deprecating smile. She stares straight past me.

My eyes swerve back to the screen. The scene hasn't changed. Fear trembles, bulges, throbs, through my veins.

I glance around, willing Stefan to hurry over and forward

the footage to the entry of a callous cleaner or a merciless member of the night staff. A sound crackles from the speaker. It's a voice. A voice I recognise.

'—it was cold that night, and Jay seemed grateful when I handed him the decaf Americano I'd laced with Rohypnol—'

I want to leap up, grab the console and hurl it to the floor but my body is no longer mine. It has stopped responding. While my eyes refuse to lift from the screen and my legs are too leaden to move, my hands flail wildly, flapping of their own accord, and when I try to open my mouth to drown out the sound of the recording, it's as if I'm pulling at the lips of a voiceless puppet, parting them jerkily, powerless to stop them from clacking shut.

Fingers grip my arms, hoist me from my seat and jerk my hands behind my back. Steel on my wrists, words in my ears, Izzy's eyes on my face; my vintage Chanel pumps slipping and sliding on the polished floor, as Watts and O'Halloran drag me through the door.

A LETTER FROM SAM

Dear reader,

If you enjoyed the twists and turns of *The Mistake I Made* you may like my other thrillers: *Her Perfect Life, Gone Before* and *A Good Mother* – and I hope that my future novels will keep you hooked. To keep up to date with my latest releases, just sign up at the link below. Your email will never be shared and you can unsubscribe at any time.

www.bookouture.com/sam-hepburn

Thank you for choosing to read *The Mistake I Made*. I've had a lot of fun creating the plot and getting into the heads of the characters. It's a story about an outwardly successful interior designer who finds herself at a turning point in her life. She's childless and newly divorced. Her ex-husband is now living with her best friend, her wild-child younger sister is away in Europe on a music tour, her mother who has early-onset dementia is in a nursing home and she's lost touch with the father she adored. She's at her lowest ebb, but instead of giving into loneliness and despair she decides to reboot her stalled existence. She forces herself out of her comfort zone and volunteers at a couple of charities where she befriends a guilt-ridden dying woman who enlists her help to put right a terrible wrong she committed as teenager; and she becomes a mentor to a newly released prisoner who is trying to put his murky past behind him. But her plans for a better, more fulfilled new life of her own implode when she makes a truly terrible mistake.

If you liked *The Mistake I Made* I would be so grateful if you could find a moment to write a review. I would love to know what you think, and sharing your thoughts in a review is a great way to help other readers to discover my books. Thank you!

I love hearing from my readers – you can get in touch on my Facebook page, through Twitter, Goodreads or my website.

All my best,

Sam

www.samhepburnbooks.com

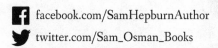

facebook.com/SamHepburnAuthor

twitter.com/Sam_Osman_Books

ACKNOWLEDGEMENTS

A huge thank you to my editors, Harriet Wade and Ruth Tross; to my lovely agent, Stephanie Thwaites; to the wonderful team at Bookouture who work so hard to support their authors and their books; and to my ever-patient husband, James.

Printed in the USA
CPSIA information can be obtained
at www.ICGtesting.com
LVHW090205091123
763460LV00037BA/622